Turn Home

Turn
Home

Eleanor R. Mayo

REBEL SATORI PRESS
Bar Harbor • New Orleans

Published by
Rebel Satori Press
P.O. Box 363
Hulls Cove, ME 04644

Originally published in 1945
by William Morrow & Co.

ISBN 978-1-60864-010-2

For My Mother and Father

All characters and all places in this novel are fictional—except the Maine Coast, which actually exists.

Part One — *July, 1943*

BUB DOLLIVER was lying flat on his back, his hands under his head, watching the big hawk fishing up the creek. The hawk would hover high over the water, keeping himself in position in the air with a slight movement of his pinions; then he'd soar off to another spot and hover again. Once in a while he seemed to be trying to back-track in the sky with a queer upward flapping, and when he did that, Bub could see the strong sunlight striking across the white bars on the undersides of those dark wings.

Suddenly the hawk sighted something. He looped down in long spirals, reconnoitering. For a second he hung motionless against the sky before he turned himself into a dark bomb of muscle and feathers and came straight down, wings folded flat against his body.

Bub saw the splash when the big bird hit the water, but it was a moment before the sound came up to him. When it did, the hawk was already in sight again, trying to take off. He had a heavy load and it was hard going, but he made it, and Bub lay watching him fade off up the tidal valley toward the hills. For a moment sunlight flashed again, this time against the silvery scales of the fish; then the hawk turned at a tangent and was merely a dark blot of dullness against the late brilliance over the mountains.

Bub grinned and eased his thin body into a more comfortable hollow in the grass. He yawned deeply, turned his head slightly, and lay looking down the creek to where the meandering line of water widened into the estuary beyond which lay the entire Atlantic.

Bub Dolliver was a queer physical combination—his body had

[1]

the long lean look that meant muscle, but he wasn't tall. The look of length was suggested by the leanness. He was long between his shoulders and his hips. The rough leather belt that held his pants up looked as it if rested loosely on his hip bones rather than around his waist. His face betrayed youthfulness in spite of the creases across his forehead and the lines around his eyes, lines that came from perpetual squinting against sunlight too bright to bear. His eyes, under the surprisingly dark brows, were a clear light hazel, and their whites were infinitesimally lined with red. His straight, short nose shadowed a mouth that looked too young for the eyes, the lips were wide and boyishly protuberant. His face widened out, too, along the jaws. His uncombed heavy light hair hadn't been cut lately, and it was long enough to shadow his forehead.

Lying there, Bub knew he was tired, but not with the grueling weariness he had come to know so well during the past three years. This was a good tiredness because he knew he wouldn't have to go on doing the thing that had made him tired. Now it was up to him just how tired he got; he could stop when he wanted to. It didn't depend any more on a disembodied voice in darkness.

He had been on his feet since sunup. Early that morning he'd started out from Freehold, twenty-five miles up the line, and had been walking all day. His arm ached from the steady tug of the canvas bag he'd been carrying. There weren't many cars on the road now, and it was a lot harder to hook a ride than it had been. The traffic that had passed him since morning had been mainly the big oil trucks with the forbidding sign "No Riders" stuck up on the windshields. That was all right with Bub. It wasn't the first time he'd walked it from Freehold to the Harbor and it probably wouldn't be the last.

He lay feeling the sun shining into him as if he didn't have any clothes on. And it was a different sun, too. It was kind, not harsh. It was sunlight you could walk out in without a hat. It didn't hit you as if somebody had hauled off with a length of two-by-four and let you have it right behind the ear.

He wondered just how often he'd thought of this place since he'd gone away. It was five whole years now since he'd shaken

[2]

the dust of the Harbor off his feet; five years, and he'd sworn then he'd never come back. But here he was again, and damned glad to be here all in one piece.

To the southeast from where he lay in the little field there was only water for as far as you could see, and beyond that. To the east, north, and west were mountains, low and blue, rounding into the sky. There had been a time when those hills had made him feel shut in, and all he'd wanted was to get out of the circle. But they were more protection than prison to come back to. South, again there was the water, but he couldn't see that.

Late July was still the height of summer, the weather hot and the sun brilliant. But already there were signs of fall—the grass browning and the out-season red of a precocious sumach along the wall. Even the air had a foretaste of fall now that the sun was getting low, a sort of tang that had been only softness in midday. The warm northwest wind drove the big clouds down over the hills, and he watched the rapid shifting of shadow over the fire-denuded sides of Pentacook.

"By the Lord Harry," Bub sat up suddenly and sat staring with his hands on his knees, "I'm some glad to be back!"

He got to his feet slowly, favoring his bad left side, and started back to the tarred road. He had three miles still to go, and the sun was dangerously close to the hills. He dug his canvas bag out from under an alder in the ditch and started south again. He didn't walk too fast because he wanted to hit town just about dusk, and he'd figured his speed to make it.

It was beginning to get dark and a few lights were already showing faintly when he passed the first outlying houses and went down the hill toward the center of town. His manner during those three miles had changed subtly. He wasn't even aware of the change himself, but it was there. He was on the defensive, wary, ready again for disapproval.

The main street was familiar in outline, but strangely different, he thought; darker than he'd remembered it. Then he saw that the lights were out. Only one street light in five burned. The front of the drugstore, that he'd recalled as a blaze of light, was covered now with a heavy dark curtain of some kind through which only a faint glow penetrated to the street. Even the row

[3]

of bare bulbs that usually blazed around the low portico of the movie house was dark, though the lobby was lighted.

What the devil! Bub thought, bewildered. Then he looked to the southeast, out across the dark space of water, and remembered. They were blacked out. He'd come through New York and had been startled and a little unnerved by the blackout there, but somehow it hadn't been half so impressive as the almost total darkening of this small town. In New York the ocean had been farther away, it wasn't right there to make you remember why everything was dark.

He stopped in front of the drugstore, set the bag down by his feet, and fumbled in a jacket pocket for a cigaret.

A couple of doors down the street Bob Haines come out of the darkened barber shop, locked the heavy door behind him, and started toward home. In spite of the fact that he was nothing but a blur in the growing darkness, Bub recognized him easily. A big man, shaped like a pear, Bob walked with a characteristic sway of his wide hips. He carried his curiously small head slightly to one side, and his arms necessarily stuck out from his side and swung in outward arcs instead of forward and backward.

From habit Bub didn't notice the man's queer physical build, but waited for the diffused light from the drugstore window to hit his small, kind face, and wondered whether or not to speak to him. Bob hadn't changed much in five years. Maybe his big, untidy mustache was a little yellower, but his face was as smooth and brown as it had ever been. He glanced at Bub curiously as he passed, but looked away without saying anything.

"Evenin, Mr. Haines," Bub said softly.

Bob stopped and came back a step or two to face him.

"Evenin, son," he said slowly, his face doubtful. He glanced down at the canvas bag by Bub's feet. "You—you're sort of a stranger, ain't you?"

"Yuh. It's been as much as five years since I left town."

Son, Bub thought. He never called me that before. Maybe they've changed. Maybe it ain't goin to be so hard, comin back. Then he saw what had happened.

"You look awful familiar to me," Bob said, the natural kind grin persisting, "but I'm sorry I can't quite place you."

[4]

"Oh," Bub said flatly, everything suddenly quite clear. He hesitated slightly, watching for the change of expression in Haines's face when he said, "I'm Bub Dolliver."

The change came. The grin faded. The voice was brusquer. "Oh, yeah," Haines said. "Remember, now." He glanced again at the bag. "Stayin long?"

"Didn't know but what I might," Bub was noncommittal.

"That so? Well, I'll probly see you again."

Bob nodded once or twice—short formal jerks of his small head —and turned away. Bub stood looking after him until his queer, wide-hipped, womanish body was dim and finally disappeared.

Well, Bub thought, I was wrong. They ain't changed a mite.

He took another deep drag on the cigaret, felt it grow warm on his upper lip, and snapped the butt away. Then he stooped and picked up the bag. Might as well go get something to eat. He hadn't eaten since early morning and was conscious now of hunger deep in his stomach.

There was a dim light in the window of the diner and he pushed the door open and went in. There were two or three people sitting at the counter—nobody he knew—looked like high-school kids. All the booths but the end one were full and he took that one quickly, sliding into the seat and shoving his bag under the table, not looking at anyone. He was hoping he wouldn't see anyone he knew. The meeting with Bob Haines had been enough for the first day. He just didn't want to see anyone else yet a while.

Bub ate ravenously. He hadn't realized until he smelled the food and saw it in its actuality before him on the plate how hungry he was. It filled him and made him feel relaxed, comfortable, his stomach a warm area of content. He leaned back, thrusting his legs out under the table and fumbling in his pocket for a cigaret before he remembered he'd smoked the last one in the pack on the sidewalk outside the drugstore.

Crossing the floor to the cigaret machine, Bub was overly conscious of eyes following him, of people watching every move he made. He thrust the coins into the slot and hated the noise the machine made vomiting the package into the tray at the bottom. He took it quickly and slouched back to his seat, realizing with

[5]

relief that he had been wrong. Nobody had turned to glance in his direction; everyone else was busy with food or conversation. He lit a cigaret and sat watching the three boys at the counter. They were hatless; their hair was bleached light by a summer of sunlight. Their faces had the clear, tanned, slightly ruddy skin of boys who are outdoors most of their time. They might have been brothers, but he didn't think they were. There was a likeness in all three, a regularity of feature, a similarity of color, that pointed to relationship. But he had seen enough kids like that in this same town to know they weren't brothers. He thought they were probably high-school kids who'd spent their summer caddying at the golf links.

What impressed him deeply was their youth, their look of extreme youngness. It was apparent in their hard young hands, the bones standing out bumpily at the knuckles; evident in the way they lit cigarets and sat blowing smoke with conscious toughness through widened nostrils. When he stopped to think, it startled Bub to realize they couldn't be much more than five years younger than he was himself. The way he felt there might easily have been a generation between them.

He was so interested in his watching that he barely heard the door open and wasn't aware that anyone else had come into the diner until he looked up with that being-stared-at feeling and saw the boy standing just inside the door looking at him.

Oh, hell! Bub thought viciously, that little bastard!

Malcolm wasn't moving, he was just standing there uncertainly, wondering if it really was Bub. Bub nodded his head slightly and watched Mack come across the floor toward him. Mack was just as dark as Bub remembered him. His skin looked oily and as if it needed a good scrubbing. He walked with the queer side-to-side lurching stride he affected, hands in his pockets, his shoulders thrust slightly forward as if he were on the verge of shoving somebody out of his way.

A few paces away Mack started to grin, still with uncertainty. Have I changed that much? Bub wondered idly.

"It *is* you, ain't it, Bub?" Mack said, easing himself into the seat across the table.

"Well, you can bet it ain't my ghost," Bub said.

"Jeez, you sure have changed!" Mack grinned widely, his mouth opening liplessly across his dark face. "You sure have changed a lot."

"That so?" Bub turned to glance at the counter. All three of the kids were watching them, looking over their shoulders. They glanced away hastily when Bub turned.

"I warn't sure it was you," Mack said.

"Well, it is." Bub couldn't think of anything he wanted to say Mack. It was too bad there wasn't something. There ought to be something you could talk about to your own brother when you hadn't seen him for five years, but he didn't have anything to say to Mack.

Mack's curious dark eyes had turned noncommittal, but they were giving Bub a thorough going-over. Bub stood it in silence, waiting. Knowing Mack, he was pretty sure what was coming. He wasn't disappointed.

"You—you ain't been in jail, have you?" Mack lowered his voice to a whisper, eying the pallor that underlay Bub's tan.

Bub laughed, a short jerk of sound, throwing back his shoulders. The twinge of remembered pain in his left side caught at him suddenly and he winced.

"No," he said loudly, "I ain't been in jail."

"Well, I didn't know," Mack said. "It's been five years since you left."

"Yeah. I didn't expect to find you around when I come back."

"I ain't been here long myself," Mack said. "Jest this summer. I been workin at the hotel since June."

"Plannin to stay next winter?"

"Like hell," Mack grinned. "You must think I'm a goddam fool. I'm gettin out jest as soon as the job's over. Sooner if they kick me out before."

Bub sat looking at his brother. He spotted the glint of silver on Mack's wrist and flicked at it with his finger. It wasn't a bracelet as he'd thought at first. It was an ordinary identification tag, but it had a social security number instead of a name. He was trying to figure just why it was he'd always admired Mack, thought he was so smart. It didn't make sense any longer.

"Still a smart alec, huh?" he asked softly.

[7]

Mack's face straightened and grew darker still.

"What you mean?"

"Ah, you kids make me sick," Bub said. "Ain't you ever goin to grow up? What's it get you, all this hossin around?"

"Well, for godsake!" Mack sat back on the bench, his face drawn into an evil impression of piety. "Since when've you started preachin?"

"I ain't preachin," Bub said impatiently, "I couldn't waste the time. I've got a lot better things to do with *my* time."

"Oh, yeah?"

"Well, what's that mean, for godsake?" Bub growled. He groped for the bag with his foot, shoved it out to the end of his bench, and started to get up.

"Hey, where you goin, Bub?" Mack said, forgetting his temper.

"I'm goin to find me someplace to sleep and then I'm goin to sleep for three days solid."

"Come on down to the hotel, I'll bed you down."

"No, thanks," Bub didn't try to hide the curtness.

He got up, glancing down at his brother.

"I'll be seein you," he said, and went over to the counter to pay his check. He knew Mack would be eying the billfold and he took out a dollar quickly, shoving the change and the wallet back into his pants pocket. He went out the door without looking back.

Outside, in the still, already-cool darkness, he stood for a moment not sure which way to turn. There was old Mrs. Barker, his grandfather's housekeeper. He'd always gone to her before —when the old man was alive. But he remembered the circumstances under which he'd seen her last and decided against it. She'd kept what she called her house money in an old cup in the dish closet. When he went away, Bub had taken the money with him and hadn't bothered to ask permission before doing it. He recalled vaguely a tourist place down around the corner. It was so strange to be back at the Harbor with money in his pocket that he couldn't quite make it real. Usually he'd waited until he was broke before he came home.

The tourist house was still there, the little sign nothing but a white blotch in the window. His knuckles had barely left the

[8]

wood before the door opened swiftly inward and a big, neat woman stood there looking at him. He saw her glance once at his canvas bag, but she waited for him to speak first.

"I—I'd like a room for the night," Bub said awkwardly, wondering if she'd know him when he stepped into the light. She went him one better and snapped on the porch light to get a look at him. Her broad, unlined, pink face was kind, but her eyes were wary. It gave him a slightly warm feeling to see her begin to smile a little.

"Why"—her voice was deliberate—"I guess we could fix you up, but—well, I have to be paid in advance."

"Oh," Bub grinned. "Oh, yeah; sure."

"Come in." She held the door open and stepped aside. Bub followed her up the carpeted stairs to the second floor. She opened a door to the right of the staircase and showed him into the room.

"Will this do?" she asked. "This one's a dollar for the night. Extra if you want breakfast."

"This is—this is fine," Bub said. He pulled out the wallet again and gave her a dollar bill. She stood there in the door uncertainly, looking at him, and Bub, hardly knowing how to act, waited for her to go.

"The bathroom's at the end of the hall," she said finally. "You can use it any time. I ain't got anyone else in the house tonight —except my husband, of course," she added, suddenly cautious.

"I guess business ain't what it used to be, is it?" Bub said, anxious to keep her there talking, enjoying the sound of her firm voice.

"No," she shook her head, "it ain't, an that's a fact. You come far today?"

"Just from Freehold," Bub said. He saw that she'd marked something familiar about him and was trying to place it. For a long moment he wondered whether or not to satisfy her curiosity and tell her who he was, but he decided against it. He didn't want to cope with that again tonight.

"Well," she said, "good night. I guess you'll find everythin you need."

"Good night." Bub didn't look at her again. He heard her

close the door carefully behind her and go slowly down the stairs. After that he could hear her voice and a man's somewhere downstairs at the back of the house. Looking around the room again, he forgot her.

It wasn't a large room, but there was something about it that made him feel as if he'd really come home. He tried to think how long it was since he'd slept in a room with curtains at the windows, and couldn't. He washed in the bathroom, hesitating over the towels and finally using a corner of one of the big white ones. He supposed that was what they were there for. There were some smaller smooth ones he didn't like the looks of. They didn't look as if they'd take up water at all, and he decided they were just for decoration.

Back in the room again, he undressed, folding his pants carefully and hanging them over the back of the straight chair. He wanted them to look fairly decent for tomorrow, because he was going to have to start hunting work. He'd bought himself the pants and a shirt in Portland on his way through. They were made of some sort of brown cotton cloth, and they were neat looking. The clerk who'd waited on him had grinned and said, "I'll bet you'll be some glad to get out of that uniform, bud."

His shoes were dusty, though, and he polished them with a dirty handkerchief.

He didn't have any pajamas, so he crawled into bed in his underwear, not liking to sleep raw. For a long time, although he was heavy with weariness, he lay there, hands behind his head, staring into the darkness. The voices were still going downstairs, but all he could hear was a slight blur of sound. The thin curtains at the window lifted into the room on the little wind, and he could hear them rasp back against the screens again when the wind faded.

He couldn't seem to get to sleep. There were so many things buzzing around in the back of his head. He'd drift to the edge of unconsciousness and then would jerk back again with that falling sensation that brings you away from the edge of sleep wide-awake and shaking with fear.

After it happened three times, he gave up and started to think about his father. Maybe he was too much like the old man. His

[10]

father had always been unsure, uncertain of himself, and that was the fault that explained him.

My old man! Bub thought bitterly, remembering the one time the old man had got up on his hind legs to tell them. It was Town Meeting Day, and by nine, when he was ready to go uptown, the old man was already half drunk. Scared, too, Bub knew, tagging along behind him. Lying there in bed he could even feel the cold of that March wind coming in across the harbor. The phrase "on the town" had never meant much to him—only that the town wouldn't let them starve. But he knew that was what the old man was going to tell them about.

Sam Benson was First Selectman then, and he was standing by the open front door of the Town Hall when Bub and his father went up the steps. Sam put his hand on the old man's chest and said softly:

"Where you goin, Tom?"

"To the Meetin—" the old man started to bluster—"to vote."

"Paupers can't vote," Sam said. "As long as the town's payin your bills, the town'll do your votin, too."

The old man looked as if he wanted to cry, but he didn't stop to argue. He just turned and went back down the steps again. Bub could remember glancing back once at Sam Benson, standing in the open doorway, looking well fed and ruddy. But the old man hadn't bothered to look back.

It was things like that that were going to make it hardest for him, Bub knew. People would say he had come from no-good stock—they would say a lot of things. Women would remember his mother as a woman who'd never been able to control her own kids and, worse, as a bad housekeeper. Men would recall his father as ineffectual and a drunk, and something to laugh at. It was going to be hard to make people forget.

Bub turned over with a sigh. It didn't seem as if it had all been so long ago. The last five years had been taken right out of the middle of his life. He couldn't believe now they'd been real. But he felt across his left side cautiously with one finger, and the ridged and scarred skin along his ribs and shoulder made him know they'd been real.

He settled down then and slept soundly, without dreaming.

When he awoke in the morning he knew it was late because he was hungry and the sunlight was hitting his window at a sharp slant. He lay for a minute watching the curtains blowing out into the room before he got up and dressed. He went cautiously into the bathroom and washed and shaved before going downstairs.

The woman had evidently been listening for him because she came out into the hall to meet him. This morning he could remember her name. It was Turner—Vera Turner.

"Well," she said, "I guess I don't have to ask you how you slept."

Bub grinned.

"I sure was comfortable," he said. "I ain't seen a bed like that in three years now."

"I didn't know whether to call you or not. You didn't say anythin about it last night."

"Nope," Bub shook his head. "That's all right. The sleep was just what I needed."

"You leavin town this mornin?"

"Nope," he said again. "I gut to find me a place to stay regular. You suppose I could leave this bag here till I do? I don't like to go luggin it all over with me."

"Sure thing," she said. "Just stick it there in the hall closet. It'll be all right until you come for it. You—you must have a job here."

Bub could sense her feeling out for something definite about him and he decided to satisfy her solid curiosity.

"Why, no, Mrs. Turner, I ain't got a job yet, but I'm lookin for one." He could see her stiffen at his use of her name.

"You ain't a town boy," she said. "How'd it happen you know my name?"

"Well, I used to live here a while back," Bub said. "My name's Bub Dolliver."

Watching her, Bub saw the instinctive change of expression when he mentioned his name. But she managed to hide it better than Bob Haines had the night before.

"Well, there, for the land's sake," she said. "I told Harvey last night you looked awful familiar. But I certainly didn't recognize you. You've changed out of all knowledge, ain't you?"

"I been told," Bub said, ducking his head slightly. "Guess I better be gettin along. Sure it's all right for me to leave this bag here?"

"Why, yes," she said slowly. "Leave it right there."

"Thanks a lot." Bub stuck the bag into the closet and closed the door. He nodded to her once more before going out. After he'd passed the front of the house, he looked back suddenly and thought he caught a slight movement of the curtains, as if somebody had dropped them and moved back out of sight when he turned his head.

MINOT'S HARBOR hadn't changed much. The streets still looked lazy and somnolent under the warm sunlight. There were fewer cars parked along the sidewalk. Before, the street had been crowded with the big cars of the summer people— Buicks, Packards, Cadillacs—with their out-of-state number plates; cars driven by the young, usually blond, boys and girls, their skins tanned to deep bronzy brown by Maine sunlight.

Now there were only three cars parked along the street, although it was nearly ten o'clock and time for the mail to be in. Bub could see the brilliant yellow and red of the mail truck by the post-office door. In front of the town hall stood the district nurse's Ford—he remembered the double-barred red cross. In the shade of the big maples before the doctor's house there was a hybrid jaloppy—a Reo roadster that had been converted into a light truck.

He stood on the corner, hands in his pockets, looking up and down the street. No, it hadn't changed much. The houses, small for the most part, painted white or brown or weathered to a silver gray, looked the same. Immediately behind the houses the woods started, young spruces and firs mixed with hardwood, an already thick scalplock, second growth, going up the hill. The houses all faced the same way, across the road toward the harbor.

[13]

It had that compact neat look of being snugged in that he'd thought of so often. It looked solid and settled, and that was what he wanted more than anything else. But he found himself nursing a seed of displeasure because it had changed so little.

There wasn't a place along the main street where he couldn't see the blue of water crawling under sunlight up the harbor; and the gulls hanging over the hill, squalling thinly, were a familiar sight and sound.

The whole town was nothing more than a double line of buildings set on a narrow shelf of rock between the hills and the water. Behind it the woods went up to the high bald top of Pentacook and the lower hills; in front, the gentler slope went down to the sea. And to the northeast the slow tides came and went up the low tidal valley where Bub had lain to watch the big hawk fishing through the late afternoon.

He lit a cigaret and stood smoking thoughtfully, trying to make up his mind what to do first. The town didn't look very active. He began to wonder if he'd been a fool to come back here thinking he could find something to do; but he shook his head impatiently. It was a hell of a note to start feeling like that before he'd even started looking.

Well, start! he thought impatiently. Just standing here, wondering, wasn't going to get him anywhere. He'd made his mind up a week ago that he would try the sardine factory last of all, but now it was the only place he could think of. He'd always been able to get work there when he couldn't find it anywhere else. His grandfather had been a sidekick of old Fred Pettigrew, and the old man had always put in a good word for him with Fred. Maybe Fred would be, after all, the person to see.

He turned slowly down the tarred road toward the harbor. Reluctance and a queer constrictive embarrassment made him go slowly, and going slowly, he could notice more things about the town. Down here it had changed. There were new houses, bright with fresh paint, small for the most part, but with nice lawns and flower gardens.

The morning was still calm. The wind hadn't blown up much to speak of, and the harbor was a smooth, opalescent sheet of water, its silver shading to gray and dark green in the shadow

[14]

of the wharves, but screeching into a blinding glisten in the direct sun.

When Bub had gone away, the sardine factory had been the largest thing along the shore. But that was different now. Across the harbor from the factory the boat yard, that he remembered as a collection of shaky shacks set around its own small tide cove, had built on until it was five times its original size. Out near the harbor mouth the old lobster factory that had leaned against the wind, ramshackle and windowless for years, was gone. In its place, on the small point of made land, a low, new-looking cluster of heavy buildings squatted on rock. Over them, on a high pole, an American flag whipped out lazily. As Bub went along the wharf road, he made out the high wire fence, and saw the pacing uniformed sentry. Recognizing the uniform, he knew the buildings must be the new Coast Guard station.

Two rawly new wharves jutted out between the station and the factory. One of them had the prosperous but somehow unbusinesslike look of public property. The other had the different appearance of prosperity given a place by the quick turnover of money. There were buildings on it and a big sign on a shed out over the water advertised sea food and marine supplies indiscriminately. He wondered who in Minot's Harbor would have had money enough to start a place like that one.

Still leering back enviously at the new buildings, Bub turned off the main road and went down the steep hill to the factory. The row of leaky shacks where the itinerant workers lived during the season was active now. Children of all ages and nationalities flocked around the buildings like seagulls after a trawler. The noise and the smell of the buildings came up to him like a familiar tide. Only one fishboat was in, tied up at the wharf and unloading. As he watched, the whistle overhead let out a shriek that stiffened him. He had forgotten just how penetrating that whistle could be when you were standing underneath it. He counted five short blasts. That meant the packers. The humming look of the place made Bub feel a little unsure of himself. Somehow this going concern didn't look like old Fred Pettigrew. A good many lazy days of loafing on this wharf had taught Bub that Fred was too easygoing for a place like this.

[15]

He went down the wharf toward the office building with that feeling of slight misgiving rapidly becoming stronger. The office was a small place, set slightly apart from the other sheds, splitting the right of way in two. To get to the wharf head you had to angle out by it, squeezing between it and the walls of the packing room.

Bub stuck his head in through the open pay window and stood waiting for the girl at the desk to look up at him. That was the first surprise. He'd expected to find Miss Blaisdell there, as she had always been, her long sheeplike face looking continually amazed; her shockingly acidulous tongue ready to blister him, as it had always done. But she was gone and in her place was this girl who looked to be just out of school.

She was pretty, though; dark, with short curly hair, and like all the young people he'd seen, she looked familiar to Bub, although he couldn't give her a name. But her familiarity was stronger than that of the others had been. He was scowling over her almost-remembered name when she looked up.

In the moment that she waited, smiling at him, Bub saw that her eyes were as dark or darker than her hair.

"Can I help you?" she asked.

"Well," Bub grinned foolishly, "I dunno. Ain't Miss Blaisdell here?"

"Oh, no," the girl shook her head. "She's been gone for two years."

"That so?" Bub said politely because he couldn't think of anything else to say. Suddenly his mind, that had been groping back to find her name, brought it up out of a mire of forgetfulness and Bub knew who she was and was surprised at himself that he hadn't known instantly. She was Lou Jellison, and she'd gone through school with him as far as he'd gone. She had been one of the group called "nice girls," not because their families had more money or were any better than other families, it was merely a phrase used to distinguish them from the kids who came from the factory camps and shacks like Charlie Barnes's.

Bub remembered her father, too, with less pleasure. The old man's name was Curtis and, as Bub recalled him, he was a big man with a big voice, and people said outside his own home he

[16]

liked to give his opinions loudly and didn't think much of having anyone disagree with him. Bub had never known Lou's mother except for one horrible moment so far back in his childhood that it was only an unpleasant feeling. He would recognize her when he saw her, but that was all. He had wondered, even as long ago as when he'd been in high school, how two people like Curtis and Edna Jellison could have had a daughter who looked like Lou.

There was an excuse for his not recognizing the girl instantly. She had lost, in growing up, that unconscious look of the snobbish little girl who's always been told that she's better than some others. She was fined down now, and her eyes met Bub's squarely, lighted with amusement but sober under the laughter.

"Well, do you know me yet?"

"Ayeh," Bub laughed in spite of himself. "I know you all right. How are you?"

"I'm fine," she said. "I recognized you the minute you stopped, but I wasn't going to let you know it until you'd made up your mind whether or not you knew who I was."

Bub glanced over his shoulder up the wharf and saw that Joe Pettigrew had come out of the storeroom door and stood there looking down toward them. Hell, Bub thought, I don't want nothing to do with that fool!

"Where's Fred?" he said hastily to Lou.

She laughed, throwing her head back.

"Anyone'd know it'd been a long time since you were around here. Old Mr. Pettigrew isn't running the factory any more. He hasn't been for a long time. But if you'll tell me what you want, I'll tell you who to see."

"Well, I was lookin for work."

"Oh," she nodded, "in that case, you want to see Joe. He takes care of all the hiring."

"I dunno whether I do or not," Bub said doggedly. "Ain't there anyone else? Let me see the feller's doin Fred's work."

"That's still Joe." Bub thought he detected a hint of sympathy in her eyes. "I'm afraid he's the one to see whether you want to or not."

"Well—" Bub started to turn away when he felt a hand descend on his shoulder and turned to face Joe Pettigrew. Five years had made Joe a little stockier and a little darker than he had been. But at ten-thirty in the morning, after he'd already put in three-and-a-half hours work, he preserved the irritating look of cleanliness that he'd always had. He looked painfully clean. The long grease spot on one leg of his faded blue denims merely emphasized the spotlessness of the rest of him. And to top the insulting picture, Joe wore a white shirt that had obviously been fresh that morning.

Joe's brown eyes were clear and steady, and his slightly thin lips had started to quirk into a grin.

"Well, Bub!" he said. "I thought it was you when I looked out the door. Been a long time since I seen you around."

"That's right," Bub said. He turned his head slightly so he wouldn't have to keep looking Joe in the eye.

"Bub," Joe said, turning to the girl in the office, "this is Lou Jellison."

"Yeah." Bub lifted his eyebrows slightly. "*I* went to school here too, Joe."

Joe laughed, a big, hearty booming of sound deep in his chest.

He don't have to act like he was God, does he? Bub thought.

"Was—er—was they somethin you wanted to see me about, Bub?" Joe asked.

"Well, no," Bub said. "I was really lookin for your old man; but I guess I got to see you instead."

Joe blinked slightly but succeeded in retaining his good humor.

"Is there any place where I can talk to you?"

"Sure." Joe jerked his head toward a pile of two-by-fours on the wharf head. Bub started toward them quickly, leaving Joe to say something over his shoulder to Lou. When Joe started after him, Bub was already seated on the pile of timber, slivering at the raw edge of wood with his thumbnail.

Joe dropped down beside him and dug a cigaret out of a crumpled pack.

"I'd offer you one, Bub, but that's my last," Joe said.

" 'S all right. Not my brand," Bub said. He took out one of his own and lit it.

"Well," Joe said, "this private enough for you?"

"Yeah, sure." Bub snorted brief laughter through his nose. He knew before he began that he might as well not bother, but he decided he'd better go through with it, just to be sure. He could see the narrowing anger beginning to grow behind Joe's eyes and, thinking back, Bub decided he couldn't blame Joe. They never had been very good friends.

"I just got back in town," Bub said shortly. "Thought I'd come down an see if they was maybe some kind of a job here."

"I see," Joe nodded slowly, staring away from Bub toward the big boat unloading along the wharf. "Well, Bub, I dunno."

"I didn't think you would."

"Now wait, Bub." Joe seemed to like to say the name. "That ain't no way to start in. Godsake, let me think, will you!"

"It ain't necessary, is it?"

"To be honest with you, Bub, no, it ain't. I'll tell you how it is. We need the men all right, but we ain't got time to put up with any shenanigans like you was always pulling. We got us a couple of Government contracts and their inspectors keep after us pretty close."

"Yeah," Bub nodded, narrowing his eyes. He'd be damned if he'd beg for anything from Joe Pettigrew. It wouldn't be worth his while. He could see that Joe had led him up to this just for the fun of turning him down and he wasn't going to let Joe see that it meant anything to him.

"We could use four or five more good men," Joe said. "You'd be just the thing, seein as how you know the job; but, well, you see how it is, don't you, Bub?"

"I sure do." Bub permitted himself to look slightly amused, to hide the bitter surge of disappointment he was beginning to feel. He had just realized how much he'd been counting on Fred Pettigrew.

"Anythin wrong with your old man?" he asked.

"Oh, no," Joe shook his head. "He just decided he needed a rest, I guess. So I took over."

"I see," Bub nodded and stood up.

"You might try the boat yard," Joe said. "They pay pretty good for unskilled labor."

"Thanks," Bub said. "G'by."

He went off up the wharf without looking back. He thought he caught a glimpse of Lou when he passed the office but he didn't hesitate or turn his head enough to make sure. When he reached the main road again he glanced back and saw the blue-and-white blur that was Joe leaning against the side of the office building.

For a moment Bub fought an impulse to go back and pound Joe's big head for him. Who the devil did he think he was, anyhow? And then the insanity of the impulse was apparent to him. What a sap he was to let that young fat-head get under his skin. Bub grinned slightly—this certainly wasn't much of a beginning. The trouble with you, he told himself, is you're too ready to start trouble. You ain't done anythin yet to make them think you're any different than you ever was.

He had been going to try the boat yard, but now he decided to wait a while. Give himself a chance to cool off. Just one turndown wasn't anything. There'd probably be a lot more before he finally got something to do. He fingered his billfold absently and hoped there wouldn't be too many. It wasn't necessary for him to take the wallet out to find out just how much money he had. He knew it by heart. There were two tens, a five, and three ones left now. And the handful of loose change in his pants pocket. Well, that was enough to eat on for a long time, and he could sleep anywhere.

Then he caught himself laughing at his own dramatics. He might as well stop right now being such a fool. Turning, he headed back down the road toward the boat yard. He found the office without difficulty, and went in.

This was different from the factory. There were three girls here, a couple of typewriters and one or two other machines that Bub remembered vaguely from his high-school days—adding machines or calculators or something like that. He hesitated in the open door, and one of the girls, the eldest, she looked, got up and came over to him.

"Yes?" she said noncommittally.

"I'm lookin for a job," Bub said. "Who do I have to see?"

"You want to see the foreman," she said. "Just a minute, I'll call the shop."

Bub stood waiting, half hearing her chase the foreman through one shop after another, finally getting him.

"He'll be here in a few minutes," she said, hanging up the receiver. "Do you want to wait here?"

"No, I'll go outside," Bub said. "What's his name?"

"Adam Barker."

"Thanks," Bub said, numbly. He went out and leaned against the warm clapboards in the sun. That tops it, he thought dully. Ad Barker! Old lady Barker's son, of all the damned things. He stood there, laxly, wondering where the dickens he'd turn next.

It was warm in the sun, and the heat waves danced back off the tin roofs of the buildings when he squinted at them. There was a screaming of saws in the air, harsh and like the ripping of heavy canvas. He could hear voices somewhere in the maze of buildings, and occasionally somebody passed him, going into the supply shop.

Bub stood up when Ad came around the corner of the shop and walked over to him. Ad was a little man, thick through, short, and he walked like a fussy woman. His red hair lay thinly over the top of his beginning-to-be-bald head, and his face was red from sun. He was grinning until he came close enough to see who Bub was, then his grin vanished as if he'd wiped it off with his hand.

"Bub Dolliver, ain't it?" he said.

"That's right."

"Lookin for a job?"

"Ayeh."

"Sorry." Ad turned and started back. He threw the last words over his shoulder like an afterthought, "Ain't nothin doin here."

Bub had been prepared for this as soon as he'd heard Ad's name, but his anger caught at him in spite of his preparedness. For a moment the sudden rage held him tongue-tied and stammering—a moment long enough for Ad to disappear around the corner of the building again. When Bub could have spoken, there was nobody there to hear what he had to say.

[21]

He grinned ruefully, tasting the brassiness of anger in his mouth. It's funny, he thought, the people who matter know me right off an don't like me. "Dam them," he said softly—and he wasn't talking about Ad Barker and Joe Pettigrew alone— "they've got to give me a chance." But the anger faded.

Already the morning was behind him and it was time to eat again. His stomach felt as if it had grown to his backbone. He fingered the change in his pocket thoughtfully. Might as well eat while he had it.

The diner wasn't full when Bub went in, and he had a chance to get the same booth he'd occupied the night before. The girl who waited on him remembered him and smiled a doubtful hint of a smile. But it was enough to make Bub feel better.

He ate stolidly, chewing steadily, his eyes fixed on the opposite seat. The food didn't seem to have much taste, but it filled his stomach and that was all he asked for. Now that he'd had time to recover from the blinding rage, he was beginning to see that this whole thing was funny in a backward sort of way. Here he'd come back all hepped up with the idea of being a nice boy and returning to the fold and, by the Lord Harry, they wouldn't let him! Well, Bub shrugged slightly, he'd darn well make them. He had as much right here as any of them. His father and his father's father, and so on back had lived here— and he was going to. His reception so far hadn't been exactly encouraging, but it had served to make him even more sure that he wanted to stay. After all, he couldn't very well blame them for the way they acted—he'd brought it on himself. And he wrinkled his mouth as if he'd swallowed a lemon—that didn't make it any easier to take.

Bub stopped chewing suddenly, his mouth full of apple pie, and looked silently at the boy who slid into the seat opposite him. Then he started chewing again and swallowed the mouthful before he spoke.

"Hi, June," he said. His eyes narrowed in concentration, taking in details of the kid. He *was* a kid, not more than sixteen; and when he'd been a little younger, he'd been a devil on wheels. Now June was a model of sartorial elegance. He wore a pair of white ducks that had apparently just come from an ironing board. His shirt was gaudy, but neat, the loose collar turned out over the collar of the brown jacket.

Even sitting still there, under the level scrutiny of Bub's wordless examination, June had a good deal of brash young swagger about him. He had developed a habit of squinting his eyes almost shut, throwing back his head slightly, and looking out through a gush of cigaret smoke that he blew up past his face with an out-thrust lower lip. He did it now, looking at Bub, and Bub had to lower his head to hide the sudden amusement in his eyes.

"Hi, Bub." June grasped his cigaret between a thumb and middle finger and leaned forward over the table. "I see Mack last night. He said you was in town."

"I just got in last night." Bub continued his inventory thoughtfully. The kid's face wasn't pleasant to look at. The lips were full and slightly slack, and the eyes, under a shock of sun-bleached, uncombed hair, were pale, almost colorless. Bub couldn't quite see how a thin face could contrive to look as heavy as June's did. The thick, light eyebrows almost met across the thin bridge of the nose, and the outer corners of the pale eyes pointed up.

"You goin to stay, Bub?"

"Yeah," Bub said heavily, looking away. "I was plannin on it. Been huntin a job this mornin."

"Any luck?"

"Not yet. Only tried two places."

"I know," June nodded wisely, grinning. "The sardine factory an the boat yard. That's where they all try."

"Yeah? Well, what's new with you?"

"Nothin much," June said. "The town ain't changed much, has it? Still jest as dead as it ever was."

"But it ain't too bad."

"Say, we used to liven it up a little, didn't we?" June grinned again. "You an me an Mack."

In spite of himself, Bub felt his face move stiffly into an unwilling reminiscent smile.

"We sure did," he agreed softly.

[23]

"Mack was tellin me you'd changed a lot, Bub. You sure look different."

"How did he mean 'changed?'"

"Oh, I dunno. You know how Mack is. Say, listen, Bub. You know, I bet my old man'd give you a job."

"Yeah!" Bub made no secret of his skepticism. "Since when'd your old man get to be givin anyone a job?"

"Well, you seen that new wharf down by the factory, ain't you?" June said. "That's his. He's doin a darn good business now. I work for him most the time. There's a bunch of other fellows, too. But he's been sayin he needs another guy just to run the wharf while the rest of us 're off somewheres."

"For pete's sake," Bub said. "I was wonderin who'd started that place. Your old man don't own it, does he?"

"Ayup."

The picture of sanctimonious Kelsey Bunker ever giving him a job made Bub say, "I can see him hirin me!"

"Well," June shrugged, "I was just tellin you. You said you wanted a job, didn't you?"

Bub nodded and got up.

"Guess I'll get along. Maybe I'll try it."

"Do that," June said. "Better than nothin."

He sat still as Bub crossed the room and went out the door; and he watched Bub hesitate just outside and then turn again toward the wharves.

Kelsey Bunker was a big, slow-moving man—he looked solid from his huge feet to his immense shoulders. In spite of the slowness of his motions, he managed to do more work than three other men. He had the strength of a bull, with the weight behind it, and he used it well. He was almost completely bald; there was only a fringe of hair left, just above his ears, and that was gray. The rest of his head and his long pious face were burned a deep, bright red.

When Bub came down the wharf all he could see of Kelsey was the sunburned top of his bald head, but that was enough to identify him. Kelsey was feet-first up under the spray hood of a big boat moored alongside the wharf, doing something with

[24]

the engine. Occasionally he slammed a wrench down on the planking and said something in a loud, monotonous voice. Bub heard the voice and recognized the anger; but Kelsey wasn't swearing. He didn't believe in profanity and went to great, seemingly impossible, lengths to avoid it. Bub stood for a moment, leaning on an odorous bait barrel, just listening.

Kelsey had subsided to a baffled muttering like a dying volcano. He spun the flywheel, the engine turned over twice, and sputtered into silence. Kelsey hurled the wrench he'd been holding at the cheeserind, missed it, and knelt, watching the bubbles coming up slowly through green water where the wrench sank.

"Sweet Jee-rusalem!" Kelsey howled.

He crawled out from under the spray hood, stood up, and looked at Bub.

"Well?" he roared. "Well?"

"I see Junior uptown," Bub said. "He said you was lookin for a man to take care of the wharf here."

"That's right," Kelsey's voice started up like a steam whistle, "I am."

"Well, I didn't know but what I might get the job."

"You?" Kelsey subsided like a pricked balloon. The immensity of the suggestion seemed to take his wind away.

Bub nodded.

"Well," Kelsey said thoughtfully, his voice returning once more to normal, a tone with Kelsey something between a buzz saw and a calliope with a booming undertone, "now, I dunno. I dunno's I was lookin for you. It's a job'd take a man with responsibility, see?"

He glanced at Bub from under shaggy eyebrows amazingly like June's. His small brilliant eyes had all but disappeared in a network of wrinkles, and the hairless expanse of his face and head shone as if they'd been polished with an oily rag.

"How much does it pay?" Bub beat him to the gun.

"Twenty-five," Kelsey said. "And I ain't made up my mind I want *you*. Seems to me you're takin a lot for granted. You warn't never what you could call responsible. Your old man warn't neither. I gut to have somebody I can trust. You'd hev to handle money an gas an I dunno which's worth most nowadays. I gut to get somebody I can trust."

"You want a hell of a lot for twenty-five dollars," Bub said.

"No swearin," Kelsey shrieked. "No swearin on my wharf. You keep your dirty mouth shut whilst you're workin for me."

"I ain't yet."

"Well," Kelsey yelled, "I can tell you right now, I wouldn't hire you if they was anyone else I could git. They's two things you gut to do: don't let me see that brother o yourn around here on my propitty—that's one; the other is, if I ever catch you pullin any shenanigans, I'll have your scalp! Hear me?"

"I don't see how I could help it." Bub straightened up. "Want me to start work in the mornin?"

"Yes, an that don't mean noon, neither," Kelsey roared. "You be here by six o'clock or you'll find you ain't been hired after all."

Well, Bub thought, going back up the wharf, there's the job, by the judast! Now all I gut to do is find me a place to stay. He thought of old lady Barker again, but remembered Ad and decided against that. No point in trying to stir things up any more than they were already. He had never realized before just how tenacious memory was, and how the things that people remembered were never the good things.

Because he happened to be passing the footpath that led up through the alder swamp to Charlie Barnes's shack, he turned and went easily up the low hill over the rooted ground. Charlie would know if there was some sort of a place he could find to bed down in. Charlie had never been snooty the way other people had. He'd married a Portuguese woman and he himself was poor white. Charlie might know of a place he could get cheap.

Charlie was sitting in front of his open door mending a net that wasn't much more than one big mend itself. He looked up when Bub came out of the fringe of alders and picked his way across the stump-littered yard.

"Hi, kid," Charlie said, without surprise. "When'd you hit town?"

"Last night." Bub squatted on the doorsill and for a while

[26]

they sat in silence. Finally Charlie picked up the stub of a cigaret from the ground by his feet, brushed it off carefully, and stuck it in his mouth. Bub watched him trying to light it without singeing the week's growth of beard he always sported.

"What you doin?" Charlie asked.

"Got me a job workin for Kelsey Bunker."

"*That* damned old fish horn!" Charlie said, and spat scornfully toward the edge of alders.

Bub laughed. "Well, he's the only man in town willin to have me work for him, I guess."

"You was always too anxious to be hell-raisin." Charlie squinted at his net and started knitting again.

"I can change, can't I?" Bub said.

"I dunno," Charlie said. "Can you? Where you been, anyhow?"

"All over," Bub waved his hand. "No place special."

"Why ain't you in the Army?"

"Maybe they ain't caught up with me yet," Bub said, remembering nights of slogging through jungle, days of lying absolutely still in steaming green water because the slightest motion brought the sharp crack of a rifle and the screaming sting of lead through the air just above his head. By god, he thought, I ain't goin to tell them any of that. They can take me the way I am or not at all.

The sound of their voices had brought someone to the door of the shack behind them and Bub turned to see who it was. Momentarily he didn't recognize the girl, she'd grown so. Nina was Charlie's eldest girl, she couldn't be more than seventeen or eighteen now, but she moved and carried herself like a woman of thirty—and it was nothing like heaviness that made her seem that old. Bub eyed her and looked down thoughtfully at the nearly naked young savage who clung heavily to her leg.

"I thought your kids'd be all grown up by now, Charlie."

"That one is," Charlie jerked his head toward Nina without moving his eyes from his work. "She's too dam big for her britches. Thinks they ain't nothin anyone can tell her. I dunno but what she's right, too. The kid's hern."   •

Nina moved out into the sunlight and sat down easily, set-

[27]

tling her back against a stump. Her level dark eyes appraised Bub slowly. She didn't bother to speak. Bub, accepting the child without comment, tried to stare her down for a moment, then gave it up—there wouldn't be any staring that one down.

"Thought you might know of some place I could get to live, cheap," he said to Charlie.

Charlie thought for a moment.

"There's that old shack of Pete's you could have if you wanted it. It ain't much. Just an old fish house. But you could use that for upkeep, I guess."

"How much'd that be?"

"Oh, two-fifty a week, maybe."

"Down near the factory, ain't it? Don't Pete use it any more?"

"The Army caught *up* with Pete," Charlie said stoically.

Bud nodded.

"Well," he got up slowly and stretched, "I'll get along and settle in. I gut to start work in the mornin."

Charlie handed him a padlock key.

"Don't let Kelsey gyp you out of your pay," he said. "He will if he thinks he can git away with it."

"Not me, he won't gyp," Bub said. He moved off down the path, rolling his hips slightly and grinning at himself, realizing he was doing it because Nina sat staring after him. She wasn't bad, he thought, but somehow he didn't want to get mixed up with a girl like Nina now. He could all right—he'd seen that much in her sulkily good-looking face before he stopped looking at her. But that wasn't what he'd come back for; and besides, he didn't think he liked the idea of sharing his girl with four or five other fellows. He thought suddenly then of Lou Jellison. Now she was more like it, but he had a pretty good idea just how far he'd ever get with a girl like Lou.

His face was wry when he came out into the road. That was another trouble with coming back like this, the girls you'd want wouldn't look at you, and the ones you didn't want were all ready and waiting.

Bub got his bag and went down the narrow footpath along the shore from the factory to the old, now unused, canning building. Somebody had told him a long time ago they used

[28]

to can beans there, but it had been empty now for years, and there was no machinery left in the place. Its door hung open loosely, the rollers stiff and useless, and he peered in as he went by. Nothing but darkness and cobwebs.

Pete's place was the smaller shed out on the end of the wharf. The only thing between it and the water was a narrow hand-rail made of peeled spruce poles. The big padlock on the door looked fairly new. Probably Pete hadn't been gone long, and he'd never used a lock when he lived there. Bub sprung it open and shoved the door wide, recognizing the musty smell of an unoccupied room before he stepped in. It was a little place, only two small rooms separated by a thin beaverboard partition that stopped short of the roof. He was surprised to find it so clean. The only dirt was the thin sifting of dust that had collected since Pete moved out.

The front room was the place where Pete had spent his time. There were a potbellied little stove, a table, a couple of chairs. Over in one corner was the sink, and above it a cupboard full of dishes and pans. He went to the door of the other room and glanced in. It was dark in here, only one window, and that small; but he saw the bed with blankets folded and piled on the bare mattress. He hauled the blankets and the mattress out and spread them over the railing to take out the smell of must. Then he built a fire in the stove to kill the dampness in the air. No point in his getting his death of cold before he even started in.

It wasn't going to be so bad, he decided, staring around him. He couldn't get over his feeling of surprise that Pete had kept the place so clean. He couldn't have been much like his brother Charlie; Charlie's place was always a mess, and on days when the wind was right it seemed as if you could smell it clear down to the road.

That night, after he'd laid in some groceries and come back to the shack, Bub settled in. The last thing he did was to bring out his dress uniform and hang it on a wooden shoulder hanger on the back of his bedroom door. He smoothed out the worst creases with his hands and pulled the trousers and tunic into some sort of shape again. Then he swung the door back so he wouldn't have to see it at all. He knew he would never look at it with any sentiment, that it would hang there until it rotted away; but he was Yankee enough to dislike the thought of it rotting in a bag in a dark corner. It was good goods, and although hanging it on the door meant nothing, it was better than thinking of it crumpled and out of shape, stuffed into a hole.

The tide was still flooding up the harbor, and when Bub stepped out the door onto the wharf, the deep, lightly colored warm night was alive with the smell of salt water and the sound of it. The smell and the sound of friendly water! He stood, hands thrust deep into his pockets, one shoulder cocked against the door frame, mooning at the wide level blackness of the water. And he could see more than his eyes saw; he could sense more than was spread out before him.

He could see the long, golden, dreamy days of wandering along the shore; could feel the hard square edges of the red granite ledges above the high-water mark, the water-worn smoothness of the boulders over which the tides came and went twice a day. He could remember the gulls wailing up, disturbed, out of the lazy tidal coves, the sharp fall days far up the estuary, the early mornings when the moss of the swamps was still crusty with frost underfoot. He felt the gray stillness before sunrise when the ducks started coming down across the sky with their sharp, hard flights, like bullets that had been given low wings; the calm winter mornings with the sea and sky gray and no breath of wind to make so much as a shadow on the water, mornings when the woods looked like those wrought-iron scenes they used to frame and hang on the living-room wall. He saw the thin slush of ice that made its hush-hush sound along the shore in the little ground swell; and somewhere, out of sight behind the bronze island, there would be a flock of oldsquaws yapping like a pack of dogs.

He had been homesick not for people but for times, colors, places. And they were all here, behind this level lowly-shining black water surface—just as they had always been and always would be.

There's one thing, Bub thought, feeling his mind groping for what he was trying to put words to, that's the biggest thing in your life. Sometimes you think maybe it's money; that's when you're young, when you ain't had a chance to get around. Then you think the most important thing is gettin money. That's because money gets dinned into you from the time you get to put any meanin to the word "money." Money, and gettin it. Get all you can. Money's what people'll judge you by—whether you've got it or not. Havin it lets you get a lot of other things. You can buy anythin with money.

That's when you're young.

When you git a little older, maybe when you're just old enough to know you ain't goin to get a lot of money and a lot of things, when you find out there's some people who git pretty happy without havin a lot of it, then you have to find somethin else important to take the place of money.

That's all right, he thought, that's just fine! But what am I goin to do? I can't just come back, I got to *do* somethin. Can't work around for someone else all my life.

But maybe he'd find out. Maybe he'd make up his mind what it was he wanted bad enough to work for it. There was time now. Here there didn't seem to be any need to hurry and shove all the time.

Lying in the big double bed that night, Bub could hear the rhythmic slapping of water against the pilings under the old wharf, and the sound made him sleepy. It had been a long time since he'd gone to sleep to the sound of water like that. He felt more at home than he had so far; safer, more comfortable, and completely relaxed.

THE AIRPLANE spotter shack was nothing but a crow's nest of rough pine boards built on a little tower above the factory. Every time Bob Haines climbed the rickety ladder and opened the trap door that let him up onto the platform, he wondered just how long it would be before he'd put a leg through the thin planks and break it. It'd be after that happened that somebody'd take it into his head the platform ought to be stronger.

Standing there silently, staring out across the bare sea and sky blackness, he shifted uneasily from one foot to the other, feeling the uncertain give of the wood under him. He was sucking on an empty pipe, and the acrid old taste of the stem was familiar to him. Everything he could see and feel was familiar through long years of constant association. The only thing that was strange was what he was looking for. And it didn't seem possible that it was necessary for him to stand here and stare out into the velvet-looking, star-spotted sky for planes that would bring death with them. That was the only strange thing.

"Hey, Bob, see any Stukas?" The raucous yell was muffled by the closed door between them, but it made Bob jump. He turned and edged quickly into the shack.

"Naw," he grinned sheepishly, shaking his head.

Hersh Baker was sitting in the straight kitchen chair under the direct light of the unshaded bulb that hung down on a length of raw wire from the center of the board roof. He had a sheet of funnies spread out on the table and was going over them with the completeness of a vacuum cleaner.

"Honest, Hersh, you're a pretty smart feller, but what you see in them things is beyond me," Bob said.

Hersh looked up. In the harsh light his big face was smooth, the skin brown and shiny, and the eyes brilliantly blue, half shaded against dazzle. His features were functional—not much in the way of beauty, but just what they ought to be to fill the purpose for which they'd been put where they were. They had a sort of handsomeness that wouldn't have been there if any one of them had been a shade different. His rough light hair looked almost red. His big, blocky figure sprawled easily in the rickety chair, and Bob eyed the long, thin, dungareed legs with a touch of envy.

"I gut to do somethin to relax my mind," Hersh said. "I can't stand outside all the time communin with nature the way you do, Bob. I gut big things on my mind an I gut to have somethin to distract me."

"You!" Bob snorted briefly. "Whatta you gut on your mind besides your hat?"

"Ida," Hersh said succinctly. His face wasn't smiling now; it

[32]

looked drawn and a little worried. He folded the funny paper carefully into its original creases and stuck it back into his pocket.

"Whatsa matter?" Bob asked with real concern. "She ain't plannin on leaving you, is she, nothin like that?"

Hersh's shocked face was all the answer he needed.

"Well, then, what's wrong with her? She sick?"

"Yeah," Hersh nodded. "She's awful sick."

"Why, Hersh, I'm sorry to hear that. What's wrong with her?"

"I dunno's I should say," Hersh said soberly, "but it seems as if I'd bust if I didn't talk about it."

"It—it ain't nothin serious is it?" Bob said, hastily. Hersh's wife was too young, she couldn't be more than twenty-three or four. She couldn't have much wrong with her, that young.

"She's . . ." Hersh said, then he stopped and looked down at his big hands; he spread the fingers out flat against the table top and drummed uneasily. "Well, Bob, she's gonna have a baby."

Laughter with Bob Haines was an unusual thing. He made it unusual. His face was straight, no expression whatsoever moved his smooth features, but he opened his mouth and the amusement came out in a long series of droning roars, beginning at full volume and ending in a faint nasal moan. The first roar stiffened Hersh in his chair, and the final ones found him beginning to be mad.

"Now, looka here, for chrissake . . ." he said heavily, getting up.

The sound of voices outside stopped him.

"What's wrong in there?" somebody yelled.

Bob turned out the light and opened the door cautiously.

"Oh, hello, Joe," he said, recognizing Joe more by his outline than by the sight of his face. "Who's that with you?"

"Me'n Batty was down on the wharf an it sounded like somebody was bein murdered up here."

"Come on in." Bob stood aside to let them pass him. "If you hadn't come along when you did, Hersh was just about ready to murder me."

He turned on the light again and they stood blinking at each other.

"An you wouldn't blame me a mite, neither," Hersh growled, but he'd begun to smile a little.

Batty stood looking from one to the other, his queer Indian face dark under his stringy black hair, his black eyes expressionless and dull. His thin high shoulders always made Bob think of a ruminative crane fishing on the ebb tide.

"What's the matter, son?" Batty said, turning his strange long head slightly and moving his entire torso to do it. "You ain't let nothin that old kooter said bother you, have you?"

"Well, I was tellin him how sick my wife was an he don't do nothin but stand there an laugh like a fool."

"She sick, Hersh?" Joe said. "I didn't know there was anythin wrong with her."

"There ain't," Bob said. "She's just goin to have a baby."

"Oh!" Joe started to grin then and sat down in the chair Hersh had vacated.

"It's all right for you to laugh," Hersh said bitterly. "You'd laugh outn the other side of your face if she was *your* wife."

"Now look, son, they ain't nothin to get excited about jest because your wife's goin to have a baby," Batty said soothingly. "Women're like that. Seems as if they just go around havin one now an then to spite the men."

"Just the same, it's an awful responsibility," Hersh said.

"Darn tootin," Joe nodded sagely.

"Well," Batty said, "jest so long's she don't go havin hankerins for things. An nothin don't happen to her to mark it. Why, I remember a woman once was goin to have a young-un an she wouldn't eat nothin to speak of. All's she'd do was drink milk from a certain spotted cow. When the baby come along, durned if it didn't have a spot over its eye jest exactly like that cow."

Hersh uttered a strangled squawk.

"Don't you let him spoof you, Hersh," Bob said. "Why, you take my mother, fore I was born. It's still a byword in the family the way she went for rabbit stew. Why, she couldn't get enough of the darned stuff. Used to eat it til the old man was

[34]

afraid it'd start runnin out of her eyes. An look at my ears, they ain't nothin like a rabbit's."

"No, they ain't, are they?" Batty said thoughtfully. "Well, I never put much stock in that story anyhow. I never see the baby myself, so I don't rightly know. But women do get cravin things to eat sometimes, the craziest things you ever heard of. You just go ahead an humor her, Hersh, an everythin'll turn out hunkey-dory."

"How come you know so much about women, Batty? I don't know's I ever saw you botherin much with them?" Joe said, grinning up into the strange, impassively brown Indian face.

"I hed me one wife," Batty said, "an ever since I've steered clear of the breed. Dunno but what I've got a couple of kids still livin off to the westward."

"That's right, too," Bob said. "I'd forgot all about that, Batty."

"I don't never talk about it much," Batty said. "I hed to make a darned fool of myself to get her, an by the judast! she warn't no bargain even after all the trouble I went to. I hed my fill of her in short time, an I guess she gut hern of me. Leastwise, she ain't been around here after me."

"What was she like?" Joe said.

"I'll tell you." Batty shifted his feet slightly and clasped his hands behind him, staring down at the unpainted floor. "They's two kinds of women. When they're good tempered, they're all alike; it's when they're mad, the two kinds comes out. One kind's sitters. They jest sit and sull like a moody cow when they're put out with you. The other kind's talkers. She was a talker, an me, I never could abide anyone who'd stand around an jaw my ear off, anyhow. I'm too fond of talkin myself to put up with that. So I up an left her. It makes me mad still when I think of what I hed to do to git saddled with her in the first place."

"What?" Bob said the monosyllable they were all waiting for.

"Well," Batty grinned slightly, and all it amounted to was a faint spark of red in his sloe eyes, "she was real interested in the west, seems like. An she found out somehow I hed Indian blood in me. Nothin would do but what I hed to git me a horse an a feather an ride up and down with her hangin on behind me and screechin her head off. Then when she gut tired, she'd git off an

[35]

set an watch me ride some more. I tell you, I gut some tired of chasin them old roosters jest to git a feather to stick behind my ear.

"She set out to make me a real war bonnet like they have in the movies, but I drawed the line there, by the judast. I said I warn't havin any and she would jest have to take what the good Lord sent her an be thankful I was near as patient as He was."

"Boy-oh-boy!" Bob said, and the long sigh he drew served to strangle back another attack of awful mirth. "That must have been a thrillin sight, now. I can just see you, Batty, riding up an down with a feather. . . ."

"Ba-*bee!*" Joe drew in his breath in simulated admiration, "D'you finally kidnap her, Batty?"

"'S matter of fact, it was jest the other way around," Batty said. "I hadn't quite gut to the point of makin up my mind I wanted her or not when I come to find out she'd gut me in front of a preacher after all, an it was too late to do anything about it."

"Schemin creatures, ain't they," Bob said. "What was her name, Batty?"

"Maud," Batty said shortly. "Jest Maud. But I'm tired of talkin about her. Jest rememberin the way she could wag her jaw makes me tired."

"You ever find out what become of her?" Hersh said curiously.

Batty turned on him with what would have been a snarl in anyone else, but was a mere lifting of the upper lip with him.

"I said I was tired of talkin about her," he said. "I don't want to say no more about her."

"All right, all right," Hersh put up his hand, palm flat out, and backed away slightly.

"I see Bub Dolliver's come home," Bob said quickly, filling in the sudden startled silence with the first thing that came into his head.

"Yeah," Joe nodded. "He was down here lookin for a job."

"Give it to him?" Bob asked with real interest.

"You think I'm crazy?" Joe's mouth drew down into a half-sneer. "I wouldn't have nothin to do with that boy. Wouldn't touch him with a ten-foot pole."

"Well, I tell you," Bob sounded thoughtful, "I hate to see people feelin that way. That kid's changed a good deal, I think. He's fined down some an looks like a real decent kid. I tell you, when he spoke to me the other night, I wouldn't a known him, he's changed so."

"He looked jest the same to me," Joe said, "an I can remember him too dam well."

"Well, you can take it from me," Bob said thoughtfully, "he ain't the same. Jest for the hell of it, I'd like to know what he's been doin since he left town."

"Yeah, an so would a lot of other people, includin me," Joe said. "Five'll get you ten it warn't nothin to brag about or he'd be braggin."

"When you get down on a guy you stay down, don't you, Joe?" Hersh said suddenly, his bright eyes blank on Joe's heavy, handsome face.

"I tell you I know him too well," Joe said. "He couldn't ever change enough to be so different I'd want to have anythin to do with him."

Batty turned toward the door and put his hand on the knob. Bob reached up without having to think, and snapped off the light. Batty hauled the door open and then stood there a moment before going out. He must have turned back to face them because his reedy voice was high and direct, not as if he were speaking over his shoulder to them, but as if he were looking at them.

"That's what's the trouble with the world today," he trumpeted. "They's too many people too darn ready to say a feller's no good. If you warn't so willin to be mindin the business of other people, the other people'd get along a lot better than they do, and so would the bunch of you."

He shut the door.

"For pete's sake," Joe said into the silent dark, "what's bitin him? I'm gettin along all right, ain't I?"

WORKING FOR Kelsey, Bub found, wasn't so simple as he'd thought it was going to be. Early in the mornings he was always busy with the men who wanted gasoline, or who wanted a coil of warp from the store, or a set of oars, or some other thing that couldn't wait. They kept him going from the time he opened up until around nine o'clock.

He liked the store building and it made him feel important to have the key on a brass ring in his pocket. It was something that Kelsey evidently trusted Bub enough to let him have a duplicate of his own key. The building wasn't really like a store. It was just a big bare room with various kinds of marine hardware and supplies stacked around the walls. And Bub had his hands full hunting things up. There was no system of any sort to the stuff. Just piled there along the walls as the shipments came in. Selling anything was a process of hunting until you found what you wanted.

After nine or ten o'clock in the morning the summer people kept him on the go. They would come down to the little shed where he kept the big kettle steaming gently over the fire and the pungent smell of lobsters and fish was always in the air. They'd want lobsters, and if they wanted them alive, he had to go off to the lobster car in the leaky punt Kelsey kept for the purpose and net the lobsters out. If they wanted them boiled, then Bub boiled them. The only difference was the boiled ones cost five cents more a pound.

He was mildly surprised at the extent of Kelsey's business. Kelsey had evidently discovered a gold mine when he put up this wharf. Everything that went on around the harbor seemed to have its root there. He was busy himself all the time and he expected Bub and everyone else who worked for him to keep just as busy as he did. Kelsey had started a sideline now that was threatening to grow beyond anything he had yet done. He was buying fish in competition with the combine and shipping them down to Portland in his own trucks. He had three, all Fords. Bub found that Junior's job consisted of driving one of the trucks. June would start off late at night, making it into Portland by early morning, sleep over there during the day and come back to the Harbor the next night. It was pretty much the kind

[38]

of job that would appeal to a kid like June, make him feel big and important.

Later in the day, when things had just begun to quiet down, the boats came in and there was the day's haul to handle. The boats, trawlers, and a few draggers came into the wharf one by one, unloaded, filled up with gas, and pulled out again. The crew on the wharf started weighing then, handling five-hundred pounds of fish at a time. They were ground fish, mostly—haddock, cod, cusk, pollack, and hake. The crew dressed them out, washed them, packed them into the barrels for weighing, and then headed the barrels up with burlap. Occasionally there were flounders, packed in flat boxes with the stenciled sign along the side, ICE IN TRANSIT; the sign at which Bert Pettigrew, Joe's younger brother, looked with open-mouthed surprise. "Transit!" Bert said. "Where the hell *is* that place, anyhow?"

There was a good stiff day's work to do and Bub found that he enjoyed doing it more than he had expected to.

Bub hadn't been working on the wharf long before he discovered how Kelsey checked up on him. Kelsey would come down in the early morning, after six, when Bub had just unlocked the store door. "Well . . ." Kelsey would stick his hands in his pockets and rock back and forth on his big toes. "Well, guess I'll go haul my traps. Gut to keep busy, you know; gut to keep busy. I wun't be back before three o'clock. Goin to stop by Sag Island. Want to hev a little talk with m' brother Jay. Be back bout three or a little after."

It seemed to Bub that the echo of his huge voice was still circling in the air when Kelsey rowed off to the mooring and started up his engine. Bub would stand there on the wharf watching the big white boat pull out of the harbor. It seemed strange to him to see the numerals painted on the roof of the coop, and repeated in black on the bow, ten times their original size. That was for easy identification by the coast patrol, he knew; but it looked funny. Messed a boat up some.

In his mind he would be carefully sorting away the knowledge that Kelsey wouldn't be back until three. That meant so many uninterrupted hours. He wouldn't start listening for the engine

[39]

until three, and that was why Kelsey succeeded in surprising him the first two or three times.

If he'd said three, Kelsey would turn up silently at two, letting his voice out to its full power the moment he came in sight of Bub.

"There!" he'd scream in justified self-pity, "What the screamin blue blazes you doin, Bub? I mighta known you wouldn't do anythin but lay around once I took my eye offn you. Ain't you gut nothin else to do? I ain't payin you no twenty-five dollars a week to loaf. I gut plenty to do, you oughta manage to keep busy. I can't go follerin you around to see you don't loaf on the job. Git goin, now, git!"

After it happened twice, Bub caught on and he never let Kelsey sneak up on him again. It was simple. All he had to do was keep at hand something he could be instantly busy with.

Kelsey had another habit that was galling until he got hardened to it. He'd open the cash drawer at intervals, always irregular ones. He'd come into the store, open the cash drawer and stare into it, blowing his lips slightly in and out, appearing to count. Then he'd stare over at Bub, his little eyes almost lost in the netting of fine wrinkles that meant he was grinning.

He never said anything then. He just looked into the cash drawer and stared at Bub. After a while Bub got used to it and let it roll off, but the first few times it was hard to do.

There was something else Bub had to stare down, though, and this was a little more difficult than Kelsey's obvious and heavy-handed baiting. Kelsey's distrust was so open that it was almost funny, he didn't even trust himself, and a thing like that was easy to face. But this other was different. This was the distrust and subtle distaste of the men Bub had to do business with daily; and the older ones were the worst. They were men who'd known his father and who remembered him, Bub, as a fresh kid with a furious temper. They never flattered him by showing open dislike, they never said anything with which he could find fault, and that was just what troubled him most. If they'd come out in the open, Bub thought, he could have answered them, could have shouted them down. But they didn't. They just looked at him, coolly evaluating, and their eyes slid easily away from his angry stare. God! Bub thought angrily, watching them, talk about women an elephants!

They obviously thought Kelsey several kinds of a fool to give Bub a job. None of them would have done it. That much their eyes said. But they were civil enough when they had to speak to him. They said "Mornin." They told him what they wanted in short brief words. They said "S' long." That was all. But their eyes, when they had to talk to him, were wary, leering away from him, always looking away. They took nothing for granted.

The attitude of the younger men who hung around the wharf, and the few who worked there, puzzled Bub a little at first, until he began to see through it. The tone of their voices when they spoke to him was always the same—a half-amused, belligerent, noncommunicative voice. They treated him with exaggerated care that almost seemed jealous. They were mostly fellows who'd gone to school with him. There was Hershel Baker. He was big, and blond, and clumsy, and his blue eyes, looking amazingly bright in his huge brown face, could never meet a glance directly. Hersh looked at you and then, out of shyness, his eyes immediately slid away and looked attentively at something else all the time he was talking. Hersh was big, his huge shoulders looking out of proportion to the slenderness of his hips, and he could pick up a hundred-and-twenty-five pound kedge with one hand, and had done it often enough.

Bert Pettigrew was another. Joe's younger brother was as heavy as Hersh was. But he was built differently—short and barrel chested, solid from his shoulders on down to his feet. From the rear he looked square, low slung, and heavy as an ox. Bert, Bub thought, meeting his jeering dark eyes steadily, was going to be the reef he'd split on if any of them were. The careful belligerence he'd noticed in the others was more than that in Bert. It was an insolent dare Bub saw every time he met Bert's eyes. And that was hardest of all to take.

At noon on the Saturday of his first full week, Bub stood around with the others waiting for Kelsey to bring out the plain white envelopes. He took his with a nod of his head and stepped aside, waiting to open it. After the others had gone on up the

[41]

hill, he stood alone on the dock with the envelope in his hand, looking out across the harbor. Then he stuck his finger under the flap, tore it open and poured the money out into his palm. There was a little paper slip showing what had been taken out for Social Security and for taxes. He read the slip carefully, straining over Kelsey's pointed jagged figures; then he stowed it away in his wallet, but he kept the money in his hand for a minute.

It wasn't much. He'd had this much before. But this was different. This was the first money he had ever earned as a civilian, doing a man's work, at a steady job. And it represented something. It meant steadiness and settling down; it meant coming home and doing something useful.

When he was a kid Bub had thought a lot about money. He had become preoccupied with the idea of money the way kids who don't have enough of it often do. Not with the thought of what he could buy with money, but just with the idea of having a lot of it somewhere, stowed safely away where he could look at it and count it over. At first the imaginary fortune had been in paper bills; then, after he found out that the paper just represented money and wasn't actually money itself, the fortune was converted into silver—half-dollars, quarters, dimes. He had wondered if there ever was one bill that meant a million dollars; one piece of green paper that meant a million dollars in gold stowed away somewhere. He had wondered what it would feel like to hold it in your hand; probably a lot different than just holding a one-dollar bill.

Money meant a lot in a small town. It meant the difference between asking a man's opinion and having him ask yours; and Bub knew that nobody had ever asked his father's opinion on anything.

Bub had pictured a room half-filled with fifty-cent pieces, he saw them on the floor like coal in a bin, and he thought of the flat chinking sliding sound they'd make when he walked on them. He'd planned to walk barefooted, and the silver would have been smooth and cool under his feet.

He looked down at the money in his open hand and then tucked it flatly into his billfold, remembering the way he'd thought about money when he was a kid. He grinned slightly at his young foolishness, but he felt unreal, a little sad, and like a ghost forced to come back to something that in memory had retained its loveliness across eternity. The sun should have cast the shadow of fleshless ribs on the white boards —but there was his shadow, solid and his own.

But the best part of being young here that he had remembered across creaking sultry roaring jungle nights was gone—and he was sad because he realized suddenly that it was gone for good and all. He had come home, but not to the same thing he had known, because he himself was not the same.

Bub usually left the wharf at five o'clock to go uptown and have his supper at the diner. Sometimes it was a little after five when he left; and once in a while Kelsey would ask him to come back and help with the checking over in the store after he'd eaten. Bub didn't much mind. There wasn't anything else to do except maybe go to the movies or hang around the drugstore, not talking, just standing around.

On Wednesday night Kelsey asked him if he'd come back after supper, so Bub left on the dot of five to go up and eat. He climbed the hill and turned into the main road before he saw the girl ahead of him. She must have come up the factory hill just before he'd left the wharf.

Bub hadn't thought about Lou Jellison particularly since the first day he'd seen her, a week or so before, but now he wanted suddenly to talk to her, not for any particular reason, but just to hear her voice. He quickened his pace and gradually overtook her. She wasn't walking very fast, just steadily. When he came up with her, she glanced up at him and smiled.

"Hello, there!" she said, before he had a chance to speak.

"Hi!" Bub swung into step with her. "Mind if I walk along uptown with you?"

"Of course not." Her voice was much as he'd remembered it from the day he'd tried to get a job at the factory—slow and sounding as if it came from some place low in her chest. It had been a hot day, but she looked as cool as if she'd just come out of a bathtub. She wore no lipstick, but Bub could see a faint film

[43]

of powder over the pale tan of her face. He liked the way her hair grew off her forehead; it looked springy and as if it would feel alive when you touched it. When she turned to look at him, he felt himself flush, and glanced hastily away.

"I hear you've got a job with Kelsey Bunker."

"Ayeh," Bub nodded. "He was the only one in town'd take a chance on me."

She ignored the opening and made him wonder if she knew what he meant.

"Do you like it, working for him?" she asked.

"Oh, yes," Bub said. "It's good enough for a beginnin."

"Then you must be planning to stay for a while."

It didn't sound like curiosity that prompted her to ask. She was only interested, and Bub didn't mind telling her what she wanted to know.

"Why, I sort of thought I might come home an settle down," he said slowly, putting the thought into actual spoken words for the first time since it had occurred to him.

"Will they let you?" she asked suddenly, looking down at the road and not at him. Surprised and startled, Bub hesitated before he said dumbly:

"I don't know's I quite see what you mean."

"You will," Lou said, and her voice sounded faint, almost bitter. "People here don't let you forget things."

"Oh," Bub said blankly, wondering what she had to forget that people wouldn't let her. He was embarrassed with the turn the talk had taken and didn't want to go along with it. He didn't want to talk about coming back home the way he had because coming back was important to him, and talking about things that mattered to him was embarrassing.

"Well," he fell back safely, "looks as if we was goin to have a long spell of this weather, don't it?"

"Yes." She accepted the change without challenge, glancing out across the calm harbor toward the islands. "Everything looks so clear these days, seems to make the harbor look smaller."

"You—you always get through down to the factory at five?" Bub asked.

"I'm the only one there that keeps fairly regular hours," she said. "Nine to five, every day. Except Saturday. Then nine to twelve."

"Must make it nice for you, havin Saturday afternoon off."

They reached the sawmill road and Bub remembered that the Jellison house was the first one on the right-hand side. The first lot was vacant and a big unpruned lilac bush shut out the main road, but Bub could see the neat white pickets of the fence. They stopped at the gate and stood there looking at each other.

"Yes," Lou answered him slowly, "but there's not much to do."

"How—how—" Bub began with difficulty, clearing his throat roughly, "would you like to go for a walk sometime, some Satday?"

He met her startled look valiantly.

"Oh, I dunno," she said, hiding the surprise under flippancy. Bud misunderstood the flippancy for doubt, and bristled.

"D'you mean, not with me?" he said thickly.

"Don't be so silly." Her eyes were like clear brown spring water, and the look she turned on him made him ashamed for having thought it. "I'll prove it, too. You can take me to the movies Saturday night."

"All right," Bub smiled delight that he didn't know how to say. He hadn't really expected her to say anything like that.

She turned away and started up the walk. "Saturday night," she said over her shoulder. Bub stood watching her until the screen door closed behind her, and then he turned and went back down the road to the diner.

BUB saw the knife one night when he was going home from work. He saw the knife in the hardware store window, tossed down with a handful of other things that didn't matter; and he was instantly twelve years old again.

That summer it had become the fashion for boys to wear a hunting knife in a scrolled leather shield on their belts, and he didn't have one. Bub wouldn't have been satisfied with just any knife. He picked out the one he wanted. It was in the window of the hardware store, stuck in between boxes of lead sinkers and fishhooks and deepwater lines. He saw it there one Saturday night in late June. It didn't have the usual great wide blade and heavy sheath. The unsheathed blade was shining steel, narrow and deadly looking. And the handle was made of something that looked faintly like ivory, and it, too, was narrow, fine, looking as if it would fit easily into a closed fist. The sheath was light leather with markings on it, and it was different.

It was a foreign-looking knife and a beautiful one. Bub twisted and strained to make out the price. Five dollars, he read, and his eyes bugged out slightly. Jeez, that was an awful lot just to pay for an ordinary hunting knife. But he knew this knife wasn't ordinary; it was different, and worth every cent of the five dollars. He wanted it.

Then he had to think how he could get the money. There was no earthly use asking his mother for it. She'd stare at him as if he'd gone crazy if he dared to mention that much money for a knife.

If he got it, he'd have to hide it. He couldn't let her see it; and he couldn't show it to Mack—if he did that, it would disappear, and sooner or later he'd see the narrow delicate sheath on Mack's belt.

Bub slouched on down the street, staring into the windows. At first it never occurred to him to work for money, but the idea came to him when he passed the grocery. There were blueberries in the window, the big ones, grown somewhere under cultivation and displayed now in quart boxes with cellophane over the top. Why couldn't he pick berries? The season would be coming in soon and he could do that and maybe get fifteen cents a quart for them.

While the impulse was still there, he shoved the screen door open and went into the store, standing there by the counter until Steve Walls got through with his last customer and turned to Bub.

"Well, kid, what you want?" Steve eyed the boy sourly. He had trusted the Dollivers until their bill had reached proportions that even he knew they couldn't pay. Usually, when the bill got that big, the old lady stopped trading with him and went to some other store. But here was the kid again, and by the looks of him, he hadn't come in to pay any on the bill.

"I wanted to know if you'd buy blueberries from me once they come in," Bub said boldly.

"How much you gonna want for them?"

"Twenty cents," Bub said, horse sense telling him that Steve would try to beat him down no matter what he said.

"Good god!" Steve said, his eyes sticking out, "I won't hardly get more than that myself. I'll give you fifteen providin they're good and clean. No green ones, and no sticks, see?"

"Yeah, sure," Bub nodded.

"I misdoubt you'll pick many," Steve said. "It's pretty hard work, you know."

"I'll pick em," Bub scowled, knowing what was in the man's mind. "I'll get them for you when they're in."

He did, too. He watched the berry plains on the hill like a hawk, spotting the ripe ones as soon as they turned blue. The first day out he got five quarts.

Steve looked the berries over carefully, his eyes hard behind his steel rimmed glasses. But he found no fault.

"These're pretty good," he said grudgingly. "Get me some more."

"Well," Bub said, "how about payin me? That's seventy-five cents."

"I don't never pay until the end of the week," Steve said. "Come in Satdy night an we'll settle up. You're goin to pick some more, ain't you?"

"Yeah," Bub nodded agreeably. He had decided suddenly that it would be just as well if Steve held off paying until Saturday. There wasn't much of any place he could keep the money around the house that'd be safe from Mack. And he didn't want to carry it with him because he'd lose it sure as shooting.

At the end of the week he'd turned in thirty-five quarts. That was just five dollars and a quarter. That paid for the knife and left a quarter over to do anything he wanted to with.

That Saturday night Steve's store was crowded with shoppers.

It looked to Bub as if everyone at the Harbor had waited till then to do his shopping.

Bub hung around for a while, hoping that Steve would notice him and hand over the money. But Steve kept pretty busy, staying behind the counter. At first Bub thought Steve really hadn't noticed him come in; but then, he caught Steve's narrow blue eyes staring directly at him.

Well, petes sake, Bub thought, why don't he pay me?

He waited a while longer and then began to edge in to the counter until finally he was face to face with Steve.

"Well," Steve came to him in the line, "what you want?"

"You owe me five dollars an a quarter," Bub said. "You said you'd pay me tonight."

"Can't you see I'm busy, boy?" Steve shook his head impatiently. "Come back a little later."

"I want it now. You said—" Bub began to get mad.

"Oh, all right. I'll settle with you. That was what I said, warn't it?"

He went to the till and took out something Bub couldn't see, leaned across the counter and put it in Bub's outstretched hand. Bub stared down unbelievingly at the quarter.

"What's that for?" he said, his lips beginning to feel stiff.

"Well," Steve explained, "your ma owes me twenty-three dollars. I figured we'd better let that five dollars go on account. The quarter's for you, son."

"You—you old—" Bub stammered.

"Here," Steve roared, "no talk like that in here. Now, git out."

Bub put the quarter in his pocket numbly and turned to go. At the door he hesitated, looking at the big baskets of Concord grapes in the window. Suddenly he leaned over, got a double handful of the grapes and squeezed hard, seeing the juice splatter. Then he went out the door like a shadow, feeling the wind of Steve's big hand whistle by his head, hearing Steve's outraged yell.

Once outside and safely away from Steve, Bub began to cry, trying to keep his head turned away so that nobody could see him. He blubbered against disappointment, shoving tears away with the back of his wrist.

"Old bastard," he whispered.

[48]

When he went by the window of the hardware store he didn't bother to look in at the knife.

Now here was a knife that might have been the same one in the same window. Bub went into the store, smelling the familiar smell of metal and tar and rope.

"How much is that knife in the window?" he said shortly to the light-headed kid who came to wait on him.

"Five dollars."

"How long you had it?" Bub asked.

"Oh, just come in the other day. You can't git what you order now, you know. Have to take what they send you."

"I'll take it," Bub said. He counted five ones out of his bill-fold, knowing that he was a fool to spend that much for a knife when he could get one that'd suit his purpose for half the money. He didn't want the knife wrapped up, he took it just as it was, closing his hand around it and feeling the handle fit into his hand just as he had thought it would. He undid his belt and thrust the tongue into the loop on the sheath, settling the knife flat against his hip.

"Pretty good knife," he said. "Well, g'night."

He heard the clanging sound of the cash register as he went out.

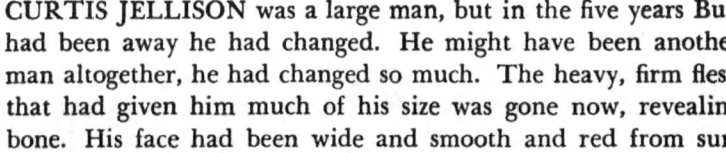

CURTIS JELLISON was a large man, but in the five years Bub had been away he had changed. He might have been another man altogether, he had changed so much. The heavy, firm flesh that had given him much of his size was gone now, revealing bone. His face had been wide and smooth and red from sun. The redness was still there, but the skin hung loose from his high cheekbones, giving him the look of a mournful bloodhound; and his large brown eyes, set deep under the heavy brows, added to the illusion.

He had been ambitious, too, once; but that had passed with the rest of his power. He had wanted things for his family, for his eldest daughter particularly, because it seemed to him that

[49]

she was much more a part of him than the other kids had ever been. The two younger ones, a boy and a girl, had always gone to their mother with their troubles; but Lou had come to him, she had always been his girl.

Curtis had hated seeing her go to work at the factory, but it was a satisfaction to him that she went as a bookkeeper and not as a packer. He knew the factory women, could tell them at sight, and they all looked alike to him—big, solid women, their hair coiled into a knot and hidden under a queer sort of dust cap they always wore. Their faces were oily and red, as if they had absorbed the grease in the steam that saturated the old buildings. But Lou didn't have to do that. Thank God he'd been able to see her through commercial school, anyhow.

Curtis himself was making good money this year, but it was the first year in ten he'd cleared enough to begin to see his head above water, and there had to be a war before he could do that. It grizzled him that this money should be made after he'd given up, after he'd lost hope altogether and decided he'd just go on the way he was doing until they put him six feet under.

Year after solid year of getting twelve and fifteen cents a pound for his lobsters; year after year of hauling less than three hundred pounds on a good week, maybe none at all the next ten days, had got him used to going without. Now that he saw the fishing industry picking up before his eyes, he neither trusted nor approved of the money he was making. It seemed almost sinful for him to have more than a dollar in his pocket at one time, and a dollar with no claims on it.

Curtis had his punt hauled up above high-water mark and was giving her a much needed coat of paint. He couldn't see how he was going to manage without her for the next few days, but she needed the paint as much as he needed her. He hadn't bothered to paint her that spring before putting her into the water, and now he saw what a fool he'd been. He'd come ashore a week ago and found his mooring apparently empty and nothing visible of the punt but the barest inch of her gunnel where she floated filled with water.

He'd hauled her ashore and dried her out enough to wiggle-nail the crack she'd developed in the garboards. She should have been recaulked, but he had neither the time nor the inclination to do it. A season of making a little more money than he had been making wasn't long enough to restore in him the old regard for a job well done. His sense of good workmanship was nearly dead and it took more than a little money to resuscitate it.

He stuck his paintbrush in the can and straightened up to look out across the harbor. He could tell from the low-lying rays of sunlight that it was getting on toward supper time. Must be nearly time for Lou to leave the factory. Maybe, if he humped himself, he'd catch her and walk uptown with her.

He covered the paint can and stuck it up on one of the thwarts under the punt. Then he turned and started along the beach toward the road that went up the hill from the harbor. The sharp rocks hurt his feet more than once, and finally he stopped to lift one heavily booted foot so that he could examine the smooth rubber sole.

"Thin as paper," he grumbled, prodding the rubber with an exploring finger. "Somethin else to spend money on."

Those boots had been new just the spring before. It seemed as if they weren't putting as good material into things as they had been. Maybe they needed it for something else, but he could remember when a pair of good boots had done him three or four whole seasons, and now these had given out before two seasons were over. Well, he'd have to go to the ration board and get an extra coupon, that was all. He started thinking defensively that they wouldn't want to give it to him. He'd probably have to fill out three or four forms to get one pair of boots. Of all the cussed foolishness!

He left the beach and started up the steep path to the road. Some darned fool had piled a lot of secondhand two-by-fours right across the path and he stood silently affronted, staring at them a moment before he started climbing over. Now what idiot had piled that junk there right where somebody'd break his neck over it, he thought, resenting the fact that it slowed him down.

He didn't see the short section of timber under him when he dropped heavily from the pile back into the path. He took a clumsy step and then stopped to look down with shocked amazement at the piece of wood that seemed to have grown suddenly to the bottom of his right foot. He set his left boot on the projecting edge of wood and pulled his foot away from it, seeing the spike that came up from the timber. He'd thought he felt it go through the boot, but he didn't feel it come out.

Crissake, he thought, now I *will* have to get them boots. Damn fool, leavin nails around like that. These young idiots'll kill someone like as not. He picked up the offending stick of two-by-four and gave it a heave into the bushes alongside the path.

Curtis went on quickly, afraid now that he might miss Lou. But when he came out of the alders into the open field, he could look across to the factory road and make out the bright pattern of her dress, moving slowly up the hill. She wasn't alone, he saw. That must be young Joe Pettigrew with her. That was all right with Curtis. If he'd gone over all the marriageable young men in the Harbor, he couldn't have found one he'd like better for Lou. Joe was a good boy, steady as they came. And there wasn't any danger of his having to go at any minute, either. He was essential, there was no question about that.

Curtis reached the road and sat down heavily on a stone to wait. The toes of his right foot felt queerly numb inside his boot and he wiggled them thoughtfully. That spike must have ticked him, then. He'd thought so at the time. Well, he'd fix it when he got home. He'd stepped on nails before.

Lou and Joe came along then and he got up and stood waiting for them. Joe didn't look any too pleased at the sight of him and Curtis grinned slightly. He didn't know what they'd been talking about, but he had an idea Joe didn't like the interruption.

"Hello, Curtis," Joe said, pleasantly enough.

Curtis nodded.

"Thought I'd wait and walk home with you, Lou," he said.

"I'm glad you did, Pa."

"Well," Joe said, a little sourly, "guess I'll be gettin back to work. Lou's the only one around the factory can keep regular hours now."

"Pretty busy, hah?" Curtis said.

"Yeah. Well, I'll be seein you, Lou."

"Sure thing," Lou said. She and Curtis stood there for a minute watching Joe walk away from them. He didn't bother to look back.

"Well," Curtis turned, "might as well be gettin along ourselves. Joe seemed sort of short."

"He was just talking mushy," Lou grinned up at her father.

Curtis snorted a short ah-hah through his nose.

"Any news?" he said, watching her hopefully. Lou racked her brain for something to tell him, knowing that he liked hearing the smallest things about her job.

"Nothing much. Oh," she said thoughtfully, "I don't know whether you've heard or not, but guess who's back in town."

"I dunno," Curtis was watching her face, his mouth curled in the beginning of an interested smile, "who?"

"Bub Dolliver," she said. "He came down to the factory a week or so back looking for a job. Joe was just talking about him, too, and it made me think to tell you."

"Well, I hope to god Joe warn't fool enough to give it to him," Curtis spluttered, beginning to be mad. "What's that young devil doin back here anyhow?"

"Oh, now, Pa, I think you're being too hard on him," Lou said easily. "He really looked quite decent when I saw him. He's changed a good deal since he was here last. Looks almost as if he'd been sick or something." She knew her father too well to mention yet the fact that Bub had walked home with her Wednesday night and that she was going out with him on Saturday; but she thought she'd better start preparing Curtis for the moment when he found it out.

"Leopard can't change his spots," Curtis said.

They were going up the walk now, and Curtis went ahead to open the screen door.

"Seems to me I remember you used to know his grandfather pretty well," Lou said.

"That was his mother's father," Curtis said stubbornly. "He was a good man. Too dam bad his daughter and his grandsons couldn't a been more like him."

"Well," Lou vanished diplomatically in the direction of the bathroom, "you never can tell."

Curtis went on out into the kitchen and stood in the door

[53]

watching his wife bend over the stove. She was frying potatoes in the spider and the smell of them made his mouth water. Her face was red from the heat of the stove and her hair was getting away from the neat bun at the nape of her neck. He looked at her for a second with a feeling of real tenderness that might have derived some of its force from the fact that she was getting his food ready for him.

"Lou says Bub Dolliver's back," Curtis said, still feeling a little outrage that Bub should come back to the Harbor.

"That so?" Edna looked up thoughtfully, noticing his anger. It seemed to her that Curtis was letting awful little things get him stirred up nowadays. "Where's he been all this time?"

"God knows!" Curtis headed for the entry to take off his boots. "These no-good kids make the rest of the country so hot for theirselves they ain't got no place to go but home."

"Well," Edna said soothingly, "his folks always lived here. Maybe he'll settle down some. He was jest a kid when he went away." .

"Leopard can't change his spots," Curtis said again, his mouth tightening unpleasantly on the last word.

Edna heard him stumble into the entry and heard his boots thump against the wall.

"I think you're gettin too upset about somethin that don't matter a hoot," she said to his silence. "After all, Bub Dolliver ain't nothin to us, is he?"

"Jesus Christ!" Curtis said suddenly from the entry, and his muffled voice made her jump and turn to stare after him.

"Curtis, what is it?"

"Bring me the iodine, will you?" he asked.

Edna took the iodine bottle from the window sill over the sink and went out to him. He had taken off his boots and the sock from his right foot. She stared down for a moment at the sodden, red-stained wool.

"What you done to yourself now?"

"Well, some young fool left a piece of two-by-four with a spike in it on the path. I thought it just went into the rubber, but it got me good and proper. Didn't even feel it, neither."

Edna leaned over his foot thoughtfully. The spike had got

him in the fleshy part just in back of the first joint of the big toe. It had come through the skin on top of his foot and the puncture was blue and puckered looking.

"That don't look very good," she said. "You better go see the doctor, hadn't you, Curtis?"

"I don't see what for. Jest pour a little iodine in it. That'll clear it out good and proper."

He stuck his foot out and Edna started painting the spot with the glass dropper.

"Oh, for godsake!" Curtis said. He took the bottle from her and splashed the stuff onto his foot.

"You'll burn it, Curtis. That ain't no way to do." Her voice sounded taut with worry.

"Got to get enough on to do some good, ain't I? Jest daubin it on with that thing don't do anythin."

He waited for the stinging pain of the iodine to reach him, but there wasn't any pain. He didn't feel anything at all. He stared at it for a moment and shrugged. Couldn't be very bad.

"Get me some of that gauze, will you, Edna?"

She went quietly into the kitchen and came back with the roll of bandage. Curtis wound it clumsily around his foot, anchoring it with his toe.

"Guess that'll do," he said. He put on the clean socks she handed him and shoved his feet into the high black shoes he habitually wore. He went, without speaking again, into the front room and settled down to his newspaper with a sigh of relief, to wait until supper was ready. He heard the two younger kids come in the front door and go through to the kitchen before he started to read.

The most important thing in Edna Jellison's life was her house. It represented her—everything she was and everything she had been was in the house. She had no actual taste, but she had a sense of color which can be easily substituted for taste. When Curtis had first married her and brought her home to the house on the sawmill road, she had been ambitious and had looked on the house as a stepping stone to a larger and better place. But during the depression, when she had realized suddenly that the house was all she owned and that it might easily be taken away from her, she developed a fierce sense of responsibility toward it. She'd called that a sense of responsibility toward her children, but actually that was the secondary emotion. The house came first.

Edna had been in a hurry tonight. She'd just come from the weekly meeting of the Ladies Aid and was hurrying now to get supper. It was Lou's night to go on duty at the spotter's shack on the factory roof, and she had to have her supper almost as soon as she got home, to make the shack on time.

Although she had been in a hurry, Edna had had to stop at the gate to look at the house and yard before she went up the walk. She looked at it with a good deal of personal pride because it represented the result of hard work on her part. She wasn't too discontented, not so discontented as she usually was on the afternoons she spent at the Ladies Aid. Usually there was, somewhere so deep inside her that it seldom came out in articulate form, a germ of discontent and dissatisfaction so ingrained that it had come to be with her continually. The desire to have things better. No specific things. Just "things." But after this afternoon's session she was wondering if maybe she wasn't pretty lucky after all. She knew well enough what a lot of the women had to put up with, and thinking about them made her feel temporarily that her own case wasn't such a bad one. Her kids were good kids; she always knew where they were and what they were doing, and she'd tried her best to bring them up so they'd be used to having things decent. The best she could do was to make them used to decency in their own home.

At moments like these Edna wasn't too dissatisfied with Curtis, either. His irritating slowness, his apparent lack of interest in the house and the kids bothered her terribly at times. But today she was charitable. He worked hard all day, he was materially responsible for the existence of the house and the things in it. He was all right in his way.

The trouble was that his way wasn't hers. Curtis was a good deal older than she, and sometimes Edna wondered vaguely if it hadn't been a mistake to marry a so-much-older man. He was sixty-three now, a bitter, defeated, and taciturn man; while she, at fifty, was still young enough to enjoy going and doing. She felt that if she could only get Curtis interested in something outside of the house in the evenings it might change him. But he always settled down with his paper in the front room after supper and there he stayed until nine-thirty, when he went to bed.

She turned with a sigh to look at Lyford and Jinnie when they came into the kitchen.

"Where you been?" she asked automatically.

Lyford's eyes slid easily away from his mother's glance.

"Just around," he said vaguely.

Jinnie came over and put her arms around her mother's warm ample waist. Looking down at her, Edna sighed again. Jinnie was going through that unfortunate stage little girls do when they look stringy and slightly untidy no matter how you tried to make them look something else. Her mouse-colored hair had lost its curl and hung lankly over her shoulders, and her thin, inquisitive face was irritatingly complacent.

"Don't you want to tell Mama where you been, dear?" Edna said, looking down at Jinnie.

"Nowhere, Mama, honest. We just been out playin around the house."

"I shouldn't think you'd want to keep secrets from your mother," Edna said, her voice taking on unconsciously a weakly carping note. "Don't you love Mama, dear?"

Lyford sighed windily and glanced at his mother out of the corner of his eye. He was only a year and a half older than Jinnie but already he had lost a good deal of his formlessness. Still lank and slightly knobby, he was beginning to fill out through the shoulders, and his smooth, rather bold face already showed the beginning of the brash good looks he'd have later on.

"That's no way to act," Edna said, seizing quickly on the sound. "I just want to know what you're doin."

"Yes, Mama," Jinnie said, not noticing, watching instead the food Edna was putting on the table.

"That's my baby," Edna said absently, turning to the door as Lou came in.

[57]

Curtis woke early Saturday morning, earlier than he'd been awake for a long time. He lay for a moment staring inertly out the window at the clear high arches of sky over the harbor. Beside him, in the big wide bed, Edna lay sleeping. He had to listen for a second before he made out the sound of her breathing. She made less noise sleeping than most people did when they were dead.

He felt curiously logy and heavy, lying there. And hot. His throat was rough and he wanted a drink of water. But it wasn't worth bothering Edna about. The first move he made she'd wake up, and he didn't want to wake her yet. He could tell from the look of the sky that it was too early. The sun wasn't up yet—there was only that still, clear, gray light that comes before sunrise.

This was going to be a scorcher all right if it was this hot so early in the morning. In spite of himself, Curtis kicked impatiently at the thin sheet that was his only covering. With the movement, a certain dull throbbing that he'd been indistinctly conscious of for minutes now centralized itself. He sat up with a startled jerk, no longer thinking about Edna. With the motion she woke and lay looking at him dazedly.

"What is it, Curtis? You all right?"

"I dunno," he said blankly.

He had pulled aside the sheet and was staring at his foot. Somehow in the night he'd managed to work the bandage off. It looked different this morning. Yesterday it hadn't bothered him much and he'd nearly forgotten it. But he'd never seen anything quite like the way it looked now. The puncture itself was a small blue spot—but the surrounding flesh was angrily red and there were streaks of white running through it. It looked puffy, too, as if it were swollen. He touched it gingerly with one finger and the red skin felt hot. The white lines ran up along the inner side of his leg toward the calf.

Edna sat up and looked.

"Oh, dear!" she said. "That looks simply awful, Curtis. I do wish you'd go have it seen to."

"Maybe I will if it ain't better by tonight."

"Well," she said, "things like that don't bear with no waitin. You never can tell what might develop in that long."

"Look!" He was suddenly angry. "I have hed all sorts of things wrong with me and none of them ain't killed me yet, have they? Well, an this won't neither. All it needs is a chance to heal. Maybe I won't go out today. It'll be all right."

The throbbing he'd noticed was still there—it wasn't as definite as a pain—it was more as if he were suddenly conscious of his own pulse beating steadily.

"Well, all right," she acceded doubtfully. For a moment she lay staring at him, then she sighed and sat up again. "Might as well get up. I won't never get back to sleep now."

Curtis stayed in bed watching her move slowly around the room. Then she went downstairs and he could hear her clanging stove lids in the kitchen.

JUNE BUNKER was seldom around the wharf during the day. The trucking job kept him pretty busy and Bub had an idea that June's off time was well taken up somewhere else. For that reason he was mildly surprised to find June at the wharf before him on Saturday morning. When he came down the hill he could make out the figure in blue dungarees and a blue shirt standing out on the head of the wharf by the big gas tank. He thought at first it was somebody waiting to get into the store, so he stopped and unlocked the door. Then he went down the wharf to unlock the gas tank and saw that the man waiting for him was June.

"Hi, Bub!" June greeted him with that typical upswing of the head, a gesture approximating a nod, but strangely different.

"Hi!" Bub said shortly. He went about unlocking the tank slowly, wondering what June wanted now. He knew June had something on his mind, that was evident enough from the single fact that the kid had taken the trouble to get down here before his father. That must have meant he'd crawled out of bed a good deal before his usual time.

Bub couldn't get rid of the dislike he'd always felt for June and the bunch of fresh kids he'd run around with, and that dislike flavored his attitude now. He moved aimlessly around the wharf head, looking the tanks over, taking a quick look at the big pump, waiting for June to come out with whatever it was that had brought him down here.

June's first words surprised him, they were so far from what he must have been thinking.

"Nice knife you got there." June indicated the carved sheath at Bub's hip.

"This?" Bub touched the sheath with his finger. "Picked it up uptown the other night."

"Don't know's I ever see one just like it," June said. "Mind if I look?"

Bub took the shining blade out of the case and handed it by the tip to June. The kid stood turning it over in his big, thin hands, trying the edge with a cautious thumb. He spat on his arm, rubbing the spittle in, and tested the blade against the wet hair; it sheared the hair off cleanly, leaving a bare place.

"God!" June said softly.

"It warn't that sharp when I bought it," Bub said. "I had to hone it quite a while to get that edge."

"You could use it to shave with!" June drew the blade lightly across his thumb again and watched with a sort of lascivious enjoyment as the thin line of red welled up on the dark skin of his finger.

"What you tryin to do, cut your hand off?" Bub said. Something in the moist brightness of June's eyes made him feel slightly sick to his stomach. The blood didn't help much, either. Bub reached out for the knife and June handed it back reluctantly.

"Guess you could always tell it was yourn," he said, "with that funny handle."

"Yeah." Bub wiped the blade on his pants leg and tucked it back into the sheath. "Well, I gut to git to work. Did you want somethin, June?"

"Oh, yeah," June said, as if he'd just remembered what he'd come for. He came a little closer to Bub and took a quick glance over his shoulder at the empty expanse of the wharf. "I come down to have a little talk with you, Bub. I wondered if the old man give you the keys to the place when you started work."

"You just seen me unlock it, didn't you?"

"Ayeh." June hesitated slightly, as if he were trying to make up his mind about something. Then he leaned over and began to whisper.

"How'd you like to make a little more dough?"

"What you mean?" Bub's eyes narrowed. He could feel himself stiffening with apprehension, but he wanted to let June finish his proposition.

"Well, you handle the gas tanks, don't you?" June said softly. "You make out the reports, too. I know because the old man told me."

"Ye-ah," Bub drawled, his eyes blank.

"Well," June said, "if you could manage to forgit to lock em some night when you went home, nobody'd know because you git here first thing in the mornin an unlock em, see?"

Bub did see and for the space of half a second he hesitated, tempted by the innate beauty of the proposition. By judast, it'd be fun to gyp Kelsey like that with his own kid in on it. June seemed to sense the momentary hesitation. He leaned forward slightly, his bright eyes fixed on Bub's face.

"Whatta you say? We'd split fifty-fifty."

June's too-bright eyes brought Bub to his senses in a hurry.

"You little bastard!" he said, stringing the words out insultingly. "You git off this wharf as fast as your legs'll take you. Let me see you showin your nose around here again with anythin like that and I'll slice it off with this knife. Scram!"

He took a threatening step, but June held up his hand. He didn't look mad.

"All right, all right," he said. "No hard feelins. I just thought I'd see what you'd say."

"I don't want nothin to do with your dam thievin," Bub said hotly, "an I ain't kiddin."

"Okay, okay," June said. "But you better not let the old man hear you swearin like that."

"He'll hear more than that if you don't get the hell outa here an let me get to work." Bub turned his back and went quickly down the gang to the float. When he looked up again, June had gone, and the first boat was curving out of the calm water of the harbor toward the slip.

Kelsey was late coming down that morning. It was nearly seven-thirty before he put in an appearance, preceded by the immensity of his voice. Bub was in the storeroom alone when Kelsey came down the wharf and stood in the door. As his big shadow darkened the room, Bub looked up in time to catch the grin before Kelsey stopped it and let his face fall into its habitual lines of sad reproachfulness.

"Well, Bub," Kelsey said, "when you first come here, I hired you because I figgured someone ought to give you another chancet. I figgured you looked as if you'd changed mightily. I'm glad to find out I was right."

Bub stiffened suddenly.

"Whatta you mean?"

"I hear you ain't goin to let nobody put anythin over on me," Kelsey said.

Suddenly the whole thing was clear and Bub shivered in a sudden chill of apprehension. What if I'd said yes to that little devil, he thought, an I darn near did.

"Did you put him up to that?" he growled. He straightened up and walked over to Kelsey. "Did you send him down here to ask me that?"

"Now, wait a minit." Kelsey held up his hand, the gesture was reminiscent of June. "Hold your hosses, Bub. I told you in the beginnin I hed to trust the feller worked for me here. If I find I can trust you, it's all the better, ain't it?"

"You—" Bub started, but he couldn't think of a word to use, there wasn't anything that meant what he was thinking.

"Don't you threaten me," Kelsey screamed. "I won't hev it. Now, you git to work."

"Of all the lowdown dirty tricks," Bub said. "My God, if

you go around settin traps like that you won't be able to trust nobody, let alone me."

"Takin the name of the Lord in vain!" Kelsey shouted. "I told you I wouldn't have any swearin."

Because he could think of nothing else to say, Bub leaned over the rope coils and heard Kelsey's heavy-booted feet go on down the wharf. Bub's brain was seething with impotent anger, but there was nothing he could say or do now that would penetrate Kelsey's thick skin. It had been a smart trick all right and it nearly caught him, but it wouldn't again. You learn fast, Bub thought.

THAT NIGHT Bub dug his one decent pair of pants out of the canvas bag, pressed them carefully, and dressed with a good deal of care. He whistled while he shaved before the small square mirror that hung over the sink.

When he'd asked Lou Jellison to go out with him he had had very little hope that she would. But when she'd suggested going to the movies, Bub had hardly dared to believe it. Lou was, he knew, what the Harbor called a "nice girl." Maybe if he was seen around in public with a girl like that, people wouldn't be so down on him.

He was glad the weather had held warm. He didn't own a decent coat to go with the pants, nothing but an old suede jacket and it was too hot to wear that. Maybe it wasn't so nice, just wearing a shirt, but he had an idea she wouldn't mind too much.

He slicked back his heavy light hair with water, took a last look at himself in the mirror, and stepped out the door, lighting a cigaret. As he went up the path toward the road, he kept swinging his left arm widely out from his side. The stiffness and soreness were beginning to leave it now, his side felt almost as strong as it ever had, and he'd noticed last night that the bright pink of the scar tissue along his ribs and shoulder seemed to be fading out a little. They'd told him at the hospital when

[63]

he'd been discharged that it would begin to feel better, but he hadn't really believed it until it did.

On Saturday night the Harbor was as festive as it ever got. The darkness was still there, even this early in the evening it was noticeable. The store fronts were shrouded in their curtains, only a faint gleam seeped through.

Bub turned up the shadowy lane under the big old elms and reached the gate where he'd left Lou the other night. He thought at first the porch was empty and felt relieved. He didn't want to have to talk to Curtis Jellison tonight; didn't want to anyway.

Bub swung the gate open and went whistling up the walk. When he reached the steps he saw that he'd been wrong. Curtis had been sitting there on the shadowed porch, but he'd hauled his chair in behind the vines so it wouldn't be apparent at first to anyone coming up the walk. He climbed to his feet and stood there staring down at Bub, who'd stopped with his foot on the bottom step and was staring back.

"Well," Curtis spoke first, "what d'*you* want?" The insulting emphasis on the word "you" told Bub what he was in for.

"Why, I come to get Lou," he said slowly. "We was goin to the movies."

"Don't know where you got that idea," Curtis said.

"Ain't she home?" Bub asked, trying to ignore the dislike in the old man's cold eyes.

"I want to tell you this right now—" Curtis didn't take the trouble to answer the question—"I ain't goin to have no daughter of mine goin anywhere with you. I wouldn't let her walk down the street with you, not where people could see her."

"Is that so?" Bub's voice was low, but his anger was bubbling up into his throat again, the old impotent anger of knowing that this was injustice, but knowing, too, there was nothing he could do about it.

"You might jest as well turn around now an git," Curtis said. "Lou don't want nothin to do with you, an if she did, I wouldn't let her."

"Curtis!" a voice said softly from the door behind him, and Bub swung his eyes slightly to look at the woman, but he

[64]

couldn't see anything but a dark blur against darkness. His anger had vanished suddenly leaving a vague feeling of sickness.

"Keep out of this now," Curtis said, not turning his head to look at her. "I'm jest tellin this boy we don't want nothin to do with him nor his kind."

"I'd like to hear Lou say that before I git out," Bub said softly.

"Lou asked me to say it for her," Curtis said, his eyes not leaving the pale whiteness of Bub's face. "She went out half an hour ago so's she wouldn't have to see you. Is that good enough?"

"Yeah," Bub said. He felt as if someone had hit him across the stomach with a board. It was the same feeling of being all gone behind his belt buckle. But it wasn't surprise really that made him feel hollow. He had known this would happen. He took his foot off the step and turned to go down the path again. He went slowly, telling himself not to hurry, because suddenly he wanted to run, he wanted to get away somewhere out of sight, where nobody could see him or talk to him. Well, I was wrong about her all right, he thought. The little—oh, hell!

Probably she'd told him she'd go out with him just so's she could get rid of him the other night. He'd been a fool even to bother asking. He had known—he really had known—this would be what'd happen.

He thrust his hands into his pockets and shuffled slowly down the lane to the main street. He didn't know quite what he wanted to do and he didn't know where he was going—what was more important was the fact that he didn't care, either. He had come to the conclusion in a moment that it wasn't worth the trouble. The Harbor had never liked him and it never would. God dammit, he felt like going out and getting so drunk he wouldn't be able to see. He would, too. As he neared the corner he started walking a little faster. At least that was a purpose and it was better than nothing. She was probably out somewhere with Joe Pettigrew right now; maybe she was even telling Joe she'd stood Bub up. Maybe they were together somewhere now, laughing over it.

At the picture he'd conjured up, Bub tightened his mouth

into an unpleasantly narrow line. He turned out of the lane and went up toward the drugstore. There'd always be some kids around who knew where you could get a drunk on. Maybe he could even find Mack—Mack would know.

He saw Lou outside the dim light from the store window. She had just stepped out of the store and was walking slowly toward him, slowly toward home, and she was alone. Bub stared at her angrily, making up his mind he wouldn't bother to speak to her. He started to pass her in silence, turning his eyes slightly away, when he heard her laugh. It wasn't really a laugh; more a low sound of amusement she made deep in her throat. And it made him mad.

"Well," he stopped in mid-stride, "what're you laughin about?"

"You," Lou said, her face perfectly sober.

"You must think it's pretty funny, standin me up like that."

"But I didn't," Lou said.

"You warn't to home," Bub said, "an your old man made it pretty clear how you felt about goin out with me."

"Oh, no," she contradicted soberly. "He made it pretty clear how *he* felt. I heard him. I was standing just around the corner of the house until a few minutes ago."

"Well," Bub began to feel a slow flooding of relief, he was beginning to see what had really happened, "Why didn't you say somethin?"

"What's the use?" she shrugged. "He just won't listen. I set out to head you off before you got to the house, but you beat me to it."

"You mean, you—you're goin out with me anyhow?" Half-unbelieving, Bub moved closer to her, trying to make sense out of her expression. Her eyes looked as if she were laughing, but her face was straight. Then suddenly it crinkled into laughter again and Bub felt himself beginning to grin reluctantly in sympathy.

"Oh, dear," she said finally, "I suppose it really wasn't that funny. But the pair of you *did* look queer—I—" she broke off suddenly, the laughter dying completely—"I didn't want to have a fight with him there. He thinks a lot of me—and he hasn't been feeling so good these last few days. You know."

[66]

"Yeah," Bub said slowly, "I guess I see. Well, if you go out with me tonight, he's bound to hear about it sooner or later. What'll you do then?"

"I'll just have to wait till he does," Lou said, "then we'll have to have it out, that's all. I said I'd go with you, Bub, and I'm going."

Somehow Bub hadn't quite believed that this was really happening until he heard her use his name. Then he did and was ridiculously happy.

The movie had already started when they went in, and the house was dark. They stumbled past reluctant feet into a couple of seats in the middle of a row. Bub sat through the show in a state of elated pleasure, not quite sure what the movie was and not greatly caring. The fact that she hadn't really stood him up was extremely important to him. He was acutely conscious of her sitting there beside him, but he made no move to touch her, didn't so much as move his arm the necessary quarter of an inch it would have taken to touch her shoulder. It wasn't that he didn't want to, he wanted to more than he had ever wanted anything, to make it come real that she was actually there.

Just before the picture ended, Bub leaned over to whisper to her.

"Would you like to go out now, before the lights come up?" It had occurred to him that if they went out now, fewer people would see them together. It might make things easier for her. He had forgotten that he wanted people to see them together, to know that there was one "nice girl" in town who wasn't too good to be seen with him.

Lou turned her head to look at him. He could feel the motion while he couldn't see it.

"No," she said, her voice clear, "I want to see the end."

Bub subsided in the seat. Well, he thought, it's her own business. He knew she had understood why he suggested leaving and had refused for the same reason.

The lights went up then and Lou stood up smiling.

"That was a pretty good show."

"It sure was," Bub agreed quickly, still not sure what he had just seen on the dead screen.

They walked slowly, side by side, down the street toward her road. Bub loitered purposely so that she'd stay with him as long as possible. There was a good smell in the air tonight, a smell like summer, and there was a faint odor of salt coming in on the light southeast wind from the harbor.

"Looks as if the weather might break after all," Bub said. "Wind's shifted."

Lou laughed.

"That all you've got to talk about?"

"Well, it's a good safe thing to talk about, anyhow." Bub felt himself grinning back. "What d'you want to discuss, Miss Jellison?" He bowed slightly.

"Whatever you do." Her voice was muffled because she was looking away from him and out toward the deeper darkness that was the harbor.

"Look," Bub said, "you don't wanna go home so soon, do you?"

"Not particularly."

"Well, why don't we go for a walk, or somethin?"

"A lady has to wait to be asked," Lou said.

"Well, I'm askin you."

"Let's go then."

They crossed the street without question and headed toward the harbor. The docks were deserted at night and there were no lights now. The street lights here at the shore had been put out. The only sign of life was the steady sound of the sentry's measured feet past the wire fence of the Coast Guard Station. Bub turned down Kelsey's wharf and Lou went with him, not bothering to ask where he was going. He dropped down on the wharf edge and dangled his feet over the side, hearing the flurry of her skirt as she sat down beside him.

"Now," Lou said easily, "you can tell me why you've come back."

"Oh, no special reason," Bub drawled, swinging his feet idly.

"I don't believe that."

"Well—" he said slowly, thinking. Suddenly he wanted to tell her, tell her why he had come back and what he was trying to do. It was important to him that she should know he'd honestly changed. "Well, look, it's like this. Since I went away the last time, I knocked around a little. I got to thinkin a few weeks ago that I warn't gettin much of anywheres. Then I got to thinkin that it was an awful waste of time. I don't know why I never thought of it before. But I remembered what this town was like—not the people, you know—just the town, an, well, I—I—" he floundered heavily.

"You what?" Lou was leaning her chin against her drawn-up knees and Bub could make out her profile, straight and remarkably steady, against greater darkness.

"Oh, I dunno. People around here never thought much of us Dollivers. But we always lived here an my old lady's people must've been different once. You know, decent people. Well, I got thinkin how it'd be if I could come back an sort of settle down here. I—I guess I changed some since I went away. I guess I musta been homesick," he shrugged, laughing to show her it was all right if she wanted to laugh, too. He felt a little silly saying things like these. But she didn't laugh. She didn't look at him either.

"I thought it was something like that," she said. "I didn't know just what it was, but I knew you were different than you used to be."

"I dunno's it's much use, though," Bub said, discouragement flooding his mind. "People around here got memories like elephants. They just don't seem to forget anythin. I guess I *was* kinda foolish—I used to raise old hell when I was a kid. . They don't let you get over that."

"Well," Lou said sensibly, "you have to make them."

"Make them, hah!"

"Talk to people. Make them see you're serious about settling down."

"No, by god," Bub said savagely, "I'm damned if I will. They can take me the way I am or not at all."

She hesitated a moment and he wondered if she was put out because of his swearing; he'd have to watch that. But when she spoke again it was about something else.

[69]

"Where'd you go, Bub, anyhow, after you went away?"

"All over," Bub hesitated. That was something he hadn't been going to tell anyone, but it was something he wanted her to know. "I been to Guadalcanal mostly."

"You—you mean, you've been in the Army?" her startled turning of the head made him jump.

"Nup." Bub whistled a snatch of a familiar tune.

"The Marines," Lou said, her voice blank with wonder.

"Ayeh, you know—'Join the Marines an see the world.'" Bub laughed suddenly. "I didn't see much of the world, but I see an awful lot of jungle."

He thrust out his chest a little, feeling justified in having spilled his secret.

"My lord!" Lou said. Then she thought of something else. "But—why aren't you still—well?"

"There, you see?" Bub said softly, the elation going out of him. "You feel the same way everyone else does. You don't think I'm much good. You're wonderin right now if I got kicked out, ain't you? Well, I didn't. I got my discharge proper an for a dam good reason."

Suddenly angry at her and at himself, he grabbed her hand. "Here," he said, "feel that!"

He thrust her hand roughly against his side so that she could feel the ridged flesh under the thin shirt. Then he let go, but Lou didn't move away. He was acutely conscious of her fingers following the scar up along his ribs to his shoulder.

"My lord, Bub," she said shakily, "you must've been—"

"I was a mess," Bub said, with half-ashamed pride. It was easy telling her now, and he enjoyed once more the being able to impress her. "They hed me trussed up like a mummy for a heck of a time."

"Is it—all right now?"

"Yes, it is now. But there was a while there I sort of wondered."

"What did it?" she asked. "How could a bullet leave a scar like that?"

"It warn't a bullet. It was a mess of em—you know—like shrapnel."

"Oh," she nodded. And then she said with sudden sharpness, "Bub, you're an awful fool."

"Whatta you mean, fool?" Amazed, he stared at her, trying to see the expression on her face.

"Well, look, why do you have to be so darn close-mouthed about where you've been? It'd make an awful difference in the way people felt about you if they only knew what you'd been doing."

"No, thanks." Bub felt again the rising of bitterness in his throat that meant anger. "I ain't goin to pull any of that hero stuff. They'll take me the way I am."

"Well," Lou said sensibly, "look at it like this. You were a hellion when you were a kid. All right. There've been others here. And the others stayed around and settled down and turned out all right. But you went away. People don't know where you've been or what you've been doing. For all they know, you've been in jail."

"So what?" Bub growled. "What business is it of theirs?"

"It's a lot of their business. Look, you've come back and you expect them to take you at your face value. They won't. You wouldn't do it yourself. Look," her voice was suddenly anxious, "what you were doing while you were away, Bub, that's—well, that's as much what you're like as anything. Tell people about it."

"I will like hell," Bub said.

"You make me mad enough to kill you!"

Lou scrambled to her feet and started off up the wharf, leaving Bub too amazed to do anything for a moment more than stare after her. Then he got up hastily and ran after her, following the retreating sound of her steps.

"Lou," he called softly, and heard her steps hesitate and then stop. He came up with her, breathing rapidly. "Look, Lou, don't go off like that."

"I'm not mad," she said. "Not really."

"I got to make them give me a fair chance, haven't I?" he said, taking her arm.

"It seems to me," Lou said slowly, "that you've got to give them a fair chance. You haven't. All they know about you is what you were when you were a kid. They've got to know what you're like now. You aren't givin them a fair chance, Bub."

"Oh—" Bub said helplessly. "Well—let's talk about somethin else; want to?"

For a moment she didn't say anything. Then she sighed lightly.

"Well," she said, "it looks as if the weather might change."

Bub laughed, throwing back his head.

"That all you got to talk about?" he mimicked. Lou laughed too, but she started walking. Bub caught up with her, and for a while neither of them spoke. Finally Bub said slowly:

"You goin to come out with me again sometime?"

"If you want me to," she told him without coquettishness.

"Well, I do if you want to."

"Then that settles it, doesn't it?"

"Not quite," he said. "When?"

"Oh, next Wednesday maybe. But you'd better not come for me again. I'll meet you by the drugstore."

"I don't like that so good," Bub said. "Your old man'll find out sometime."

"I know it, but let's wait a while."

"What for?"

"Now I'm being stubborn," she said. "I don't want to start anything. I don't like fights, that's all."

"Your mother love me as much as your pa does?"

"Mother's different," Lou ducked her head slightly, looking at him. "She's willing to be easy-going. She'll give you a fair chance." Her voice underlined the words and Bub's face felt hot.

They had reached the narrow road where Lou wanted to leave him and they stood together in a slightly uncomfortable silence. Bub knew what he wanted to do, but he couldn't get up his courage. When he finally looked at her, she had moved away.

"Good-night, Bub; I'll see you Wednesday."

"Well, good-night."

Bub stood on the sidewalk watching the light blur of her dress going away from him growing fainter, and finally he saw it swallowed into nothing.

When Bub turned away from watching Lou leaving him, he

[72]

felt tired. He wanted to go home and go to bed. He walked slowly at first, thinking about the things Lou had said to him and wondering if maybe she wasn't right after all. Maybe he couldn't come back and say "Well, here I am. I've changed. I'm going to be good." Maybe that wouldn't go over. He started turning over in his mind what the people in this town could remember about him, and there were some pretty raw things. Thinking back he wondered vaguely why he'd done them. There had to be some reason for doing some of the things he'd done. A few of them might have been funny; but most of them were the nasty sort of fresh things some dumb and not too scrupulous kid might think were smart.

He had to pass the new high school building, and looking up at its long low bulk against the sky he remembered the old building, the old barn of a building where he'd gone to high school for just two months. Two months! Bub thought. That's all it took me to get kicked out. Remembering the things he'd done, he felt angry and disgusted. They weren't funny and they weren't smart.

He remembered, too, the showdown. They'd all been called into the Assembly Hall and old Abel, the principal, got up and stood looking at them for a long minute. Bub, in the back row, knew quite well that Abel didn't have any idea who'd started the minor reign of terror. When Abel started to talk, the room was as still as if the entire school held its breath.

"Some things have happened here since school started," Abel began. "Things that have to have something done about them." He proceeded to list the worst of them: the twenty-five dollars missing from the English teacher's desk; the defaced pictures and clock in the Main Room; the ruined coats in the girls' cloak room.

"This is out of my field," Abel said, his voice expressionless with distaste. "It's too big for me to discipline whoever's responsible. If any of you know anything about it, I want you to tell me. Not now. Come to me afterward and tell me then." Something in his face showed that he knew they wouldn't come, but he had to say it.

"If you don't admit it or tell me anything you may know

[73]

about it, I will be forced to go to the superintendent of schools and then the matter will be out of my hands. That's all."

Bub didn't know when Abel started talking just what he was going to do. But when Abel finished, he stood up, hearing the creaking of seats as the kids all turned to stare at him. His hands were cold, but he was mad, too. He didn't even see their startled faces.

"Yes?" Abel said huskily.

"I done it." The sound of his own voice startled him. When nobody moved, he said it again—"I done it." The silence broke and surged into whispering.

"Go down to the Commercial Room," Abel said softly. "I'll talk to you there."

Bub left the room and went down the stairs noisily, cursing himself for being a dam fool. Here he'd gone to work and spilled the whole thing just because he'd thought it'd be smart to do it in front of the whole school. He wasn't scared of that old fool of an Abel, but when he passed the front door, he hesitated and took a tentative step toward it.

"If you ain't scared what're you runnin for?" he said aloud, and went on into the Commercial Room.

He heard Abel coming downstairs then and settled his shoulders firmly against the wall. He was leaning there, scowling, when the man came into the room.

"Dolliver," Abel began without preliminary, "will you tell me if you had any reason for doing the things you've done?"

"I'll tell you." Bub thrust his head forward slightly. "I done it just for the hell of it! I don't like you an I don't like this goddam school. An you can do what you want to about it. I ain't ascared of you, you old sonovabitch."

"You don't show much originality in your profanity, Dolliver." Bub was silent. "You know, don't you," Abel went on, "you've done something that would mean jail if you were older?"

"So what? You can't scare me."

"I'm not trying to. I'm just telling you. It probably *will* mean reform school."

"They'll have to get me first."

"Oh, for the love of God," Abel said bitterly, "stop talking

[74]

like a third-rate movie. They'll 'get you' all right—sooner or later."

"Ah, go to hell," Bub said, intoxicated by the sound of his own voice.

Abel moved to the door and held it open.

"I want you to get out now," he said. "You'll hear later what we intend to do about this."

Bub went by him like a shadow, glancing back once. When he saw Abel still in the doorway, he thumbed his nose. Abel vanished and Bub went on down the sidewalk, swaggering.

God! Bub shook his head and moved hastily along toward the wharf and bed. Of all the fool things to do, he thought. I must have been a little baster. Now he couldn't even remember the impulse that had started the whole thing. All he remembered was that he hadn't given them time to come and get him. He'd left town for the first time and had been gone six months. When he came back, the incident wasn't forgotten but it had died down. He felt now a deep sense of shame and a sort of dumb thankfulness that Abel had long ago moved on to another school.

Maybe Lou was right after all. Maybe he wasn't giving them a fair chance. He'd been a terror of a kid and they were in no position to be sure he'd changed any.

When Lou went up the darkened walk into the house she knew instantly that something was wrong. There was about the house itself that indefinable hushed atmosphere as if everyone were somewhere behind closed doors, whispering.

Her mother came heavily down the stairs, and when she saw Lou, she stopped on the landing and stood there, her hands waving aimlessly, her thick underlip beginning to shake.

"Ma, for heaven's sake, what is it?" Lou said, feeling apprehension stiffen in her throat.

"Oh, it's your father," Edna said, her voice a combination of fear and exasperation. "He's gone and done it now."

"Well, what?"

"He's got himself an infection an I can't make him go to the doctor."

"He looked all right tonight," Lou said, remembering Curtis as he'd stood on the porch talking to Bub.

"Well, he had a fever and his foot was all swollen up this mornin," Edna said weakly. "He said he'd go to the doctor tonight, but now it's worse an he won't go. He's just lyin there in bed sayin it'll be all right."

"I'll go up and see him." Lou started up the stairs past her mother. When she came up with her, Edna took her arm lightly and turned her so that the light fell on her face.

"Don't tell him where you been if he asks."

"What—what d'you mean?"

"Well," Edna looked away, "I was out town to the drugstore an I see you comin out of the movies."

"Oh," Lou said softly. Then she turned and went on up the stairs.

Curtis was lying, still fully dressed, on his bed. There was no light in the room, but light came in dimly from the hall. His eyes were open Lou knew, because she could see them shining in the darkness.

"Dad," she said softly, hesitating in the doorway, noticing the dry sick smell of the closed room.

"That you, Lou?" Curtis moved his head to look at her. "Come on in."

"How you feel?" She came in to stand beside the bed.

"All right," Curtis said. "They ain't nothin wrong with me. Lord, you cut your finger an your ma thinks the world's comin to an end. If I run to the doctor with every little thing that happened to me, we wouldn't never get caught up on his bill."

Lou saw that he had apparently forgotten all about Bub in thinking about his own troubles, and she was thankful that he had.

"Let me see your foot, will you, Pa?"

"No," Curtis said. "Now, Lou, for heaven's sake don't go gettin like your mother. They ain't no earthly reason for you lookin at it. I'm takin good care of it. I jest got done soakin it in creolin. That'd ought to kill any germs."

"I wish you'd let me see it."

[76]

"Well, I won't," he said shortly, "an I don't want to hear any more about it tonight. Go on to bed."

He didn't bother to ask her where she'd been. He just closed his eyes and lay there waiting for her to go away. Feeling useless and scared, Lou went out, closing the door behind her. Edna had come back upstairs and was hovering outside the door, her wide, crumpled-looking face worried.

"He all right?" she asked.

Lou shrugged. "I don't know," she said. "He won't let me look at his foot an he won't go to the doctor. Is it really bad, Ma?"

"Well, it was startin to turn sort of yellow and blue," Edna said thoughtfully. "I gut a look at it just before he went to bed."

"Oh, lord!" Lou said, the beginning of terror hitting her. "That's bad."

Edna nodded dumbly and turned toward the door.

"I'd let him alone tonight, Ma," Lou said quickly. "Come on in an sleep with me. He needs his rest bad."

"Well, all right." Edna turned back and followed Lou along the hall to her bedroom.

JUNE BUNKER was sitting in the driver's seat of the light Ford truck out in front of the drugstore, just watching the people going by. It was Saturday night and there were quite a few people on the street. He could tell what they were doing by looking at them. There were the families of the men who worked at the boat yard. They'd just got the weekly pay check and were heading for the A. & P. to do the weekly shopping. Then there were the ones who were going to the movies. The movies did a land-office business on Saturday night.

June was dressed up to the nines. Since he'd started working regularly for the old man he spent every cent he could get his hands on on clothes. His mother took five dollars out of his pay every Saturday night for board, but that left June nearly fifteen

[77]

dollars to do what he wanted to with. He had it in his pocket now, one ten-dollar bill, four ones, and some loose change.

Jeez, he thought, I sure was smart to quit school when I did and go to work for the old man. It sure makes a difference when you're working. People think you're more important then. The kids he'd gone to school with, what a bunch of suckers they were, sticking around that schoolhouse. And what would they ever do with their Latin and their bookkeeping. June certainly hadn't ever been called upon to use anything he'd learned in school.

It was beginning to get dark when somebody loomed up at the truck window, and June thought for a moment it was Bub, and wondered what he wanted. But it wasn't Bub. It was Mack. In the darkness the color of his hair wasn't so apparent and his build was very much like Bub's.

"What you doin, June?"

"Hi!" June jerked his head in greeting. "Nothin much. Just sittin."

"How about a ride?"

"Where'd we go on the gas I got?" June asked sarcastically. He lit a cigaret, bending his smooth head down to the match and drawing down the corners of his mouth as he sucked in the smoke. He didn't offer Mack a cigaret, and after a moment Mack took out one of his own. He lit it and climbed into the cab.

"Whatcha doin for excitement?" June said.

"Lookin around."

"Where's Bub?"

"How the devil should I know?" Mack growled. "Lissen, I ain't havin nothin to do with Bub, see; not since he's turned preacher."

"Funny how he's changed," June said thoughtfully. "He ain't half the guy he used to be."

"You tellin me?"

"Say, where's he been, anyhow? I can't git nothin out of him. He's as close-mouthed as a clam."

"I dunno," Mack shrugged, staring out the window. "He ain't talkin much. If you ask me, he got into some kind of trouble somewhere an he's come back here to lay low till it blows over."

"Yeah?" June pricked up his ears. "Spose it was anythin bad?"

"Musta been," Mack said, "or what else'd he come back to this goddam graveyard for?"

"Hmmm," June said, and snapped his cigaret into the street.

"Let's go have a beer," Mack said suddenly. "Come on. I'll stand."

"Where you gettin the dough?" June shoved the truck into gear and kicked the starter.

"I ain't dumb," Mack said. "I can pick it up when I see it layin in front of me."

"Yeah?" June's voice was scornful. After that they were silent. June drove fast, but he made up for it by shoving the truck out of gear on every downslope.

Barron's Beer Parlor was the only one in the Harbor, and it was about a quarter of a mile beyond the factory. There was a narrow parking place in front of it, but there weren't many cars. June swung the truck into the space on a wide half-circle, leaving it so that its radiator pointed down the main road toward the sea wall. They got out and crossed to the door, June's long-legged stilted walk looking meticulous beside Mack's swinging slouch.

The room they went into was low-ceilinged and thick with smoke. Along the left side of the open floor space was a converted soda fountain, now liberally called a bar. One or two men were sitting there on the high-legged, wicker-bottomed chairs, and they turned to look as the two boys came in; but the majority of the patrons were sitting back along the wall in booths or at tables. The few lamps that hung along the walls at rare intervals had low wattage bulbs in them and their dirty orange shades made the dimness even thicker. June wanted to brush his hand before his eyes, it made him feel as if he'd walked into a mess of cobwebs and he couldn't see. He slid into a booth after Mack and they both ordered beer from the single waitress who was making the rounds of the various prospective customers.

"You know," Mack took a swallow from his glass and set it down to stare at June with his dark eyes narrowed, "I been thinkin how a couple of guys could make a pretty good thing in this town if they warn't too particular how they done it."

[79]

"What you talkin about?" June's face was puzzled and began to show alarm.

"Well, now Bub's back," Mack began, his voice low, "people'll sort of expect things to happen. If we was to take care of the things, now—"

"Wait a minit," June said. "Whatta you mean 'we'?"

"Oh, I was jest talkin. Of course, I didn't expect you to come into it with me. I got to have someone I can depend on not to spill the whole business the first time anyone starts askin questions. I can't do business with a kid like you."

"I'm as old as you are," June said defensively.

"Yeah, maybe; but you ain't been around much."

"What kinda business?" June decided to ignore that last because there was no good answer.

"I can't spill everything to somebody who ain't gonna want to come in with me," Mack said. "That'd be dumb, wouldn't it? If I was to tell you an then you decided you didn't want nothin to do with it, why where'd I be?"

"Spill what?" June said. "If they's anythin goin on I want to be in on it. This burg is dead enough to give anyone the creeps."

"Once I tell you," Mack said, "you're in an no questions asked. Okay?"

"Is it against the law?"

Mack nodded, stuck out his underlip, and took another swallow from his glass.

"Well, I don't know's I want to get mixed up in anythin like that, now. What if we got caught?"

"Ah, hell, don't be such a dam baby. Can't you get it through your thick head? If anythin happens, people ain't goin to say 'Now, June Bunker done that.' What they're goin to say is, 'Bub Dolliver's back an the trouble's startin.'"

June stared, nodding.

"Ayeh, maybe. Well, what's this big idea, anyhow?"

"Maybe I'll tell you later," Mack said. His eyes had slipped past June's shoulder and were now staring across the dim room toward a booth on the opposite side. June turned his head to follow the direction of Mack's gaze. His eyes met those of the girl squarely, and June flushed and looked away.

"Who's she?" Mack said. "I ain't seen her around before."

"Aw, she's just a kid," June said. "Her old man just moved to town. He's that new engineer on Joe Pettigrew's biggest boat."

"Yeah?" Mack smiled, still looking. "She ain't bad. You could have some fun with her."

"Now, look, I ain't gettin mixed up in no funny business," June said desperately.

"Aw, shut up. I know what I'm doin."

Mack got up and crossed the room, adding a swagger to his walk. June saw him stop beside the girl, who sat alone in the booth. He said something to her, and to June's horror she got up and came back with him.

"She's come to have a beer with us," Mack said. "I told her we was lonesome."

"You looked lonesome," the girl said in a queer, roughened voice. "I see you come in an you looked awfully lonesome."

She sat down and June stole a quick glance at her. She was pretty, there was no getting around it, but she had that look around her eyes that June had been brought up to call tough. Her face was a pale tan against her dark hair that curled down to her shoulders in the back. She caught him looking at her and raised her dark eyebrows suddenly, smiling when June blushed and looked away.

"My name's Dolliver," Mack said to her. "Seein as it's you, I'll let you call me Bub."

June grinned suddenly.

"Bub? That's a kid's name," the girl said.

"We'll see whether it is or not," Mack said. "What's yours?"

"Patsy," she said. "How about him?" She nodded at June.

"His name's Pete," Mack said.

"Well, what about that beer you promised me?" Patsy asked. "I can't sit here talkin with my throat dry, can I?"

"Sure not."

Mack got up and went over to the bar, coming back with three full glasses. June sat with his on the table in front of him. He didn't drink any of it, he just sat there making little circles on

[81]

the dark painted wood with the bottom of the glass that hadn't been wiped completely dry. Mack and the girl were talking, but June wasn't listening to them, he was just sitting there wishing to god he hadn't bumped into Mack tonight. He had a certain fastidiousness about him that was offended by this performance because he knew pretty well how it would end and he wasn't liking Mack very much.

The sudden movement of the other two made him look up. They were standing up, waiting for him. Mack's eyes had begun to shine and his mouth looked loose and wet. June felt his nostrils widen with distaste as if he could actually smell something unpleasant.

"You comin?" Mack said. "We can't take the lady for a ride without you."

"Okay." June got up. It'd be better than sitting around here, anyway. He was glad Mack hadn't told her their real names, but he was wondering what would happen if Bub ever heard of this. He climbed into the truck, but Patsy stood staring.

"A truck!" she said. "Whatta you think I am?"

"Lissen," Mack put his hand on her arm, "nowadays you take what you can git, see? Come on."

She hesitated for a moment and then got in. She sat between them and when Mack shut the door it pushed her against June. A billow of perfume came up to him and his nostrils widened again. He tried to hitch himself away from her, but the seat was too narrow and he couldn't move any farther.

"What's the matter?" she looked up at him. "You scared of me?"

"Not much," June said tightly. "Where to?" He looked across her at Mack, his hand on the gear shift.

"Down to the sea wall," Mack said. His voice sounded strained and rough to June. June could feel his hands getting cold on the wheel, but there was nothing he could do. She was old enough to take care of herself, he figured. It was up to her what happened.

Their truck lights hit the big white sign that said Restricted Area and June switched to parking lights, leaning forward over the wheel to see the road.

[82]

"This is good enough," Mack said finally, and June swung the truck over into the woods, backing it into a side road so that he could start it up without turning.

He switched off the heavy motor, and in the silence he could hear the steady beat of the ground swell against the ledges. When his eyes got used to the darkness he could make out the white dim line that marked the edge of the incoming tide. There was a smell of freshness in the air, and a light wind, soft and warm, from the southeast hit his cheek.

Mack and the girl were sitting in complete silence until Mack moved impatiently.

"Well, come on." He got out and stood beside the truck. Hesitating for a moment, Patsy looked at June before moving.

"What about him, Bub?" And June jumped, to hear her use Bub's name.

"He'll keep an eye out for us," Mack said impatiently. "Come on, will ya?"

She got out then.

"Hey, Pete," Mack said, "gimme a blanket from the bunk, will ya?"

June reached up to the sleeping space that was built in over the back of the seat, hauled out a blanket and threw it at Mack. They disappeared and he sat there stiffly, listening. They went around the truck and June felt the springs sag slightly as they climbed into the back. He sat there trying not to imagine what was going on behind him. He could feel his face getting hot and cold by turns. The truck moved once or twice, and he could hear their voices, low and monosyllabic; then they settled into silence. And June began to feel himself getting sick. He got out of the truck and went out toward the sea wall. He stood there looking out across the water, his hands clenched in his trouser pockets. What he saw and smelled and felt was so clean and free and without complication that the thought of the two back there in the truck nauseated him. He was still standing there when Mack came looking for him.

"Hey, where'd you go?"

"Right here."

[83]

"Holy old mackinaw!" Mack whispered. "She's all right. It's your turn. Just give her a buck."

"Nuh," June clenched his teeth on rising sickness. "Not me."

"What's wrong with you?" Mack peered at him. "You all right?"

"Yeah," June said. "Yeah, sure. I just don't feel like it tonight."

"Okay," Mack shrugged. "You don't know what you're missin, though."

He went back to the truck and June stayed where he was until he could hear them talking. He saw a match flare up in the front seat and there were two lighted cigaret ends when the match went out. Then he went back and got into the driver's seat. Patsy was settling her skirt carefully around her knees, looking as if nothing had happened. She glanced at him curiously as he got in.

"What's the matter, sonny?" she said. "Say, how old're you, anyway?"

"What's it to you," June said. He started the truck and slammed it into the road. He didn't say anything until he'd pulled up before the beer parlor again. Mack and the girl got out but June stayed where he was.

"Ain't you comin in?" Mack said.

"No," June shook his head.

"Okay," Mack said. "I'll be seein you." He shut the door and followed Patsy across the parking lot.

June didn't look after them. He horsed the truck out into the road and raced it for home. He felt queerly stiff as he garaged the truck, and after he got out, he went around by the side of the garage, leaned his hands on the rough wood and was violently sick into the burdocks and pigweed that grew up around the cedar supports.

ON SUNDAY morning when Lou's alarm went off, she dressed quickly, woke Edna, and went down the hall to the door of the front bedroom. The door was closed and she couldn't be sure whether or not her father was up. She pushed it open silently and stood looking in. Curtis wasn't up. He was lying there in the bed, fully dressed as she had left him last night. His brown face looked queerly flushed against the crumpled white pillow case, and his breathing was loud in the quiet room.

She went over quickly and put her hand on his forehead and then snatched it away again, her eyes wide with fear. His head had felt like a furnace under her hand. He opened his eyes and stared up at her. His eyes were brighter than she had ever seen them, and for the space of a minute he didn't seem to recognize her. Then he did and sat up, swaying slightly from the waist.

"My head," he said thickly. "God, what a headache!"

"Pa, you lie down," Lou said sharply. "You lie down and don't you so much as wiggle till I get back."

"Where you goin, Lou? Now, I ain't goin to have no—"

"Lie down," Lou snapped. "Lie down an stay there."

Curtis groaned and subsided onto the pillow. He closed his eyes again and lay breathing heavily through his mouth.

Lou went quickly downstairs, not bothering to look at him again. Edna was already in the kitchen getting breakfast, and when Lou came in she looked up, her eyes a mixture of sleep and fear.

"What—how is he? What you goin to do, Lou?"

"I'm calling the doctor," Lou said.

She cranked the telephone angrily, spoke into it shortly, and hung up again.

"There! He'll be right over. Pa's awful sick. We were foolish to let him get away with not going to the doctor yesterday."

"Well, he's comin now. It'll be all right," Edna said, with great faith in the ability of the doctor. She poured coffee into cups already on the table and sat down heavily. "Come on an eat."

Lou sat down and started drinking her coffee. The Sunday morning silence of the house was thick around them as they ate. Neither of them broke that silence until Lou heard the first sound of feet on the front porch. She got up quickly and went to the door. A moment later Edna followed her and was standing by the foot of the stairs when the doctor came in. He was an old man with a big, square wrinkled face, and his eyes, electrically blue, sunken into queer deep bony pockets, went over her face as if it had been a sign to direct him.

"Well," he said brusquely, "what's the matter with him now?"

Edna who had grown up under the auspices of this man and who called him Don when they met on the street, observed the unspoken rules of the seriousness of his business by calling him Doctor Simmons when he was occupied with that business.

"He's awful sick," she said helplessly.

"Infection," Lou said succinctly.

"Oh god!" The doctor picked up the small black bag and started up the stairs. He knew from experience which room he'd find Curtis in and he went in without bothering to knock.

"What the hell you trying to do, Curtis, kill yourself?" he said loudly.

"Hello, Doc." Curtis raised himself in the bed and slumped back again. "Didn't see no need to call you. Only them fool women done it when I warn't lookin."

The doctor glanced casually at his face, suddenly gaunt, covered with three days' growth of stiff gray beard. He noted, without seeming to, the abnormal brightness of Curtis's eyes and the flush of red under the weather brown on his high cheekbones.

"Well, what is it? Hand? Foot? What?"

"Foot," Curtis gestured weakly in the right direction.

The doctor pulled the blanket away and jerked lightly at the makeshift gauze wrapping. It came away in his hand and for a long silent moment he stared down at the foot. His face was a blank and his eyes looked as if they'd settled a little deeper into the amazing sockets.

"Crazy women," Curtis said. "I coulda took care of it myself."

"Well, you sure did. How're you goin to like an artificial foot, Curtis?"

"What the hell d'you mean?" Curtis's face was a spasm of unbelieving horror.

[86]

"Well, I'll tell you," the doctor said bluntly, looking away, "that one ain't ever goin to be much more good to you."

Through a maze of fever and pain, Curtis heard Edna at the door. She was sobbing weakly and that was the only thing that made him believe he'd actually heard what the doctor had said to him.

Part Two — *August, 1943*

〜〜〜 〜〜〜

THE WEATHER held fair through July and early August. Usually, along about the last of July or the first of August, there'd be a spell of fog and rain and nasty easterlies that made people think the sun would never shine again. Not that summer. Occasionally the fog came in but only for a day or two.

The high, limitless blue skies of fair days rolled over the land endlessly. The heavy cumulus clouds poured down over the hills before the northwest wind each afternoon. Sometimes late at night heat lightning developed into a roaring thunderstorm; but by morning the water had soaked into the ground and vanished except for dark stains on the old wood of the wharves. The woods got dry and the windfalls were full of brittle dead limbs like bones, and the wind brought the hot smell of spruces and pines down from the hills over the town. At noon the red granite ledges along the shore were too hot to touch.

August felt as if winter had never been and would never come again—but the water knew it would. The water held chill within itself as if it were never far from ice floes. On some days the morning's illusion of peace would be shattered by the thunderous distant explosions of depth bombs on the practice ground out by the Ship and Barge—deep sonorous roars that rattled loose glass panes in the windows. And each night and morning the coast patrol planes went over, flying low.

It was weather that led to trouble. The steady, unshifting heat made people restless and uneasy for no reason. There was a tenseness in the atmosphere that hung over the wharf. Bub could sense it in the air; it was like something he absorbed through his pores. And it was highly uncomfortable to know that the men he worked with disliked and resented him, and for no particular reason. Their feelings were magnified by weather and constant association. Their dislike was crystalizing into something uglier and more active, and it made him feel as if he walked a narrow path on the edge of a cliff below.

Bub had been thinking about Lou off and on all day. Early in the morning, from the wharf, he'd seen her go down the hill to the factory. How he was sure it was Lou he'd picked out at that distance he didn't know. She was just another light spot, one brightly colored dress among the many that went down the hill. But it was Lou he'd picked—he didn't doubt it for a minute.

Thinking about her had put him in a mellow mood that was unusual even to his naturally easygoing temperament. He found himself visualizing her face with its warm brown color—and he could see the way the sun made the light down on her cheeks shine when she turned her head. Now, away from her, he could remember a trick she had of drawing her upper lip in between her teeth and creasing her forehead when she was thinking. He couldn't remember actually having seen her do it, but he could remember the trick itself.

He spent the morning down on the slip painting one of Kelsey's punts that had been hauled out to dry a week or so before. It was lazy and hot down there in the direct sunlight and he felt sleepy when he went up to the storeroom at noon to pick up his lunch box. Bub made it a point not to sit with the others when they ate. They sat along the big timber by the storeroom door, but Bub went down to the end of the wharf and ate, dangling his feet off over the water. After he finished and stuffed papers back into his box, he lay down on the hot boards, half dozing in the sun.

He was nearly asleep when he heard Kelsey's big voice shouting somewhere up the wharf.

"Come on, you lazy bums. I ain't payin you to sit around an chew the fat all afternoon. Come on, git to work."

Bub got up slowly and started back up toward the sound. When he got there, nobody was around but Art Blundin, caching his lunch box inside the office door.

"Say, Bub," Art said, hearing his step.

[89]

"Yeah?"

"I was workin up on the road this mornin, but Kelsey wants me to go out haulin this after with him. I left my crowbar up there. Be a good guy an go pick it up for me, will you?"

"Sure," Bub said. He put his lunch box in back of the counter and started up the hill. He could see the bar from the wharf. It was leaning against one of the big rocks Art had been prying out of the tracks. Bub picked it up without thinking, and in the moment of shock before he dropped it again, his hand tightened unconsciously around the iron. Then he let it go with a clang and did a brief two-step, shaking the burned hand.

"Judast priest!" he said out loud. "That musta been lyin there all mornin."

He took a quick glance down at the wharf. Art wasn't in sight, but by some miraculous coincidence, everyone else was. Bub could see their grinning faces, and with a grimace at his own foolishness he realized he'd been taken again. He looked the hand over but it wasn't as bad as it had felt. There was a slight redness along the palm and the inside of the thumb, but he'd seen worse.

It wasn't the first time something like this had happened, or the second—it was always happening, and Bub was beginning to wonder when he'd get wise to them. Evidently it was going to go right on happening until the inevitable showdown came.

He could remember the first time clearly. Kelsey had been in on that one, but he hadn't since. It was soon after Bub had started work for him. Right after he'd had his lunch that day, Kelsey had said:

"Bub, I left a bait tub on the head of the wharf. Bring it down to the slip, will ya?"

Bub knew where the bait tub was, he'd seen it early that morning and it had been sitting there all day. He went up to the wharf head and stooped to pick up the bucket, using his left hand. It came freely for six inches and then stopped with a jerk that sent tongues of pain licking along his side.

"Judast!" Bub said heavily and let go the bucket. It clanked over on its side and he could see what had happened. Somebody had put a rope through the bunghole, anchoring it with a turk's

[90]

head, and nailed it to the wharf on the off side, and Bub hadn't noticed the rope.

Bert Pettigrew had been coming down the wharf behind him and Bub knew the story of how he fell for the bait tub gag would be all over the wharf before night.

"What's the matter, sonny," Bert said, grinning with hearty good humor, "too heavy for you? Here, I'll give you a lift."

Bert picked up the bucket, expecting the tug of the rope, and giving it a good strong pull. The nail came away and Bert, looking as if he hadn't even noticed it, handed the bucket to Bub.

"Here you are," he said. "Jest let me know when you need help."

"I'll do that, Bert. Thanks a lot," Bub said. He took the bucket and went down the ramp. The unexpected yank at the muscles of his left side when he hadn't been set for it, had started them tuning and he didn't want Bert to see his face until they'd calmed down a little.

Kelsey peered at him when he handed over the tub.

"Have any trouble?"

"Not a bit." Bub tried to keep his voice mild, knowing suddenly just who it was who'd fastened that tub down. "Not a mite, Kelsey."

Kelsey never pulled another one; it wasn't exciting enough for him. He liked fireworks to follow his practical jokes. But he'd pulled the first one and after that Bub was fair game. It was as if Kelsey had sanctioned anything and Bub could never be sure what they'd try next.

They did nasty little things, the sort of things that kids in grammar school do when they don't like another kid. Bub made up his mind that he wouldn't let them get his nanny. He'd choke first. And he nearly did. It made him careful. He got to the point where he never took a swig from his thermos bottle without a preliminary cautious sniff. He never took a bite from one of his sandwiches without opening it first to be sure it was still what it had been that morning. He never left his cigarets lying around the storeroom after he got the first good drag off the package they doctored.

As far as he could see, Hersh Baker was the only one who

hadn't had a try at him, and Hersh acted as if he didn't give a damn one way or the other.

Oh, Hell! Bub thought. Well, I won't let em know it hurt. That devil of an Art. Well, maybe I'll learn sometime.

More cautiously, this time using his gloves, he picked up the crowbar and went slowly down to the wharf again. There was nobody in sight when he stood it by the open door, and he heard the swelling roar of the motor as Kelsey's boat shot out from the slip. Art was with him—Bub recognized the blue shirt—and just before they vanished around the Coast Guard Station, Art looked back. He was grinning.

During the long afternoon Bub nearly forgot about it, except when he had to pick something up with the scorched hand. A small blister developed on the inside of his thumb and broke, making a tender place. Whenever he hit that it made him mad. But the trick was on a par with the others they'd pulled and he thought they'd forget about it sooner or later.

They didn't, though. He knew that at five o'clock. He knew, coming up the wharf from the tanks with the keys in his hand, that they'd been cheated. He hadn't said anything and he hadn't lost his temper, and they had been cheated of their fun once too often. Now they were out for it.

Bub heard the low mumble of voices before he went around the corner of the building, and when he did round the corner into the midst of the knot of men sitting there, he stopped as suddenly as the talk did. There were five of them sitting on the big eight-by-twelve just outside the door of the store. There were Bill Seavey and Art Blundin. There were Hersh Baker and Joe Smalley and Bert Pettigrew. And in the open doorway beside them, his legs straddled and his hands shoved deep into his hip pockets, Kelsey was standing looking out, his face noncommittal and slightly amused. He looked as if he was interested, but was having nothing to do with whatever would go on.

This is it, Bub thought. He didn't speak, waiting for them to begin it; but his eyes circled the crowd quickly and came to rest on Bert's smooth, red, insolent young face. Bub knew from the matter-of-factness of his mind that he'd been expecting this ever since he'd come home. Sooner or later this was bound to

[92]

happen and he'd be just as glad to have it over and done with.

"Why, hello, Bub!" Bert started it. "Set down. We was jest sittin here gabbin."

"Sorry," Bub shook his head and took a step backward so he could face them all at the same time. "Ain't got the time."

"What's the matter, Bub?" Bill Seavey's voice was still good-natured. "You ain't thinkin you're a little too good for us, are you?"

"Why, no." Bub's throat started to thicken. He didn't want a fight but they were setting the stage for him. He only hoped to god he'd be able to keep his temper. Once he lost it, he'd undo all the good he'd done by behaving himself. He shoved his hands into his pockets to hide their shaking. He knew how he'd come out after mixing with any of them, but it wasn't fear that made his hands shake, it went deeper than that; and he didn't want them to see it. He shook his head slightly and stood there waiting.

"Guess you caught us that time, all right," Bert said. "We was sittin here talkin about you—" he paused—"you know, 'speak of the devil.' "

Bub met Bert's eyes squarely and they didn't move away. There was the beginning of an ugly look in them that belied his smile. Bub knew what they were doing. They'd done it mildly before, but this time they meant business. They were going to make him fighting mad if they had to slap him around to do it.

"That so? Hope you warn't sayin anythin you didn't want me to hear," Bub said smoothly, thankful that his voice wasn't trembling the way his hands were.

"We mighta been," Joe Smalley said. "You come up mighty quiet. You didn't hear nothin, did you?"

Bub managed a slight tight-lipped smile and shook his head no. He looked fleetingly at Hersh Baker, wondering just where he came into this. Hersh met his eyes for a minute, grinned sheepishly, and looked away again.

"Art was just sayin he was sorry you gut such a burn offn that bar," Joe said.

"Yes, you s.o.b.," Bub turned on Art, "you knew that thing was hot."

[93]

"Anyone with any sense woulda knew it," Art said coolly. "I didn't think you'd be goddam fool enough to pick it up in your bare hands."

There was silence while they waited to see if that was going to make him mad. The hope was too evident in their watching eyes, and Bub, warned, sidestepped, managing a grin. He started forward, stepping carefully over the feet shoved out before him.

"If all you boys got to do is gossip," he said, "I guess I'll shove along."

He had passed them and gone a few steps up the wharf toward the road before anyone spoke. Then Bert's voice came clearly after him, the words carefully articulated.

"The goddam son of a bitch is scared," Bert said.

Something exploded silently with a shower of white sparks behind Bub's eyes. He turned and started back, moving slowly, his hands low at his sides and his eyes steadily on Bert. Bert got up clumsily from the timber. He stood loosely, waiting for Bub to get within reach. Coming in, Bub knew instinctively how this was going to end. Bert had a fifty-pound advantage and his arms were a good deal longer than Bub's. But he kept on going and the shower of sparks had melted into a glow that made his face feel warm and stiff.

"Guess you meant me to hear that, all right, didn't you?" he said. His voice was low but there was something in the tone that wiped Bert's grin off and jerked the heads of the others around toward him sharply. Their faces looked like a lot of featureless balloons.

Bub came in to arm's length and started his swing low, knowing that the first blow was going to be the important one. Bert stepped back, bringing up his left to take the swing; his heel came down hard in a little puddle of oil and he started slipping. Bub's fist grazed his jaw lightly and gave just the right impetus to his fall. Bert went down, not fast, and the solid klunk his head made against the length of timber was a heavy sound in the startled silence.

More surprised than any of them, Bub stared down at Bert's silent figure, his anger fading out in amazement.

"For godsake," he said, breathing hard, "I only grazed him."

[94]

Kelsey bent over Bert and straightened up again.

"Out coldern a haddock," he said. "He hit that timber mighty hard."

Bub walked away and left them clustered there like a flock of excited gulls around Bert's heavy prostrate figure. He walked away admitting to himself that was more than he'd expected to be able to do. He was halfway up the hill to the road before he heard steps and turned, instantly on the defensive. Hersh Baker was climbing the hill, about fifteen feet behind him, and when Bub stopped, he did, too.

"Well?" Bub said.

"Thought I'd come along with you, if you didn't mind," Hersh mumbled, looking anywhere but at Bub.

"Pretty late in the day to choose sides, ain't it?"

"I figgered you was doin all right by yourself back there," Hersh said. "I didn't see no need for mixin in. Besides, it takes me a reasonable time to make up my mind which side I'm on."

"You done it yet?"

"Ayeh," Hersh nodded. "That's why I come along. How about a beer?"

"Good idea," Bub said.

After the sixth beer, Bub stopped long enough to look around him at the joint. He hadn't been to Barron's before, but evidently it was an old haunt of Hersh's.

"This ain't so bad, is it?" he said.

"Nope." Hersh's fine air of discrimination made Bub wonder how many beer parlors he knew intimately. "Old Steve has pretty good beer." He took a large swallow, and Bub, watching with fascination the rugged apparatus of Hersh's Adam's apple, realized that Hersh had already had ten to his six.

"You trying to git drunk?" he asked.

"Might's well." Hersh's taciturnity wasn't anger; it sounded like the depths of wordless despair.

"Whatsa matter?" Bub glanced around behind him, looking for the door to the men's room. He began to realize it had been quite a time since he'd had more than one glass of beer at a time.

[95]

"Oh, nothin," Hersh said. He sighed deeply, finished the glass, and crooked his finger at the girl behind the bar.

"All right," Bub said recklessly, "I can do it if you can."

He thought a minute, trying to remember what it was he'd wanted to ask Hersh. It came to him.

"Say, what was the idea of that business tonight?"

"Oh, they was jest settin around without enough to do, an they sort of figgered they could have a little fun with you."

"That so?"

"They would of, too," Hersh managed a weak grin, "if the kid hadn't of slipped jest when he did."

"Might have been fun for them," Bub said. "It wouldn't for me."

"Bert *is* pretty sizeable," Hersh said judiciously. "Howcome you don't get on so good with the Pettigrews?"

"Joe an me never got along from the beginnin," Bub said. "I guess his kid brother's carryin on the family rows."

"It's gonna be worse now," Hersh grinned. "Joe ain't goin to like it much when he hears what happened to Bertie."

"I can't help it," Bub said. "I never hardly touched him. Just my luck, I guess."

"Ayeh."

Hersh pondered a minute and then said weightily:

"How'd you like to come out haulin traps with me Sunday?"

"I sure would like it," Bub accepted hastily. "You haul every other day?"

"Yup."

"Howcome you're workin for Kelsey anyhow, if you got a boat of your own?"

"Aw," Hersh groaned deeply, "I wouldn't. But my wife says I better have a steady job besides fishin. She says you can't make a decent livin just fishin. I gut to humor her right now."

"That so? Howcome?"

"Well," Hersh looked impressed and a little embarrassed, "she's goin to have a baby, see? It's the first one, an it's a lot of responsibility, see? I got to handle her pretty careful."

"I should think so," Bub nodded heavily as if he'd had endless experience with mothers of babies about to be born.

[96]

"You know," Hersh said, "it's enough to drive you to drink. It ain't no wonder I come here an drink like this. I know I oughtn't to do it, an I don't like doin it, but if I didn't I'd go nuts."

"What're you goin nuts for, Hersh?" The slightly hoarse voice made Hersh jump and Bub looked up with a grin as Nina Barnes dropped into a chair between them. "What's the matter, anyhow?"

"Oh, it's jest Ida an the baby," Hersh said.

"I didn't know you had a kid," Nina said. Miraculously a glass of beer had appeared on the table before her and Bub eyed it, wondering who was going to be stuck for that.

"Well—I—er—" Hersh gargled slightly, trying not to seem indelicate.

"Oh, you mean it ain't quite here yet?"

"That's right," Hersh said, relieved and beginning to be slightly tearful. "If it don't hurry up I'm the one's goin nuts."

"Well, now," Nina said soothingly, "you don't want to go feelin like that, Hersh. I been through it an it ain't so bad."

At this open reference to something he'd always mentioned in whispers, Hersh looked slightly shocked, almost as if he'd thought an illegitimate baby was born in a different way.

"We-ell."

"That's right, Hersh," Bub said stiffly, feeling as if his tongue had a lead weight hung on the end of it. "She's right. Every word of it."

"Now, how d'you know so much about it?" Nina turned on him with a teasing grin. "You ain't a papa, are you?"

"No," Bub said hastily.

She sat looking at him for a moment as if she hadn't seen him before, and looking back at her, Bub realized foggily that he actually *hadn't* seen her. He'd noticed before only the slatternly house she kept and the baby pulling at her skirt. Now, divorced materially from her background, Nina was well worth looking at twice. She was clean and she wore a neat light suit that had just been pressed, from the looks of it. Her curiously wide face, narrowing down to a very small chin, gave her the look of a young, but not an innocent, cat. Her eyes met his glance squarely, and

Bub, reading easily what Nina was thinking, looked quickly away, feeling the growth of warmth under the band of his collar.

"I don't see why not," Nina said thoughtfully.

"Here, that's enough of that." Hersh got clumsily to his big feet. "I'm goin, Bub. You comin with me?"

Bub glanced back at Nina and found her still watching him with that queer, steady, knowing look. He got up and followed Hersh outside without looking back again.

"That's not bad," Hersh said. "If you want to stay, it's okay with me."

"Unh-unh," Bub shook his head. "That ain't for me."

"That's what you think," Hersh said with drunken directness.

"That's what I know."

There was a long silence. Bub felt as if the road went back under his feet an inch at a time. The laborious steps beside him told him that Hersh felt the same way.

"God, that's an awful thing," Hersh said suddenly, out of silence, just before he turned up the drive that took him to his back door.

"Wha's that?" Bub stared.

"Curtis Jellison," Hersh said. "Ain't you heard?"

"Heard? Heard what, for godsake?" Almost sober, Bub glared at him.

"Why, he gut a blood poisonin in his foot and they hed to take it off just above the ankle. That's an awful thing for a man to have happen to him. On top of that, he went an got ether pneumonia. He's awful sick."

Hersh lurched away and disappeared into the darkness, leaving Bub to realize that he'd come way uptown here without even noticing it. Feeling a little foolish, he turned back down the road again, toward the wharf.

When he left Hersh and went down the road to the shack in a pleasant and foggy daze of beer, all Bub could remember of the evening was Hersh's telling him about Curtis Jellison.

He leaned on the railing looking out into blackness, his head swirling slightly. God! it would be tough on a man to lose a part of him like that, especially a man who had to make his living on his feet. Bub himself had had an awful fear of being maimed, losing an arm or a leg, maybe an eye—and when he'd finally been hit, the fear of the seriousness of his wound was partially drowned in relief that it hadn't been a foot or a hand.

It's always the decent, hard-working ones who have a thing like that happen to them, he figured idly. The others just go along in perfect health until something final happens to them. He remembered his own father, whose health had been as good as it possibly could be until he came home late one night and stumbled into an old disused well. They hadn't found him for two days. He remembered the Old Man, too. The Old Man had been his mother's father, his grandfather. The queerest thing about this return to the Harbor, to Bub, had been the Old Man's absence. Always before he'd been there, to talk to, to be with. Now he wasn't.

He had died the summer Bub was working on a farm way upcountry near the line and nobody had known where Bub was to let him know about it. Late in the fall Bub had got sick, and as soon as he was able to walk again, had lit out for home and the Old Man, forgetting that just three months before he'd sworn never to come back to the Harbor again.

Bub got there late on Sunday night and reconnoitered the house before knocking on the door. Old lady Barker had been alone in the big kitchen. When she opened the door, she stood behind it so he couldn't come in.

"I want to see the Old Man," Bub had said.

"I never thought to see you again," she'd said. "I thought probly you'd heard an wouldn't be back."

"Heard what?"

"He's dead, Bub. He died over a month ago."

Bub could remember coming to on her kitchen floor. She'd managed to drag him into the house and had propped up his head with a pillow. When he could stand up, she'd fed him. She had taken him in as she always did, when he came back. Except this time. Now he was on his own and it was pretty hard.

[99]

JINNIE AND LYFORD had both gone to the movies and Edna was sitting alone in the front room with a magazine in her lap when Lou came down the stairs to the front door.

"Good night, Mom," she said. "I won't be late."

Edna looked up as if she'd just noticed Lou.

"This ain't your night for the warden, is it?" she asked, knowing perfectly well that it wasn't.

"No," Lou said. "I'm just going for a walk."

"Dear, I wish you wouldn't be so secretive. I wish you'd tell me where you're goin without makin me ask. What if somethin happened an I wanted to find you in a hurry?"

"I don't know exactly where I'm going," Lou explained patiently. "Just for a walk. And I'll be home early."

"Well, with your father so sick an all—"

"He's coming along all right, Mom. It wouldn't do him a bit of good in the hospital over there if I stayed around the house here all the time, and you know it. Now, don't be foolish."

"I'm just tryin to think what's best, dear. I'm sorry if you think I'm foolish. I'm just doin my best."

"Yes, I know. That's not what I meant," Lou said. She sighed, standing waiting for her mother to finish.

"You meetin Joe out town, Lou?"

"No, Mom. I'm not going with Joe."

Edna's full underlip quivered.

"Well, be careful, won't you, Lou?"

Their eyes met fully and Lou saw that her mother had known all along that it wasn't Joe she was going to meet.

"I wish you'd have people call for you here to home," Edna said.

"I thought Pa was going to be here. I didn't feel like starting a row over something that doesn't—that isn't worth it."

Edna said nothing more. She picked up the magazine, and Lou, with a sigh of relief, went out and closed the door softly behind her.

She hadn't been exactly truthful when she said she hadn't let Bub come to the house because the whole thing wasn't worth the row Curtis would kick up. That wasn't true, and she was ashamed of herself for having said it. It was because she just didn't want to face that row before she was sure of herself.

Lou wasn't sure yet just how she felt about Bub, but she knew herself well enough to know that if she hadn't liked him she wouldn't be bothered to see him again. She remembered him from high school as an unpleasant, too-loud boy with a bad complexion and an ill-tempered face. She hadn't liked him then at all. And she couldn't understand why she had quite suddenly felt actual liking for him when he'd appeared at the office window that first morning.

She wasn't dumb and it was obvious to her how Bub could feel about her if he wanted to let himself. His face was impassive enough when he looked at her, but his eyes weren't; being a woman, she felt warm at the thought of that half-concealed admiration.

She didn't even know how far she wanted to let that admiration go. Lou was enough her mother's daughter to have absorbed a certain amount of Edna's respect for actual possessions. But Lou had a sneaking suspicion that there was something more to look for than that. Joe represented unadulterated material prosperity, but there wasn't much else there. She certainly had no desire to grow old, as her mother had done, in an atmosphere of discontent and unhappiness. There had to be something more to look for than just that.

From a distance she could see Bub's thin figure outside the dimly lit drugstore, and she quickened her pace unconsciously. He turned to face her, hearing her steps.

"I didn't hardly expect you to come," he said.

"You're talking just like my mother. I don't see what good it can do Pa if I sit around the house waiting for him to come back."

"Can't do none, can it?" Bub said. "I never thought of that. Well, where d'you want to go?"

"Let's go for a walk. I don't feel much like sitting inside tonight. And it's a lovely night."

"It is nice." He breathed deeply as if he'd just noticed that he could. "Want to take a walk down an see where I'm livin?"

Lou looked at him, amused, wondering if this was the beginning of Bub's line.

"I'd like to."

"I was sorry as hell to hear about your father." Bub stuck his hands into his pockets. "It's sort of hard to think what to say when somethin like that happens. Is he—how is he?"

"He's coming along all right now. At first it was sort of touch and go. It's too bad, but what bothers me is he'll always keep remembering it was his own stubbornness to blame for the whole thing."

"Well, that don't help much when you lose something like a foot," Bub said. "We turn off here," he gestured toward the little lane that ran down through the alders to the shore.

"You probably think I sound hard," Lou said, "but it isn't as bad now as it would have been—they can do wonderful things now. He'll get an artificial foot that'll be—well, the doctor said nearly as good as his old one."

"That's all right," Bub growled, "maybe he will. But it won't be the same. Losin part of you like that, you always know what you got to replace it ain't really you."

"Well," Lou said shortly, "it's done. We can't do any good by having it over. Pa'll just have to make the best of it. But I do feel sorry as the dickens for him. It'll change a lot of things, this happening. It'll make a lot of things harder for him."

She stopped talking and looked down, thinking of her father and how much difference it was going to make for him. If she hadn't stopped talking, she knew she would have started to cry, thinking of him, and she didn't want to do that. That lump in her throat always meant tears and she swallowed hard, feeling the lump dissolve painfully.

Here under the big old alders it was shadowy, and the unused cart track was grass-grown and smooth. Their feet made no sound on it. The green silence made her think of swimming underwater and how everything was unreal and furry looking and dark when you opened your eyes. Bub was still walking with his eyes steadily on the ground when she looked over at him, and she thought his face looked almost disapproving, as if he thought she hadn't shown enough emotion. Well, he'll just have to put up with me the way I am, she thought.

They came out of the narrow road, crossed the field, and went down onto the small wharf, their feet sounding loud by comparison on the punky old wood. Bub unlocked the door and pushed it open. Lou went in by him silently, glancing around her at the neat small room and peering into the bedroom beyond it.

"My gosh, Bub," she said in mock amazement, "I didn't realize you were such a good housekeeper."

"I guess it's Pete's example." Bub sounded surprised himself. "It was so clean when I come here I've just gone ahead keepin it that way."

"It's nice. I like it. Not too many doo-dads around."

"Ayeh," he said brusquely, and stepped back out onto the wharf, standing aside at the door to wait until she came out. A little surprised, Lou followed him. He closed the door and went over to the railing. Lou stood by the door momentarily, watching his back and the straight arms that held him stiff as he leaned there.

"What is it?" she asked. "There's something wrong with you tonight."

"No—" he didn't turn to look at her—"there ain't really. But I just got to thinkin about your old man an what it's goin to be like for him—you know. Why I sounded so het up about it," Bub said, "I remembered how I used to think about gettin wounded, an the worst I thought could ever happen would be to lose a foot or an arm like that. I was scared to death somethin like that would happen an I couldn't think of anythin that'd be worse."

"Please stop talking about it." Lou's strangled voice made him jump. "I don't want to talk about Pa, don't you see?"

But still he went on thinking, not so much of Curtis as of himself and the horror he'd had of losing some part of himself, and what it was like waiting to be killed.

"What was it like where you were?" Lou said, as if she'd been able to see what he was thinking.

Bub heard the question turning over somewhere in his mind.

What was it like, anyhow, he thought, groping for the memory of what it had been like. He was silent so long that Lou finally spoke again.

"What are you thinking about?" she asked, and Bub felt his attention come back with a jerk so sudden it almost hurt him.

"I was thinkin about what you said. You asked me what it was like. I was tryin to think."

"If you don't want to talk about it, it's okay." Lou took his hand and held it lightly. "They say men don't sometimes when it was bad."

"I don't mind," Bub said. "It ain't that. I was jest thinkin how to tell you how I felt. It was queer."

"Were you—scared?"

"Ayeh," he nodded. "I was so scared most of the time I couldn't have moved if I'd wanted to. But I guess most of the rest of em was, too. There was so much waitin. You waited around and it was dark an you wondered what was goin to happen."

"I should think it would have been hard for you—" Lou's voice was slow as if she were trying to think out the right words —"you're so easygoing. You—well—I've never seen you really mad."

"I guess I used up all my mad," Bub grinned. Then he turned serious again. "That's what it was," he said, trying to pin down the thought. "You had to get mad. You had to think about somethin that maybe meant a lot to you—an then you had to think about what they'd do to that thing. Then you lost your temper an it warn't half so hard to go out an kill a mess of em. When you seen a bunch of em comin at you all ready to kill you, then it was different. You got scared as hell an *then* you could kill em. But when you go *after* em, you have to be mad."

"What did *you* think about?" Her voice was so low he could hardly hear it.

"About the Harbor," he said reluctantly. "I'm darned if I know why, either. It never meant nothin much to me till I got to thinkin how I'd feel if they made a mess of it like we done there. An I got so darn mad thinkin about it, they just didn't

[104]

look real an it wasn't so hard." His voice slowed and trailed away into reluctance. It embarrassed him to reveal himself, even to Lou, and he was beginning to see he'd said an awful lot.

She seemed to sense his not wanting to say anything more about it and she half-changed the subject.

"If only you'd get mad now," she said with sudden vigor, straightening up and moving slightly away from him. "Lose your temper. Tell people what you've been doing. Raise hell once in a while."

Bub chuckled.

"It sounds funny when you swear."

Lou actually slatted.

"You're laughing at me," she protested.

"No, I ain't really. It's funny about gettin mad. After—well, I used to when I was a kid. It was always gettin me in trouble. Then I did there, too, I guess. And I guess it makes this look like just not enough to get mad about."

"Yes," she said slowly. "I can see how that would be. But, look, when you were fighting and you had a gun, you didn't put it down and use your bare hands, did you? Well, it looks to me like that's what you're doing now. You've got a gun, you just aren't using it."

"Oh, Lou," Bub moved his shoulders impatiently, "I can't go spillin all that junk I told you. People wouldn't b'lieve me in the first place. If they did, even, just bein in the war don't mean I'm a hero or somethin. I've tried to tell you how I feel. You've got to let me do it my way or it'll never work out right. I've *got* to do it my way."

"Why, Bub Dolliver, you nearly lost your temper."

"Humph!" Bub felt his mouth quirk into an unwilling grin. "Dunno, maybe I did."

"Well," Lou said lightly, "at least you've proved you've got one. That's better than nothing."

When he left her at the door that night and went alone down the dim street, it seemed to Bub as if what he'd been thinking and talking about to Lou had made the Harbor unreal again. It didn't seem possible that he was back here, walking down an alder-lined lane toward his own bed under a sky that would not be split and torn by the whining climbing sound of planes.

He felt as if the years since he'd left the Harbor had been taken bodily out of the middle of his life. He could almost taste the mud that had gritted in the inky water he'd drunk on jungle islands that were so far away from the Harbor and so detached that they might have been on the other side of time as well as the other side of the world.

Momentarily he was back in that time, and the Harbor had gone. The sense of peace and quiet he'd felt since he came home was gone, too. And he wanted it back. He didn't want to think about anything but the Harbor. But when he undressed and crawled into bed and shut his eyes, he lay for awhile drifting to the edge of sleep and jerking back away from it again.

Finally he got up, pulled on his pants, fished a cigaret from his pocket, and stepped barefooted out into the cold still crispness of the clear late night. He leaned on the railing and smoked, watching the red coal flicker faintly in the moving black oil of the water beneath his feet.

It was half-tide, and below him, on the scrawny old pilings, the barnacles and winkles made soft sucking noises in the darkness, waiting for the tide to come again. This silence had a different texture, it was friendly instead of inimical. It was peaceful.

There was a smell of distant fog in the quiet air, and what wind there was came from the east. The slow, regular tolling of the bell buoy on Sinker's Ledge, just outside the mouth of the harbor, was loud; and as he listened he heard the first low, protesting, thumping growl of the foghorn from the Hog Point Light.

Beyond the regular flash of the Light itself there was darkness on Old Point. Somewhere over there the summer people were sleeping. "The summer people!" He half-whispered the words, remembering what they'd meant to him. People with more money, better houses, better cars, better clothes. People who always had more fun and did less work. Well, they were all alike when they were asleep and they were sleeping now.

Behind him the town was dark, too. And there the natives were sleeping. No matter how good or bad they were, he thought, they probably looked pretty much alike when they were asleep.

Under the faint silver light the whole harbor seemed to move with a slow, almost invisible movement, like the great, smooth, exposed heart of the land itself. The town was at his back, and behind the town there was a whole continent of living, sleeping, laughing, working people—doing whatever they wanted to do or had to do at the moment without wondering when death would spray on them out of the sky itself. Three thousand miles of land covered with people who weren't thinking about death. Three thousand miles of silent people behind him and he wasn't afraid to turn his back on them.

But he started and turned suddenly at the sound of an incautious foot against wood.

"Who's that?"

"Don't git excited, son, it's jest me. Come down to see if you was still up. Bein your neighbor an all, thought I better visit you."

Bub grinned.

"Come on down, Batty. Pretty late, ain't it?"

The queer, tall, twisted figure came out of the gloom and stood looking like a malformed crane. Bub could make out the hawklike head, thrust forward and turned a little to one side, and knew the peering eyes were going over him invisibly.

"Well, I tell you," Batty said, his reedy voice growing like an organ note, "way it is with most people, all they do's worry about the time. Either it's too late or it's too dam early for em. You'd think God set up in heaven jest gettin time to go too fast or too slow jest to spite em. Now take me, I don't care. Me'n God come to a sort of agreement. I take my time an He takes hisn, an neither of us don't go botherin the other one about it."

"That's right," Bub said. "You're right, Battty."

"Right? Course I'm right. They ain't no question about my being right or wrong. I ain't one of these people have to git up and eat an drink an go to bed by a clock. I ain't even gut a clock. Don't need it. Man warn't never meant to run his life like a dam railroad train anyways. If they was less worryin about gittin places on time they'd be a lot less indigestion an cancer."

"Time don't cause that, does it?"

"Well, I tell you—" Batty came a step closer and shoved his hands into the pockets of his ragged pants. "You ain't got an extra cigaret, have you?"

Bub handed him one and stood waiting for the crooked head to come down to the match he held cupped in his hands. Batty's face in the flickering light was strange and wild. His bones were covered only by a taut layer of dark skin. His shining eyes were half closed against the match flame, but Bub could see them gleaming between the slitted lids. His thin brown cheeks, unmarked by line or wrinkle, puffed in and out strongly, and he shot clouds of fragrant smoke into the air before he was satisfied with the light.

"Thanks, son." He straightened again. Bub watched the light die away from his face with reluctance. The last gleam left the thick black hair and Batty refaded into a shape.

"I'll tell you, like I said," he started again. "Civilization now ain't nothin but a squirmin mass of disease and democrats. Politics an cancer, there ain't a mite of difference, exceptin with one it's a person that has it an with the other it's the whole dam country. An it ain't nothin but time that causes it —no matter how much people talk about tomahters."

"Is that right?" Bub could remember just where to interject in order to keep Batty going.

"You bet it's right. You take the word of a man's seen a lot of things come an go. Me, I been sittin right there in that old shack of mine watchin things go by now for near fifty—sixty— years, an they's a lot of people that's died of being in a hurry —an they died young. I ain't never been in a hurry an look at me."

"You *ain't* changed much, Batty," Bub said. And it was true. The Batty he was talking to now looked exactly the same as he had ten or fifteen years ago. He hadn't changed by so much

[108]

as one gray hair. It made Bub feel good to find that there was something alive that was still untouched and unchanged.

"I been tellin you why. You take it from me, all you hev to do is let things go by an don't hurry an don't worry." He stared off over the water for a moment. "Where you been these last few years?" he asked suddenly.

Bub jumped, the unexpectedness of the question taking him off guard.

"Oh, all over," he recovered quickly.

"I bet," Batty said. "You young fellers go hellin off an be gone god knows how long. But I notice you always come back in the end. What you gonna do?"

"I'm goin to get me a boat," Bub said, surprising himself. "I'm goin to get me a boat an go lobsterin an fishin."

"They's worse things you could do," Batty said. "They's better, too."

"That sounds pretty good to me," Bub said thoughtfully. It did, too. It was what he'd been floundering around after. Now, listening to this half-crazy old man talking about time, he'd made up his mind what he wanted to do.

"You probly seen some pretty excitin things whilst you was gone," Batty said. "How d'you know you kin settle down doin somethin like that?"

"Whatta you mean, excitin?" Bub said slowly.

"Well, you been in the Army, ain't you? Buncha the fellers was talkin the other day an said you'd either been there or in jail."

"I ain't been in neither, an you can tell the next bunch that for me."

"Touchy, ain't you?" Batty chuckled. The performance was weird. His thin, high shoulders writhed visibly and his head jerked up and down between them. He topped it off by raising one knee and cracking it heartily with his open hand. "Anyways, I see you've picked up with Curtis Jellison's girl. Nice girl, ain't she?"

"Ayeh."

"Jeez," Batty groaned, "warn't that awful about Curtis losin his foot?"

"Ayeh."

"I tell you, it all comes of bein in too much of a hurry. They ain't a single ill or ailment you can't trace back to hurryin. Honest, it's a wonder to me people don't strain their innards right out, hurryin." His voice trailed off to a mere whisper of sound. He sucked greedily on the end of the cigaret, flung the final brilliant fragment over the rail into the water, and turned away.

"Guess I'll git along. Feelin sleepy. Don't know what time it is an don't give a dam. I'm jest sleepy."

"Well, sleep good," Bub said.

Batty didn't answer. He ambled up the wharf, hesitating for a moment by the door of the shack, almost turning, it seemed to Bub. He kept on going, though, and Bub stood watching until Batty's tall, thin figure crossed the clearing and disappeared shadily into the shore path before he turned back to lean on the railing again.

He hadn't thought before just what he wanted to do eventually, but now he had put the mere ghost of an idea into words and had found what he wanted. Fishing wasn't an easy job and nobody knew that better than he did, who'd been brought up in a fishing town and who'd lived there most of his life. But he wasn't looking for a job that was easy. He was looking for something it took a man to do, something that other people respected you for doing, and something that took skill and knowledge. There were times when you hardly got your seed back, fishing, but that was a chance you had to take, and Bub figured if you knew what you were doing, you stood more than a fair chance of breaking even. You didn't do more than that in the end no matter what you picked out to make a living at.

Now everything was all right for him again. His perspective had come back, and with it a deep weariness that made him feel lax with the weight of sleep. He yawned deeply, groaning, dropped his cigaret overboard and heard it hiss out in the water. He went sleepily back to the door of the shack and stood looking down, without surprise, at the empty space beside the jamb.

"By judast," he said softly, "that old devil musta took my clam hoe with him. I know I left it right there."

He didn't feel mad—just amused. He could get that back all right. He went into the shack and was asleep as soon as he hit the bed.

Bub woke early on Sunday morning, coming to suddenly in the pale light of the early summer dawn. He got up and glanced out across the harbor. The mist hadn't cleared yet and the sun was a faint glow through grayness. Everything was faintly opalescent against gray. Even the deep, clear green of the water under his window had a cast of shifting elusive color, like the fading moving tints of oil film, but not so vivid. The old unpainted wood of the pilings was dark and wet looking. Out on the harbor the faint shapes of boats loomed hazily. He couldn't even make out the other shore.

Bub dressed hastily and ate his breakfast standing in the window. When he'd finished, he rinsed the dishes out at the sink, stacked them on the wooden drainboard, and stepped outside, closing the door behind him. The thin air was still cool, but later on it was going to be hot. While he had been eating, the sun had come up above the mist and it was gone now, leaving only a few ragtails floating aimlessly just above the surface of the water.

It was still early enough for the morning to have that elusive smell of clean clothing just after it's come in out of the wind. It was a smell like the odor of wind blowing across distant fields of snow; the faint, almost sharp perfume of glaciers and pines and winds that blow down from high mountains.

Bub lit his first cigaret, enjoying the knifing of tobacco smoke through the air as much as he savored the lungful of smoke. He was leaning on the rail waiting when he heard the motor start spasmodically on the other side of the harbor. The noise was explosive and shattering. He could see the white hull detach itself from the grouped boats at mooring and edge slowly out into the channel. It came feeling its way slowly up the harbor. He could make out Hersh's big shoulders past the spray hood. Then Hersh's face, brilliantly tan and widely grinning. The boat drifted slowly in to the wharf and Bub dropped lightly to the bow and fended her off.

"Gee," Hersh said tautly above the engine chatter, "I didn't know's I could make it. This place sure has filled in since they stopped usin it."

He took a quick glance over the stern. Bub, coming aft, saw the yellow tinge of mud where the propellor had hit clam flats and stirred them up.

"Dunno but what I'll have to make you git out an push," Hersh said.

His big hands were as smooth as silk on the controls as he put away from the wharf and headed out for the channel again. Bub watched him with a feeling of envy, envy for the hands that looked so clumsy—that were so clumsy—but that could handle a boat as if there were nothing to it but an easy turn of the wrist.

Hersh hit the channel and opened the throttle. The little boat surged forward, raising a following wall of water just astern and sending great spreading "V's" of her wake growing out across the silvery harbor.

They passed out of the harbor mouth and rounded Hog Point, and instantly the character of the water changed. It was calm outside, but it was calmness that held no promise of safety; it was calmness that could be instantly furious and raging. Against the rough spruce growth on the Point the white painted bricks of the lighthouse shone with an intensity that was too much to look at long. And along the following shore Bub could make out the big ramshackle summer cottages, built back among the spruces, their shingles weathered and their roofs stained brown to blend with the land.

Hersh's traps were up near the estuary, and Bub watched with growing pleasure the shore they were hugging. It was all familiar to him, but this was the first time in years he had seen it from a boat. The spruces grew raggedly down to the beginning of the great red-brown ledges, and beneath them the green water came in deep. Presently, though, the spruces began to thin out and grow smaller. The country became swampy and low, and the land took on that shield-like look of wide salt

[112]

marshes. Though he couldn't see it, Bub knew how the salt water channeled through the land along the river mouth. You could go for miles in a punt up and down those winding, shining arms of water and not hit the same arm twice.

Gulls screamed lazily upward and circled before the splitting sound of their engine; and once a big crane, disturbed, went clumsily flopping away across the sky.

Hersh picked up his first buoy skillfully and started hauling the trap.

"Fill me a bait pocket, will you, Bub?" he asked over his shoulder. Bub took a pocket from the bunch and stuffed it with ripe herring from the bait tub. He wrinkled his nose slightly at the ruddy, cheesy smell of the fish, but that too was something he remembered.

The trap came murkily out of water, a weed-wound mystery of laths and barnacles and queer water sounds and strange flapping noises. Bub watched, fascinated, as Hersh explored the trap with a gloved, cautious hand. He scaled a handful of small crabs off into the quiet water, extracted two small lobsters and three counters, tied in a new pocket, and let the trap go with a splash. The boat moved on slowly to the next buoy.

All morning they hauled, in the wide, flat silver. Bub watched with silent pleasure the way Hersh went about his business. It was something to watch. It was good to be around somebody who could make a hard job look easy just by knowing exactly how to do it. Hersh never wasted a motion. Each seemingly slow move of his big shoulders was for a purpose, and it was good to see.

Toward noon they went ashore and boiled a pailful of shorts Hersh had kept out, eating them out of the shell with their fingers. After he'd eaten, Bub peeled off his shirt and lay back against the rocks with a sigh of deep and abiding content. The sun seemed to go right through his body, he thought his bones could feel it, and the ledges under him were warm with stored heat.

"You heard how Curtis is?" Bub asked.

"Oh, he's comin along all right now. They thought at first he was a goner, but I guess he's jest as tough as he looks."

There was silence, then Hersh said mildly:

"You wanta be careful. That sun can give you an awful burn, specially after it burns through a mist the way it done this mornin."

"Ayeh," Bub turned lazily. "I'll watch it."

"You gut a pretty good tan, though," Hersh said. "I never—" His voice stopped on a quick, surprised gurgle of sound. Too late Bub realized that his turning had exposed the livid scar tissue along his side. He flopped back instinctively, but one glance at Hersh's face told him it was too late.

"What in god's name's wrong with your side?" Hersh sounded strangled. "I never see a scar like that in all my life!"

"I—I—" Bub muttered, groping for something to say. Then he shrugged mentally. "That's somethin they let me bring home with me from Guadalcanal."

"Jesus Christ!" Hersh said, and his mild eyes were wide with astonishment. "You don't mean to say you was in that mess?"

Bub grinned and nodded.

"I see some of it before that happened," he said. "Afterwards they figured I wouldn't be much more good to em, so they let me go."

"Well, god!" Hersh was almost whispering. "That warn't no ordinary bullet done that, son."

"No, it warn't exactly. It was a mess of shrapnel, I guess. At least, that's what they told me after they gut through pickin it out of me. Boy, I tell you, I musta weighed ten pounds lighter when they gut that stuff outa me."

"I'll bet," Hersh said. "For pete's sake, whyn't you tell anyone about it?"

"I just don't want to. An I don't want you to neither, Hersh."

"Well . . ." Hersh said doubtfully, "it's your business, an if you say don't tell, why I won't. But it's foolish, seems to me. Jeez, if I'd a been in anythin like that I'd want people to know about it, an you can tie to that."

"Well, I'm funny," Bub said rather shortly.

"Ayeh." Hersh was silent for a second, then he edged a little closer, his eyes curious.

"What's that country like, anyhow? Is it worth anythin?"

[114]

"No," Bub said explosively. "I never see why anyone'd want it bad enough to fight like that for it. It ain't nothin but a mess of little islands. And wet! Rain? I never see rain like that before. Honest to god, Hersh, one minute you'd be in the middle of a cloudburst an the next you'd be steamin away in sunshine. An bugs! More than you'd ever think they was made. I *never* see nothin like that place an I don't want to again. Talk about the place God forgot—well, them islands is made out of the leavins of what He forgot in the first place."

"Hunh!" Hersh made the sound through his nose and shook his head slowly. "I figured they was somethin like that, but of course you can't really tell unless you've seen em or talked to somebody that has."

"Mud!" Bub exploded. "Up to your knees an sometimes deeper an them hills, jest like the side of a glass house; so slippery a fly couldn't walk up em. You had to crawl, an b'lieve me, when you crawl in mud that's up to your knees when you're standin up, you look like nothin on God's green earth."

Hersh said "Ugh" in a satisfactory tone of disgust.

"What was you, a Marine?" he asked. He got to his feet and stood looking down, his big hands poised on his hips. Bub nodded and got up too, swinging his shirt in one hand. "That's some tough job," Hersh said. He headed for the punt.

They pulled back to the boat in silence. But during the long golden afternoon Bub noticed something that was pleasing to him in spite of the fact that he hadn't wanted people to know where he'd been. Hersh's attitude toward him had undergone a subtle, deep change. It was entirely unconscious, and for that reason flattering. There was no longer the unintentional but openly apparent patronage of the man who has done things for the man who hasn't. There was none of that competent attitude of "You'd better move. I've got to be where you're standing because I can do it better than you can." That was gone as completely and suddenly as if it had never existed; and it had been replaced by the respect one hard-working man will always have for another who has worked as hard or harder than he has.

That night, after supper, while it was still light, Bub went up along the shore path to where it came out into Batty's clearing. Batty's house was dark, but Bub could make out his thin figure slumped on the doorstep.

"Hello!" he said.

"Hello, son," Batty said calmly. "I thought you'd be turnin up."

"What'd you think I would for?" Bub asked.

"Well, I figgered you'd probly be missin your clam rake an come up here after it. I dunno why it is, people always come around here lookin for everythin that's ever missin. I can't understand why it is. They always come arunning to me for everythin under the sun. I can't keep track of their things."

"Where'd it be apt to be?" Bub glanced around at the immaculate yard.

"Why, if it's anywhere, it's probly over there jest inside the shed door alongside of mine." Batty gestured lazily and Bub walked over to the open shed door. He retrieved the clam hoe and came back.

"How d'you suppose it got to be there?" He stared down at the old man.

"Blessed if I know," Batty shook his head heavily. "Beats all the way things turn up, don't it?"

"It sure does." Bub chuckled without noise, put the clam hoe over his shoulder, and turned back to the path.

Batty yelled at him just before he entered the wood's edge.

"Hey, son!"

"Ayeh." Bub turned and waited.

"That's a real nice clam rake. If I was you, I'd take it in o nights."

"Thanks, Batty, I'll do that."

"You better. Someone's apt to make love to it, you go leavin it around careless like that."

IT was over a week before June saw Mack again, and in that time his disgust had had time to simmer down. It had turned queerly to a sort of grudging admiration of Mack and shame for himself. That Mack! he thought. He'd dare to do anything! And June felt ashamed that he himself couldn't be the same way. He wanted to be devil-may-care like Mack; he wanted to be able to do things the way Mack did and never stop to think what might happen. That was the way to be, all right, June told himself. He began to see what a good joke Mack had pulled on Bub telling that girl his name was "Bub."

Looking back on it now, June forgot his sickness and knew that he wanted to be like that. Mack was big for sixteen—you'd think he was a lot older really, and June resented that, too, knowing that he himself really *looked* sixteen.

For that reason he greeted Mack with a greater hospitality than he would have shown earlier when Mack came slouching down the road to the wharf and found June sitting there dangling his feet over the water.

"Where's your old man?" Mack said cautiously, letting himself down beside June.

"He went to Portland this mornin," June said. "He probly won't get back till sometime tomorrow."

"Aw, hell! I was hopin you could ask him for the truck. Maybe we could find somethin excitin to do tonight."

June looked thoughtfully off across the harbor. His mind was turning over cause and effect, and he decided quickly that he couldn't have Mack thinking him any more of a baby than he already did.

"Hell," June said, "you don't think I have to ask him whenever I want the truck, do you?"

"Yeah." Mack's dark eyes were curiously amused. "Yeah, that's what I thought."

"Come on, I'll show you." June started to get up.

"Hold your hosses," Mack said. "We don't want to git started yet. It ain't dark enough."

"Dark enough for what?" June was suddenly suspicious.

"Anythin you wanta name," Mack said. He didn't move, and June sat down again, cautiously.

[117 [

"You—you ain't said nothing about the other night, have you?" Mack asked, after a moment's silence.

"You think I'm crazy?"

"We-ell."

"Say, Mack, you seen her since?"

"Nu-uh." Mack shook his head. "I ain't an I ain't goin to. I got what I wanted, didn't I?"

"What'd you do after I left you?" June asked, his mind avid for detail.

"You can imagine," Mack grinned. "I took her home an her old man was workin that night. We was all alone there at the camp."

"I should think them camps'd be dirty," June said thoughtfully.

"Who cares? We hed a good time."

"What'd you do?" June persisted.

Mack turned his head just enough to see June's face and he grinned at the expression in June's eyes.

"You coulda found out for yourself," he said, "only you was too scared."

"Ah, go to hell!" June stopped asking questions, his ears warm and bright with embarrassment.

It grew dark slowly as they sat there, and finally Mack got to his feet.

"Well, let's go. Let's see how you get the truck when your old man ain't around."

June didn't answer. They went up the hill to the big garage and June went in, started the truck, and backed her out. Mack shut the sliding doors and swung lightly onto the running board as June slowed for him. June had barely got the truck into high when Mack moved suddenly, looking around.

"Hold it," he said. "Swing in here. I got to see a man."

June swung the wheel over and the lights circled on the sign that said J. B. PETERSON GENERAL STORE. Mack got out and stood for a moment looking around, his hand on the door.

"You turn her," he said. "I'll be right back."

He disappeared into the growing dusk and June turned the

[118]

truck around and cut the motor. There was nothing but silence and gathering darkness around him. He couldn't even hear the sound of Mack's feet.

Once he thought he heard a slight tinkle of glass, and he stiffened in the seat, listening; but it didn't come again, and he relaxed. He lit a cigaret and sat holding it, forgotten, in his hand. Only when it had burned down until it was warm against his fingers did he realize that Mack had been gone an awfully long time.

"Where the dickens is he?" June muttered softly, turning in the seat to crane his neck, trying to see Mack out the side window. The bulk of the store was dark and silent. In the other direction he could look down the road to the Coast Guard Station. The guard was pacing along the gate but he was too far away to make a noise June could hear. He was just on the verge of getting out to go hunt for Mack when he heard the muffled thud of feet alongside the truck and Mack climbed into the seat beside him.

"Okay," Mack said, "light out. But fast."

Without thinking, June started the truck and slammed it, weaving, into the road. He could hear Mack's breath coming fast and unevenly.

"How long does it take you to button your pants, for pete's sake?" he said.

"Don't be a dope." Mack's voice was thin and sharp. "What'd you think I was doin?"

"Well, what were you?"

Mack didn't say anything. He unzipped the dark jacket he wore and the open front spilled loose packages of cigarets and candy onto the truck seat between them. June gasped, his eyes on the stuff, and the truck weaved crazily across the road.

"Watch what you're doin," Mack yelled, and June hauled the heavy wheels back to the right side. "That ain't all, neither," Mack said. "The old boy's cash register sure let me hit the jackpot tonight."

"You mean you broke into that store?" June felt his face getting stiff with terror.

"What'd you think I was talkin about the other night?"

[119]

"Well, jesus! what if they catch you?"

"Me?" Mack said scornfully. "They won't. An besides, I don't like that 'me' business. You're in this just as deep as I am. You helped me get away. An you're takin part of the haul."

"Hey, wait a minute," June said. He could feel his breath begin to come and go faster. He felt as if somebody had knocked his wind out. "I didn't have nothin to do with it."

"Try an make anyone b'lieve that," Mack said. "You tell anyone that an they'll sure b'lieve every word of it. For godsake, don't be such a little dope. You're in it up to your eyebrows now an you might as well get use to it, see? Because there's goin to be plenty more."

June put the truck away that night not forgetting to turn the speedometer back so Kelsey wouldn't know he'd had her out. It was a warm night, but his hands and feet were icy when he walked up from the shore. Once safely in his own room, he stood wildly staring around him, wondering where to hide his share of the stuff. Finally he hauled a high laced boot out of the closet, put the crumpled bills flat inside the foot, and poured gum and cigarets in on top of them. It had occurred to him that the money could be spent, but he knew he couldn't do it. With the closet door closed between him and the boot, he felt a little better—but he lay shivering in the bed for a long time before he fell asleep.

Joe Fennely's eldest boy, Ted, was in the Army somewhere in the South Pacific. On Monday night his mother sat up late writing her regular weekly letter to him, and because she'd written it Monday instead of Sunday as she usually did, she went down to the post office first thing Tuesday morning to get it off in the quarter-to-seven mail. She dropped the letter in the chute and then, although it was only six-thirty, went on to the Red Front in hopes it might be open. She'd forgotten to get coffee the night before and she didn't feel right, not starting her day with a good cup of black coffee.

In front of the barber shop Bob Haines was swiping off his concrete sidewalk with an old broom dipped in a bucket of water.

[120]

"You look kind of sober, Bob," she said, slowing down a little.
He glanced up as if he hadn't heard her coming.

"Well, I am, sort of, Abby."

"Anythin wrong?"

"Jack Peterson jest called me up. Says someone busted into his place last night an cleaned out his cash register."

He watched her eyes go big with titillated horror.

"Land!" she said, her mouth round with prolonged amazement. "You don't say so!"

"Ayuh," Bob nodded. "That's *just* what I said, Abby. Just exactly."

"My goodness, we ain't hed nothin like that since Haynes Turner left town. They any idea who done it?"

"Why, we really ain't had time to go into it yet. I guess it was some kid, though. Lot of candy an stuff taken."

"There!" She gave the word a prolonged, satisfyingly nasal sound. "I ain't a mite surprised, what with the way people let their youngsters run the streets now. All hours of the day an night, any time at all, you can see kids on the street. If I hed my way, we'd put em all to work the minute they get out of school at night. And the way girls take up with these Coast Guards, too! It ain't decent. I certainly ain't surprised to hear this's happened. It won't be no time now till we have murders an Lord knows what all."

Bob nodded sadly. When he looked up to say something more to her, she had gone. He noted with a certain amusement that she seemed to have forgotten whatever it was she'd been coming downstreet for and had headed for home like a racing mare.

Abby *was* headed for home, and as she went she was thanking her lucky stars she hadn't had the telephone taken out last winter when she'd been thinking the expense was too much. Things like this made it worth while having a phone. The letter to Ted was forgotten, the coffee forgotten, all she could think of was who she'd call first.

When she went by Celia Newman's, she saw a flash of blue out near the barn. Now there was Celia out seeing to the hens most likely, and Abby turned in the short drive to the house and

[121]

caught Celia just as she came up to the back door with the panful of eggs in her hand.

"Celia," Abby caught her breath, "I want you to bear witness ain't I always said no good would come of havin all these Coast Guards an people comin in to work at the factory an boat yard an all?"

"What's happened?" Celia turned a little pale, and her knuckles whitened suddenly on the rim of the pan. Abby remembered just in time that Celia's boy Joey had got into trouble over a missing skiff just a month or two before.

"Well, Bob Haines told me jest now somebody's broke into Peterson's store, down by the wharf, and cleaned it right out. They even found a pile of rags all soaked in kerosene out back, but they couldn't of hed time to light it. Last night it was. They broke in through a window an there was blood all over the place where whoever it was must've cut theirselves on the glass. Oh, Bob said it was a mess. They didn't leave *one thing* in the whole store."

"My lord!" Celia said, properly impressed. "Last night, you said it was?" She put the pan of eggs down on the doorstep and lowered herself to a seat beside them, her knees weak with relief. Joey had spent his evening in the back room, she remembered, fooling around with his model planes, and he'd gone to bed without going out. "Ain't that awful! We ain't hed nothin like that here in the Harbor for a long time."

"Not since Haynes Turner left town," Abby confirmed, nodding. "Just what I said to Bob. Well, I got to get along and do my work. I just see you out to the barn an thought I'd tell you about it. I got to go tell Alice Scott. She'll be real interested."

"I warrant she will," Celia said with a touch of dryness. She sat watching Abby bustle away down the drive. Just as she picked up the eggs to go into the house with them, she saw Ida Baker come out into the yard next door to hang out some dish towels.

Celia went slowly over to the fence, her eyes resting calculatingly on the younger woman's distended stomach. It wouldn't be much longer now, she figured, before there'd be a young one running around over there. Ida saw her coming and half-turned to go back into the house, but Celia called to her.

"Ida, Abby Fennely's jest been here an she told me the awfullest thing." Celia told the story with relish. "And," she finished triumphantly, "someone see the fire last night jest in time to put it out before it really got started."

When Ida went back into the house, Hersh was just finishing a last doughnut. She told him the story as he was getting his cap from the hook behind the stove.

"I wouldn't put much stock in all that blow about fingers all over the floor," he said mildly. "Maybe someone broke into the store, but it ain't likely they cut a hand or two off, doin it."

He fell in with Bub going down the hill to work. They walked along together for a moment before Hersh said:

"You heard that wild yarn goin around how someone broke into Peterson's store last night?"

"No." Bub's startled glance was proof that he hadn't. He looked first at Hersh and then, involuntarily, looked over toward the group of buildings that housed the store. "What's it about?"

"Well, Ida come in with it this mornin, all excited. Seems it's all over town already. I never see nothin like the way talk travels in this town. God amighty, it's worse than fire in a blowdown. She hed a lot of talk about somebody settin the place on fire an how there was bloody fingers all over the floor where they got cut breakin the window to get in."

Bub laughed shortly and said the thing people usually said first:

"They got any idea who done it?"

"No, and they never will have. You know's well as I do they never catch up with anythin like that. Why, everyone in town knew Haynes Turner was gettin his everlastin whack off stuff like that. But they couldn't prove nothin."

"What'd they do about him, anyhow?"

"Well, they *did* make things so uncomfortable he up and left town finally. But there never was anythin said to him. Guess he musta had a guilty conscience."

"Hunh! I don't like it so much, this happenin right now."

"It *is* sort of unfortunate," Hersh said mildly.

Turning to look at him, Bub saw that they were both thinking the same thing, so he decided to bring it out into the open.

"They're bound to think of me sooner or later," he said.

"Ayeh. That's why I thought I'd let you know about it, so's you'd know—"

"Thanks," Bub said dryly. "But they'll let me know, too."

"They sure will."

"All I hope is, it don't happen again." Bub left him and turned down the wharf to unlock the gas tanks. Hersh stayed where he was, leaning against the storeroom door waiting for Bub to come back and unlock that.

His gaze was contemplative. Anything like this was bad enough, but if nothing more happened and nobody got caught, sooner or later the talk would die down, although Hersh knew well enough it would never be forgotten.

Edna liked to hurry about doing her work in the morning and getting it out of the way as soon as she possibly could. That way it left the whole afternoon free for whatever she wanted to do. But she enjoyed doing her housework, too. It gave her a deep and complete feeling of satisfaction to see the house clean and shining around her and to know there were no dusty corners anywhere. She was the kind of woman who couldn't be comfortable in a cleanlooking house if she knew there were dust kittens under the beds and dirt pushed out of sight into the corners. Everything had to be just so.

Lyford's room, the small room off the kitchen, was the bane of her existence. It seemed to her that she and Lyford were forever battling over that room and that she was fighting the losing end of the war.

She stood in the door looking at it now, and an unwilling half-smile of amusement made her lips twitch upward. She always left his room until last and it was always the worst. But she had to admit it certainly looked lived-in. The blankets on the narrow cot bed along one wall were, surprisingly enough, spread up. But he'd played that one on her before. She jerked them back.

"I thought so," she said aloud in mild expostulation, her voice, now that there was nobody to hear it, almost warm with impatient amusement. There, crumpled in between the sheets was the white shirt she'd ironed yesterday and told him to save until next Sunday. He'd managed to get a streak of green paint down

[124]

one sleeve and the inside of the collar was disgraceful. She had half a mind to make him wash it himself, but she knew she wouldn't do it.

She made the bed, dusted, and gave the room a general straightening around, dodging, out of habit, the black-painted model airplanes that hung from the extension cord across the ceiling. She'd torn four or five hairnets to pieces on propellers and wings before she'd learned when to dodge.

When she'd finished, she stood in the doorway a moment looking back into the room. It looked some better. Lyford always said he could never find anything in the room after she got through cleaning it, and Edna always answered him, "A place for everything and everything in its place." She said the words over softly to herself. That's what her mother had brought her up to believe and she would have been uncomfortable if the same thing hadn't been true of her own house.

She glanced thoughtfully at the row of calendars that rounded all four walls of the room, so close together that their edges lapped. Every December the school kids had a sort of contest to see who could get the biggest collection of new calendars. Each store in town had several different designs printed and they were given away free to customers. Lyford must have one of each kind from every store in a twenty-mile radius. The biggest one was a huge, wall-map size picture of a brown bear. Underneath it the printing read, COMPLIMENTS OF THE NORTHEASTERN LUMBER COMPANY. There was another, almost as large—ROSENTHAL'S FIVE, TEN, TO A DOLLAR STORE. That picture showed the torso of a lovely blonde in a white bathing suit. Her face was decorated with a large black mustache. Lyford had taken great pains to decorate various other parts of her anatomy, but Edna had made him erase these. The black smudges were still faintly apparent, pointing up her charms.

"Tch!" Force of habit made Edna click her tongue sharply against her upper plate. "And him only twelve years old! I don't know how these kids get started in their deviltry so young."

If bedrooms reflected personality, Edna thought, Lyford certainly didn't have any lack of it.

The knock at the back door startled her and she dropped the

dirty shirt she'd been dangling from her hand. Picking it up again, she stuffed it hurriedly into the string-and-paper bag on the back of the pantry door. Then she glanced quickly into the mirror over the table, thrusting at her already neat hair with both hands before opening the cellar door and peering down the entry way to see who it was.

She made out vaguely, through the curtained door window, the sharp, almost foxlike face of her nextdoor neighbor. Thank the lord I had time to get the kitchen cleaned up, she thought, going down the steps to unlock the door.

"Alice Scott!" she pretended amazement. "Whatever made you come to the back door?"

"Well—" the quick, snapping voice always made Edna feel the way she did when somebody scratched a fingernail across glass— "I come to the front first an knocked an knocked. I guess you couldn't a heard me. You musta been busy out back here somewheres. So I come around here."

"Well, come on in now you're here," Edna said wryly.

She led the way up through the kitchen and into the front room, knowing that behind her Alice's sharp blue eyes were examining everything along the way. Edna sighed slightly. Alice could always make you feel as if everything was just a little off center even if you knew perfectly well it wasn't.

"I hed to come over to ask how Curtis was." Alice settled herself comfortably into the big upholstered chair and folded her thin restless hands in her lap.

Edna looked with well-concealed distaste at the gray dustcap Alice wore, knowing quite well that it hid a row of steel curlers and a mass of uncombed gray hair.

"Why, there's nothin much new," she said slowly. "He's comin along as well as could be expected. And that pneumonia and all didn't make it much easier. He'll be in the hospital about a month. Of course it's harder for him because he's quite old. A younger man, it'd be different."

"Yes, they's that," Alice said. Her pale eyes slid curiously over Edna's face. "I often wondered just how much difference they was between Curtis's age and yourn. You always seemed so much younger."

"Six years," Edna lied snappishly. In spite of the fact that she herself railed at the difference in their ages, it made her mad as hops to have anyone else mention it, and she preferred lying about it to telling the truth and facing the pity of a woman like Alice.

"I should have thought it was more than that," Alice commented. "You can't show your age much."

"That's all," Edna said, meeting Alice's gaze without trouble. She figured that when somebody came poking their noses into other people's business, it served them right to get lied to, and she felt no compunctions about doing it.

"I spose you've heard the news," Alice said.

"Why, I ain't been out today to do anythin," Edna said easily. "I been doin my housework all mornin," she added softly.

Alice ignored that.

"Well, Peterson's store was broken into last night. Whoever it was cleaned out the cash register and took all the cigarets he had in stock. Gum an candy, too."

"Heavenly days!" Edna was shocked enough to show it. "You don't mean it?"

Alice settled back in her chair with a satisfied bump.

"I thought you probly didn't know about it. It's awful, ain't it, anythin like that goin on right here in the Harbor?"

"Did they get who done it?" Edna asked.

"No," Alice shook her head regretfully, "they didn't. I guess it's what we got to expect now what with strangers comin in here to work at the boat yard and all—people that never was nothin but trash an never will be. Why, it'll get so we won't be safe in our beds at night. Why, it's got so bad now a decent girl can't go out on the street alone at night."

Alice leaned forward slightly and her eyes grew suddenly brighter. This is it, Edna thought, knowing that now Alice's real reason for this visit was coming out.

"Well, there now! I knew they was somethin else I had to come see you about."

"Perhaps you better tell me what it is," Edna said into the waiting silence. She felt curiosity and a constrictive amusement, watching Alice's face.

[127]

"It's Lou," Alice said flatly, and settled back again as if that were all she had to say.

"Now, wait a minit, Alice," Edna said quickly. When her children were in her sight, she treated them to a constant saccharine criticism and a long series of rhetorical questions that always began, "I don't see why you don't—" or "I should think you would want—." But when anyone else mentioned them to her she was as fiercely proud and maternal as a mother cat. None of the kids would have known what to make of it, seeing her now. "I don't want you to come to me with any gossip about Lou. It's probly gossip or you wouldn't look so like the cat that ate the canary."

"Edna, you know I'm your best friend," Alice looked deeply injured, "an I don't want you gettin mad at me, but this ain't gossip because I see it myself an I come straight to you with it. I didn't want you to hear it from anyone else who wasn't your friend like I am."

"All right. I'm not mad," Edna said. "An I see you're bound to get it out, no matter what. So go ahead."

"Well, all right, but you don't have to treat me as if I was a child. Me and Harold went to the movies the other night—first time I been outa the house in more'n a month now—an I see Lou out with Bub Dolliver. He's just come home, you know."

"Well, what were they doin?" Edna asked, placidly. "Weren't they behavin the way you thought they ought to?"

Alice looked blank, and her mouth went lax with disappointment.

"Why, yes, I guess so. Afterwards they went off somewheres down the road an I don't know where they was goin. But I should think you wouldn't want Lou runnin around with anybody like that, after the way you talk about them factory people."

"I shouldn't think you'd want to leave your mornin's work, Alice, just to come over here an tell me somethin I knew already. If you'd been watchin a little earlier, you'd a seen him call here for Lou," Edna lied stoutly. "An I guess since you're worried about it, I better tell you somethin. I trust Lou. She ain't ever done anythin to make me not trust her. I don't have to worry about what any of my kids do because they always come an tell me. They've got a decent home an they been brought up right and I don't worry about their doin anythin to shame me."

"Oh," Alice said weakly. "Well, I thought you probly knew, but I come over just in case you didn't."

"That's right, Alice," Edna nodded her head, a short little jerk of confirmation, speaking as she would have to a child. "You did just right. Anytime you see anythin you think's wrong, you just come an tell me an we'll straighten it out right away."

Alice glanced once at Edna's calmly impassive face and got up quickly.

"I got to be runnin. I knew you wouldn't get mad."

"Why should I?" Edna smiled broadly. "Nothin to get mad about. Come in again, won't you, Alice?"

But after Alice had gone, she sat on there in the stiff-backed chair, her hands folded tightly in her lap. It was going some when people came to her with tales about Lou! And the fact that she actually had known where Lou was that night and that she'd been out with Bub since then didn't serve to make things any better. She was ambitious for Lou as she had once been for herself. All the things she had wanted and had failed to get were embodied completely in her idea of what she wanted for Lou.

Her own disappointment in the physical side of married life she had at first laid to the fact that Curtis was so much older than she was. She wasn't sure now. But with that reason wavering, she couldn't think of another to take its place. She had come to the conclusion that everyone who contemplated marriage must face the probability of that disappointment and must make up for it somewhere else. With her it had been in the acquiring of material security. She had failed there, too. She was going to see to it that Lou wouldn't fail.

Lou was so much like Edna herself had been at twenty-one that sometimes Edna felt as if she were living her own life over again, watching Lou grow up. She hated the idea that Lou would grow old as she was doing, disappointed and without much hope. Her pride in her children was fierce and completely maternal, but it wasn't unusually possessive. Now that Lou had reached the age when she would begin to think about marrying, Edna felt none of the usual pangs mothers were supposed to feel at the idea of her children leaving her.

She was proud that they could start out from the vantage point of having been *her* children; and she didn't like to have them do anything that could let people like Alice Scott come to her with tales, thinking she didn't know what they were up to.

At twelve o'clock when Lou came in for her lunch, Edna had two places set at the table and was sitting down to drink a cup of tea while she waited.

"Hello!" Lou washed her hands at the sink and sat down. "Aren't the kids eating here?"

"I gave them their lunch early, Lou. I wanted to talk to you when you come in and I didn't want them around. You got home early."

"Yes, Joe brought me up. He had to go to Freehold on business, so he gave me a lift to the corner." She looked curiously at her mother, seeing with foreboding distaste the slight trembling of the full underlip. "What is it? Nothing about Pa?"

"No, it's about you," Edna said. She had fallen automatically into the half-tearful tone she used to the kids and to Curtis when something had happened; she had learned to use it against Curtis's determination because it worked better than determination of her own. It had become so much a second nature that she was hardly aware of doing it. Now she told in detail her conversation with Alice.

"Oh my god," Lou said bitterly when her mother stopped talking. Lou's face was red and her eyes were sullen with temper. "Honestly, I should think that woman wouldn't be able to live with herself."

"Lou, I won't have you swearin," Edna said sharply. "I don't much blame you where Alice's concerned, but you don't have to swear."

"I'm sorry," Lou said shortly. She looked down at her plate, waiting. When she saw that Lou wasn't going to say anything more, Edna started slowly:

"Lou, I ain't ever encouraged you to be snobbish because I don't think it's right; but they's a difference between bein snobbish and bein particular. I'm not tryin to pick your friends for

[130]

you, but I want you to pick ones you can be proud of. That's all."

"You're judging Bub by what his people were like, aren't you?" Lou said carefully.

"Well, that's all I've got to judge him by. We don't know nothin about him except what his family was like an the things he used to do and we have to judge people that way."

"I don't see why we have to judge at all." Lou sounded bitter. "I don't see who we think we are, setting ourselves up as good enough to judge someone else."

"Now you're just talkin," Edna said with a hint of impatience. "That's all right to say, but when it comes right down to cases, it doesn't mean a thing. An there's another thing, too. What's Joe goin to think about you runnin around with this Dolliver boy? You don't want to go an spoil your chances with Joe just because of thinkin you like this Bub. An a fine name that is, too, for a grown man!"

Lou got up slowly and put her fork down on the oilcloth beside her plate so softly that Edna couldn't hear the sound it made touching the table. She glanced up in surprise and saw the expression on Lou's face. She gasped and could feel tears gathering in her eyes.

"I wish," Lou said evenly, giving each word equal emphasis, "you would stop talking as if Joe owned me. He doesn't yet an I'm not so sure he's going to. Honestly, Mom," her voice broke and shook slightly, "if you don't stop this eternal ranging, I'm a good mind to run off with—with a Portergee!"

She went out the door, leaving her mother with the convenient tears still unshed. Edna wiped them away with the clean corner of her apron and started clearing away the dishes, not thinking anything.

IT didn't take Bub long to find out there were times when the shack was too quiet for him—especially at night. The still evenings coming down easily over the hills, the gradual quiet darkening of the sky, the fading gray water outside his door, were all *too* quiet. He didn't quite believe it was so even when he felt it most, and when he couldn't believe it actually existed as he saw it, he felt restless—he did not think of it as loneliness.

He learned from experience just how many long steps it took to get from the front door to the bedroom door; how many from the stove to the sink. Then he varied it and found out how many shorter steps it took, both ways.

He would sit in the old Boston rocker by the window, smoking one cigaret after another and feeling his nerves grow tauter and tauter by the moment until he felt as if his legs and arms were fastened on with piano wire and somebody was tightening the wire, turn by slow turn.

At those times, because he couldn't help it, he'd start thinking about Lou. That bothered him. He didn't want to think about her, not in the way he did. Lou had taken him unawares—she was completely new in his experience and he found no way to docket her. He'd seen her once or twice since the night she'd come down to the shack with him, and he still couldn't believe in her friendliness.

She was a swell girl and he liked her. When he came to that point in his thoughts Bub nodded his head. She was the sort who could look you in the eye without giggling because you were a man and she was a girl. There were some girls who kept you thinking about one thing all the time you were with them; but Lou didn't. She let you forget it, and it was nice to be with her. When you didn't feel like talking, she didn't seem to expect you to talk; and she didn't keep up a string of chatter to fill your silence, either. You didn't keep wondering if she was bored because you didn't feel like doing or saying anything. It was just nice.

Yes, Bub tried to tell himself, it was just nice. But he knew there was something else; there was another thought that he'd forced into the back of his mind and kept there—until these spells of sitting and staring brought it out of hiding. Lying night after night in the jungle, thinking about the Harbor and everything it represented—security, happiness—everything he wanted, he'd thought about a girl, too. No particular girl, just a decent,

[132]

quiet, nice-looking one—not too pretty. Now he knew he'd been thinking about a girl like Lou.

He'd thought a lot about how nice it would be to settle down here in the Harbor, find some girl like that and marry her and maybe raise a family. But then, when he'd been thinking about it, it had been remote, so far in the future that he hadn't even wondered whether her hair would be light or dark. Now he knew—it would be just the color of Lou's hair; and her eyes would be the color of Lou's; and they'd look at him straight, just the way Lou's did. Now he'd found her, and there wasn't a thing he could do about it. Lou had offered him friendship of her own free will, but Bub knew that the first time he asked her for anything more than friendship the whole uneasy structure would go over like a card house.

That friendship meant a lot to Bub and he wanted to hold onto it. There was another reason, too. He thought too much of Lou. Even if she were willing, he thought too much of her to drag her through the mess of gossip and talk that would start up like a forest fire if they ever thought of getting married. There was Joe, besides. Joe could give her everything she might want; Joe had money, and people thought highly of him. Joe would be the one her parents would pick for her. Joe and Lou were going together and that in the Harbor amounted to an out-an-out engagement.

God dammit, Bub thought, all my life I've either been too late or not good enough. He looked down at the cigaret he'd been holding and saw that it was mashed between his fingers. The palms of his hands were damp and clammy with sweat, and there were beads of perspiration along his upper lip. He ran his tongue along the lip, tasting salt, threw the dead cigaret at the stove, and went out slamming the door viciously behind him.

Halfway up the road he remembered that he hadn't locked the door, hesitated, half-turning, and then went on. Let them steal the whole pesky shack if they wanted to. There were times when he didn't give two hoots in hell if somebody did, and this was one of them.

The August night was cool blue velvet around him and the stars hugely brilliant in the moonless sky, and he was going to have himself a glass of beer. I got to get busy, he thought. I got to snap out of it and get me that boat. I got to show them I mean business.

On Friday nights Barron's Beer Parlor was quiet, almost somnolent. The men at the yard were low on cash, they weren't paid until Saturday, and on Friday night there were few of them who had one dime to rattle against another. There'd be one or two fishermen, a couple of engineers from the factory fish boats, and an aimless slatternly woman or two. The dim lights and Steve Barron's barrel-like drowsing figure behind the bar made the place look doubly sleepy.

Bub shoved open the door and glanced once around the room before going over to the bar.

"What'll it be, son?" Steve pushed himself with an obvious effort off the high stool and leaned across the bar as if he hadn't enough strength in his backbone to hold up his immense stomach.

"Glass of beer," Bub said.

Steve put it in front of him and scooped up the dime Bub laid on the wooden counter. For a preoccupied moment Bub sat making interlocking circles of wet on the black wood, then he turned to face the room, feeling more comfortable when he could see what went on behind him. He grinned mirthlessly at the feeling; that must be a hangover from a long time of not knowing which way death would come from.

He had no particular desire for the beer. The first mouthful tasted horribly bitter in his throat and he took another quick gulp to get rid of the bitterness. The quicker he got it down and ordered another, the quicker he'd begin to feel better.

There was nobody at the tables that he knew and the people in the booths were out of sight. He caught himself wondering whether Nina might be there. The fact that there were other people in the room with him began to make his nerves loosen up. A woman wavered out of the shadows at the back of the room and wandered idly toward an occupied table. After a slight effort of memory he knew who she was. Gladys Jennings, her name was. She'd been sponging drinks when he was a kid in school, and as far as he could see she hadn't changed much since

[134]

then. She still had the woebegone, frail wistfulness she'd always had; her pale, almost dead-white face was still lovely, and her silky hair was nearly red and quite alive under the dim light. She hesitated, glanced once in his direction, started toward him. Bub grimaced and spun his stool away quickly, facing back to the bar again.

He gulped the rest of the beer and looked at Steve, raising his eyebrow.

"Want another?" Steve wanted to make sure before heaving himself again off his high seat. Bub nodded just as the hand came down on his shoulder. He turned his head just enough to look down into Gladys's face. At close range he could see the lines around her eyes and mouth and the network of tiny red veins that marred the whites of her eyes.

"Know you," she said. "You're Bub Dolliver. You oughta buy me a drink on the strength of that."

"Not now."

"Aw, now, be a sport. I remembered you, didn' I?"

"Oh, all right." He gave in because it was simpler.

"One for her?" Steve looked at him, jerking his head at Gladys.

"You heard him, didn'chou, you old suds bucket?" Gladys said rudely. Steve hesitated, ignoring her, watching Bub. Bub nodded.

Steve put the full glass down in front of her with a slam and the foam shot over the edge onto the bar.

"Go easy with that," she grabbed it away from him.

"I oughta pour it over your head," Steve said. "She's been at it since noon," he said to Bub. "You don't know what you're gettin into, son."

"She'll only get one out of me," Bub said. "That's all the dough I've got with me."

"You're kiddin," Gladys said. "You all kid me all the time. You keep sayin you ain't got any more money and then you always manage to have enough for one more beer." She drank thirstily, holding the glass in both hands like a child, eying him widely over the top.

"Not me," Bub looked away. Gladys leaned over toward him, trying to catch his eye.

"There's a lots would think it was somethin to buy me a beer," she said. "You know what people tell me? They say I look just like a movie star. I bet you can guess which one."

"It's been a long time since I been to the movies," Bub said evasively.

"They say I look jest like Norma Shearer," she told him.

"God!" Steve said, "it musta been many the long day since anyone said that to you."

She eyed him malevolently for a second, and Bub held his breath; then, to his horror, she started to cry. He watched, spellbound with dismay, the big drops of water forming in the corners of her slightly bleary eyes and followed the first one down, to watch it splash on the dark wood, leaving a little circle of dampness.

"Oh, for pete's sake, don't do that. Don't listen to him," he said. "He didn't mean nothin."

"I guess I know what he meant," Gladys said. She was beginning to cry in earnest now and Bub was really getting bothered. The hard, smooth voice behind them made them both jump and turn with almost identical expressions of surprise.

"All right, Gladys, that's about enough."

Bub saw with relief that Nina had appeared as she always seemed to and was standing behind them, her hands on her hips, her pointed chin set hard, her narrowed eyes ignoring him and holding Gladys's fascinated stare. Bub hadn't ever thought he'd be glad to see Nina, but he was now. She was a breath of fresh air compared to Gladys. Gladys opened her mouth to say something but Nina beat her to it.

"I said that's about enough," she repeated. "Now git."

Wordless, as much with astonishment as anger, Gladys picked up her glass and got. Nina took the vacated stool and grinned up into Bub's blank face.

"Five more minutes, old son," she said, "an you'd a had all you could handle."

"What's wrong with her, anyhow?" Bub said.

"Oh, nothin much. She's just another poor bum like the rest of us."

"Hunh," Bub grunted. "I guess I better buy you a glass of beer for rescuin me from a fate worse than death."

"An you ain't kiddin," Nina grinned.

Gladys, from the post she'd taken up a few feet down the bar, watched Steve get up and draw two more glasses of beer. She started sidling back up toward them but Nina caught the first motion. She put her glass down carefully, turned to face Gladys, and jerked her thumb toward the door.

"You better be goin," she said. "I don't want to have to tangle with you tonight." Wordlessly Gladys set down her empty glass and headed for the door. Nina watched it close behind her before turning back. Steve shook his head in speechless wonder.

"Honest," he said to Bub, "Nina here's the only one can manage her. I never see the beat of it. Anyone else talk to her like that an she'd start screamin the house down."

"I got just the right touch," Nina said. She turned her back pointedly on Steve who went grunting back to his stool. "Pa was talkin about you just today," she said, "sayin he ain't seen you since the first day you got back."

"I been busy."

"Too busy for your old friends?" she mocked. "Seems to me you're in pretty low company tonight, ain't you, after hob-nobbin with the higher-ups?"

"Whatta you talkin about?"

"Oh, things get around," Nina said. She watched with obvious relish the slow flush that crept up his thin cheeks. "Course, if she was to find out you'd been drinkin beer with people like Gladys an me, she wouldn't think much of it, would she?"

"Oh, hell!" Bub exploded. "You women're all alike. Nothin suits you."

"How d'you know nothin suits me?" Nina protested. "You ain't never tried to suit me yet, have you?"

"No," Bub said flatly. "I ain't. An I ain't goin to."

He set the half-full glass he held down on the bar with a slight click, turned the stool, and slid off it to cross to the door. Nina sat looking after him, held momentarily still by surprise. Then he heard the quick tapping of her high heels as she came after him. He got outside the door before she caught up with him, and there they were both stopped by a high, agonized wailing.

Somewhere out there in the dark a woman was screaming thinly, steadily, apparently without stopping for breath.

"God amighty," Bub's voice jerked suddenly in his throat, "what's that?"

"Ha!" Nina said. "Now, my lad, you're goin to see just what it was I *did* save you from."

Bub's eyes, growing used to the darkness, made out the knot of men standing indecisively around the car parked on the far side of the graveled parking space. They just seemed to be standing there doing nothing, staring at the car. And from the front seat, came that high, steady, thin wail.

"There's something wrong with her!" he said. "Why—ain't they goin to do anythin?"

"There's nothin wrong with her." Nina sounded impatient. "That's your little girl friend, an she's celebratin."

The men seemed to reach a simultaneous decision and somebody opened the car door. Immediately the wail rose to a screech; there was a concerted tug of war, and Gladys came out of the car the way a tight cork comes out of a bottle, all at once. She landed sitting down on the gravel, her hands palm down behind her. After the sudden crescendo of screaming as she fell, she was silent for a stunned moment. The owner of the car seized his opportunity, started up, and went out of the parking space as if the devil himself camped on his trail.

Gladys got to her feet and shook both fists after the disappearing taillight.

"You big coward!" she shouted hoarsely. "You dirty coward, you hadda get a gang to do it. You couldn't a got me out alone. You lousy coward!" She stopped shouting when the car disappeared, and turned to face the circle of men who watched her. She looked down dazedly at the bleeding palms of her hands and up at them again.

"I guess he didn't know what I wanted," she explained. "I just wanted to go for a ride. You know," she put her head on one side, smiling, "he use to tell me I looked just like Norma Shearer."

"Come on." Nina jerked at Bub's elbow. "The party's over. When she starts lookin like Norma Shearer she's all right again."

Bub gulped, fighting against gathering sickness. He couldn't say anything. He turned blindly away, half-aware that Nina came with him, and started up the road toward home at a quick walk.

"Judas," Nina gasped in his ear, "you goin to a fire?"

"You don't have to come," Bub said rudely. "I don't remember askin you."

"That's all right," she said breezily. "I don't have to be told more than once. Maybe I jest wanted company up through these woods. Gets kinda dark, you know; an lonely."

"You've walked it before."

"Oh, blub! Don't be so bad tempered."

Car lights picked them out just as Nina grabbed his arm and brought him about to face her. The machine slowed, came to a stop beside them, and Bub saw the white blur of a face peering out at them.

"That you, Bub?" Joe Pettigrew's voice said. "Wanta ride uptown?"

"No," Bub said shortly. "I'll walk."

"Oh!" Joe sounded knowing. "Sorry. Thought that was Lou with you."

"Well, it ain't, nosey," Nina said icily. "An now you know, don't you?"

"No hard feelins," Joe said. He put the car in gear and drew slowly away. Nina, momentarily silenced, walked beside Bub, who had turned back to the road. When they came to the path that led up through the alders to Charlie's shack, she stopped.

"Look, Bub, I—I hope this won't make no trouble for you."

"Trouble?" Bub set his jaw and looked away from her.

"With Lou Jellison, I mean."

"No reason why it should," he said tightly.

"Well, I just hope it won't make trouble, that's all. 'Night."

Bub heard her running feet go up the dark path as he walked away.

LATE FRIDAY night when the last light on the shore road had blinked out and the entire district was in darkness, a truck circled the parking space in front of Barron's and pulled along for a few hundred feet up the road, where it stopped. As soon as the engine died, the lights were snapped off and for a moment nothing happened. Then two figures detached themselves from the bigger mass of shadow that was the truck and went silently down through the woods and circled up around through the blackness to the back of the building.

As soon as Mack felt the rough shingles under his hands, he stopped and stood listening. His muscles were taut with the effort of making as little noise as possible, but his breath came quickly with a slight whistling sound between his teeth. Excitement always made him shake a little and he was shaking now, but he managed to hide that fact from June.

June was right behind him, and when Mack stopped suddenly, June came up against him with a little grunting sound of dismay. He was sick. He could feel himself getting sicker by the minute with fear and utter shaking horror at what he was doing.

"Shut up," Mack hissed at him. "For chrissake, you'll have the whole place down on us. I wish to god I hadn't started you in on this. I coulda done better by myself."

"I wisht you hadn't neither," June muttered.

"Well, shut up. You're in now. All you have to do is follow me an not make any noise, and for pete's sake don't try to do anythin on your own. Just wait an let me do it. All you have to do is stand still an hold things, see?"

"I wisht you'd let me wait in the truck."

"Nothin doin. Think I want you high-tailin it off the first jack rabbit you see an leave me here? You're comin with me."

Mack's slowly moving feet found the first step of the rickety stairs that went up to the back door. He started up them slowly, his hand on the rail, testing each board before he stepped on it. June followed him so closely that Mack could feel his hard, uneven breathing through his thin shirt.

"You tryin to blow the door down?" he asked unpleasantly.

June immediately held his breath, but that was worse because when he was finally forced to let it go, it came out in a mighty uncontrolled whush of air.

"Oh god!" Mack said.

He found the door knob and tried it softly, then he bent over, feeling around the lock. June heard his knife snap open and there was a light grinding noise, then silence. Mack swore once, under his breath, heaved, and the lock clicked. To June the noise sounded as loud as a shot. Mack vanished into the yawning blackness where the door had been and June stood straining his eyes after him.

"Hey, where'd you go?" he whispered.

Mack materialized out of blackness and grabbed his arm.

"Come on, you damn baby." June let himself be pulled into the room and then Mack let go. "Now stay there an don't move, so's I'll know where to find you."

June froze where he was, following Mack's progress around back of the bar by the soft thuds and the string of whispered swearing. He heard the glass door of the cigaret showcase slide back and the rustling sound as Mack stuffed his pockets. He heard, too, the faint click of the wooden money drawer beneath the counter, the flat rattling sound of silver, and then silence.

He listened, trying to place himself, but there was nothing to hear. He almost screamed when Mack ghosted out of the stillness and thrust an armload of cigaret cartons at him.

"Go on back to the truck. I'll be right along."

Without asking questions, June went, thankful only to get out of the place and as far away from it as he could. He stumbled back through the woods and got heavily into the truck, throwing the cigarets into the catchall behind the seat back. Then he put his hands on the wheel and leaned his forehead on them, feeling the diminishing chills fade along his spine.

"Judast," he groaned, "why'd I ever let myself in for this?"

He'd protested against this business tonight, but Mack had turned ugly and June admitted he was as much afraid of what Mack would do to him as he was of what would happen if Mack talked.

"You'll come an shut up about it," Mack had said. "I'll spill the whole thing if you don't. I ain't gettin mixed up in this alone."

"If you tell, it'll get you in as much trouble as it will me," June had showed a spurt of rebellion.

"Not the way I'll tell it, it won't." Mack's smile hovered before June when he closed his eyes. "An I'm a better liar than you are."

All June could think now was what would happen to him if Kelsey found out about this.

Mack came silently up through the woods five minutes later and got into the truck without saying anything. But June could smell the wave of beer on his breath and knew without asking what it was Mack had stopped for. As he started the engine, he heard the first muttering of thunder from the north.

IT was late on Saturday morning when Joe came down the hill to the factory. At one o'clock that morning a thunder storm had blown up from the northwest, and even at nine the still August heat hadn't been strong enough to bake the lingering memory of fresh rain and wind out of the air. The grass was bright and the bushes along the road shoulder hadn't started to grow their gray fringes of dust yet. Everything Joe could see was just as clean as he was himself, and he was spotless. His white shirt was dazzling in the sunlight, and his swarthy face and hands were as clean as he could get them with a stiff brush and strong soap.

His grin was nearly wolfish as he went slowly down the wharf toward the small office building where Lou was already hard at work. Joe didn't believe in mixing business with pleasure, not in the usual course of events, but there were times when he felt justified in sprinkling a little pleasure in with the routine, and he was looking forward to this. He stepped in the open office door and stood there until Lou was forced to look up from the ledgers she had spread out over the desk in front of her.

"Busy?" Joe said.

"Why, yes, Joe; but if there's something you want—"

"Oh, no," he said, elaborately casual, and knew that she was watching him closely as he circled the desk and sat down on the far corner. "Just come in to pass the time of day."

"For goodness sake," Lou straightened in her chair and stretched her arms over her head, "you're usually earlier than this. How come you're taking the morning off?"

"Just felt lazy, I guess. You know, the end-of-the-week feeling."

"I get it myself on Saturday."

"I see your boy friend last night," Joe said, watching her, to note the quick disappearance of her smile.

"Who?"

"Bub. Thought you told me he wasn't so bad."

"Why, as far as I know he isn't. All I know's what I can see for myself."

"That's what I figured," Joe said, and stopped as if he didn't intend to say anything more about it.

"Why, what made you ask?" Lou said finally, her own voice as purposely casual as Joe's had been.

"Well, if he's turned over a new leaf, he certainly picks funny people to do it with, that's all I got to say." Joe nodded his head thoughtfully and turned his face just far enough away so he could pretend to be looking out the window and still keep her within his range of vision.

"I don't see why you think I'd be interested."

"Well, I didn't know's you'd want people talkin about you the way they talk about the two he was with last night."

Joe swung his sneakered foot evenly and the regular soft thud of his heel against the leg of the desk was the only sound in the office. Then, just above their heads, the whistle shrieked twice, tearing the air.

"I can see," Lou said, after the hoarse yell died away, "you're just sitting there waiting for me to ask you who they were."

"Why, lord, Lou," Joe's amazement was almost good enough, "if I'd hed any idea you'd be interested, I'd a told you right out. I see him with Nina Barnes an later someone told me he'd been foolin around with Gladys Jennings down to Steve Barron's place."

[143]

"Now we're both satisfied, aren't we?" Lou's coldly even voice really startled Joe, and for a quick moment her eyes, when he met them, looked just the way the voice sounded.

"Why, Lou, I didn't mean to upset you. I just figured you know how people are. They sorta judge you by the company you keep. I thought you'd like to know about Bub, that's all."

She grinned up at him widely, her eyes friendly again. There was more than a hint of laughter in her voice.

"It's real nice of you to worry about my reputation, Joe; but I guess it'll work out all right. Matter of fact, Bub and I are going to the movies tonight. Maybe that'll counteract whatever happened last night."

Joe saw the whole idea had been a mistake from the very beginning. He might have known it'd take more than a little gossip like that to put Lou off anyone she really liked. And Joe was beginning to be afraid she liked Bub. That wasn't going to do at all. He hadn't figured it had got to the point where she didn't care what Bub did but trusted him in spite of it. That was going a little too far, and Joe wasn't concerned with Bub when he spoke again. He was thinking merely of himself, and a cold, light mist of intuition told him that what he had planned as an exposé of Bub had backfired a little.

"Look, Lou, whatta you see in him anyhow?" he said pleadingly, leaning over slightly so he could meet her eyes.

"Oh, he's just a nice kid," she said carelessly, her very tone stiffening Joe's premonition.

"He ain't no better than I am, is he?"

"I don't know's I said he was, Joe."

"Well, then, whatta you want to spend so much time on him for? Your old man don't like him."

"My dad isn't the one who spends the time with him."

"Look, there's only one thing a feller like Bub wants from a girl," Joe said, "an he can get it a lot easier from Nina Barnes."

"How d'you know what he wants? You aren't a girl."

"Oh, Lou, for pete's sake, don't talk like that. You talk circles right around me. I wish you'd stop laughin just for once an take me serious."

"All right," Lou said. "I'm not laughing now, Joe."

"Well, will you marry me?"

Lou sighed and looked away without answering.

"Will you?" Joe said. He got up and came around the desk to stand in front of her, and she had to look up at him. "I know I've ast you before an you always said you warn't ready to think about gettin married. But couldn't you just say that when you were, you'd marry me?"

"I don't know whether I would or not, honestly," Lou said. "And you wouldn't want me to lie to you, would you?"

"Well, you got to make up your mind sometime."

"All right. Maybe I have. But you'll just have to wait till I do. Ask me again—later on."

"Give me a kiss to seal the bargain."

"I haven't made any bargain. And besides, there are people all over the wharf this morning."

"I don't give a dam for the people or the bargain," Joe said. "All's I want's that kiss."

He leaned over, holding Lou in the chair with one wiry hand, and kissed her hard. Then he straightened up and went out without looking back. He left her breathless and a little surprised.

IT was nearly two o'clock that afternoon before Joe got up to Bob Haines's barber shop. Usually Joe shaved himself but he stopped in at Bob's every Saturday. He noticed with pleasure that the occupant of the other chair was Steve Barron. For Joe's purpose there couldn't have been a better man to be in it. He recognized Steve's huge mountain of stomach although Steve's head was swathed in an anonymous white towel. Joe hung his soft hat on the hook and climbed into the empty chair as Bob came out of the back room where he'd been practicing pool shots under the green-shaded lights.

"Gimme a haircut an shave, will you, Bob?" Joe settled back.

Bob whipped out his white cloth and got the clippers. He said nothing. He had a pretty good idea that Joe was loaded for bear and he was going to let Joe shoot first.

Joe did, finally.

"Bob, I been thinkin today, since I heard about Steve's place."

Steve reared up in the other chair.

"For chrissake," he said, "ain't that enough to make you sick? It's got so a man can't even make an honest livin without havin some dam thief come along an rob him. If that warn't bad enough, the guy had the nerve to drink my beer an leave the dirty glass standin right there on the counter. He left the tap runnin, too."

"Ayeh," Bob said. "What was you thinkin, Joe? I'm always glad to have suggestions."

"Well, I'm a property owner," Joe said, "an although I ain't got it yet, if things keep on this way, it stands to reason whoever's doin it will git to me sooner or later. I figure we ought to do something about it before instead of sittin around afterwards suckin our thumbs."

"If you think that's all we been doin, Joe, maybe you'd like to take over the sheriff's job."

"Now, wait a minute," Joe put his hand up soothingly. "I ain't tryin to make you mad, Bob. I'm jest tryin to figure out some way of gettin him. You know, an ounce of prevention."

"Yeah, yeah. I know all that."

"Well, why don't we get up a citizen's committee, or somethin like that, an run the feller out of town."

"You talk," Bob said cautiously, "as if you was pretty sure who done all the shootin."

"Well, for godsake, ain't you?"

"No, I ain't," Bob said flatly.

"You must be blind then. Don't you ever listen to talk?"

"Too much."

"Well, now look. We ain't had nothin like this in the Harbor for years. An now that a certain feller's come back, it starts right in. Ain't that good enough?"

"Look, Joe," Bob clipped furiously, "if you'd been away for a week an the night you come home somebody's barn burned

[146]

down, I wouldn't figure you'd set the fire just because we hadn't had one for a couple months."

"That's a hell of a lot different, an you know it. You ain't as dumb as you put on, Bob. You know as well as I do there ain't nothin this feller wouldn't do if he was amind to."

"That may be," Bob said. "I don't know, but it may be. But there's one thing I *do* know, Joe. If you're willin to swear out a warrant we'll arrest this "certain feller" who you don't think so much of. But the thing I was tellin you I did know was what they can do to you for false arrest. Why, he could take everythin you owned an *then* some. I tell you, you need proof. You can't go around arrestin people because you don't like em, or because people talk a lot about em."

"Seems to me you're stickin up for him."

"I am till I'm showed different." Bob flicked the cloth and Joe stepped down from the chair. "As far as I know, he ain't done nothin wrong and it's got to be proved before I'll b'lieve it. If he's doin it, he's dumber'n I think he is."

"What you mean?"

"Well, there's an awful lot of people's goin to figure just the way you do. It's all started happenin since he come back. Now, if he was goin to do anythin like that, he'd either wait a while, or else he'd take the trouble to make it look like someone else was doin it. An these both look like he might be doin it. A man'd be a fool to make a thing look like he done it hisself."

"Maybe he's got it figgered out people'll think the way you do, Bob. Maybe he thinks if he makes it look like he done it hisself, people will think he couldn't be that dumb an somebody's tryin to plant it on him. Maybe he's smarter'n you think an he might be jest a thought or two ahead of you."

"Maybe he is," Bob shook his head. "But I still got to see proof. I ain't goin to put my foot in my mouth just because you talk a lot, Joe."

"Hey, you look," Steve was sitting upright now, staring first at Joe and then at Bob. "Who the hell is this wise guy you're talkin about? I got a right to know, ain't I? After all, he's had some free beers on me."

"Maybe he has an maybe he hasn't," Bob said.

[147]

"Figure it out for yourself." Joe sounded impatient. "Who is it who's just come home an who's reputation ain't been very good if I remember right?"

"Oh, yeah," Steve said, a great light dawning. "Why, he seems like quite a nice young feller now. Goin around with a good girl, too. I don't know—"

"Oh, you don't," Joe snarled, the reference to Lou setting him off. "I suppose the pair of you'll set around and let him steal your eyeteeth before you see I'm right. Thank him for takin em, too, probably."

"He's right," Steve said after Joe had gone. "We ought to do somethin before anythin else happens, not after. Why, that young feller'll think he can get away with murder if we don't stop him."

"How d'you know it ain't Joe's doin it?" Bob said idly. "You ain't got no proof one way or the other. An he seems mighty anxious to see somebody else get the blame."

"You think it is?" Steve said, the idea taking him.

"Oh my god, no. I don't think it is. But they's jest as much proof. What I mean is, you ain't got nothin to go on but talk —an that just ain't enough."

THAT NIGHT when Bub went uptown to meet Lou at the drugstore he was feeling good. He was impatient, too, wanting to tell her what he'd done that afternoon.

After he'd got through work at the wharf that noon he'd gone over to the boat yard to look around just on the chance he might be able to find something to suit his needs in the way of a small boat. He thought he knew Ad Barker pretty well and that the idea of getting money out of him might be strong enough to overcome Ad's dislike. But at first he thought he'd been wrong.

"We ain't got anythin here *you* could ever want," Ad had said.

"You might let me decide that," Bub said shortly. "How about lettin me look around. No law against that, is they?"

"Not that I know of. But I'm tellin you, there ain't nothin here you could ever touch."

Resenting the scorn in the older man's voice, Bub took his time. He stood for long minutes staring at the gleaming mahogany sides of Chriscraft that he didn't want and couldn't afford if he did. He walked up and down the long rows of racing craft, hauled up in storage, admiring the sheer of their bows and the forest of bowsprits nearly meeting overhead, knowing that Ad fumed and fussed behind him.

"For godsake," Ad said finally, "what're you plannin on doin, lobsterin or yachtin? There ain't nothin in here you'd want anyhow, if you're goin fishin."

"I know it," Bub said equably. "I'm jest waitin till you get around to showin me somethin I *do* want."

"Oh god!" Ad threw up his hands in disgust. "All right, come on."

He started at a quick trot for the wharf, and Bub, grinning, tailed along behind him.

"There," Ad said, pointing as if he'd hauled the boat out of his sleeve. "A young feller from one of the Islands is goin into the Army. I took that one off his hands yesterday."

"That's more like it," Bub nodded. "Now, see all the time you coulda saved if you'd showed me that in the beginnin." He went down the gangway to the slip to get a closer look at the little boat moored there. He was disappointed in her at first. She didn't look like much—a short, wide boat, built like a pumpkin seed; but when he had a chance to give her a good going over, his opinion went up rapidly. She was a good buy, within his reach. Solid and seaworthy as a boat that size could be.

Ad said without hesitation that he wanted two and a quarter for her.

"One seventy-five," Bub said laconically, and stuck to it until Ad, with a disgusted grunt, said:

"All right. Take her. But I want a hundred down."

"Seventy-five," Bub said, "an you needn't act like you was doin me a big favor, neither. You couldn't git that much for her from anyone else."

[149]

"Judast priest," Ad howled, "what d'you think I'm in the business for, my health?"

"She needs a lot of work done on her."

"Hell! Well, take her an then get the pesky thing out of my sight."

Together Bub and Hersh had towed the little boat across to the old wharf and moored her securely. And tomorrow Bub wanted to get busy and build himself a way so he could ground her out properly and get to work on her. Looking her over after she'd been moored, he grinned at himself. He couldn't have felt better if he'd just bought himself a yacht. He knew where he could pick up an engine, too. For a long time he had had his eye on an old Ford motor Kelsey had kicking around the garage. He ought to be able to get that cheap.

That night, of all nights, Lou was late, and he got more and more impatient to see her and tell her what he'd done. He strolled slowly up the road toward the sawmill lane, hoping to meet her before he reached the big lilac bush by the corner. But she was nowhere in sight when he rounded the darkening bulk of the shrubbery and glanced up the side road. He took his courage in his hand and started up the road. He went slowly from the beginning so that his walking by the house slowly wouldn't seem unusual.

The first night he had come there after Lou he'd been too upset by his meeting with Curtis to give a thought to the house itself. But now he gave himself a chance to look it over, and he liked what he saw. It wasn't an impressive house, but there was something solid and settled in the way it stood there against the background of spruces that came down to the lawn edge on the uphill side. The flower beds that surrounded it hid the foundation and made the buildings look rather as if they'd grown up from the ground itself than as if they'd been put there by a more nearly human agency. He knew the name of the big shrubs that stood at each corner of the wide porch along the front. Hydrangeas, they were; their big massy blooms were already turning bronzy with a foretaste of fall. The lawn itself was cut, and it looked like a lawn that was well cared for. And the pickets in the straight white fence were perfect. The vine that grew on a lattice of wire over the porch made a deep bower of shade, and Bub caught himself wishing he had a right to sit there with Lou.

He went far enough up the hill to be invisible from the house, then he crossed the road and came back past it again, this time on the near side. He had just reached the gate when he heard the front door open softly. He didn't hurry himself, but he didn't look up, either, keeping on his slow saunter.

"Just a minute, young man."

The voice was unfamiliar where he had expected Lou's voice. Surprise stopped him in his tracks. He glanced back once at the woman standing on the porch, looked away, and then looked back at her again.

"You mean me?" he asked dumbly.

"Yes, you. Come in here a minute."

Bub fumbled with the gate latch, keeping his eyes on her face. The features grew more distinct as he went up the walk toward her. He knew who she was, knew her by sight, but this was the first time for nearly fifteen years that Edna Jellison had spoken directly to him. He realized that she had called him "young man" because she couldn't think just what else to call him.

"You wanted to see me?" he asked.

"You're waitin for Lou, ain't you?"

Bub gave himself a moment to look at her before he answered. He saw the thick trembling underlip and the lines of worry and indecision in the pale, slightly flabby face. But he saw her eyes, too, and they were a surprise in that face. They were clear deep blue and very steady; and the way they were looking him over now was very like the way Lou had looked at him that first morning at the factory. He liked the directness of that gaze, knowing that there was little that would get by a woman who could look at you like that, and he grinned up at her engagingly.

"Yes'm, I'm doin just that."

He watched, fascinated, the unwilling way her drooping mouth quirked up at the corners into a wry answering smile.

"Well," she said, "I wisht you'd come inside an wait. I don't like to have my girl meetin people on street corners."

"I'd be pleased to," Bub said seriously. "I don't like it any more'n you do; but I figured with Curtis feelin like he does it was simpler."

"Well, he ain't home, so you might's well come in. Besides, I'd like to get a close look at you. I ain't seen you since you were knee high, not really to look at you."

"I'm a little higher'n that now," Bub said, stepping in through the door she was holding open for him, "but I dunno's it's much improvement."

"Come in an set down." Edna motioned toward the front room and Bub followed her through the door that led off the hall. He waited for her to sit down, then settled himself in a straight chair that he realized suddenly must have been put where it was for this very purpose. She see me go up by the first time, he thought, moving his head slightly, trying to get out of the direct light from the west window.

Edna sat facing him, but a little to one side so she wouldn't obstruct the light that fell sharply on his face. Bub could see her looking at him, but he couldn't tell much about her expression because her face was in shadow.

"Lou tells me you're plannin on settlin down here," she said, and he could hear the slight tremor of nervousness in her voice and immediately felt more at ease. If she was nervous, that meant two of them, and misery was certainly glad of company in this case, he thought grimly.

"Ayeh," he let it go at that, preferring to make her carry the battle to him.

" 'S funny. A strappin young feller like you. I should think you'd be in the Army or somethin."

"Maybe I got out of it like Joe Pettigrew did," Bub said, half angry.

"Joe's got a heart murmur. Besides, he's essential."

"Well," Bub evaded lamely, "I got hurt a while ago. They figured I couldn't be much use to em."

"That so?" For a moment he thought she sounded sorry. "Were you hurt bad?"

"Oh, I was laid up for six months or so."

"My land!" Edna straightened up and shifted her chair a little. "What on earth happened?"

"Well, there was a sort of explosion and I guess I was standin too close when it went off." And that wasn't any lie, he added silently.

"Don't you know you ought to tell people that so's they won't go thinkin anythin funny? You can do yourself a lot of harm not tellin people things."

"I figured it warn't anyone's business," Bub said shortly.

"That ain't the attitude to take. You got to live with people. They got to know somethin about you."

She looked at him when he was silent. The light on his face made the bones stand out, made him look thin, and a little pitiful. But she could see from the way he had set his jaw that he didn't ask her for pity. He looked resentful and was beginning to look sullen. Edna couldn't make up her mind whether she liked him or not—one minute she did and the next she didn't. She sat wondering what Lou could see in a boy like this—remembering what he had been and what his parents were.

They both heard Lou coming downstairs and turned to her at the same moment. Lou stood on the landing goggling at them speechlessly.

"Hi!" Bub said, enjoying fully her amazement.

"Well!" Lou let out her breath in a long, silent whistle. "I certainly never expected to find *you* down here."

"I got tired waitin and your ma invited me in."

Lou looked quickly at her mother, her slow smile beginning to grow in her eyes.

"Well," she said, "what d'you think of him, Mom?"

"That ain't fair," Bub said before Edna could answer, and after he'd spoken she didn't say anything. "You ready at last?" he said to Lou.

"Why, I guess so," Lou said. She came down the remaining stairs and stood waiting for him. Bub glanced uncertainly from Lou to Edna and then back at Lou.

"Well, good night, Mrs. Jellison," he said, bobbing his head stiffly.

"Good night," she said solemnly. "You'll have to come in again sometime, when you can stay longer."

"I'd like to." Bub wasn't sure whether or not he meant it, then

[153]

decided he really did. This house and the way it was taken care of and furnished and the people who lived in it were really what he'd been thinking of when he thought of the Harbor. Not this exact house, but houses like it. Not these particular people, but just hard-working, decent people with a definite place in a real peaceful world to which they were important. Women who kept their houses clean even if they weren't palaces; men about whom other men said, "He's a good man to have on a job." Respectability was what he wanted more than anything else in the world; and that meant he had to be respected by people like these.

"I'd like a lot to come again," he repeated. But he saw by Edna's face that whether he came again would depend very much on what Curtis had to say about it; and Bub knew without question just about what Curtis would say.

They went down the walk to the gate in silence. But once out of earshot of the house, Lou said:

"Well, what'd you think of my mother?"

"I like her a lot. She makes me think of you."

"How?"

"Her eyes, I guess. You ever notice the way she looks at you? Straight."

"I guess I must be used to it," Lou said slowly. "There's not much gets by her, though."

"I'll bet," Bub agreed heartily. He hesitated and then said, "I didn't think I was goin to like her."

"Why on earth not? You never knew her very well, did you?"

"Well, there was somethin happened a long time ago—an I hated her for a while. But I guess you get over things that happen to you when you were a kid."

"What *are* you talking about? What did she ever do to you when you were a kid that you can remember this long?" Lou looked at him in wide-eyed amazement.

"It was silly." Bub grinned at the memory. "It was Christmas when I was—lessee—I musta been about ten or twelve, I guess. She was president of some club or somethin, and they made up a big barskit full of stuff for some poor family. Well, we got it. I remembered it a long time."

"Didn't you like the stuff?" Lou asked.

[154]

"Well, it warn't a question of likin it or not likin it," Bub said flatly, feeling as if his whole story were going down like a balloon. "Matter of fact, I didn't get none of it. I wouldn't eat none and Mack said I was a dam fool. I remember how sick he made himself."

"But I don't see—you were just a kid."

Her complete lack of understanding baffled him for a minute.

"It was just bein poor an havin to take charity like that from anyone. I guess I sort of thought your mother was responsible. I never liked her after. But I guess I do now."

"When you were that young?" Lou said. "You felt like that? Oh, my poor Bub!"

He looked at her suspiciously and saw that she was smiling, but her eyes were sober. With growing warmth he knew that she understood what he'd been trying to tell her.

They had turned the corner and were going slowly down the road toward the dimmed-out portico that sheltered the entrance to the movie house. Bub, walking in silence now, his thoughts busy with the idea of that Christmas, became increasingly conscious of the car that had come up behind them and now, slowed almost to a fast walking pace, was drawing by. He glanced up just in time to see Joe grinning at them before the car shot ahead. It turned in a driveway and came back, swinging wildly to the wrong side of the road and drawing up with a protesting screech of brakes. Joe stuck his head out the window. To Bub his teeth looked almost too white in the clean darkness of his face.

"Hi, Lou!" Joe said, his voice conversational; but he was watching Bub.

"Why, hello, Joe." Lou's voice was mingled curiosity and irritation.

"Wanta come for a ride?" Joe asked her, still watching Bub. Bub crooked his mouth into a wry grin and looked at Lou. She glanced at his face and turned to Joe. Bub walked on a step or two, leaving her beside the car, but he took care not to go so far he couldn't hear what Joe said. He just stood there, waiting, listening to their voices.

"Joe," Lou said sharply, "I told you I was going to be busy tonight."

[155]

"Well, you know about the woman's privilege," Joe laughed, and the hearty rich sound of his laughter made Bub's hackles rise like a dog's.

Dam him, Bub thought, he's got a nerve to ask her like that, right in front of me.

But he couldn't think what he ought to do. He felt momentarily like going back there and pulling Joe out of the car by the scruff of his clean neck and winding him around the nearest telephone pole. He knew he wasn't going to do it, though. The impulse passed almost as quickly as it had come. After all, he couldn't blame her very much if she preferred Joe to him. It mattered, though; it made him stand there clenching his fists, waiting to see what Lou would do.

He glanced back when he heard her voice lower to a mere thread of sound. He was just in time to see her turn away from the car. Joe reached out and grabbed her by the wrist, bringing her about sharply, and Bub heard Lou's sharp startled exclamation. That was the last thing he heard before the frightening anger burst redly behind his eyes. When the anger cleared, he was standing beside Lou and they were both staring up the road after Joe's twinkling tail-lights.

"Dam him," Bub said unsteadily.

"I guess he's drunk." Lou's voice sounded uncertain, but when he looked at her he caught the subdued twinkle in her eye. "You're mad, aren't you?"

"I—I—yes, I am."

"I don't blame him for running," Lou said, letting her laughter go. "Honest, Bub, I never saw anything like that before in my life. I think if you ever came at me the way you just did at Joe I'd be too scared to run."

"I'm sorry. I guess I made sort of a fool of myself."

"Oh, for heaven sake, don't apologize," she said snappily. "I tell you, I liked it."

Bub simmered with recurring waves of reminiscent anger all through the movie, and when they left after the lights came up again, he wasn't quite sure what he'd just seen. He'd been telling himself what a fool he'd been to let Joe get away with anything like that. He was telling himself he'd been a fool not to haul him out of the car when he'd first thought of it.

When they reached the white gate, though, his anger had gone and he had remembered suddenly what he'd been so anxious to tell her.

"Hey," he said, "I bought me a boat today."

"Bub, did you?" She sounded so pleased that he had to laugh.

"Well, she ain't no yacht, but she's a good little hooker. I'm goin to haul her up alongside the shack to do some work on her. You can come down an see her."

"You can't keep me away," Lou said. "I think that's an awfully smart thing to do, buy that boat."

"Well, it'll show people I really mean business," Bub said thoughtfully, "an that ought to make a difference."

"I know it will."

He said good night then because he didn't want to stay so close to her, not with Lou looking at him the way she was. He was nearly twenty feet away from her when he heard her voice.

"Oh, Bub," she said.

"Yeah?" He turned quickly and saw dimly that she was leaning out over the gate looking after him.

"Well, come here a minute. I can't yell at you."

With strangely reluctant steps he came back and stood there dumbly, looking down at her. Just looking at her like that made him forget Joe completely. In the dim light her face was lovely and mysterious to him, shadowed by the irregular shapes of leaves.

Don't let this happen now, he thought. It's too soon. It can't happen.

"You certainly make anyone carry the battle to you, don't you, Bub?" Lou said, and her usually calm voice sounded uneven to him, as if her breath had started to get away from her. She leaned forward and kissed him lightly, and because it was so different from what he'd been thinking, it left him breathless. His lips felt numb—and the palms of his hands tingled slightly.

"Thank you for getting mad," she said, and left him. Bub stood with his hands clenched around the gate pickets watching

[157]

her go up the walk. He said her name once and knew that she heard him say it, but she didn't turn around.

HE could still remember that kiss and the way it made him feel when he turned down the narrow path to the shack. In spite of the way it made him feel he was telling himself over and over again that it hadn't meant a thing to Lou. She was an attractive girl and she was probably used to having fellows kiss her good night. Maybe she thought he'd wanted to and couldn't get up the nerve to do it and she was just being nice to him. But it didn't help him much, and the idea of Lou kissing anyone else good night like that bothered him. It'll be all right, he thought, just so long's I don't let it get away from me. Why, she'd probably kiss anyone like that.

But she had kissed him, and that was the way it always began. Lou just didn't realize how foolish it was for her to get mixed up with anyone like him. She just didn't see what she'd be letting herself in for, he told himself. She couldn't see how different they were—how impossible it was. But the memory of her as she'd leaned over the gate toward him was something he couldn't put away without thinking about it a little. It couldn't do any harm if he just let himself think what it would be like if he and Lou could be in love; how nice it would be if it were possible.

"But it ain't," he said softly, and it wasn't any use really thinking about something that couldn't ever happen. He knew pretty well how Lou would react if he ever let himself go. She felt sorry for him, and maybe she liked him a little; that was all he could expect from her and, feeling grateful enough for that, he looked forward with regret to the time when he *would* let go. Because it would happen, just as sure as his name was Dolliver! It would happen because he wasn't going to be able to help it, and after that it'd be all over. He didn't try to think of what else there might be left for him after it was over, because *it* was suddenly the most important thing in his life and he couldn't think of anything big enough to carry over from the time when he had known Lou to the time when he wouldn't know her any more.

Bub looked up as he came out of the path and stopped in mid-stride, his eyes on the dark figure silhouetted against the slightly less-dark harbor. There was somebody, a man, standing there on the wharf waiting for him. Evidently he hadn't stopped soon enough, and whoever it was waiting there had heard him coming. The man turned and came slowly up the wharf and across the narrow grass space toward him.

"Bub?"

"Ayeh," Bub said, realizing with dismay, now that his anger had cooled, that Joe had come down here to wait for him. And the taut heaviness the sound of his own name made in the air between them told Bub that Joe was still mad.

"Come out where I can see you," Joe said.

Bub stepped out of the shadow of the woods and walked toward him, stopping just out of arm's reach.

"Didn't expect you, Joe," he said, keeping his voice even with an effort.

"I come to tell you somethin," Joe said heavily. "I thought you better know. You been makin pretty free with other people's belongins since you come back—I thought you better know you can't pull that on me."

"What the hell d'you mean, making free?"

"Think it over," Joe's voice was a mere whisper. "Maybe it'll come to you what I mean."

"You ain't by any chance sayin I'm the one that's been breakin in those places, are you?"

"You're right on the beam tonight," Joe said. "I don't give a dam what you steal from anyone else. But, by god, I ain't goin to let no paddy like you come along and take my girl right out from under my nose, see? I never had any trouble with Lou til you come along."

"You don't think you're goin to tell me what to do, Joe?" The anger was back now, this time it came slowly and was cold. The muscles around his mouth felt stiff and his eyes smarted.

"I know I am."

"What you gonna do if I disagree?"

"I'll show you." Joe came a step closer. "I'll knock the sweet jesus right out of you, Bub. I been wantin to for a long time."

Bub heard the grunting exhalation of breath when Joe leaped, and he felt the hard edge of Joe's fist scrape along his jaw. The blow took him off balance and spun him halfway around; but he came back, feeling his leg muscles coil under him. He let himself go with a snap, knowing if he could once get Joe down they stood even chances. His hands closed on Joe's throat and he dug his thumbs in deep. Joe gave way slightly and then went over with a crash before the impetus of that jump. But he wouldn't stay down. He seemed to bounce when he hit the ground, and came up again stronger than he had been before. His fists felt like sledges to Bub, and they let loose a flock of pinwheels inside his head every time they landed, and they landed with increasing fury. Along his bad side pain stabbed—but he was surprised that he'd managed to stay on his feet this long.

Joe came at him like a windmill. Bub crouched away from the flailing fists and came in under Joe's guard with a long lunging right. He heard the grunt and felt Joe give; but he still came back. He always came back. The sobbing sound of his own breath drowned the bursting pound of Joe's fists. Then Joe stepped back a little and let go with one that came from the ground. It caught Bub between the chin and the point of his jaw.

He fell with his arms out and lay there, unable to move but conscious enough to know that Joe stood leaning over him for a moment, watching, and then walked away up the path with slow, uncertain steps.

The steps faded and Bub lay, seeing the sky swing in great tented circles above him. After a very long time he found he could drag himself along somehow. His legs wouldn't work well, but he could drag himself. He thought vaguely he knew what a snake feels like when you step on it. He pulled himself into the shack and onto his bed and lay there face down, not thinking anything, just feeling the steady throbbing of his aching body.

LYFORD preferred the house when it was empty and there was nobody around who would say to him: "Be careful how you go through the living room. I've spent the whole mornin in there clearin up after you kids. I don't see why you won't learn they's two doors to a house an the back one's the one to use when your feet're dirty."

There was nobody to say: "Lyford, there's no call for you to be goin upstairs, now. I won't have you rummagin around in the upstairs rooms. It does seem as if I could trust my own children, but I won't have you rummagin."

He stood in the lower hall listening, his head cocked to one side. The standup piece of hair on his crown caught the dim sunlight that leaked through the vine-shaded front-room windows. He knew there was nobody there to hear him, but it suited his purpose to pretend there was.

At two o'clock that afternoon Edna had gone out, down to the Parish House to work for the Red Cross. Lyford didn't know what it was she did there and he didn't care much. It meant only that she would be out of the house and that he would be there alone. He'd waited cautiously in the fringe of alders along the woods until he saw her go out. Briefly he'd thought that she looked neat in her light summer dress, her hair fixed just so in the even unnatural waves. He knew how she'd smell, too, if he got close enough to her—faintly of the gardenia perfume she kept in a little atomizer in her bedroom, stronger of powder and plain bath soap.

The moment she'd turned the corner out of sight and he was sure she hadn't forgotten anything and was coming back, Lyford flattened himself against the even grass of the lawn and practiced doing the Indian crawl across to the house. Then he ghosted along the wall to the back door and went in.

There was something mysterious and exciting about an empty house when you knew somebody might be coming in at any minute. Edna always locked the front door when she went out, but she'd got into the habit of leaving the back door unlocked in case it rained and the kids wanted to get in. That made it more exciting for him.

He went up the front stairs lightly, two at a time, knowing just

[161]

where to put his feet so there wouldn't be any noise. It paid to keep in practice with those things, so Lyford did it every time he got the chance. Many a time he'd gone up these stairs with Edna right in the room below him and she hadn't heard.

Lou's room came first, and he went in, closing the door behind him, and stood looking around the quiet bedroom. There was never anything much to rummage into in Lou's room, but he believed in doing a complete job. He tried the closet first and stood looking at the row of light dresses and suits hung along the rod in the back. Lou was always too neat. There wasn't anything in her room you couldn't see at first glance.

Lyford crossed to the dresser and eased the drawers out one after another, lifting the neat piles of clothing to run his hand under them just in case there might be something interesting there. There wasn't, and he straightened up, being careful to put everything back into the position it'd had before he'd touched it. Once or twice Edna had caught him that way, finding things that weren't just as they'd been left. Sometimes Lyford thought she left things just so to trap him, maybe putting something small on top of the clothes and remembering so she'd notice if it had been moved. He'd caught onto that, though, and took pains to put everything back exactly as he'd found it.

He stood before the bureau, noticing the powder box, the pin cushion along under the big mirror, the brush, comb, and mirror set put out straight on the clean scarf. He lifted the hand mirror and stared down at the loose change under it, his face expressionless as he counted. Fifty cents in dimes and nickles. He laid the mirror down carefully, just as it had been, without disturbing the money, and went out of the room silently.

He had been saving his mother's room until he'd gone through Lou's, because there was always something interesting in Edna's room and seldom was in Lou's. Edna kept small fascinating things in the little left-hand drawer of the dresser; things that made his fingers itch. There were little boxes filled with old jewelry, rings from which the stones had vanished long ago, old stickpins, strings of beads, and a few loose stones she'd always planned to have put back in their settings but never had. In a little box by itself was her most valuable piece of jewelry—it was a complicated gold pin that came apart in ten little pieces, and her mother had given it to her years ago. They weren't ever allowed to touch it, but Lyford had figured the combination the first time he'd come across it. There were three or four rough pieces of carnelian his grandmother had brought back from the time she went to Wisconsin or out West somewhere in the covered wagon. Nothing very valuable, but all fascinating.

Lyford had turned the knob and started to push the door silently open, when the voice stopped him in his tracks. Frozen, he stood listening.

"Why don't you come right in?" Jinny said cordially somewhere behind the door. Too startled and mad to move, Lyford stood gaping, and in the next second realized she wasn't talking to him because she answered herself.

"Why, I'd love to, Jinny," she said graciously, making her voice as deep as she could.

For pete's sake! Lyford thought. Somewhere inside his mother's room the dialogue went on.

"It's been so long," Jinny said.

"Two hours, dear, and it's seemed like two years."

"Oh, Jack!"

That did it. The laugh that had been burbling up in Lyford's throat came out in a strangled giggle.

"Oh, Jack!" he groaned. "Oh, Jack!" He staggered into the room, waving his arms wildly, got one good look at his young sister, gasped once more, this time in horrified amazement, and said, "Oh, jesus!"

"I'll tell Ma," Jinny shrilled. "I'll tell her you swore at me! You were rummagin again an you swore at me!"

If Lyford had ever seen anyone look guilty, Jinny did. She'd been standing before the mirror watching the expressions on her own face, and when he came in she'd spun around to face him. She had crammed onto her thin arms and fingers every ring and bracelet she'd found in the drawer. She wore the long, clear, brown earrings that looked like drops of spring water with dead leaves under it—Edna kept those for best. And Jinny had plastered her face with rouge and lipstick until it would have been difficult to say what the actual color of her skin was.

Lyford covered his eyes with his hand and staggered backward.

"My good lovin god," he said, "ain't you a lookin sight!"

"I certainly don't look any funnier than you do, old Mr. Nosy."

"What'd Ma do if she ever see you?"

"No more'n she would to you," Jinny said tartly. "You ain't got a bit more right in here than I have."

Lyford, seeing the logic of this, resorted to ridicule again.

"Oh, Jack!" He ogled at her, his voice syrupy. "Who's Jack? What silly old fool'd even look at you? You look even worse with that goo on. Wait'll I tell the kids."

"You dare, Lyford Jellison, an I'll tell Ma you was up here stealin her things. That's all you do, just steal things."

"I spose you ain't?" he inquired scornfully. "I spose you can put all that stuff on your face back in the boxes again! I spose you ain't stealin, are you?"

Jinny, the eternal woman, started to cry, and the resultant mess was more than Lyford's stomach would bear. He made a rude retching noise and closed his eyes.

"All right, all right. I won't tell no one, but you shut up, too. If I hear any more of you bein such a good little girl, I'll spill it, see?"

He left the room without looking back at her and went downstairs shaking his head wonderingly. These women! He had to giggle again, though, when he thought of Jinny's face, red under the slathering of makeup, and how she'd looked when she found out he'd been listening. I guess that'll be somethin to keep her down, he thought happily. I'll just have to remind her of that every now an then.

On his way out, Lyford stopped in his own bedroom to pick up his new sling-shot. It was a beauty and it had taken him a whole morning to make it. He'd found just the right stick he needed up on the hill the other day and it had taken him an hour and a half to carve the decorations on the handle. He tested the piece of inner tube he'd used to give it spring and nodded at the answering twang of taut rubber.

It took him nearly fifteen minutes more to pick out a pocketful of ammunition from the gravel road shoulder in front of the house. He liked stones of just a certain size and weight.

[164]

When he started up the hill toward the woods his mind was blank, but he was seeking inspiration. He passed the old sawmill, looked contemplatively at the heaps of dull yellow sawdust, and went on.

There were only two buildings above the sawmill. One of them, a gambrel-roofed house, was uninteresting. Old lady Atherton lived there all alone, and she didn't like kids. Lyford had been screamed at often enough when he crossed her yard to know that. She didn't like kids, him least of all. He went on thoughtfully, the road growing narrower and more gravelly under his feet.

He had nearly passed the other building, which every year snuggled deeper into the forest of young spruces that were rapidly surrounding it, before he stopped. Lyford had got so used to seeing the old Congo Church that it barely made any impression on him. But now he stopped and looked. The only things that would make you know it was once a church were the colored-glass windows and the empty steeple where the bell had hung. He could remember going there to Sunday School years and years ago, but the building had been empty since they'd had the Federation in the Harbor. It wasn't safe any longer for more than a few people at a time. The last time they'd tried to use it, the old floor timbers groaned and sank under the startled congregation. So they'd let it go and used the other church now.

Somebody must be using part of the big room to store hay, because Lyford could see it through the few missing panes in the crude purple, green, and brown windows. The missing panes bothered him. It didn't look right, like sores in the old long-unpainted clapboards, those windows like that. It would even look better, Lyford thought, if the glass were all gone.

He reached for his slingshot, selected the first stone, and let it go. The sensation that followed the first crash of breaking glass was a good deal like the one he got from eating lemon pie—it made his mouth water. He found another stone.

When he went back down the hill an hour later, the afternoon was still and somnolent and hot with nothing stirring, only the heat waves shimmering over the top of Pentacook. But as he passed the gambrel-roofed house, old lady Atherton knocked on her front window, and when he looked up, she shook her fist at him angrily.

"Oh dam," Lyford said, "she musta seen me."

But he forgot about it.

The telephone rang just before supper. Lyford, who was sitting by the radio, absorbed in a funny book and listening to the adventures of Dick Tracy, didn't move. Edna came in from the kitchen and before she took the receiver off the hook, looked at him plaintively.

"Lyford, can't you tune that down a little? My lord, I can't even hear myself think with that thing screamin. Sometimes I feel just like throwin it as far as I can heave."

Lyford sighed windily and tuned the radio down a fraction. He didn't listen to his mother's telephone conversation, finding two things sufficient to absorb his whole attention. Edna hung up and said musingly to herself:

"Now what d'you spose *she* wants? She ain't been in this house more'n twice since we moved here."

"Who?" Lyford looked up quickly.

"Why, old Mrs. Atherton lives up on the hill. She wants to come an see me tonight. Asked if I'd be home."

"Did you say you would?" Lyford's eyes darted past his mother toward the back door and freedom.

"Course I did. I got to find out what she wants. If I didn't I'd just about die of curiosity."

A moment later, when she'd gone back to the kitchen, Lyford sneaked past her and headed for the sanctuary of outdoors; but she caught him.

"Lyford, where you goin now? It's close to supper time an I don't want these dishes hangin around all evenin while I wait for you to come home. You go wash, then come down here an eat your supper."

Meekly, to avoid her talk, Lyford washed at the sink and sat down to eat. By the time Jinny and Lou and Edna joined him, he was nearly through. In the middle of their talk he said, "Excuse me, please," and went out.

"I don't know what ails that boy tonight." Edna stared

thoughtfully after him. "He never said 'excuse me' before without havin to be told."

"Maybe it's having some effect," Lou said.

Jinny looked up and started to add her two cents' worth, but some thought caught her just before she gave tongue and she sat for a moment with her mouth open, her waspish little face thoughtful before she closed it again, silently.

Edna knew old Mrs. Atherton the way you know somebody who lives on the same street to whom you speak occasionally but whom you don't meet often. The old woman was big and clumsy through lameness; she didn't get around much. As far as Edna knew, she sat up there alone in her house from one year's end to the next, not bothering anybody and not expecting anyone to bother her.

Edna was sitting out on the porch behind the vines when she heard the wheezing, thudding sound that preceded the old lady's heavy progress down the hill. When she got up to meet her, she thought at first it was breathlessness that made the broad face under the skun-back white hair look so red. But it wasn't. It was anger, and Edna, recognizing it at last, drew back, puzzled.

"I'm a good Congregationalist," Mrs. Atherton began, when her foot hit the bottom step, "an both my mother an my father was before me. They went to that church all their lives an they was buried from it. I've went to it all *my* life, an I don't hold with this Federation business anyhow, an I never set foot inside any church but that one."

By that time she'd reached the front door. Not waiting to be asked, she pulled the screen door open and limped into the shadow of the front room. Dazed and completely at a loss, Edna followed her. The old woman let herself down cautiously into the biggest chair and sat there glaring, her wide shelf of bosom heaving dangerously.

"I don't believe—" Edna began, standing in the door.

"I spose you don't know what I'm talkin about. Well, I've come to tell you, I had to sit up there this whole afternoon an watch your boy raisin his ructions with that church, an I tell you it chilled my blood."

[167]

"Lyford?" Edna said stiffly.

"I don't know what his name is an from what I see this afternoon I don't want to. But it was your boy."

"What's he done?" Edna said sharply. "Why don't you tell me instead of just talkin like that? What's he done?"

"Jest talkin? I'm tellin you about sacrilege an you call it jest talkin!"

"Oh, please, for goodness sake, how can I tell what you mean?"

"Well, I set there this afternoon an watched him smash every window out of the side of that church with a sling shooter!"

"Good heavens!" Edna clutched at her throat to stifle back the relieved laughter. "I thought it was somethin bad," she said before she could stop herself, and for one awful moment thought the old lady would strangle.

"That is the house of the Lord!" Mrs. Atherton's voice shook. "Your son desecrated it an you have the nerve to sit there an say you thought it was somethin bad! What would you call somethin bad?"

"Now, wait. I didn't mean that to sound the way it did. It *is* bad an he'll have to be punished."

"I should hope *so*."

"But it's not really so terrible, is it? After all, it's been a good many years since that old barn was used for a church. It ain't really as if he'd smashed the windows out of a church. Why, your boy Pete is usin it to store his hay in this year, ain't he?"

"Once a church, always a church. An it don't make no difference one way or the other who's hay's stored in it. Besides, think of the glass in that hay an the rain comin in the broken windows. But that ain't here nor there. The point is, that young hellion ought to be put in the reform school, goin around destroyin others' property like that. He ain't fit to be let loose where there's decent people around."

"Just a minute," Edna got up from the piano stool where she'd slumped in relief. "Lyford's not a bad boy. He just smashed some windows out of an empty old buildin. Probly every boy in this town's done that at some time or other—I wouldn't be a bit surprised if yourn had once. I want you to

[168]

know he'll be punished proper—but it ain't nothin to go talkin reform school about."

"I never knew a mother could see anythin wrong with her own kids! I spose if they committed a murder or somethin, you'd say it wasn't anythin bad!"

"Well, I don't think they will," Edna said. "Breakin a few windows ain't murderin anyone." She was holding her patience with a rough hand.

"One thing can lead to another. Start out breakin windows, like as not end up breakin into banks." Venomously the old woman snapped the words out, and Edna, with a shocking upsurge of injured innocence and anger, realized that she actually hated—she really did feel what Lyford had done was as bad as murder.

"Why didn't you stop him instead of settin there watchin him do it, like you said?" She kept her voice deceptively low.

"You might've noticed I ain't as spry as I once was. I couldn't get over there. An I *did* yell a couple of times, but he was too busy. Now, what I wanta know is, what're you goin to do about it?"

"I'll put back every window if I have to do it myself," Edna said, her patience gone at last. "Now, go on home. I'm tired of this rantin around. He'll be punished all right. But you ain't goin to see me do it, so you might's well go on home."

"Well, I certainly will!" Mrs. Atherton groaned to her feet. "I must say, this hill is comin to a pretty pass when we got young toughs like that runnin wild all over it."

"Go on," Edna said. She made a shooing motion with her hands. When she heard the old lady panting down the steps again she felt a twinge of shame at the way she'd acted. Poor old thing, she thought, that's probly all she can do for excitement, sit around waitin to stir up trouble. But then she started thinking about Lyford and forgot the old woman until it was too late to go after her and say how sorry she was for acting so.

Useless destruction was something that made Edna angrier than anything else she could think of, and when she got over being mad at the old woman, she started getting mad at Lyford. That kid! Going up there and smashing those windows out!

[169]

There wasn't any need for him to go doing things like that and the lord knows he'd been taught different. Honest, she thought, it seems as if that boy set out to do the most devilish things he could think of. Having other people come to her with tales about her own kids bothered her more actually than the deeds that inspired the stories.

She got up and went into Lyford's bedroom. Fifteen minutes' search it took her to find the slingshot, but it was there and she found it. It was in his pillowcase, under the pillow itself. Panting with anger, Edna took it down cellar and made kindling out of it with the hatchet that stood by the furnace.

There, she thought, now let him try that again!

But chopping up the slingshot hadn't been enough to cool her off. She was still good and mad. The idea of that kid doing a thing like that to shame her in front of everyone. Wouldn't Alice Scott lick her lips over that! And Edna wasn't fooling herself it was a thing you could keep quiet. She'd seen feuds start up over less than this in the Harbor, feuds that started twenty years ago or more and the families still weren't speaking to each other.

She was so mad she went back upstairs and started cleaning the kitchen. She tore it apart, delving into cupboards and cubbyholes that had been cleaned thoroughly just that spring; but if she didn't do something, she was going to be too mad even to talk to Lyford when he came in.

At nine o'clock it was nearly dark, and she started watching the clock. At eleven he hadn't turned up and she was beginning to get less angry and more worried. When at one he finally sneaked in through the backway, she'd got over being anxious and was mad again, clear through.

"Lyford Jellison, you come in here! I've got somethin to say to you!"

He came and stood in the cellar door, looking at her with his smooth, expressionless young face, his eyes coldly watchful. It was what she called his "fresh" look, and it always made her furious.

"I spose you know you've fixed it so I can't walk downtown again holdin my head up?" she said, and waited.

Lyford said nothing.

"After the way I brag about how nice my kids are, after the way I go around tellin people my children never done anythin to make me ashamed of them an never will—now I got to go thinkin everyone knows what kind of a son I've got."

Lyford said nothing. He shifted slightly, changing his weight from one foot to the other, but he kept his mouth shut tight.

"Well, I want you to know I'm ashamed of you, an if I was stronger I'd give you the worst hidin of your young life. As it is, we're goin to have to replace them windows you broke an you're not goin to get another cent out of me til it's done an paid for. What've you got to say to that?"

"Nothin." Lyford skidded around her and headed for his bedroom.

"You needn't go lookin for your slingshot, neither," Edna said. "I took it down cellar an chopped it up."

Lyford stopped short, but he didn't turn, so she couldn't see his face.

"It took me a whole mornin to make that slingshot," he said.

"Yes, an it'll take you a whole lot more than a whole mornin to pay for the damage you done with it, too, young man. An you're goin to do it. 'N don't you ever let me see you with one of them things again. If I can't trust you, then I'm goin to watch every move you make. Now, git into your bed. The idea, stayin out til one o'clock in the mornin. I guess you knew all right what it was she was comin down here to see me about."

Part Three — *September, 1943*

EARLY in the month, when the woods had lain under the hot August weather until they were dried down to the beginning of the rich black loam under the leaf mold, the forest fires started. The first sign was a light yellowish haze that drifted in over the hills and stayed. After that the air began to have a thin pungent smell, faintly bitter and exciting. It was the thin smell of death for acres of firs and pines upstate and to the westward. The smoke would grow thicker on the hills, and in the late afternoon it would be a brown-gray bank like low-lying clouds in the west. And the sun going down into it was a bloody coin and you could look directly at it without squinting.

Once, years ago, the fires had been so bad that one day at noon the sun was almost obscured behind the flying scud of yellow cloud that wasn't cloud at all. Since then the smoke made people nervous. Late August and early September made nervous weather with the smell of smoke like a storm-warning everywhere.

It was summer still, summer of perfect hot weather that you knew couldn't last. Someday soon you'd wake up and find a chill in the morning that hadn't been there before; but not quite yet.

The summer people began packing up and the big houses over on Old Point had wooden shutters at their doors and windows. The day after Labor Day, school opened and the kids who'd haunted the shores and the estuary all summer disappeared.

In late July the doctor had taken Curtis to the hospital over in Wells. There had been two days of which Curtis could remember nothing but the smell of antiseptic and the white shifting delirium they called "coming out of ether." He had been abjectly sick, and immediately afterward his stomach was normal.

Then he was bad again, he knew he was seriously ill—pneumonia was no joke, especially to a man of his age. There was a long night of which he could remember nothing. The next morning, once more weakly sane, he heard the awed stories of how it had taken two orderlies to hold him in his bed—of how Edna and Lou had walked the corridor outside his door—of how the doctor had twice given him up. But now he was sane again, the crisis was past, and he knew with inert regret that he was going to live. Maimed for life, a part of him gone for good, he was going to live.

He had had a series of days through which he lay staring at the smooth unmarked ceiling, listening to the sounds around him in the ward, watching doggedly the rays of sharp sunlight coming in the brilliantly clean windows. He lay there looking at anything that could possibly draw his attention from the round hummock of basketwork under the bedclothes that marked the place where his foot had once been.

After that he had time to worry about how they'd get along, what they'd use for money. Thank God he'd had a chance to stash a little away before this'd happened to him.

Lou and Edna had come to see him several times, whenever the doctor happened to be driving over, but they hadn't been able to come often and Curtis had been just as glad of it. Edna's soft voice, dulled with muted sympathy, and Lou's constant tense brightness were almost too much for him, the way he was feeling.

But now he was coming home and he'd have to face them all—Edna, Lou, and the kids. He began to wonder just how it would be. Lyford had recently developed a deep reverence for physical strength and had been spending his spare time doing exaggerated and complicated exercises to develop obscure muscles. Curtis wondered how he'd feel about having an old man with only one foot.

Then the thought of it started to make him squeamish. He looked down, avoiding the doctor's sideways glance, to the neat closed trouser leg. They could talk all they wanted to about

[173]

artificial feet and stuff like that. Curtis knew it wasn't going to be the same.

The car drew up before the house, and almost before it stopped, Curtis was fumbling around with the crutches. He hated them. Their polished brown padded wood was so damned durable. They looked as if they'd been built to last a lifetime.

Doc Simmons got out of the car and came around to Curtis's side and held the door open. He didn't offer to help with the crutches, and Curtis, getting out heavily, knew that it wasn't lack of sympathy. They were supposed to let him do for himself everything he possibly could. But he could see Lyford on the porch watching him, and his own sense of his clumsiness made him move more slowly.

Edna came to the door, saw the car, and came running heavily down the walk to meet them. She started to put out her hand to help him and Curtis could feel his mind curling up inside him. He drew back, scowling.

"You ain't supposed to help me," he said gruffly. "I got to do it all myself, Edna."

Her full underlip started shaking and she looked pitifully at the doctor. He nodded shortly without speaking, and she drew back to let Curtis go ahead of her up the walk. His shoulders, hunched up high on the crutches made her think of some kind of distorted bird, and she covered her mouth quickly with her hand so that nobody could see the betraying tremble of her underlip grow worse.

Lyford opened the door and held it aside for his father to go in. Curtis hesitated a moment, looking down, trying to find some sign of feeling in Lyford's face, but there was none to see. The clear hazel eyes looked back at him as easily as if he'd been a stranger.

"Why ain't you in school?" Curtis said automatically.

"Satday," Lyford said.

"Oh. I forgot."

Time hadn't meant a great deal since It happened and he was already referring to the loss of his foot with a capital "I." He went on into the house and let himself down heavily in the big chair by the front room window. Edna hadn't come in,

[174]

and he could see her still talking to Simmons. Finally she turned away; the doctor's car started up, and Curtis watched it turn the corner into the main road and disappear.

When Edna came into the front room, Jinny was with her, sticking close to her mother's side; and her eyes were as coolly detached as Lyford's had been. She stood looking at Curtis as if he were some queer exhibit that should be examined carefully. Her thin, brown face was expressionless until she looked down and saw the closed trouser leg. Then Curtis thought some expression appeared in her eyes, but it passed so quickly he couldn't be sure what it was.

Edna gave her a little shove, and Jinny came over and kissed his cheek carefully, moving back at once as if he were fragile and something to be touched with great care.

"Goddammit," Curtis said helplessly, looking at Edna, "what's the matter with you, anyway? Don't I look the way I always did? For godsake, Edna, I don't haveta be treated like I was a dozen eggs or somethin, do I?"

Jinny started to cry then, and when he turned to stare at her, she flipped around and ran, gulping hiccoughing sobs wildly as she went.

"There, now," Edna said, staring haggardly after her, "I told them kids to be sure an behave good. Jinny's been so worried about you, Curtis. I don't know what she thought. She's been askin every day when you were comin home. I'd tell her today an then the very next day she'd ask me again."

"Well, I didn't know that was it." Curtis felt a surge of absurd warmth and then surprise that the youngest one of the kids would be the one to feel the worst.

At noon that Saturday Lou stood at the open office window watching the road. She was waiting to see Joe leave the factory and go home to dinner. She didn't feel like talking to him today. He'd be sympathetic and kind about her father, and she didn't want him to. It was going to be hard enough to face Curtis now without having to face all the people who would be kind about him. She wondered vaguely why it was that kindness was so difficult to take. It was a good deal the way charity must be, she thought; a lot of people who meant well, normally hard and almost grudging with sentiment who, when they gave way to it, were too pliable, too giving.

Joe came out of the furnace-room door and stood hesitating there, looking down toward the office. Lou ducked back out of sight, hoping he hadn't caught a glimpse of her. Evidently he hadn't because he went off up the road. She waited until he'd reached the main road and turned left along the top of the ridge. Then she went up the hill quickly and turned right.

At noon, even on a Saturday, the road was deserted except for a car or two, and the high, dry, early September sunshine brought the smell of sweet fern and spruce clearly from the woods. Lou walked slowly, almost loitering, watching the big clouds pile up behind the mountains to the northwest. The shadows they made over the sides of the hills passed quickly, giving way to sunlight again. There were heat waves against the sky after they had gone.

She went slowly up by the drugstore and turned left along the sawmill road, past the huge, uncared-for hedges of lilac, to the neat picket fence. The gate squeaked a little when she swung it open, and she saw her father sitting in the front window. At the sound, he turned and leaned forward in his chair to see her. Lou grinned and waved her hand, and Curtis smiled, nodding at her. He mouthed something she couldn't understand and beckoned widely.

Sighing, Lou went up the steps and into the house, hearing his voice as soon as she opened the door.

"Come on in here an see me," Curtis shouted.

"Sure, Dad." She went into the front room, and then, seeing him closely for the first time, stopped short. The change in him was startling. When she'd seen him at the hospital it was in the company of other sick people and he hadn't looked so horribly sick himself. But here in the oppressively normal atmosphere of his own house, Curtis looked as if he'd been knocking at death's door. Lou set her face stiffly into a smile, determined not to let him see that the sight of him had terrified her. But his thin face grimaced and she knew she'd been a little too late with the smile.

[176]

She went over and kissed his cheek, feeling the beginning of his beard stiff against her face.

"Well," he said heartily, "well, what you been doin while I was away? Set down an tell me all about it now."

Edna came to the door uncertainly.

"That you, Lou? Curtis, you oughta let her have her dinner before you make her sit talkin."

Lou looked at her father and saw in the sudden disappointed drop of his face that he'd been sitting there just waiting until she would get home from work and could talk to him. It was going to be hard for him to spend his time sitting around waiting for somebody to come and talk to him.

"It's all right, Ma," Lou said. "I'm not very hungry."

Edna went away again. Lou leaned back in her chair, perching her feet on the rung and folding her arms around her knees.

"It's been pretty quiet since you went away, Pa. You know how the Harbor is, you just go on from day to day."

"Ayeh," he said dully.

"Oh, there *was* something."

The starting of interest in his deadened eyes made her gulp for a minute.

"Yeah? What?"

"Well, we've actually had a robbery—two, really."

"Is that so?" Curtis straightened. "Nobody said nothin to me about it. What happened?"

"Well, first there was that little store of Peterson's down by the Coast Guard station. Somebody broke into that an took a lot of candy and cigarets and cleaned out the cash drawer."

"They find out who it was?"

"No," Lou shook her head. "They think it was some kid, though, because of the candy and stuff. It's the sort of thing a kid would do."

"Maybe." Curtis pursed his lips and Lou thought she could almost see what was going through his mind.

"They had the sheriff down from Freehold and everything," she told him, "but they didn't find out a thing. And then, just when they'd got quieted down over that and thought it was all

[177]

forgotten, somebody broke into Barron's Beer Parlor early one morning and pulled the same trick."

"Is that so?" Curtis said again. He was watching her closely, trying to see if her face showed any expression, and Lou carefully held her slight smile. "They don't have any idea atall who done it?"

"Well," Lou shrugged, "you know how it is as well as I do. There's always somebody willing to air his feelings. There's been talk."

"Bub Dolliver!" Curtis let the words explode as if he'd been holding them back with an effort.

Lou nodded slightly.

"That's what they're saying, but it seems to me they're bein a little premature about it. They haven't any proof. Nobody *knows* anything."

"Mighty funny! We ain't hed nothin like that in town for years, and now, jest as soon as he comes back, we start havin trouble."

"I guess a lot of people feel the same way you do, Pa." Lou looked away from him momentarily. "But you know that's no way. It's, well—it's not fair to make up your mind just from that. There's any number of people would do a thing like that an you know it."

Her control over her voice must have slipped a little, there must have been some tone there that Curtis's ears, sharpened by suspicion, had caught, because he straightened up sharply and sat staring at her.

"Lou."

"What is it, Dad?"

"You ain't—you remember that night he come here for you?" She nodded, not bothering to speak. "You ain't been seein him since, have you?"

"If you want me to lie to you, I will. But you haven't made me yet."

"Then you have." Curtis's voice started to rise. "You been goin around with him." Accusingly his heavy eyes stared at her. Lou nodded again.

"I never thought I'd see the day you'd defy me like that, Lou," he began. "I—well—you know how I feel about them Dollivers an how I always will."

"Look, Dad," she said sharply, "I wasn't goin to bring this up today. I didn't think you'd want to. But you're making me, so we'll have it out right here and now."

There was a note in her voice that Curtis had never heard before and he heard it now with a constrictive surprise that Lou, of all the kids, would be the first to talk to him like this. He wasn't angry then, just surprised and beginning to be hurt.

"You always told me," Lou said, "if there was anyone I wanted to see or talk to, you'd rather I brought them home here than go out on the street and see them there, didn't you?"

"Yes," Curtis said, "but I never thought you'd take up with anyone I couldn't think much of, Lou. I always figured you had too good sense for that."

"Well, one of us is wrong, Pa. I don't know for sure which one. But I've got a feeling you are this time. I've seen Bub quite a lot since he's come home. We've gone to movies and things. And he's never so much as touched me."

"By god," Curtis yelled, stirred to anger, "he dam well better not!"

"I spose you think I'd better stick to Joe?" Lou's voice was dangerously quiet.

"Joe's a nice boy. You can't compare him to a do-less good-for-nothin like this Dolliver kid."

"Well, Joe may be a nice boy," Lou smiled with her mouth, leaving her eyes cool and level against her father's clashing stare, "but I'm telling you now, I never go out with Joe but it ends in a free-for-all."

"Why—" Shocked and unable to accept her words, Curtis searched her face for some sign that she was lying to him, but he knew she wasn't. Her eyes were like clear water and they met his angry stare easily, without slipping away. "I—I didn't know that, Lou."

"I know you didn't. But you know it now. I'm not complaining. I'm just telling you. A gal gets pretty much to expect something like that. It usually happens. And I'm telling you, too, it's a relief to go out with someone like Bub for a change.

[179]

When I'm with him, well—" she looked thoughtfully at her father and then said with calculated brutality—"I don't have to beat him to it every time my skirt blows up over my knees."

"Why, Lou," he said. His anger had drained out, leaving him lax and a little sick. "I never knew. I'd—I thought Joe was a nice boy."

"Joe *is* a nice boy," Lou said patiently. "Can't you see that's the way even the nice boys act? Maybe they didn't in your day, Dad—I don't know—but they do now. You see, they think a girl expects it. It's—oh, I guess it's sort of a reflection on them if they don't act that way."

"Oh my god," Curtis groaned, thinking of her—and the thought of her rumpled and angry, the idea of his girl having to go through anything like that made him sick at his stomach. She saw what he was thinking and smiled suddenly.

"Don't look like that, Pa. It's really not that serious. I can manage. You see, you get so you can turn off anything like that, you develop a defense that works pretty well. But you can see why I was surprised at Bub."

Curtis said nothing.

"Well," Lou tried to soften it, "Joe means right by your Nell." Her mouth twisted wryly. "He's asked me to marry him."

"He has?" Curtis's look was relieved. "Well—"

"I haven't said I would and I haven't said I wouldn't. I don't want to get married for a while yet."

"Oh." Curtis looked at her curiously. She wasn't looking at him. She was watching her own hands with an intent and steady stare. "Joe's a pretty good provider, Lou—he's in a good spot. He could give you a lot of things."

"That's what Joe says," Lou agreed. "But I'll wait a while." She got up and went toward the door slowly. Then she turned to look back at him. "What I've been trying to tell you is, I'd like to have Bub come to the house when he wants to see me instead of having to meet me on a street corner."

Curtis set his jaw and stared stonily out the window.

"I won't say he can't because I'd rather, if you're goin to see him, you'd see him here to home where I can keep an eye on him. But I want to tell you, Lou, I don't trust him and I ain't

[180]

goin to act like I did. I never liked him nor anythin I ever heard about him."

"Well, do I go on meeting him outside?" Lou asked when he stopped.

"Look, Lou, if I was to ask you, would you stop seein him? Would you for me?" Curtis was watching her face now and he saw it set in the heavy, almost sullen lines of her anger.

"No, I don't believe I would, Pa."

"All right," he said, "all right. Then he can come here. But you'll see, Lou; an when you do, I want you to come an tell me I was right."

She nodded, beginning to smile.

"When I see I was wrong, I'll come," she said.

Curtis sat for a minute watching the empty doorway where she'd been a moment before, as if he expected her to come back. He was thinking maybe it was just as well to let Lou have the Dolliver kid here to the house if she was going to see him anyhow. Wasn't there something about "give him enough rope"?

He was surprised and, against his own inclinations, deeply shocked at the things Lou had said to him. He hadn't thought it was like that. Once more the thought of her wrestling with young Joe Pettigrew in the back seat of a car somewhere came vividly to his eyes and he felt sick. Goddam, he thought—and then shrugged. The way Lou talked, she could take care of herself. There wasn't much he could do about it anyhow. But the idea bothered him deeply. He sighed and shook his head, thinking, These young brats!

HIS FACE was a mess, Bub thought, looking peeringly into the mirror. Here it'd been a whole week and the colors were just beginning to fade. Joe had certainly got in some good licks while he was at it. It was a long time since Bub had had a shiner like the one that turned half his right cheek purple and blue. By now the whole surface of his cheek was a dirty saffron that was even worse than the purple had been. The steady aching of his left side was beginning to die out, but the skin over his ribs was still sensitive to touch.

Bub had taken a good deal of razzing about that eye in the past week. The men at the wharf seemed to take actual pleasure in the fact that somebody'd beat him up. They were curious enough to know who'd done it. He wouldn't tell them that. Evidently Joe hadn't said anything about it either, because they didn't seem to know who was responsible.

"Who won?" they said, their eyes narrowed and amused.

Bub had an answer for that one.

"You don't see no one else runnin around with an eye like this, do you?"

"Well, you never was a one to mix it with anybody offered to bat you down." Bert Pettigrew appeared in the store door and Bub knew he'd been there listening in. Bert's small eyes still turned bright red when he looked at Bub, or they seemed to, the pupils narrowing down until they disappeared completely.

"I should think," Hersh said placidly, "you'd be the last one to say that, Bert."

"I keep tellin you, I slipped. If they's any more talk about that, by the Lord Harry I'll take the pair of you out and prove it."

"Big talk," Hersh said.

"Ayeh? Well, I was jest wonderin if maybe it was a mad papa give you that eye, Bub?" Bert's grin turned more evil, and premonition stirred uneasily somewhere behind Bub's breast bone.

"What's that crack mean?"

"Ain't you heard? Seems to me you're in as good a position as anyone else to know what it means."

"Well, I don't know," Bub said tonelessly, "so climb off your high hoss an tell me."

"Why, sure. They's some little young girl down around the factry's havin it over how you made a pretty good pass at her one night."

"Oh god! If there's one more thing anyone can think of to say about me, I wish to pete they'd say it all to once an get it over with."

[182]

Bub was thinking about that, too, as he turned away from the unpleasant reflection in the mirror and went out to stand looking down on the boat beached below the wharf. Bert hadn't said anything more; he'd just grinned knowingly and disappeared again. But the premonition of trouble was still with Bub. If there was anything more I needed, he thought, that's it, by judast. To get a story like that started now would be just exactly what I need. And wouldn't it sound great, getting back to Lou!

Sometimes he wondered whether it was worth the trouble, trying to get these people to admit there was something more to him than a bad word. He wanted security, but he didn't want it at the sacrifice of his peace of mind. And he wasn't sure now that what he meant by security was here for him to find. He was unsettled enough in mind over those robberies without having something like this crop up now.

It was evenings like this that made him uncertain and uneasy. Late in the afternoon the wind had risen, northwest, blowing up the big cumulus clouds from the hills again. The harbor was violently blue and there was a windy sunset, with gulls screaming wildly against it and great streaks of insane color riding up the sky. It made him feel restless and unsettled and trapped—held down by things that had never been able to hold him before. The desire for respect, mainly; but material things, too. Things like a job and a boat and a girl.

The boat was grounded where he could look down into her cockpit from the wharf. He had to admit she was a pretty sorry-looking craft—but she wasn't really a bad little hooker. She was like a singed cat, he thought, a lot better than she looked.

Lou hadn't been down to see her yet, and Bub hadn't been any too anxious for Lou to see him either. It would probably have finished her off to see him in his present shape and to find that the boat he'd been so proud of looked the way she did.

He knew Curtis was coming home today, too, and that would probably keep her occupied for a while. When he looked up and saw her coming down across the clearing it was as if she had walked in out of his own mind.

He saw her hesitate and almost come to a full stop when she got her first good look at him. When she came closer, though, he saw she wasn't looking disgusted. Her eyes were almost black.

"Bub!" she said, and the whole question was there.

"It ain't what you could call pretty, I know," he tried being amused, "but I thought it was quite a good job."

"What on earth?" she touched the puffed place under his eye lightly, but that was enough to make him wince with remembered pain.

"Ask me no questions."

"Bub, for heaven's sake, what happened? What did it?"

"A darn good pair of fists," Bub said ruefully.

He saw Lou start to swallow her questions; but he saw something else, too. She had, without trying, turned over in her mind the various people he might have had a fight with and she'd picked out the right one. The knowledge was as clear in her eyes as if she'd said the name.

"Are—you're all right, aren't you?"

"Well, if I was goin to be laid up with a black eye, I'd a been done for long ago."

"If you won't talk, I spose you won't. Well, I came down mainly to get you to come up and have supper with us tonight."

"You mean, to your *house?*"

"That's right."

"Why, I can't—didn't your father come home today?"

"That's right." Lou looked demure, but he could see the deep twinkle behind her eyes.

"What's the joke?"

"Unh-unh," instantly serious, she shook her head. "No joke. Dad and I had a talk today, that's all. I just said I'd rather see you there at the house than out on a street corner. He saw the point. But I'll have to admit, he probly won't like it much, either way. Can you stand it?"

"Well, gosh, Lou, I dunno. Look at my face, for pete's sake. I don't want to go lookin like this."

"He won't be a mite surprised," Lou grinned. "He might as well see you at your worst; he will anyhow."

She was laughing at him again, and when she did that there was little Bub could say or do but agree with her.

[184]

"All right, I'll do it." He started into the house for his jacket. "Take a look at the boat there."

When he came back out, Lou was leaning over the railing giving the boat a thorough once-over.

"She's smaller than I thought, but she looks quite good."

"You don't think much of her, do you?"

"It doesn't matter what I think of her," Lou said. "She's only the beginning. If she was only a skiff, she'd be just the beginning—"

"Ayuh," Bub said slowly, thinking how right she was, how she always knew the right thing to say to him. "Well, I'm ready. But I'm goin to come right away after supper. I'm gonna say I got to work on the boat while there's light."

"All right," she agreed, without question. "This probably won't be much fun for anyone, but it'll be a beginning, too."

After it was all over, Bub thought that Lou had understated when she'd said it wasn't going to be much fun. It wasn't fun at all. It was horrible. Curtis had taken one look at his face, grunted, and refused to say anything at all through the meal. Edna, pale and a little nervous, tried hard. Bub could almost see her straining for something to say to him. It was the reaching way she turned her head from him to Curtis and back again —as if she were begging them to find something they could talk to each other about. But Curtis wouldn't do it. And the two younger kids, scrubbed until they gleamed, sat staring and poking each other and giggling. Lyford was deeply interested in Bub's eye, but after one cautious reference to it, he caught his mother's glance and subsided so suddenly that it wasn't funny.

Maybe this'll show Lou, Bub thought. After this, she'll see.

He could have got mad, but he didn't. He could see too clearly just how the whole thing looked to Curtis. There was Lou, the oldest one and obviously her father's favorite— Curtis looked more puzzled than he did angry whenever he looked at Lou; as if he couldn't understand what would make a girl of his pick up with a Dolliver.

Very carefully neither Bub nor Lou mentioned the strain after they left the house. They went down to the wharf and Bub worked on the boat until dark, with Lou sitting watching him, and neither of them said anything about Curtis.

There had been two blackouts since Bub had come home, but this was the first one that had ever caught them together. The dark had come down and they were sitting there talking and smoking—talking about the work that still had to be done before the boat would be seaworthy. The quiet harbor was a well of impenetrable black around them as they sat there, their backs against the smooth shingles. At the moment they happened to be looking up toward the row of dim lights that marked the center of town.

Then, out of infinite silence and peace, the siren started blowing. Bub could sense Lou getting stiff. It was as if he could feel her shoulders get taut under his hands, but he wasn't touching her. They stayed silent, listening to the single long, steady shriek of the fire whistle. Then the lights started going out, one by one, along the row of houses. The few street lights still left were the last to go, and they went all at once, leaving a darkness so profound that it seemed to have a material existence. It was as if somebody had covered everything with a thick black blanket, through which even the air itself had difficulty in passing. Bub could hear himself breathing hard, as if he couldn't force air into his lungs.

"Jesus!" he said softly. "I never saw it like that before."

"It's enough to scare you to death," Lou said. "It makes you feel as if all the rest of the world had just died in a minute and you were the only person left alive."

"Ayuh."

Two planes of the Coast Patrol droned in over the harbor and circled to go down the shore. Their lights were the only apparent moving things against a low starless sky.

"That doesn't help much," Lou said. She shivered and stood up. Bub waited without moving, and felt her shoulder against his.

"What's the matter?"

"Oh, I don't know," she shrugged. "It's so darned lonely. It really scares me, Bub. What if it turned out to be the real thing sometime?"

[186]

"It won't."

"How can you tell?" She was facing him, he knew, because he could make out the white blur of her face against the darkness.

"What good would it do em to bomb the Harbor?" He tried to say it lightly. "There ain't nothin here they'd want to bomb."

"If they do bomb us," Lou said, "they won't be able to try for the important places. It'll be just the idea of bombing here. That's all they want. To be able to say they've bombed the East Coast, too."

Bub tried to laugh, he tried to think of something foolish to say to her, to change her mood somehow. But he couldn't. All he could think of was: What if they do? What if we get killed here? And the idea of losing Lou came upon him suddenly, finding him with no defense against it.

"Lou," he said sharply, just for the satisfaction of hearing her answer.

Her voice, when she said: "Yes," was low and unlike her.

"What is it?" he asked, trying to see her, turning his head to try and bring her expression into focus.

"I'm afraid. We wouldn't have anything to remember, would we?"

"No—everythin we *could* have."

She slapped him without warning. He hadn't seen her hand coming, and the palm smacked him hard across the cheek, making him wince with pain and see a galaxy of stars.

"What the hell?" He was angry in a minute, but anger went out of him like sand running out of a hole in a sack, leaving him sorry and feeling sorry for her.

"I didn't mean to do that, Bub, but you make me so dam mad!"

"Mad?" he echoed dumbly.

"You always take things the way they come. You never try to do anything."

"Don't, dear," he said. He put one hand on each side of her, against the wall, feeling the wood smooth with weather under his palms. When he bent his head to kiss her, he meant to do it the way they had before, lightly, and as if it meant nothing. But it got away from him. Her lips felt different—willing, eager

[187]

under his. She put her arms around him and pulled him so that he was caught off balance, and his weight came upon her, pushing her hard against the wall. In the second before he forgot to be gentle with her, he heard her breath go in sharply.

"You little fool," he said, finally, shoving himself away from her. "What d'you think you're doin?"

He could feel himself shaking and she must have been, too, because her voice was unsteady.

"That was different, wasn't it?"

"You mustn't do that." He could hear his voice, sounding dull and ominously heavy, the way he felt. He knew quite suddenly that this was the end. He'd been a goddam fool, kissing her like that. Now there'd be an end to this easy friendliness they'd had, whatever it had been. It was gone now and they'd never get it back. He felt as if she had cheated him somehow, had taken something valuable away from him and he could get nothing from her to replace it.

"Don't you see?" she said.

"I see what you've done—I guess I done it, too."

"Well—what?"

"Lou, you can't be *that* dumb."

"I know how you felt just then," she said, whispering, "but I didn't think you'd try to make me think you didn't feel that way."

"Well, an what if I did?"

"That's up to you, Bub." He could almost sense her smile, slow and beginning at the corners of her eyes, going slowly down to her mouth. "You're supposed to say it."

He turned on her angrily, feeling her, startled, move away. His laugh was an agonized thread of sound.

"All right," he snapped at her. "It's up to me to say I love you now, ain't it? Well, I do. And that's that."

"Bub, are you going to be foolish about this, too?"

"What d'you mean?"

"Don't be noble and forgiving all your life, Bub. You won't be fit to live with."

"You'll never get the chance to find out whether I'm fit to live with or not," he said fiercely. "You better get any idea you got in your head right out of it, Lou. Now, you listen to me—"

"Wait a minute—" she interrupted him forcibly with her hand across his mouth—"I guess you aren't goin to say it, so I've got to. I love you, Bub. I want you to—marry me." The last two words came hard, he could feel the effort it took to get them out.

"Yeah?" His hands were faintly damp with sweat and he clenched them into fists and thrust them into his pockets. "Now it's your turn to listen, Lou. You're nice people, see? There's a difference between you and me an always has been. Far's I can see there always will be. I warn't any good when I lived here before, an you can't be sure I'm different now. All you got to go on is my word. My people warn't any good, neither."

"I don't care," she said. "I don't care."

"You got to," he insisted with a queer desperation, not sure whether he wanted her to agree with him. "It'll make things awful hard for you, Lou. People will think you're crazy—even thinkin of marryin me."

"It's not people," she protested. "Look, I don't care what your father was or your mother, either. I don't even care what you were like before. It's what you're like now that matters to me. And I *know* what you're like now—it's not a matter of saying you've changed. I can see for myself."

"I make twenty-five dollars a week," Bub said. "You make that much yourself."

"Well, that's fifty a week. We could live on that."

"There's your father, too. He'd raise holy hell if he ever heard about this. You saw tonight—we won't never get along."

"He wouldn't be marrying you," Lou said. "I would. I'm old enough to know what I want." For the first time there was hesitation in her voice. "Wait. Maybe you're trying to tell me I've taken a lot for granted? Is that it? You're trying to say you don't—feel the way I do."

"Yes." Bub grasped harshly at the straw. "I didn't want to come right out and say it, Lou."

She was standing in front of him trying to see his face. Then, before he could move, he felt her hands, one on each side of his

[189]

head, pulling him down. He had neither the wish nor the ability then to stop her.

"I'll find out," she said softly before she kissed him.

He didn't move, hoping by his quiet to keep her there, but when she started to move away from him, he put his arms around her to hold her. Caught, she stayed there, laughing a little breathlessly.

"You ought to know you can't lie to a woman and get away with it," she said.

"No, I guess not; but, Lou—"

"No."

"Lou, listen—"

"No."

"Oh my god!" Bub groaned, "you're nothin but a cussed dictator."

"I'm going to *have* to be with you. Now I'm going home and you're going to stay right here."

"You can't go alone in this blackout."

"Why, Bub!" She laughed again in deep amusement. "Didn't you notice the lights come on? The blackout's been over for five minutes now."

In desperation he said, "Will I see you tomorrow?"

"Tomorrow night," Lou called back over her shoulder.

Bub stood watching her walk away from him. She would disappear into a patch of shadow and then come out into a patch of light and he'd see her again. Finally she disappeared for good, but the sound of her steps, steady and even, came back to him long after she had gone.

The wind had shifted and the fog was coming in. Bub could hear the Hog Point Light—its long thumping whistle tentative at first, then when the faint stirring of east wind quickened, it was stronger—it wove an in-and-out pattern with the buoy on Sinker's Ledge.

Maybe it would rain, he thought stiffly—and up-country that was what they were waiting for. What he was waiting for himself, he wasn't sure now.

BY MORNING, Bub's restlessness and uncertainty were back. It was still restless weather and he felt it. He kicked savagely at a coil of warp lying alongside the storeroom door, and the pain in his foot didn't make him feel a bit better. Early that morning when he'd got up, the harbor was lost under stifling fog, and the big horn on Hog Point kept going all morning, its steady long whump rising and ripping through the fog, the only thing strong enough to tear it apart.

Just before noon the wind had changed and come down in gusts from the northwest. Before it the fog drew out, uncertainly, leaving reluctant tatters along the shore and low down over the water. Now it had cleared out of the harbor altogether and the little whitecaps were beginning to kick up on the shallow water inside the channel. Low under the side of Pentacook there was still an arm of fog following the water inland. And outside the harbor mouth it lay still and waiting on the eastern horizon. The wind had backed around and that meant the gray fog would be back in again as soon as the calm settled down.

But at noon, here in the harbor, it was clear and blue and dazzling, and the gulls squabbling in droves above the factory were too bright to look at.

Bub had Lou to think about now—the way she'd been last night and her saying she loved him. He remembered how he'd been afraid of this happening because afterward she wouldn't want to look at him; but now all he could think of was, What am I letting myself in for?

"What's the matter?" Kelsey came to the door, his hair tousled and the glasses he wore to do his bookkeeping slipping down on his big nose. "Feelin sorta restless, ain't you?"

"Oh, I dunno."

" 'S this weather." Kelsey glanced to the eastward, sniffing, as if he expected his nose to tell him what the wind would do. "It's enough to give anyone an itchin heel."

He looked curiously at Bub's scowling face.

"You can't afford to go around feelin restless, son. Not if you're plannin on settlin down, like you say. You got to get over that business of pickin up and goin whenever you feel like it."

[191]

"Who said I was goin?"

"Why, nobody's I know of. I was just tellin you. When a man starts to have an investment in a place, he can't just pick up an get out from under. When you got an investment that means you got responsibilities, too."

"Investment!" Bub snorted. "I spose you mean that boat. Honest, sometimes I wonder if I'm crazy tryin to do anythin with that old tub. Besides, money ain't everythin, is it?"

"It's an awful lot." Kelsey took the glasses off and used them to gesticulate with. "That reminds me, I been meanin to talk with you for the last week or so. Come on inside, will you?"

Wondering, Bub followed him into the little cubicle of office Kelsey had. The plyboard that cut him off from the store didn't go all the way to the roof, it barely topped Kelsey's billiard-ball head when he stood up.

"Set down, set down," Kelsey said, and Bub settled loosely into the chair across the desk from the old swivel. For a minute or two neither of them spoke. Bub was resolved that Kelsey couldn't make him ask what this was all about; he was pretty sure it was unpleasant and he wanted Kelsey to bring it up first. So he sat there waiting, and watching with a certain resentful amusement Kelsey's big hands fumbling around with the loose time sheets on the desk. Kelsey's hands, the fingers thick and stubby and their backs covered with reddish hair, looked out of place handling papers. He kept glancing at Bub under his heavy brows, and when he found Bub staring back at him, he'd drop his eyes quickly to the desk. He put the glasses back on, pretending to hunt for something, and took them off again, twice. Finally he leaned forward over the desk, but he still wasn't looking directly at Bub when he began to talk.

"Bub, I got to tell you I'm surprised at you."

"That so?" Bub said cautiously, sure now that whatever was coming would be unpleasant. If he fires me, by god, I'll light out; I'll shake the dust of this place off my heels before I can spit.

"Yeah. How long ago was it you started workin here?"

"July."

"Yeah, that's right. Well, I'll tell you, I never thought for a minute you'd ever last out as long's you have."

"Or you wouldn't a hired me, that it?"

"No, that ain't it!" Kelsey shouted. "Whatta you mean, tryin to tell me what I wanta say?"

"Sorry." Bub's voice was light.

"When I say I'm surprised, I mean good, see? I'm pleased at the way you took hold, see? An you buyin this boat an all makes me think maybe I wasn't such a fool hirin you, after all. You know, don't you, what people said when I give you a job here?"

"I guess I got a pretty good idea. I ain't had much time, though, to listen to talk."

"You'd be better off if you would. You wanta know what people think of you, don't you?"

"Well, I know that too, pretty well," Bub said, surprised at himself for the loosening feeling of relief that went through him; he could feel his taut muscles letting go. Pete sake, he thought, looking at Kelsey's warm red face, who'd ever of thought he'd start talkin like this!

"Yeah, but d'you know what they're sayin about these robberies?"

"I heard about that. Hersh was tellin me," Bub grinned. "He says they're bound to think I done it. I can see why. I'm the only one's just come back to town and there warn't nothin like that goin on before I come. I never done it, though."

"All right," Kelsey said. "That's good enough. They's one other thing, though."

"Well, let's have it all to once."

"They's this girl down to the factry. Says she's goin to have a baby. Says the feller responsible told her his name was Bub Dolliver. Anythin to say about that?"

"That's what Bert was sayin just the other day." Bub felt his ears get warm. "Honest to god, Kelsey, I don't know nothin about it."

"I b'lieve you," Kelsey howled. He brought his fist down on the desk top with a crash that scattered papers wildly and made Bub jump. "I b'lieve that, by the Lord Harry. I been watchin you almighty close, Bub, an I don't think you been actin like a feller with a guilty conscience. But I just wanted to have it out with you an hear what you hed to say for yourself."

"Now you've heard."

"You got any idea who'd be doin things like that? Looks like someone didn't like you an was tryin to get you into trouble."

"I figure sooner or later whoever's doin it'll get his come-uppance, an then it'll be my night to howl," Bub said.

"Well, all's I hope is, you git the chance," Kelsey said. "That brings me to what I was intendin to say. How much you gittin, Bub?" He didn't wait for Bub to answer. "Twenty-five a week, ain't it? Well, I'm goin to give you a raise. I'm goin to give you thirty from now on."

I will be condemned! Bub thought. Kelsey handin out money and I never even asked him for it! He wasn't sure whether he was pleased or not, he was still feeling trapped, and this would make it worse.

"It may break me," Kelsey said mournfully, "what with taxes and everyone wantin more money an prices goin up. I'll probly be sorry. But I'm gonna give you thirty a week. I want to tell you right now, though, I want my money's worth out of you an this ain't gittin it." He got up and gestured widely toward the door. "Go on, git busy. From now on you work five dollars a week harder, see?"

Bub went without a word. He felt like laughing, but after a minute, he didn't. Hell, he thought, all that talk an then he had to go an spoil it in the last minute. If that ain't just like him. Just when he'd started feeling good and expansive about the whole business, Kelsey had to go and say the wrong thing and make him feel resentful and shut in again.

The gulls were still screaming, dazzling white, above the factory; the harbor was still that bright, bristling blue; but the foghorn had started up again, heralding the return of the thick, dripping whiteness. The long low arm of fog along the foot of the mountain hadn't gone out at all.

Bub was too busy that afternoon to think about his raise, but when he started up the hill at five o'clock he had the chance. And he was thinking, For twenty-five a week, I could afford to leave; for thirty, I can't.

[194]

He could see what had happened to him. That extra five dollars a week was like a gate closing behind him, a gate shutting him into respectability and responsibility. It was shutting him in with what he had wanted since he came back—but it had taken the gate so long to close that Bub wasn't sure he didn't feel more like a prisoner than a man who's got what he wanted.

He crossed the road to the garage, locked the gas tanks, and took a look inside before shutting the big rolling doors. He'd always looked inside since the night he'd found the uncovered tubful of gasoline Kelsey had left standing by the work bench. Bub had taken care of that, remarking bitterly to himself that Kelsey might have good sense about engines but he certainly didn't have it about gas.

He hesitated for a moment, his head stuck in through the door, sniffing. It seemed to him the smell of gas was stronger than it should have been. But he took a quick turn around the garage floor and found nothing that would make it stronger. The two big snowplows the town stored there were dim monsters in the unlighted dusk; and beside them stood one sheeted car and another uncovered. Kelsey kept one of his trucks here, too, but that stood down in back, near the mechanic's bench that ran along the windowed end of the building. Nowhere could he find anything that would make the strong smell of gas, and he decided it wasn't so strong as he'd thought at first.

Bub thought he was alone in the place until he sensed the shadow that crossed between him and the door, and turned, his heart going faster with surprise.

"Oh, it's you!" he said.

"Well, for pete sake, you don't sound very happy to see me. I ain't seen you since the first night you come home."

"That's all right with me, Mack," Bub said. "I thought you'd be gone by now. Ain't the hotel closed up?"

"Well, everyone's gone, but I'm stayin on there with a couple of other guys, just doin the things like puttin up shutters and stuff like that."

Bub watched Mack's eyes covering the garage, and there wasn't a thing Mack missed.

"Where you been keepin yourself, anyhow?" Mack asked.

"I been workin."

"Yeah, yeah, I know that; but I don't never see you around."

"I guess it's a good thing you don't. People see me around more, they'd spend even more time talkin about me."

"Why, what's up?"

"Oh, there's some kid down the factry's got in trouble an says I'm the one to blame." Bub stiffened, his eyes on Mack's face. There was a slight gleam in Mack's dark eyes that vanished almost before he saw it. "I don't spose—" Bub started slowly, watching, suspicion beginning to grow in his mind—"you'd know anythin about that, would you, Mack?"

"Judast," Mack said loudly, his eyes meeting Bub's soberly now and perfectly level. "I tell you, I wouldn't do a thing like that, Bub. Sides, when I have to go around them camps, it'll be the day. I can find better girls anywhere I want to."

"If I ever thought you done it, Mack, I'd have your hide," Bub said.

"I told you I never!" Mack was a picture of injured innocence. "Pete sake, I wouldn't get my own brother into trouble like that. You crazy? Come on, now, I never come down to fight with you. I just wanted to see if you was still alive."

"I am," Bub said. He went out and started closing the doors, forcing Mack out of the building.

"Ayeh." Mack thrust his hands into his pockets and waited while Bub snapped the lock shut and gave it a try, then he swung into step beside him. "Look, Bub," he said, "I'm—I come to see if you could let me have some dough. I'm pretty short right now."

"What the devil d'you do with it?" Bub turned on him. "You're makin more'n I am. No, I can't let you have none. I got me a boat I got to pay for now and I ain't givin you any of my dough to hell around on."

"Honest," Mack said, "you ought to hire you a church. You started preachin that first night and I see you ain't stopped yet."

"I ain't goin to neither. I know where I'm well off."

"I should say so," Mack said. "I hear you're walkin off with Joe Pettigrew's girl. Say, how is she, anyhow?"

Bub turned on him sharply, and Mack stopped in his tracks, his mouth gaping open.

"You shut up about her. If I hear you mention her again I'll knock your head off, Mack, an if you think I'm foolin, you just try it."

"Judast!" Mack said. He stopped where he was and let Bub go on without him. When Bub looked back, just before he turned the corner, Mack was still staring. He raised his hand in a mocking salute and turned away when Bub didn't answer it. As soon as Mack was out of his sight, Bub forgot him.

It wasn't Lou's night to watch at the spotter's shack and they'd planned to see each other, but something had happened, somebody got sick or something. Lou had called him that morning to say that she had to substitute for a woman who couldn't make it and would he mind. He did mind, but there hadn't been much he could say.

You'd think they really expected to see a flight of bombers coming in off the Atlantic, the way they acted. It seemed to him their eyes got a little brighter when they talked about it, almost as if the idea was exciting, maybe even pleasant. Not Lou, but some of the others he'd talked to—the fellows on the wharf, most of them were spotters or air raid wardens, and it made Bub a little sick to his stomach watching them talk about it. He agreed with the philosophy of Billy Newman. Billy wasn't much good but he was making his living now taking over the four-hour stretches of others at the spotter's shack. He got seventy-five cents an hour for it and most of the hours Billy slept.

All that time being wasted, Bub thought; for pete's sake, there's any number of things they could do that'd bring in results instead of just sitting around on their tails waiting for German bombers that won't come.

He felt superior about it, knowing what he did of war, and once or twice he'd made the mistake of saying something revealing to Lou. The first couple of times she'd snapped him up on it, getting riled and telling him just because he'd seen real action there wasn't any need for him to go around feeling he could make fun of those who couldn't fight but were trying to do the best they could at home.

[197]

"It ain't that," Bub had protested, "but they talk as if they'd be pleased if it really happened and maybe a plane dropped a couple of bombs on the Harbor. They look as if it was somethin to look forward to; and it ain't. It's awful!"

"Oh, don't be so superior," she said hotly. "They don't know what it's like. How could they? But they're trying to do a good job. You can't do anything about it, so why not let them have their fun?"

"Fun!" Bub protested. "My god, if that's their idea of fun!"

After that Lou seldom mentioned the plane spotting to him, but if she called him at the wharf and said she was going to be busy that night after all and they couldn't go to a show, or for a walk, or do whatever it was they'd planned, he knew what it was she was going to do instead, and it made him mad.

He ate supper at the diner thinking, sullenly, if she thought more of her foolish spotting than she did of him, maybe it was just as well he was getting out. Then he remembered that he wasn't getting out. He'd got a raise and he was going to stick it.

After he finished eating, instead of going home to work on the boat, Bub turned back down the wharf road and went on to Barron's place. He was getting thirty dollars now. He could afford a couple of glasses of beer.

The fog was back, thicker than it had been that morning, and the air felt cool and thick and hard to breath, like cotton wool soaked in cold water.

Bub went into the parlor defensively, making his face expressionless. He'd begun to notice people looking at him more curiously than they had, as if he were some peculiar breed, as if they were looking at him to find some mark that would tell them their suspicions about him were right. And the whole attitude was brought to a head by Steve Barron. Steve looked at him uncertainly now, as if he were trying to decide whether or not to let him in.

Bub found an empty booth, sat down, and ordered his beer. When the waitress brought it, he looked up at her and it wasn't the waitress at all. Nina had pulled her appearing act again.

"You must live here," Bub said, and watched her start to smile. "Mind if I join you, or would you rather be alone?"

"Set down." Bub made a quick backward motion with his head, meaning invitation. "I'd just as soon have company tonight." I'll show Lou, he was thinking, glad that Nina had turned up; I'll show her she can't go on standin me up forever.

He looked at Nina approvingly. She had on wide-legged slacks of some soft material that made them look almost like a skirt. And the fine wool shirt she wore with them made her brown skin look browner and cleaner than it usually did.

"You're the only woman I ever see could make pants look dressed up," he said appreciatively.

"I'm smart, that's why." She settled into the seat opposite him, her eyes appraising. "You on the town tonight?"

"Ayup."

"Well, that ain't no reason, is it, for lookin so down in the mouth?"

"Didn't know I was."

"You mean you could come in here lookin as if you was goin to a funeral an not know it? My gosh, I was almost afraid to speak to you at first."

"Funeral, hell!" Bub said sharply. "This here's goin to be a party."

He crooked his finger at the waitress.

"I'll pay mine," Nina said, reaching for her purse.

"Unh-unh. Got me a raise today. This's my party."

"For heaven sake, you mean you got more money out of Kelsey?"

Bud nodded.

"Well, *that* is swell. If I was you, I *would* celebrate. First time on record anyone ever got anythin out of him."

"I was surprised myself," Bub said. He felt suddenly like talking to her. He had a good mind to show Lou she wasn't the only girl in the Harbor. "I was surprised the way he talked. He said somethin about places bein broken into an I'll be darned if he didn't say he didn't think I done it."

"You ought to get that in writin," Nina said. "There's a good deal of talk goin around about that."

"So I heard. That don't bother me none."

"Well, it ought to," she said. "I've had enough of it an I know

[199]

it ain't nothin to laugh at. If you think the everlastin gossip in this town is somethin to laugh at, you jest take a look at Gladys Jennings."

"I should think they would talk about her." Bub glanced surreptitiously at the table in the shadowy corner where Gladys was busily starting her evening. "She gives em plenty to talk about."

"The talk," Nina said harshly, "started before Gladys did."

Bub glanced at Gladys again, and Nina made a sharp noise with her tongue.

"Don't let her see you lookin or she'll be over here to tell you the story of her life. An it ain't pretty. She was, though. You wouldn't b'lieve it to look at her now, would you?"

"Oh, I dunno," Bub said. "She wouldn't be bad-lookin now if she'd lay off so much drinkin."

"No, but she really was pretty—prettiest girl in town, once." Nina lowered her voice and leaned over the table so nobody could hear what she was saying. "She married Joe Coffin—you remember him? They got married jest after they got out of high school. An that warn't what Joey's mother was plannin for him, so she done it. His own mother!

"She started the story goin around how Gladys wasn't no good —you know, how she'd go out with anyone come along, an go out an stay all night, not gettin in till mornin. Joe hed a job then, drivin for Fred Pettigrew, so he was away a lot of the time. He didn't know what she was doin while he was gone, an he b'lieved his own mother. I guess you couldn't blame him.

"Then somebody wrote him a letter about how the baby wasn't his at all—it b'longed to an oiler off one of the sardine boats. An what with everythin, Joey b'lieved it. So he kicked her out—that was near ten years ago. The letter warn't signed, but I been willin to bet old lady Coffin knew where it come from."

"Oh, god," Bub said, "I remember now. I remember hearin about it when it happened, but I forgut."

"They don't care what they say so long's they can rip someone up the back." Nina finished her beer angrily. "It has to be somethin good an dirty, though, or it ain't worth sayin."

"How come they ain't got after you?" Bub raised a curious eyebrow.

"They have," Nina grinned suddenly. "The only difference is, I don't care what they say an I guess Gladys did. You know, the funniest part about it was, she really did use to look like Norma Shearer, almost exactly."

"Judast!" Bub shoved his glass away. "Come on, let's get outa here. Jest sittin here where I can watch her makes me sick."

"Where's there to go?"

"Come on down to my place." Bub didn't know what made him say it; then he looked at Nina again, and did know. "I got a boat now. You come on down an look at her."

"Well—" Nina hesitated thoughtfully, and Bub had an idea she knew what was going on in his mind. "All right. But I wouldn't want to get you in wrong with—anybody."

"Lissen—" he leaned over heavily—"I'm my own boss, see? The last time you was willin enough to come—so get a move on."

"All right—all right."

She got up and followed him across the room and out the door. Bub had the feeling that everyone in the room was watching them, he could sense eyes narrowly on his back, and Nina's silence made him think she felt it too.

"You see what I mean?" she said, once they were outside. "The men's every bit as bad as the women. There ain't one man in there tonight who won't go home an tell his wife you come in alone and come out with me."

"So what?"

Bravado made him say that, and now that he was out on the road alone with Nina, he wasn't so sure he wanted to be alone with her. She was one of the ones who kept you busy thinking about just one thing; she even had him busy thinking about it and it wasn't the way he thought about Lou. Dam, he thought viciously, I don't even want to think about Lou now. I'll show her she can't stand me up like that. Trying to reason it out, he thought, she'll see now when this comes out, she'll see I ain't what she thought I was.

"You goin to stand there all night? Much longer an it'll be so dark I won't be able to see that boat."

"You sure you want to?"

"I wouldn't be here if I didn't."

They went up the road and cut down through the gray mist-dripping alders. Their silence, Bub felt, wasn't even the same kind of silence he and Lou could have. This was tight and hot and unpleasantly alive. He was so acutely conscious of Nina moving along beside him that when his swinging hand touched hers and he felt the hot dryness of her palm, he snatched his hand away suddenly. Then he put it back again, trying not to let her see he'd snatched it away because it touched hers.

"What's the matter with you?" Nina said evenly. "Sort of nervous, ain't you?"

"Black flies," Bub said. He made another swipe through the air. "They bother me a lot."

"Pretty late in the season for them," Nina said thoughtfully. "You sure you want to show me this boat?"

"I'm old enough to know what I'm doin," Bub said, and they both knew he wasn't talking about the boat. I'm into this now, he thought, I might's well—

Nina leaned over the railing to look at the boat, just as Lou had. But when she straightened up, her face was disdainful.

"It's only a little one, ain't it?"

"Well, hell," Bub said defensively, "it's somethin. It's a beginnin. I got to start somewhere." He cut the words off when he remembered that was what Lou had said. He couldn't seem to get her out of his mind, the way she'd been down here just last night, how he'd felt when he kissed her. And here he was with *this* dame, here where he had been with Lou just the night before. Maybe I ain't such a good guy, he thought. Maybe I was the one was wrong an everyone else was right. But he didn't really want to act this way. There was something dark and resentful growing up in him and it made him do the things he was doing tonight. He felt as if he stood outside himself, watching with an inconclusive amazement the way he was acting.

He crossed over to Nina, who was standing back to him looking down at the boat again, and put his hands on her shoulders to turn her around.

"Now I know what you think of my boat," he said tightly, "tell me what you think of me."

"You know, dear," Nina said. "I've told you that. I told you

[202]

the first night down at Steve's. You ought to know that." Her eyes were half-shut, sleepy looking, but at the same time bright. She made it easy for him to kiss her, the way she melted against him and leaned back against his arms to look up at him. So he did it hard, trying to hurt her; but her lips were hot and soft, and he couldn't seem to hurt her at all. He felt her hands along his back, the fingers burning him through his shirt. She didn't have much on besides the shirt and slacks. Bub didn't know how he could tell that so easily. When he took his arms away and lifted his head, Nina didn't move; she just stood there against him, but she put up her hand, looking surprised, and touched her underlip lightly.

"It's bleedin," she said. "You tried to do that, didn't you?"

"Yeah."

"Darlin, darlin!" she said. "I hoped you'd—you need someone like me. You can see that. You don't want to go wastin your time—you wouldn't with me. See?"

If only she didn't push so, Bub thought weakly, feeling the way she grew up against him. This time the excitement was gone and he just felt sorry for himself—waiting for her to get through, to get tired and let go of him again. She was doing something with one hand, and when she took his wrist and brought his hand up, Bub found he'd been right. She didn't have anything on under the shirt.

"Here!" He pulled himself away, the word coming out sharply.

"What's wrong with you anyway?" Nina looked at him narrowly and her eyes weren't sleepy now. "Whatta you want?"

"Well, for godsake, what if somebody comes along? Button that shirt up, will you?"

"All right." Her voice was perfectly normal, but he could see she was blushing and her hands were uncertain on the small buttons. Thoroughly ashamed of himself and feeling a little sick, Bub reached out and tilted her head up so he could look at her. She looked as if she wanted to cry and he wasn't disgusted with her or with himself, now, just tired.

"Look, I'm sorry," he said. That didn't sound the way he'd wanted it to.

"I was afraid it wasn't any use," Nina said. "I could see from the beginnin it wasn't any use. I guess I just ain't her, ain't that it?"

Bub didn't answer and his silence told her more than she'd asked for.

"Well, this is right pretty," Batty said suddenly, appearing around the corner of the shack and beaming down on them.

Nina jumped and started to laugh helplessly.

"I don't know what it's like," she said, "but Forty-second Street and Broadway can't be much busier."

"What are you snoopin around here for?" Bub spun on Batty, grateful for something to take his feelings out on. "What the devil do you want, anyhow?"

"Now, now; calm down, son. I jest come down to pass the time of day with you. Maybe I oughter say night. It's quite near dark, ain't it. Didn't know you was gonna have company. Don't see how I could of."

"How long you been standin there listenin?" Bub took a long step toward him, and Batty backed away. Behind them Nina was laughing again. Batty held his hand up, palm out, pacifically.

"I jest come this minute," he said. "I jest got here. You ain't got no call to git excited. I ain't a talker an I don't go around spilling my guts, son. Not old Batty. I'll git along now. Sorry to interrupt."

"It's all right," Nina gasped, "I was just goin."

"Don't hurry." Batty waved his hand gently and Bub nearly started after him again. But he vanished into the woods and they could near him crashing noisily away through the under-brush. Apparently he'd missed the path and was taking a short cut.

When Bub turned to face Nina, she was laughing again.

"I don't see what's so funny," he growled.

"Well, if you don't, I can't help you out. But it really was funny, in a way."

"Maybe."

"All right," Nina said. "I'm goin."

"You don't have to hurry." Bub let the conventional phrase go before he thought, and then hoped she wouldn't take him seriously. She didn't. She said good night and started up the path.

"Wait a minit," he called after her, "I'll walk back with you."

"No need to," Nina said without turning her head. She lifted her hand slightly in what might have been a wave and went on unhesitatingly into the alder path. Bub stayed where he was, looking after her, relief strong enough to be an actual taste in his mouth. Judast, he thought, what a fool I am!

He had just turned away to go into the shack when he heard the quick sound of someone coming along the path where Nina had disappeared, somebody coming at a run. He glanced back to see her flash out of the woods, slow down, and come down across the field at a walk.

"What's the matter?"

"Well," Nina got her breath back and started to laugh again. "I guess you better walk back to the road with me, after all."

"What's wrong?" Bub tried to read her face, but she was laughing too hard.

"I don't know how long he'd been there," she said, "but I guess he thought he'd finish what you started. Batty's up there along the path waitin for me."

"Why, that old kooter!" Bub began to see the funny side of it, too. Laughter made his face feel tight. "That old devil. I'll fix him!"

"No, wait a minit." Nina put her hand on his arm restrainingly. "No need to start trouble. Just walk up with me. He won't do nothin with you there."

Batty was there all right. Bub made him out, standing beside the path waiting, but when he heard their voices, he disappeared, melting back into the darkness of the trees.

"Well, good night," Nina said, when they hit the tarred road. "You forget this tonight an we can still have a glass of beer together now and then, can't we?"

"Don't see why not," Bub said. But he knew that he never wanted to set eyes on her again. Even at that, she'd been a lot decenter than a lot of other girls would have, he thought, turning to go back down the path alone.

THE LADIES AID met every two weeks at the Parish House. Ostensibly they were there to work together; they were knitting sweaters now to go overseas somewhere. But there were a few of them who liked to get there a little early to get in a hand of bridge before they settled down to knitting.

Alice Scott and Celia Newman were playing partners against Ida Baker and Abby Fennelly at the table set up in the big front window. It was nearly one-thirty, and Abby, looking out on the street as she did whenever she got the chance, spotted Lou Jellison just going back to work.

"There goes Lou Jellison," she said.

They all turned to look after Lou, who was in a hurry and had already passed nearly beyond their range of vision.

"Had her dinner late today most likely," Celia said.

"Oh, I don't know. She usually comes up about twelve-thirty. I see her go by my window every day," Alice Scott nodded her head vigorously.

"Well, I spose she can keep what hours she wants to on that job, seein Joe's so soft on her."

"I think Lou'd be real smart to take him," Celia said thoughtfully. "Joe must be pretty well off—will be, anyhow, when his father dies—an he's certainly a good steady boy. You couldn't ask for a better."

"Lou's pretty choosey, though."

"Choosey, humph!" Alice said. "If Joe knows where he's well off, he'll be the one to be choosey."

"What d'you mean, Alice?"

"Well, of course you ought to know who it is Lou's been goin around with, to the movies and walkin and all. Bub Dolliver."

"Yes, I know it. An Edna so strong against all them people. Why, she'd never so much as speak to one of them. You suppose she knows Lou's taken up with him?"

"Says she does," Alice said smartly. "I thought it was only fair to tell her about it an she nearly snapped my head off. Said it was Lou's business and *she* didn't have nothin against Bub."

"I guess you know, don't you, they's a girl down to the factry goin to have a baby an it's his?"

"My lord, didn't take him long, did it, once he got back."

"Well, she was sayin it," Alice Scott said regretfully, "but I guess it warn't so. They say her father went draggin her down to the wharf one day to face Bub with her. An she took one look at him and starts to cry an says he ain't the one at all."

"How'd you know that?"

"Kelsey's wife told me. They asked Kelsey where Bub was, so Kelsey pointed him out. But when the girl see he warn't the one, she wouldn't go near him. I guess Bub never even knowed they was there."

"If it warn't Bub, then who was it? Seems funny she was so sure it was him."

"He, Kelsey, says the girl said the feller done it was darker than Bub an not so thin—know what I think?"

"Maybe it was the youngest one."

"I don't b'lieve it," Celia said. "Why, he's a real nice boy—always with a smile an a polite word. I don't know where he ever got his manners. Besides, he ain't no more'n sixteen."

"Sixteen or sixty," Abby said tartly, "he's a male, ain't he? And *I* think he's the one. Probly said his name was Bub just to make trouble."

"Well, I don't know—Bub was always the troublemaker of them two—always into somethin from the very beginnin."

"Yes 'n I can tell you, if I was Edna Jellison, I'd keep an eye on any girl of mine had anythin to do with that trash."

"You know," Abby looked complacently at her partner, "I always said it was a mistake to send kids away to school. Especially girls. Now you take mine. Not a one of em's been beyond high school, an here they are, all married to good boys an settled down. An Ted, of course, he's overseas."

Alice Scott didn't say anything to that, but behind her sharply watchful eyes she was figuring hastily. It always had seemed to her that Abby's girls had been in an almighty rush to get married. She'd done some counting then, and she was pretty sure why it was.

"I think you're right," Celia said emphatically. "I tell you what, I wouldn't want no daughter of mine to go traipsin off to the city for two years, schoolin or no schoolin."

[207]

"You never know what they're doin while they're away from you that long."

"She was livin with her cousin, wasn't she?" Ida said easily.

"Yes, but—well, maybe nothin happened, but they get funny ideas sometimes, goin off like that. Wouldn't it be awful for poor Edna if Lou passed up Joe an took up with Bub Dolliver —maybe even married him?"

"Are you goin to play bridge or are you goin to sit here rippin everyone up the back?" Ida's voice was cool.

"Well, I don't know's you'd call it that, Ida," Abby put her cards down. "I've got sort of a headache, though. I don't know's I feel like playin cards today."

"All right—" Ida got up and stood leaning her hands on the table—"but I want to say this. My Hersh works at the same place with Bub Dolliver an he sees him every day. He says he's a decent kid an works hard and I don't know what more you can ask for. That's a lot more than you can say about a lot of the boys who grew up in this town." She turned and left them staring after her.

"Mercy!" Celia said quickly, covering up the reference to other boys, "what ails the girl?"

"Oh, you know how they are when they're carryin," Alice said easily. "I don't hold nothin Ida says against her now. It's only to be expected, specially with the first."

"Speakin of boys," Abby said, leaning over the table, "I spose you've heard about what young Lyford Jellison done the other day."

"I did," Alice said, "an I think it was the awfullest thing I ever heard. Not decent."

Celia looked down at her cards and laid them on the table, preserving the fan shape carefully.

"I didn't hear," she said. "What was that?"

"Well, he went up to the old Congo Church there above the sawmill with a slingshooter and he busted every single one of them lovely stained-glass windows out of it."

"The Congo Church!" Celia gasped, unbelieving.

"Yes, ma'am, the church. Mrs. Atherton was tellin me about it. She hed to sit there an watch him because he didn't hear

[208]

her when she yelled. She said he was just like a madman. He just stood there an shot them out, one after the other."

"Honest," Abby said, "I think somethin ought to be done about a thing like that. After all, we all got an interest in anythin like a church, an that's the oldest one in town."

"That church's been a landmark in this town for years. It's shameful to let kids get away with anythin like that."

"That's just how I feel," Alice said. "That old church's really important to the histry of this town. Why, if we let kids do things like that, there'll be no stoppin em."

"Yes," Abby nodded, "'n if it was any kid but Edna Jellison's he'd be in the reform school before you could say Jack Robinson. As it is, I guess they ain't goin to do nothin to him. Exceptin make him pay for the windows."

"There won't be no replacin that old colored glass—that was unusual. It's pretty awful when the property of the church don't get any respect."

"Well, what can you expect from these kids growin up? Not one of em worth the powder. I don't see how Edna Jellison gets to brag about her kids being so nice. Seems to me they ain't a bit better than a lot of others I could name, nor so good."

"Ssst," Alice said sharply, getting up. When Edna passed the big window and went toward the door, they were busily putting the cards away; they looked up to smile at her and she smiled and nodded back. But she recognized the pleased air of satisfaction about them and knew what they had been doing.

ON WEDNESDAY NIGHTS the barber shop was open late, until nine o'clock, and Hersh usually went in after supper to have his weekly store shave and haircut. He was late that Wednesday and it was nearly closing time before he opened the screen door and tossed his cap over one of the long row of hooks.

"I was afraid you warn't comin in tonight, Hersh." Bob

busily wrapped the bib around his chest and started messing around with the shaving soap.

"Don't mean to say my half-a-dollar'd make that much difference, do you, Bob? My gosh, if I thought you was in such a bad shape financially I'd a been in sooner, so's you wouldn't have to worry."

"Course that's most important," Bob said. "But I been meanin to see you for the last week or two. I was beginnin to figure I'd never git around to it. They was too many in here last Wednesday to talk to you."

"Nope," Hersh said.

"No, what?"

"I ain't runnin for no school board."

"Wrong again; I wouldn't even try to make you run for that just in case you might happen to win. I'd be scared of what'd become of the school." The razor made its first rasping sweep across Hersh's face, leaving a smooth pink stinging track behind it. "No, I been meanin to talk to you about Bub Dolliver."

"What you got to say about him?" Hersh's voice wasn't amused any more. "I better tell you, I like that guy."

"That's why I picked you to talk to," Bob said. "I'd rather talk to somebody likes him for a change."

"Well, then—go ahead."

"It's about this trouble we been having. People are getting to talk quite a lot around how Bub's doin it. I want to know right straight whether you think he is. You're pretty level, Hersh, what you think?"

"I think he ain't." Hersh's voice came so quickly after Bob's stopped that if it hadn't been for the difference in tone, it might have been the same voice going on without pause. "I don't know who is, but I know it ain't him."

"Joe Pettigrew seems to have a different idea."

"Joe! For chrissake, what's he got to do with it?"

"He's been havin it around how he wants somethin done before Bub takes it into his head to go breakin into the factory. Joe wants him run outa town."

"Why wouldn't he?" Hersh asked angrily. "Here Bub comes back and gets hisself a job an starts settlin down, bought hisself a boat, too. Then he starts walking off with Joe's girl right under Joe's nose—an he knocks Joe's young brother galley west in a fight, even if he was wounded. It warn't much of a fight, the kid hit his head on a timber, but Bub walked away."

"Wounded! What the devil you talkin about? Bub hisself's been sayin he warn't in the Army."

"Oh, judast!" Hersh shouted, "I warn't supposed to spill that, an now you've gone an made me. Honest to god, you talk wors'n an old woman. I spose I better tell you the rest of it now. He was in the Marines. He got hurt on Guadalcanal, an he's jest been outta the hospital a little while. I see his side where it got him an it looks like he'd been chewed up in a thrashin machine."

"I be damned! You mean to say he's been through somethin like that an never said a word about it?"

"He said he didn't want to trade on that. I think he's nuts. Anyone been through what he has an come back to try and settle down ought to be give a decent chance to do it. An he would, too, if he warn't a Dolliver."

"We-ell, where'd he git the dough to buy a boat, if he's been behavin?"

"Oh, for pete sake, you ain't no better than the rest of em. He's been workin, ain't he? It ain't much of a boat; it only cost him a hundred an seventy-five an he only paid seventy-five down on her. I spose he could come by seventy-five dollars honest, couldn't he?"

"Don't go gettin huffy, Hersh. You jiggle around so I might cut your throat. I just wanted to know about it, that's all. I just wanted to see what was going on so's I'd know what to say to Joe, see? I ain't any fonder'n you are of seein a man get kicked around when he ain't got it comin to him. But you know just because a man fought in the war an got wounded, that ain't any reason to take it for granted he's perfect afterwards."

"I know that," Hersh said impatiently, "an Bub knows it, too. That's probly why he ain't done any talkin. But jest the same, Joe wants to look out before he goes takin the law into his own hands. He has to prove something like that before he

[211]

goes around shootin his mouth off. He can't jest say someone done it because he don't like him."

"Ayeh," Bob wiped the last of the soap off and folded the cloth, "that's just what I told him, Hersh. Just exactly."

BUB waited a whole week before trying to see Lou again. He had a lot of thinking to do, and besides, he wanted to get the taste of Nina out of his mouth before he went near Lou.

That business with Nina had taught him one thing he couldn't forget, and the thing he couldn't forget was Lou, no matter what he did—and now he didn't want to forget her. All the time he hadn't been thinking about Nina at all, he'd been remembering Lou and thinking what a fool he was to try and make a mess of something it had taken him this long to build up. He had known it wouldn't be fair to let Lou think he meant one thing while all the while his mind was busy wondering how he was going to get out of the trap he'd walked into. But it had taken him only a week to know the trap wasn't a trap at all—it was something he'd built himself and walked into with his eyes wide open.

He'd done his thinking and he'd made his mind up once and for all—and here he was right back where he'd started. He wanted Lou. But there was a difference now. He not only wanted her, he'd made up his mind he was going to get her if he had to kidnap her to get her away from Curtis.

Curtis was going to be the hardest nut to crack. Bub knew where he was with Lou all right, and in about five minutes he was going to tell her where she was with him.

He was sitting on the ledge just in the edge of woods that made a narrow lock up the factory hill to the road. Pretty soon now she'd be coming up to go home to supper. Now that he was going to see her again, he could tell how much he'd missed not seeing her this last week. Pleasure at the thought of talking to her again, mixed with relief that he hadn't ruined the whole business, made his knees feel rubbery and weak.

Funny, too, how much difference five dollars a week could make to the way you looked at things. That wasn't much money, really, but it made an awful big difference. It meant that he was making more than she was for one thing, and he had to have that assurance. It wasn't just more money, it was a sign he wasn't going to be stuck in a rut all his life.

He'd sort of started looking at things different, too. That talk Lou'd made about how it wasn't her father who wanted to marry him, and how she didn't care what his family was like, that was straight. It was foolish to talk about anyone being better than anyone else just because of what his people were like. That didn't make any never mind.

After all, he knew better than Curtis did what he felt and thought like now. He wasn't a kid any longer, he wasn't a fresh kid who didn't know where he was or what he was doing half the time.

And he was getting what he wanted, little by little, but getting it. In this last week he'd got something more, he'd got a self-respect that he'd never had before. He didn't know what it was, but he knew it made him feel different, it was something that made him feel calm and sure. It made him feel as if he was as good as anybody and he didn't have to bow down to anyone.

He saw Lou coming up the road then and he got up to meet her.

She didn't look surprised to see him, just happy. He stood without speaking for a minute to see her slow smile start up. When it came, he felt faintly a stirring of the same feeling he'd had the other night when she kissed him.

"Hello, darling," Lou said. She came over and took his hand openly. "This is nice."

She didn't look embarrassed and he liked her for that. She just seemed glad to see him.

"Seems as if it's been an awful long time since I've seen you."

"A whole week," she said—and she didn't say, Where've you

[213]

been? She waited to show him he could tell her or not, just as he pleased.

"I been workin hard," he said, with a flash of laughter. "I got to earn my five dollars more a week."

"Oh, Bub, how swell; you got a raise."

"Umhum. Thirty bucks a week now."

"That's one of the best things that's happened to you since you came back," Lou said musingly. "I think it'll turn out to mean a whole lot more than five dollars more a week."

"It has already." Bub looked down, watching her eyebrows wrinkle the way they did when she was being serious.

"You're making more than I am now. Let's see—thirty a week —Why—you could—we could—"

"What?" he said, knowing perfectly well what she'd started to say and wanting to hear her finish it.

"You could support a nice economical wife on that, couldn't you?"

"Maybe," he grinned. "Know anyone fits the description?"

"You mean you want me to pick you out a wife?"

"Ayup."

"Well," Lou looked thoughtful, "there are a lot of nice girls."

"I'll settle for one."

"Then I know just the one for you. She's not too pretty, but she'd be a very good cook. And economical! You wouldn't believe it. She thinks you're sort of homely, too. But—" Lou's voice lost volume suddenly and she looked away—"she loves you very much."

"Sounds nice when you say it that way."

"Oh, Bub!" She snatched her hand away from his loose grasp.

"Sure she ain't after me for my money?" he teased.

"Well, that's definitely a consideration," Lou said stiffly.

"What's her name? I have to have one with a pretty name. In fact," Bub stared thoughtfully into distance, "there's just one name would do."

"Whatever it is, it'll be hers," Lou said. "She's accommodating. She'd even change her name if you didn't like it."

"Sounds sort of wishy-washy to me."

"No, she has a vicious temper and she's very bossy."

[214]

"Well, it's all off then. You can tell her to go jump in the lake. I can't go takin up with a domineerin woman."

"You're too particular. You won't be able to find anyone to fill the bill," Lou said. "I guess you'll just have to go on being a bachelor."

"Nope," he shook his head, "you just ain't very good at pickin wives for me. I was foolin you all along, I got the one picked out already."

"Oh, just leading me on."

"Ayuh. All I got to do now is get up my courage to ask her an then go tell her old man I'm going to marry his bee-yew-ti-ful daughter."

"Hmm. Well, do you want me to tell you what to say to her?"

"Nope. I got that all thought out, too."

"Well?"

"Curious, ain't you? Well, I'm goin to say to her 'Lissen, babe, take it on de lam wid me an we'll git hitched.'"

"You think she'd like that?"

"She better."

"Why don't you try it on her, then?"

"All right. Will you, Lou? It seems I just can't get along without you to boss me around."

"Yes," she said. "Yes, I will, before you change your mind."

"I won't change it. It's made up for good and all."

"Are you sure?"

"Course I'm sure, for pete sake."

"Well, then, I've got a little surprise for you."

"So soon!" he reeled back in pretended dismay.

"Now be serious," she said, but she was blushing. "It's just that I—well, I'd like to be married at home."

"Now, Lou, look," Bub started, his face completely serious now, "I don't think that'd be the smart thing to do."

"Well, what *do* you think?"

"What we oughta do, seein how your old man feels about me, is go off to Freehold and get married there and then come back an tell him about it when it's all done—not before, like this. If we tell him now, you know what kind of a fuss he'll put up."

"I don't like that," Lou said. "It's sort of like sneaking off, as if we had something to be ashamed of an we haven't. Besides, you don't know Ma. If any one of us kids did a thing like that it'd kill her."

"Well," Bub thought that over, "course, there's that. My gosh, I never realized gettin married would be so complicated. I wisht I was a cave man, then I could just come an drag you off."

"You know how it'd be, too, if we went off to Freehold that way. Everyone in town would have it over an have his little say, and they'd all decide just why it was we had to do it that way. That'd be worse for Ma than any other part of it."

"It wouldn't be so hot for you, neither, would it?" Bub kicked viciously at a stone and watched it bounce away along the tar and peter off into the ditch. "People never seem to let other people alone. Well, all right, but you know what kind of a rig we'll have to run before your father'll let me in the house."

"I'd rather run it before than after," Lou said. She grabbed his hand and held it tight. "Come on, now. We'll talk to him this very minute. Let's start it as soon as we can and it'll be over sooner."

"Gosh, I didn't realize we come this far," Bub looked up. Without noticing it, he had followed her to her front gate. And when he glanced up, he could see the curtains move hastily in the front window where Curtis sat. "You think I better see him now? He's settin in there watchin us."

"I know he is," Lou said. "He's always waiting there when I get home at night. And I don't know any better time than now, do you?"

"I spose not. But he's still pretty sick," Bub managed a pale grin. "I feel like I was goin to the dentist. I'm scared."

"So'm I." Lou's voice didn't sound like her—it sounded shadowy and as if it might fade out. "You coming?" Without looking at him, she started up the walk, so he followed her. They reached the door and it opened inward before them, telling Bub that Curtis hadn't been the only one watching them. Edna looked at them curiously, her eyes beginning to be worried.

"What is it, Lou?" she said nervously.

[216]

"Nothin, Ma. We just want to talk to Dad is all. Maybe you better come along too, because I want you to hear it."

Edna plucked at her loose full underlip, her eyes on Bub.

"It's all right," he said, because she looked more nervous than he felt.

Curtis was sitting in the heavy chair just to one side of the front window and his eyes were fastened on the door through which they had to come. Lou went first and Bub followed her. Behind them, Edna peered over their shoulders, her face puzzled and beginning to look sad.

"Hello, Pa!" Lou went over and kissed his cheek. Curtis bore it, but he was looking at Bub.

He don't look very well, Bub thought. He still looks like an awful sick man. In spite of himself, his eyes flashed down to the lax pant leg where there was no foot. He'd planned not to look at that but he couldn't help himself.

"How's Joe?" Curtis asked, his eyes level and bright on Bub to see how he was going to take that.

"Joe's all right," Lou said. "He wants to come in and see you soon's he gets the chance."

"Guess he don't have much time for lallygaggin around, does he?"

"He's pretty busy, Pa."

That was for me, Bub thought. He stepped forward and stood looking down on Curtis.

"I dropped in just for a minute," he said. "I wanted to talk to you, Curtis."

"You didn't have much to say the other night," Curtis said evenly. "I don't know why you'd have more now."

"Pa—" Lou sounded worried.

"I told you he could come here," Curtis said to her, "but I never said I'd talk to him when he did."

"You ain't got to talk to me," Bub said. "All you got to do is listen." He was getting a little tired of this. After all, Curtis didn't have anything to be so high and mighty about. "I got somethin to tell you."

"Well, I can't very well stop you." Curtis looked at Edna,

[217]

who was still standing in the doorway tugging at her lip. "You know what this is all about, Edna?"

"No, I don't. But if you'd listen instead of makin so much fuss, maybe we could find out," she said.

Bub looked at her in surprise. That sounded a little more like the way her eyes looked; that sounded more like Lou.

"All right," Curtis said. He looked out the window, away from Bub. "What is it?"

Bub took a deep breath, sensing that Lou had moved back until she could just touch his limp hand with one finger.

"I want to marry Lou," he said, the words coming out louder than he'd intended them to.

Behind him, he heard Edna's breath go in in a sharp explosive sound, and then, for so long a time that he was afraid nobody was going to say anything, there was absolute silence in the room, thick and stifling silence. Nobody said anything. Nobody moved. Then, when the stillness had started to scream in their ears, Curtis reached down and got his crutches. It was an effort for him to hoist himself out of his chair, and Lou made a motion as if to help him, and then stopped. He made it at last and stood erect on the crutches, his shoulders pushed up and his big head sunken between them.

When he finally looked at Bub, his eyes were small-looking and red in the dim light. Judast, Bub thought, I thought he just didn't like me. But he wasn't facing dislike now and he knew it; it was hatred that was so deep it was almost speechless. He could see that Curtis was trying to say something, the thick cords in his throat moved but nothing came out. When he got his voice back, it was thin and reedy.

"I thought they was somethin like this comin. That'd be jest what you wanted, wouldn't it? Marry some girl like Lou, somebody too dam good for you. My daughter may be a fool—I never thought she was—but I'm afraid this shows she is. But I ain't. I wouldn't let her marry you if I thought she'd never git married, and that's final."

"Pa," Lou said, "you can't talk like that. I'm of age."

"Curtis, that ain't no way—" Edna began.

Curtis swung his head from one of them to the other like a bull.

"Shut up," he yelled, losing control of his voice completely. "I'm the one who's sayin. An I say if I ever catch you around here again, Dolliver, so help me God, I'll take after you with a shotgun. Now, you git outa here and you let my girl alone."

Bub glanced at him steadily, his eyes calculating, then he said, "All right." He didn't look at Lou or Edna; he brushed past them and went out the door and down the hall. He thought he could hear the silence closing in again when he closed the front door carefully behind him.

For a moment, in the startled hush after Bub had gone, Lou was too shocked to move. She hadn't expected this—anything but this; and now that it had happened, she was too surprised to think. When realization of what Bub had done hit her, she spun with a quick little gasp and ran for the stairs.

"Lou!" her mother called after her.

"Lou, you come back here," Curtis shouted.

She heard them both but she kept on going up the stairs and into her bedroom. She shut the door and locked it before going over to the window. She was just in time to see Bub's thin straight back disappear around the corner.

She started to cry and didn't realize it herself until the warm wetness on her hands made her put one hand up to her cheek slowly. She turned away from the window and lay down flat on the bed, her hands under her head, staring at the ceiling. Over the bureau was the pale brown stain that made the map of Africa and that always came back no matter how many times they fixed it.

Outside on the landing, Edna stood silently, straining her ears for some sound from Lou's room. She'd followed her upstairs and had been standing there listening ever since. She'd heard Lou move to the bed. Now there was nothing, and Edna stood listening and wondering just what she could do.

For the first time in her life one of her children had raised a situation that left Edna speechless and at a loss. Before this there had always been a formula solution for family rows; but this time there wasn't, and Edna's mind was one that worked best to a formula. Now she just didn't know.

She knocked on the door lightly and stood waiting. At first there was no answering movement inside the room, nothing but that oppressive dead silence. Edna knocked again, and Lou's voice came faintly in answer.

"Mother?"

"Let me in, dear."

"Look, Moms, go away. I don't want to talk right now."

"Lou, please let me in."

"Oh, all right," Lou said impatiently, and Edna heard the springs creak as she got up and came across the room. She turned the key in the lock and evidently returned to the bed without opening the door. For a long moment Edna stood with her hand on the knob wondering whether she'd be smarter just to go away and let Lou alone. This entire affair had been embarrassing to her and she had an idea it would be more so if she did what her heart told her to and opened the door. She dropped her hand from the knob, turned half away, and then, with the suddenness of impulse, turned back and opened the door.

Lou was lying face down on the bed, and she didn't move when her mother came in. Edna realized that Lou had been hoping she wouldn't come in and had been purposely rude, relying on her rudeness to make Edna change her mind. Edna stood there wanting to go over and sit down on the edge of the bed and take Lou in her arms as if she were still a baby. But you can't do that when your kids are old enough to be thinking about getting married—that automatically removes them from the children you could still treat like babies.

"Lou, dear," Edna began tentatively. There was no answer, but Lou's whole back stiffened as if she had set herself against the words. In a sudden flood of embarrassment Edna looked away from her, glancing around the room, barely noticing what she did but thinking that its impersonality was like Lou. The room hid itself beneath a lot of things that could have belonged to anybody; it was like a room in a tourist house, unrevealing, taciturn, and not giving anything away. It was like Lou herself and, realizing that, Edna thought she saw how to handle her.

"Look," she said again. She went over to the bed and stood looking down at the girl without touching her. "This ain't like you, Lou. And this ain't no way for you to act. You're behavin like a baby that can't have the first thing it wants."

Lou gasped at the unaccustomed tone of firmness in her mother's voice and sat up, staring. Edna saw immediately that for once her intuition had been right, but she didn't know quite what to say next.

"Wh- what?" Lou said blankly.

"Well, why don't you behave sensible," Edna said briskly. "Instead of gettin all upset and rucked up, why don't you set down an see if there ain't somethin you can do about it?"

"What on earth can I do?" Lou protested. "Both Pa and Bub are actin foolish, like a couple of roosters."

"Well," Edna settled slowly down on the edge of the bed, "I got to admit I think your Pa's wrong about Bub. But are you sure you're right, Lou? This gettin married, well, you got to realize it's for good an all. And you got to give yourself time to be sure."

"I am sure," Lou said. "I've known Bub since I was a kid."

"Well, that's not the same thing, is it? You never use to like him as I remember."

"No. You're right. It's not the same thing at all. But I'm sure. He's different than he was. He's like another person, Mom. He's not the same at all."

"He does *seem* different, I'll have to admit that. But they's so many things we don't know about. He's been away five years, Lou. He's what? Twenty-three now? Them's usually the most important years in anyone's life—what a person does durin those years is apt to be a pretty good way to judge what they're goin to be like. We don't know anythin about that with Bub."

Lou straightened up and shoved her hair back impatiently.

"I know where he's been," she said. "He told me that first night. Didn't you ever wonder why he wasn't in the Army? Well, I'll tell you. He was on Guadalcanal. He was wounded. And he'd just got out of the hospital when he came back here."

"If that's so," Edna said judiciously, "I should think he'd be

[221]

proud of it enough to brag about it instead of actin like it was something to be ashamed of."

"I told him that. But he thinks people'll say he's being too big for his own good, swelling around like that. He wanted them to take him the way he was."

"There's all this trouble that's started, too, since he come back."

"Look, Mom," Lou got up and stood looking down at her mother, "I guess you don't see how it is. I know what Bub is like now—and that's all that matters. I don't care what his people were, what he used to be like, or what people are saying about him now. I've made up my mind and that's all there is to it."

"You mean that, don't you?" Edna, looking up at her daughter's sober, set face, felt somewhere so deep inside that it hardly reached her senses, a stab of something she couldn't quite analyze. It made her wish momentarily that she herself could have felt like this about somebody once, no matter who it was. She had always been able to consider various outside things; but never in her life had she felt the way Lou did now, and she recognized it and wanted to change it. Her long lifetime spent in search of something better than she had, made her say the wrong thing.

"I wish you didn't, Lou. He may be all right—but he's not good enough. He hasn't had the education you have either. You'll see someday how right me and your Pa were, sayin no."

Once and for all she had aligned herself with Curtis and now it was too late to go back. Regretfully she watched Lou's face harden against her. She got up from the bed feeling older and clumsier than she was, and went out, leaving Lou alone.

WHEN BUB had walked out of Curtis's house leaving the silence behind him, he had done it because of that one revealing look at Curtis's face. He knew then where he stood with Lou's father and where he would always stand unless he did something more active than talk to him. He wasn't afraid of Curtis and he wasn't deeply surprised that things had turned out the way they had—he'd been expecting something very much like it. But he was sorry he couldn't have said something to Lou before he went. Leaving her alone there without a word, that had been bad; but it would have been much worse if he'd tried to speak to her then. He could remember her unbelieving eyes on his face when he went past her, and that wasn't good, either.

At five minutes past nine the next morning, as soon as he was sure she'd be in the office, he called the factory. Her voice over the phone sounded dull and as if she didn't care what happened. It was sort of new, Bub thought, for him to be the one to pick *her* up. Usually it was just the other way around. Now that it was different, it seemed to him he loved her more than ever.

"Lou, this is me," he said.

"I didn't know whether you'd call or not." She managed to sound a little huffy, and Bub's mouth quirked up uncontrollably, but he kept his voice sober.

"Don't go soundin as if this was the end of the world," he said. "That was just the first battle."

"Looked like the last one to me."

"Well, don't depend on that. How can I see you tonight?"

"I don't know," she hesitated. "D'you want to?"

"You devil," he said. "If I could reach you right now, so help me, I'd turn you right over my knee. An you deserve it, too. Now, you come down tonight—we better go down to my place. I'll be there waitin and you come down as soon's you can."

"Well, I'll try. He won't like it if I go out. I could say I was meeting Joe. I never was very good at lying to him."

"Well, you try anythin just so long as you get out. I'll be there all night, an you better turn up."

"We'll see," Lou said, and hung up.

Bub was still smiling when he put the receiver back on the hook. By gosh, she still had the pep to stand up to him. He liked that.

Bub went directly home that night. There was still an hour and a half of light that he could use. He had started painting the boat now and was anxious to put every spare minute into working on her. He was so interested in what he was doing and

[223]

so positive that Lou would come that he didn't start worrying until the patrol planes went over. They were late, too, he saw. It was nearly eight o'clock and there were no signs of her.

He sat up and stuck the paintbrush into the can. Maybe she's not coming after all, he thought. Moodily he started taking paint off his hands with the turpentine-soaked rag. Maybe the old devil wouldn't let her out of the house for fear she'd try to see me or I'd try to see her.

But he heard her feet on the wharf above him, recognizing her step, and knew that she'd waited just to make him wonder whether or not she was coming at all. She went to the door of the shack and evidently looked in. Then he heard her come back and over to the edge of the wharf.

Bub got up and climbed up the ledges to the wharf. Lou wouldn't turn her head to look at him, she kept staring down at the little boat.

"She's beginnin to look like somethin now she's got a little paint on her," Bub said. "I'm real encouraged."

"You didn't want to talk to me about that, did you?" Lou still sounded a little touchy. Well, he knew how to handle that. So, he did. And he knew that no matter how much she wanted to be angry with him, she couldn't be. Her face felt wet under his, and Bub let her go and lit a match to hold it up.

"You're cryin," he said unbelievingly.

"I am not," Lou denied so fiercely that he blew the match out quickly.

"Look, darlin, nothin's happened yet. You don't have to go feelin bad."

"You let him scare you," Lou said. "You ran away from him."

"Well, I'll be damned," Bub said helplessly. He'd thought she might be thinking a lot of things, but that wasn't one of them. "Look, you little idiot, I didn't run away, darn it. But I see his face, Lou, an you didn't. I've seen people look the way he did before. And when they look like that, it just ain't no use tryin to talk to them. They just get worse."

He stopped but Lou was silent.

"I been thinkin about it. It simply ain't goin to be a bit of use tryin to wear him down, Lou, because he won't wear. You

[224]

see, he's still sick, an he's sort of not feelin good, an he won't be till he gits back to work again. If you want to wait till then, why we might stand some chance talkin to him, but not now. Do you want to wait?"

"You know I don't," Lou said, and all the traces of anger with him were gone. "I want to do what you do."

"Well, that's all right then. Now, I been thinkin—" Bub stopped short. When he'd first thought of this, it had seemed the solution. But now that it came to telling Lou about it, he just couldn't find the words.

"You said that before." She sounded as if she was smiling.

"Yeah, I know. Look, Lou, how much do you trust me?"

"You ought to know that."

"No, that ain't what I said. I said 'trust' me."

"More than anyone else."

Bub put his arms around her and pulled her against him hard.

"There's one way we could get him to let us get married, an you could be married to home, with them both there. There's always one way in a town like this."

She knew what he meant. He could feel her cheek getting warmer against his.

"Look," he said hastily, "you could spend the week-end with a friend somewhere—you know anyone in Freehold? An then you could tell him you'd been with me somewhere an we—well."

"I can't—I can't tell him a lie that big without him knowing."

"It—this is why I asked you how much you trusted me, Lou— because it don't have to be a lie. You could be tellin him the truth."

Lou said "Oh," and twisted away from him. Bub stood watching her move down the wharf until she reached the railing and couldn't go any farther. He went after her slowly, his hands cold with apprehension.

"Lou," he said, "that's just a way, see? I don't want to get started wrong with you because we're goin to have to put up with each other a long time. But I just want to tell you I'm goin to have you no matter what happens."

I hope to god, he thought, I ain't spoiled everything.

"You see, he's the only one'll have to know. You won't even

have to tell your mother, because if Curtis comes around, she will too. I could see that. But you can do anythin you want to and that'll be what I want to do too."

"I guess that's the way I feel," Lou said, but her voice was doubtful; it was there in her voice.

"Look, Lou," he said harshly. "I'm goin to promise you somethin. If I ever say or do anythin you don't like, you tell me. That's all you'll have to do."

She was trying to see his face, to see what he looked like. She couldn't have seen much in the darkness, but it must have been enough.

"When—what time d'you think—" Lou faltered and stopped.

"I'll borrow a truck from Kelsey. I'll pick you up Friday night. Can you get Satday morning off?"

"Yes."

"Okay; then I will, too. An you take the bus as far's Dennisville. That takes about fifteen minutes, an the bus leaves here about seven. So I'll meet you in Dennisville at quarter past."

"You've got it all planned out," she said.

"That's right." He was purposely saying little, figuring she'd feel better the less he said or did. "If you ain't there, I'll wait till eight."

"All right," Lou said. "Friday night. I think I'll go now, Bub. An I'd sort of like to walk home alone."

"Okay. You better let me go up through the woods with you, though. I'd feel better."

Just before they reached the road, Lou let him kiss her goodnight. Bub didn't make much of it, trying to show her it would be all right.

"I'll see you Friday," Lou said. "And I do trust you, too."

"Good." Bub grinned at her and let her go, turning back down the alder road when the sound of her steps had faded.

Bub was standing in front of the old mirror by the sink trying to make his hair lie down in some fairly civilized way. A couple of months of sun and salt water had done queer things to it. There were three strands right on the crown of his head that stood straight up in spite of the water he applied lavishly. Actually the hair was an excuse. He was trying to get his courage up to the point where he could go out the door and get into the truck that was parked in the little clearing.

The queer mixture of apprehension and elation in him held him there before the mirror as if he'd been chained to the wall. His legs felt queer and his mouth was dry. He kept wondering what Lou would be like, how she'd act. And what if this was the wrong way. That bothered him more than anything else; if this was the wrong way and afterward Lou would feel different about him.

Then the elation caught him and spun him around so that he was facing the open door and grinning like a fool when Joe Pettigrew poked his head around the jamb and looked in. Bub collapsed, his smile going out.

"Hi!" Joe said. He stood in the doorway waiting for Bub to say either "Come in," or "What the hell—"

"Hello," Bub said cautiously. He circled slightly to one side, wondering just what was coming. Joe didn't look formidable. As a matter of fact he looked sheepish and a little ashamed, which was something so new that Bub wondered just what the game was.

"Mind if I come in an talk to you?" Joe took a tentative step forward.

"Nope," Bub pointed to the Boston rocker. "Set down if you want."

"Guess I'd rather stand up," Joe said. "Just in case you decide to take a poke at me."

"I ain't goin to take no poke if you don't poke first."

"Well, I didn't come to do that." Joe hesitated, fumbled around in his pocket and brought out package of cigarets. He shook a couple up loosely and shoved the package at Bub. "Smoke?"

Completely at sea and because he didn't know what else to do, Bub took one and bent his head to the match Joe held for him.

"Guess I might's well get it over with," Joe said gruffly, his face a brilliant dusky red. "I come to say I'm sorry about the way I acted."

"Uh?"

[227]

"It's a little late in the day, sort of. But I have to have time to think things over. First place, I was drunk that night we had the brush-up. Second place, I figured you'd come back here just because other places was too hot to hold you. I found out different."

"What's that mean?"

"I got talkin with Bob Haines. Dunno how he knew it, but he told me about where you'd been the last couple of years. Figured I hadn't given you a square deal."

"Oh, he told you, did he?" Bub's eyes narrowed. "Where'd he find out?"

"I dunno," Joe shrugged. "That ain't important. What is, is I was wrong. I—it ain't very easy for me to admit."

"No, I can see that."

Bub was halfway between being pleased and being mad. He knew pretty well where Bob had got his information and he was getting set in his mind just what he was going to do about it. That dam Hersh wasn't any better than a funnel. Pour something in his ears and it come out his mouth before you could say Jack Robinson.

"Aw, hell," Joe blurted, "you don't have to be like that. I've said I'm sorry. I ain't goin to lick your boots. But I would like to shake hands with you if you'll call it quits."

The being pleased, in combination with his elation, won out, and Bub smiled.

"Okay, Joe. I sorta hoped I'd get a chance to give you a mouse as good as the one you hung on me that night. But I guess I can forgit it."

They shook hands solemnly, not looking at each other as they did it. There was something native to both of them that made this situation embarrassing and they both wanted to get it over with as soon as possible. When the hand-shaking was done they were on solid ground again. To wash out the memory of what had just happened, they both started talking at once, but Joe won.

"How about comin out to have a couple of beers?" Joe said.

"Gorry, I'd like to, but I'm sort of goin out tonight. We'll have to make it later on."

[228]

"I figured you probly was when I see Kelsey's truck outside," Joe jerked his head toward the door. "He a pretty good feller to work for?"

"He's all right as far as workin for anyone goes, but I dunno, I'd sorta like to be my own boss." Bub went back to the mirror and started combing his hair again. "Set down, Joe. I'll give you a lift in a coupla minutes if you're goin uptown."

"Right." Joe went over and sprawled in the straight chair by the table. Then he said, "Bob was sayin you got invalided out."

"Ayeh."

"Pretty bad?"

Bub nodded. Joe gave a grunt that might have meant anything.

"See you got yourself a boat, Bub."

"Tha't right." Relief at changing the subject was evident in the lifting of his voice. "I thought I'd have a try at it."

"The boys are doin good now," Joe nodded judiciously. "Good time to get started."

"Get started!" Bub repeated dazedly. He snatched out his old Ingersoll and glanced at it. "Judas Priest, it's late. I got to go. Come on." He snatched his jacket and headed for the door. Halfway up to the truck he stopped. "Hell, I forgot my belt. Wait a sec, will you?"

"That's a pretty serious thing to go forgettin," Joe called after him.

Bub saw the belt on the table, grabbed it, and started threading it through the loops at his waist, buckling it on the run. Joe was sitting in the cab when Bub climbed behind the wheel, and he looked over with a curiously slanted smile.

"You act kind of excited."

"Ayeh," Bub said noncommittally. He horsed the heavy truck up through the narrow lane in second and slammed her out onto the main road. It was just a minute to the drugstore and Joe got out there, raising his hand for good-by. He stood watching the truck pull away from him and he kept on watching until he saw the tail lights vanish up the road. He noticed that Bub kept on past the sawmill road without stopping.

LOU came down the stairs with her overnight bag in her hand and went into the front room to say good night to Curtis. He put down the paper to look up at her.

"Where you off to now, Lou?"

"I—I'm goin to spend the week-end with Mary Freeman up to Freehold, Pa."

"Oh," he said.

"I have to get the seven o'clock bus." That was true enough and she could face him when she said it.

"You be real careful, won't you, Lou," Edna said.

"I will, Mom."

"You see to it you behave, Lou," Curtis said, and it had been a long time since he'd said anything like that to her.

"Oh, Dad!"

"That's all right, Curtis," Edna said. "She'll be all right."

Curtis didn't answer. He picked up the paper again and started to read. Edna and Lou went to the door together.

"Good night, dear," Edna said. She didn't offer to kiss Lou good night because it would have embarrassed both of them, and she didn't want to do that. She opened the door and held it while Lou went out.

Lou glanced back once and waved to Edna, who stood in the door watching her. She just made the bus as it went up by.

It seemed to her the driver went faster than usual tonight—it took only ten minutes before he hauled into Dennisville and stopped. For a second she wasn't sure she was going to get out, then she knew she would.

She was just as glad the bus was early, then nobody would see Bub pick her up. She got off and the bus pulled out again immediately. Nobody else had got off in Dennisville, and, as far as she could see, the little street of narrow houses was empty. It might have been a dead town for all the people there were on the road. There was little traffic, and whenever she heard a car coming from down Minot's Harbor way, she could feel herself try to look smaller than she was.

Between ten-past and quarter-past seven, three cars had passed her. She had looked at her watch five times. When the minute hand ticked the wide black mark behind the three, she picked up her bag and stood there looking wildly up and down the road, wondering where she could hide, where she could go so that he couldn't find her. She was frightened and she was thinking of all the things her father and mother had said about Bub and all the talk that was going around the Harbor about him. She was thinking that he'd been back only a little longer than two months—that actually that was as long as she'd known him because all the time before didn't count.

The truck was upon her before she saw it, she'd been so deep in what she was thinking. The truck was there, stopping before her, and she could see Bub's face looking out. He got out and came around to take her bag and stow it in the space behind the seat. While he was doing that there was one second in which she still might have run, but she couldn't move. When he got down and turned back to her, suddenly she didn't want to run any more.

"Climb in," he said, "unless you want to spend the night here."

He was smiling, and the smile was something she'd known for a very long time, a longer time than could be measured in days.

He didn't say anything more to her until he'd turned the truck and they'd hit the main road again. Then he started to speak, but she got in ahead of him.

"Where are we goin, Bub?"

"Well, we'll go anywhere you want to; but Hersh Baker's got a little shack in to Spectacle Pond an I told him I wanted to do some fishin this week-end, so he let me have the key. If you want to go somewhere else, though—"

"No," she said hastily, "that sounds nice."

She was silent for so long after that that Bub found himself wondering if she'd gone to sleep, but she hadn't. She'd been sitting there thinking and he knew just what her thoughts had been when she spoke.

"Bub," she said suddenly.

"Yes?"

"Are you scared?"

For a minute he didn't answer, wondering whether it would be best to say no or to tell her the truth. He tried to think how

[231]

each answer would make her feel, tried to reason out what she was feeling now.

"Yes," he said, then. "I am."

It was the right answer. Lou didn't say anything, but he felt her move slightly and she put her hand on his knee. After a minute, not too suddenly, he put his own hand down and covered hers, feeling her fingers uneasy under his.

SPECTACLE POND was a tiny, irregular, shallow dish of water off on an old tote road that branched off two or three miles above Freehold. It couldn't have been more than two miles long and a mile wide at its greatest. But it was a lovely little lake. Around the southern shore where the feed brook ran in, the land was low, and birches grew down to the small sand beach. Hersh's cabin stood on a small rise in the birches. At night it was a mysterious and lovely place, with the pale boles of the trees marching down to the low, faintly silver mystery of the water. Along the eastern shore the dark hill went up steeply; to the west there was nothing but darkness; and the faint elusive scent of the pond itself, fresh and quiet, filtered up to them.

They sat there in the truck after Bub cut the motor. The lights shone on the rough walls of the cabin, making pools of liquid of the two small windows. Lou moved first. She got out and stood looking down toward the water.

"These trees!" she said, her voice like a protest and sounding thin in the quiet. Under the birches, down as far as the water, the carpet of fallen yellow leaves was light. Overhead, the yellow leaves that hadn't fallen yet were light against the misty looking sky. And all around them, the thin, straight, silvery boles looked almost as if they were moving in slow gracefully regular strides down the hill. "I've never seen anything like them," she said.

"It's nice." Bub felt a compulsion to speak in a whisper.

She took his hand and her fingers were cold and shaking, and they made him feel as if he held something very much alive and small and frightened. He knew how she was feeling, knew as well as she did herself, because the same feeling made him stiff with uneasiness. But, not knowing how to make himself feel more at ease, he didn't know what to do for her.

He dropped her hand, went back to the truck, and took out her small overnight bag. Lou had turned and was watching him; he could see her face faintly in the unearthly light that filtered down through the birch leaves. He started for the cabin. When he brushed past her, he hesitated momentarily.

"Don't be scared, Lou," he said softly. "You don't need to be scared."

She didn't answer, but Bub heard her slow steps behind him as he headed for the door. The key turned easily and he shoved the door open, groping around him for a lamp and finding it on a small table. He bent over it carefully, making a good deal of lighting it and seeing that the wick was turned down far enough so the flame wouldn't stream up through the chimney. Lou had stopped in the door to take stock of the small room. It was just large enough to hold an old sofa, two chairs, and the table. At one end there was a field-stone fireplace, not a large one, and a pile of logs stood beside it. On the lake side two windows looked out on darkness. There was a door at either end of the room. One, Bub found, led into the bedroom. He took only a cursory look at that and came back to the other, glancing at Lou when he passed her. The other opened into the kitchen, and he stood looking in, noting its compactness and cleanness.

The whole cabin had that elusive, almost-musty smell of rooms not often used.

"Come on an look," he beckoned to her. "Hersh certainly b'lieves in doin himself proud. You could stand at that stove an reach everything you'd want without takin a step."

She came to look over his shoulder, and he could hear her breathing, loud and uneven with nervousness.

"Hersh uses this place for huntin every fall. I dunno how he come to build it, but he done it all himself, just the way he wanted."

"Golly," Lou said steadily, "it couldn't have been neater if

[233]

a woman'd planned it all out. Everything's just where you'd need it."

"Come on," Bub snatched at her attempt to be natural. "Whatta you think I keep you for? Here's a broom." He grabbed the old broom that stood in the corner by the stove and thrust it into her hand. "We got to air things out and stuff."

Lou grinned at him widely, and she looked so much more like herself that Bub began to feel a slow tentative return of that elation he'd felt earlier in the evening. He went in and started a fire in the fireplace, hearing the steady swish of the broom over the small kitchen floor. When he had the fire going and had hauled bedding out of the tiny bedroom to spread before it, Lou was working on the living-room. She had a space all cleared for him, and two chairs were standing back to the fire so that all he had to do was to drape sheets and blankets across them.

"Goodness," she said, "if you could only cook!"

"I can see that I'm going to surprise hell out of you. I fry a mean slice of bacon. You had supper?"

"Lord, yes. Hours ago. It must be nearly nine o'clock."

"Well, then, I won't surprise you tonight. I'll get your break-fast tomorrow. But I don't want you to get thinkin I'm goin to spoil you like that for long, though."

"What'll you do if I won't get up an get yours when we're—later on? Beat me, I suppose."

"Ayeh. With a split lath so it'll hurt worse."

"Oh, you brute," she said, and threw the broom at him, bushy end first.

"Well," Bub shrugged philosophically, "I'm jest as glad to be learnin these things now. You'd a thrown it if it'd been a flat-iron, wouldn't you."

"Yes, dear," she smiled with mock humility. Bub wanted more than anything to go over and kiss her, but he decided against it. She was free with him now, but he knew the mood was so thin that the least thing would break it and they would both be strange and monosyllabic again.

"Well," he glanced around, "we can't do anythin more for a while. I'm goin out and have a look around. Want to come?"

[234]

"Try and leave me here alone!" Lou grabbed her jacket from the hook.

Outside a light breeze had come up from the northwest. It was scarcely more than a moving breath of air, but it was enough to start the dry leaves on the young birches. They made a crisp soft sound, almost like a clicking, but not quite loud enough.

They went together down the little rise to the lake shore where the narrow sand beach glinted palely. Standing there with the sand firm and wet under his feet, Bub felt the wind, stronger here with the whole free sweep of the lake, lift his hair. It made something inside him crinkle with pleasure and excitement. Because he couldn't stop himself, he turned on Lou and kissed her soundly.

"There," he said, letting her go again, "I've been wantin to do that all along."

"It seemed to me you were taking your time," Lou said softly. "If it hadn't been for the wind, you wouldn't have done it then, would you?"

"How'd you know that?"

"I could tell, just standing beside you, how you felt."

"I can see I ain't goin to have many secrets from you."

"Do you want to?"

"You ought to know that, if you can tell the way I feel."

"I guess I do," she said. She grasped his hand firmly and her fingers were warm now. "Come on. Let's walk down the road a piece."

As soon as they hit the hard-packed tote road, Lou started to run. Bub stood still and let her go, knowing she'd come back; she wouldn't keep on going. When she had nearly passed beyond his sight, she whirled and came back again, this time at a walk. He fell in beside her silently and they went up past the truck to the cabin door. As soon as she had come up with him, Bub realized with dismay that she was afraid again and nervous. There was an air about her that made him think of a wire stretched too tight. He thought he knew the sound she'd make if he offered to touch her. He opened the door and she went by him silent and light as a puff of air.

[235]

Suddenly as he stood there in the doorway watching her, Bub knew what he ought to do. He was surprised at himself for not thinking of it before and saying something to her. Then his own disappointment, coming up in him like a tide, told him why he hadn't thought of it and why he hesitated now.

"The bedding's warm now," Lou said tautly, testing it. "We might as well make up those beds."

"Ayup." Bub started to haul the quilts into the bedroom. He tried to look very matter of fact, knowing that no motion he made was lost on Lou. In complete silence they started making up one of the beds, Bub on one side, Lou on the other.

"There," Bub said in satisfaction, "now, you climb into that."

"But—" Lou stammered. "Where are you—the other—"

"We won't need to make that one," Bub said and then saw that she had misunderstood him. She was blushing furiously, but she said nothing. She just stood there waiting for him to go out.

Bub left the room, closing the door behind him. He sat down on the old sofa and lit a cigaret, smoking slowly, staring at the fire that had burned down to a fiercely hot brilliant bed of coals. He smiled slightly at himself, realizing that this wasn't any mistake. Lou was the only girl in the world who could make him want to say what he was going to say to her and not feel cheated. This was all right with him.

He waited until he heard the springs creak in the other room and then the silence. Then he got up and went over to knock lightly on the door.

"Yes." Her voice was low. Bub shoved the door open and went in. He couldn't see her at first, after the light, but then he made out her hair, dark on the pillow.

"Lou, I come to tell you somethin." He sat down on the edge of the bed, feeling her convulsive and involuntary movement. Her hand was lying outside the cover and he picked it up, lacing his fingers through hers. "I jest wanted you to know that I don't want anythin you don't, that's all. And if you want to wait, that's all right with me. I thought of this when we were talkin it over first. I meant to tell you before," he lied evenly, making her believe him. "You see, if you ain't ready, I'm not either, an there wouldn't be much point in that. Besides, think of all the time we're goin to have."

"Oh, Bub, I—dammit!"

"It's all right. Don't feel like that. We got to be able to see how each other feels, ain't we? If we couldn't, we'd drive each other crazy in less time than it takes to tell. Besides, just knowin we were here alone will work with Curtis."

"I love you."

"Yes, an I do you, too, an don't you go forgettin it, old girl. Now go on to sleep and keep quiet so's I can." He got up hastily, leaned over to kiss her lightly, and grabbed his bedding off the unmade bed. "I'll sleep out on the sofa. See you in the mornin."

Lou let him go. She said, "Good night, darling," just as he closed the door.

BUB woke early in the morning, coming to with that start of terror you have sometimes on waking and finding yourself in a strange place. It took him a minute or two to get his bearings again. Then he got up quickly, dressed, and stepped outside, taking care not to wake Lou. He got his cheap telescope rod from the truck and angled down through the birch woods toward the lake shore, turning over stones as he went. By the time he reached the water he had half a handful of angleworms and a few succulent-looking white grubs. On the shore he stopped long enough to thrust his face into the icy water, coming up red and gasping from the shock of it. Then he set up the rod, baited his hook, and started cautiously toward the feed brook that emptied into the lake a hundred feet down from the beach.

The water of the brook was brown from the layers of dead leaves. Only in the middle where the slow current speeded up could he see the bright gleam of gravel. Intent and oblivious, he cruised slowly up the brook, his eyes searching the mysterious golden water. He stopped where a water-soaked log made an eddy in the brook. Directly opposite him a sign read, "This

[237]

brook and water within fifty feet of outlet closed to all fishing."
Dropping the baited hook lightly into the water on the down-
stream side of the log, Bub watched the struggling worm sink
slowly and disappear. It had barely vanished before he felt the
light tug that meant trout. Bub didn't fish for the sport of it
—he couldn't see the sense in spending minutes playing a fish.
He belonged to the set-and-jerk school. And the jerk was mainly
a nervous reflex. The fish went sailing over his head and set up
an immense scrabbling in the dry leaves somewhere behind him.
Bub scrabbled too, and came up with the trout clutched in his
hand. It was one of those short, deep, heavy trout, firm and
thick through. It felt icy in Bub's hand, and it was like trying
to hold a piece of charged steel spring.

"Boy," he said aloud, "another one like you's all I need!"

He cracked the trout firmly on the head with a rock, and
when the flapping had stopped, he strung a short length of
twine through its gills and hung it from his belt. He dropped
the hook again into the same pool, but there was nothing there
now. Fifty yards upstream he found an overhanging bank,
though, and from that pool took two slightly smaller fish.

Satisfied, Bub took down his rod and headed back to the lake
to clean his catch. The sun had risen higher in the short time
he'd been gone and was up enough now to make those dancing,
irregularly shaped light-patterns on the sand under the water.
Bub knelt down and reached for his knife. Then, for the first
time, he missed it. It wasn't on his belt and he couldn't remember putting it there the night before. Well, he must have left
it home. He got up and went up to the cabin to clean the fish
in the kitchen.

He already had them frying over the wood fire and the coffee
was nearly done when he heard Lou come out of the bedroom
and cross to the kitchen door. He looked up smiling, to find
her rosy and still sleepy-looking, standing there watching him.
She'd put on an old robe over her pajamas, but he saw with
pleased amusement that she hadn't been too hungry to fix herself up before she came out. Her face looked scrubbed and her
hair was neatly combed.

"I thought this'd bring you out," he said.

[238]

He saw, too, that she could easily start to be embarrassed with him again, but he knew about her now and refused to let her.

"You've been fishing already," Lou said. "What are they, trout?"

"Yup," Bub said, skillfully transferring one to the platter on the back of the stove.

Lou started to steal a piece of the bacon he'd fried, but he cracked her lightly over the knuckles with the handle of the fork.

"Out of that!" he said. "You don't get a smell till you start a fire in the other room."

"Hmmm," Lou raised an eyebrow at him, but she disappeared, and he heard her moving around in the living-room. Presently, when he brought the coffeepot in and put it on the little table, she had the covers spread up on the sofa where he'd slept and there was a crackling fire going. Lou was sitting demurely on the sofa waiting for him, her eyes bright with amusement.

"You really can cook, can't you?"

"You mean to say you didn't believe me?" Bub looked hurt.

"Darling," Lou said without looking at him, "after what you told me last night, I'd believe you from here to Jericho."

Bub sat down happily, surprised again at how right he had been and wondering what good spirit had made him see what to do and how to do it.

The day was high and golden and almost warm when they went out into it. It was the beginning of a day out of the middle of summer that they couldn't have expected and could hardly believe now that it was here.

They spent the morning climbing the cliffs that went up sharply from the lake to the east. From the top they looked off over miles of country, over the low tawny fields to the west—and to the east over spruces to the far blue plateau of water.

All through the long afternoon they lay sunning themselves on the little sand beach below the cabin. They wrote each other's initials in the firm wet sand and watched the little waves coming in to melt them away. Bub drew a big heart and wrote 'Bub loves Lou' inside it, and she made him do it again, farther up the shore, where the water couldn't change it. He even went swimming, splashing in and out again quickly, thin and brown, almost the same dark brown of his swimming trunks, to stand over her showering her with water.

They did all the foolish things they'd never had the time nor the opportunity to do before. Then, when the sun went down, they went quickly up through the birches to the cabin again.

After supper, Bub came in from the kitchen to find Lou lying on her back in front of the fire. He lay down beside her, loosely, keeping her profile between him and the flames so that he could watch the light across her face. He propped his head on one hand to see her more clearly, and his free hand barely touched her arm. He knew now that the last of her shyness had disappeared, and that it wouldn't come back. She could be honest now without embarrassment, and he knew that what they had both been thinking about would come out.

"I feel as if I'd been poured here," Lou said. "Oh, I'm weary!"

"All that sun this afternoon. Makes you awful sleepy."

Suddenly she turned her head to see him and said without preamble:

"You never talked to me like last night before."

"No, I know it. I couldn't seem to do it before. Honest, Lou, this sounds funny, but I don't feel as if I'd really known what you were like before. I know you better after today."

"I guess there's not so much difference between the way a man feels and a woman feels after all," Lou said thoughtfully. "You must have been feeling just the same way I was."

"Were you afraid we were wrong—about us?"

"I was scared to death," she said deliberately. "I was so scared I couldn't even look at you. But after you came in and sat there on the bed last night, I wasn't scared any more."

"I stopped bein, too, all of a sudden."

She twisted around so that she could put her head down on his chest, as on a pillow.

"I can hear your heart beating."

"I ain't a bit surprised."

"You're grumbling, too."

"Listen," he protested, "don't be gettin too personal with my innards. It's that bacon you give me for supper."

[240]

"Hmmm," she said. Then, "What are you thinking about?"

"You, I guess."

"What about me?"

"I was thinkin about how you stopped bein scared. You were awful scared last night."

"Yes."

"You look nice there," he said. "You look all sort of limp like a kitten. You know, as if your skin was loose, the way a kitten's is."

"That's how I feel."

"You aren't scared right now, are you, Lou?"

"No." She turned her head fully this time, to look at him, and he saw her face foreshortened by nearness. He could kiss her, he thought, without hardly moving. He discovered he was right—he hardly had to move at all.

She was so still that it frightened him until he saw her heart beating—there was a little place in her throat that showed it; he could count each beat.

"Lou," he said. "Lou, please."

"Go put out the lamp," she said huskily, "and then come back here." Bub could feel her lips moving against his cheek. He felt weightless when he went across the room, and he tried twice before he managed to blow out the lamp. There was just the fire-light and Lou lying there waiting for him when he went back.

"This won't make us any different, will it?" she said, her voice drowsy.

"No, it won't, not the way you mean," Bub told her. He reached out for her blindly.

IT was nearly twelve o'clock Sunday night when Bub stopped the truck in front of the big lilac bush at the corner of the saw-mill road. After spending this Sunday with Lou, he knew he'd been right. There was a difference, but not the way she had meant. The change was there, the change was in both of them, and it was all right. No matter what happened from now on, they were all right. There was a certainness about them, a deep confidence that flowed like a strong river between them.

"Well," Bub said inanely, "I guess I better be goin. I'll see you tomorrow. I'll call you first thing in the mornin."

"You see you do. Good night, darling."

" 'Night, Lou." He tried hard to keep his voice level, but it broke slightly on her name. "Hey, Lou, you know what we forgot?"

"What?"

"We never decided when we were goin to get married."

"When d'you think?"

"Lord," Bub reached out for her, "I don't care so long as it's soon."

"We'll talk that over tomorrow," Lou said. "I—I guess I just can't think tonight."

"Well, just so's you don't go forgettin."

"I'm not apt to. Now, let me go." She was laughing when she got out of the truck and Bub grabbed at her, but she dodged him. "Idiot," she said fondly, "go on home now."

Edna was still up when Lou went into the house.

"Ma, why aren't you in bed? It's twelve o'clock."

"I got nervous when you didn't come on the bus, so I thought I'd wait up for you."

"That was foolish. I didn't come on the bus anyhow. I met Bob Haines in Freehold and he was comin down later, so I waited and drove down with him."

"Well, I'll sleep better," Edna said, "knowin you're in all right."

"Well, I am," Lou said, wondering at how easy it had been to say she'd come down with Bob. It satisfied Edna, and Lou went upstairs to bed leaving her mother to turn out the lights and lock the door.

That Sunday evening Lyford had gone to his room early, and when Edna looked in at eight, he was sitting at his bench carefully glueing paper on a narrow balsa-wood frame.

[242]

"It's nearly your bedtime, Lyford," she said. "School day tomorrow."

"I know it." Lyford didn't bother to look up. "I wanta get this glued so's it'll be dryin overnight."

"Well, all right," she said, and went away again.

At nine Lyford got into bed and turned out his light. He heard Curtis come into the kitchen half an hour later and then go back again. That meant he was going to bed and, if Lyford was lucky, Edna would go soon afterward. But she didn't. He could hear her moving around in the front of the house. Sometimes she sat and read, but tonight she couldn't seem to settle down to anything.

Cautiously he got up and switched on his light. He dug a comic book out of a pile of them he kept in the corner, and started reading. Maybe she wouldn't notice his light, and he had to do something to keep from falling asleep.

Lyford was the instigator and leader of a gang known to themselves as the Midnight Raiders. They were having a meeting tonight and he had certain things to do before he went. They'd picked the old hulk that lay on the tide flats below Batty's house as a clubhouse and they could hold meetings only at twelve o'clock at night. Each member had to bring something sustaining in the way of food, but it was against the rules to get it legitimately. It had to be stolen or it didn't count.

He lay waiting hopefully for the creaking of the stairs that would mean his mother had gone to bed. But it didn't come, and at eleven o'clock Lyford knew that he couldn't wait any longer. He got up and moved slowly around the room, making no noise, testing each board with his foot before he let his weight down on it. Working quickly, he stuffed a pillow down under the bedclothes, trying in the best manner to make it look, in a dim light, as if he were still lying there. Half out the window he hesitated, looking back. It didn't look much like him, he thought, but maybe she wouldn't look in; maybe if she did, she wouldn't look too close.

Once outside the house, Lyford flitted across the yard like something less than a shadow and disappeared into the labyrinth of the lilac. He went through it by his own secret path, crossed the road and, keeping well behind the dark houses, headed for the shore. He had decided long ago what he was going to steal. He passed the center of town, crossed a field, and hit the shore path. He went along it at a dogtrot, stumbling now and then when the writhy root of an old fir made the going uncertain.

He crossed cautiously the little open space above Bub's shack on the wharf, but there was no light there. He angled down again to the shore, and came out on the factory road. For a moment he stood in the underbrush staring down at the still buildings. There was no sign of a light in the factory itself. Lyford had been a little afraid they might have a watchman there after the robberies. But there was nothing but silence and darkness. He might have known old Joe wouldn't go around paying anyone for just sitting and watching.

The camps were dark, too, for the most part. There were only two lighted windows down there, one far down the line and one in the camp next to the road. But the curtains were pulled down against glare and no trace of direct light showed anywhere.

Keeping well in the gutter and ready to disappear into the woods at the slightest sound, Lyford went down the road slowly and reached the wharf. Once beyond the camps, there was less danger; but he flattened himself out against the wall with his back to it and his arms out, edging along in the best movie manner of those who are hunted men.

A little to his disappointment the door of the cartoning shed was held closed by an open padlock stuck carelessly through a hasp. He would have preferred having to open it with a rock, but of course this made it simpler for him. He decided if Joe was careless enough to go around leaving doors unlocked like that, he deserved everything he got.

Lyford stuck the padlock into his pocket and went into darkness, closing the door carefully behind him so that nobody happening to pass by would notice anything about it. He headed for the big wooden trays where the tins of sardines came down through chutes from the sealing room. He'd seen the shed often enough in daylight to know where he was going without anything to guide him.

The trays were nearly empty. He got several cans from along

the edges where they'd been pushed under the apron and over-looked. Hauling his belt tighter around his waist, Lyford stuffed the flat cans into the front of his shirt and went on to the next tray. He got twenty cans before he was satisfied. That meant two apiece if everyone showed up, and he wasn't too sure they all would. He looked like a misshapen gnome when he started back for the door.

He'd been so absorbed in what he was doing that he hadn't heard anything, but when he passed the lighter patch of the window, Lyford spotted a figure moving slowly down the wharf. In spite of the fact that nobody could see into the room from outside, Lyford, wise in the best tactics of marauders, dropped to the floor as if he'd been poleaxed. Emitting a slight clanking sound, he wormed across to the window and pulled himself up by his hands until he could just see over the sill. From this vantage point he watched with deep curiosity the unusual actions of the other occupant of the wharf who, quite obviously, didn't want to be seen any more than Lyford did .

It was too dark for him to make out who the other marauder was, but he could tell that it was a man and a big one. Keeping so deeply in shadow that once Lyford was afraid he'd lost him, the man went down the wharf to the still, dark bulk of the office. He stopped before the window, Lyford saw his arm move quickly, and heard the muffled sound of glass breaking.

Suddenly he thought what it was he was seeing. This was the robber, and here, right before his very eyes, a robbery was being done. Cold, unpleasant chills started chasing themselves up and down his spine, and he had an impulse to let go the window ledge and cower down under the protecting wall until whoever it was had gone. But curiosity was stronger than discretion. Lyford thought of the glory that would be his if he could only get a good look at the burglar's face. If he could only tell people who it was—he'd be the hero of the town! So he stayed where he was, watching, fascinated.

But the procedure the dark figure went through didn't look much like robbery. He didn't seem to want to get into the office. He stayed outside the broken window. He just leaned in over the sill, and there was a dim light as if he had a partially obscured flashlight. He did something with his head and shoulders inside the little room, then straightened up, and turned off the flashlight.

The second of time between the straightening up and the turning off of the flashlight had been just long enough. Lyford knew who the man was. Scared and rather puzzled, he let himself down softly to the floor and sat there waiting. Now what the devil had that performance been about, and what was that guy doing around here breaking windows? Lyford didn't see very well how he could be the burglar. It just didn't make sense any way you looked at it. But it was unusual enough to have frightened him thoroughly. Whatever it was, it was something nobody had been intended to see, and Lyford didn't want the man outside to know he'd seen it.

He waited where he was, hardly breathing, until he heard the shuffle of cautious steps going back past the window. They faded, and Lyford got up quickly. He went over to the trays and dumped the sardines he'd stolen back into the wooden containers. He just wasn't going to have anything to do with this. He didn't care what the Midnight Raiders would think, he just wasn't having any. It looked too darned funny.

He left the shed, putting the padlock back as he'd found it, and took out for the woods. He vanished into the brush just in time to miss the change of watchers at the spotter's shack. Funny, he thought, that's Bob Haines coming up and he couldn't have seen a thing. Lyford didn't give another thought to the Raiders. All he wanted at the moment was to get back to the sane safety of his own bedroom.

He reached the lilac bush and cowered into it just as Bub stopped the truck. Lyford waited until Lou got inside the house before he moved; but three minutes later he was in his own bed, and he lay there stiffly trying to keep his breathing even when Edna opened the door and peered in at him.

ON MONDAY morning early, Joe Pettigrew left the house and went slowly down the hill to the factory. It was going to be another clear day with the sky a deep penetrating blue over the northwest wind that was already stirring the harbor and pouring down over the hills. It was colder today, as if the year regretted the softness it had shown these last few days. The wind was still light enough to have left shreds of mist that had risen off the water during the night.

Joe stood for a moment at the junction of the roads, looking off over the harbor. He glanced casually over at Kelsey's pier, looking for signs of life, and saw the thin, distance-shrunk, khaki-colored figure that was Bub come down the wharf to unlock the tanks. Joe grinned slightly, triumph as apparent on him as a new shirt.

Bub's distant figure disappeared and Joe turned to look over at the boat yard. It was just seven o'clock and the night shift was coming off. He could see the crowds of aimless-looking men leaving the sheds and moving slowly toward the parking space. Others were coming in the opposite direction. Boy, he thought, they must be doing a lot of business. A year or two ago that yard hadn't been anything but a couple of old sheds you could shoot peas through anywhere and a wharf that looked as if it needed a lot more than moral support to hold it up. Now look at it. It sprawled over as much as five acres, and that wasn't bad for a town like the Harbor, with maybe seven hundred people. Not bad at all.

Joe hitched unconsciously at his belt, pulling his pants up a fraction of an inch on his lean waist, and went down the hill toward the factory. He walked with a slight suggestion of a swagger, and well he might. The factory itself wasn't anything to be ashamed of since he'd taken over. It was doing more work than the old man had ever dreamed of handling, and doing it well. Yes, Joe thought, he might well be proud of what he'd accomplished.

It was quiet on the wharf this morning, nothing moving. They'd got in a load early Saturday morning and the packers hadn't gone home until Sunday afternoon. Joe went down the long length of oil-soaked freeway to the office. He was within a few feet of it before he seemed to notice the broken window. When he did see it, he hesitated and then went on slowly.

Inside the office was dry and still, the dusty air of the week-end sending up startled motes brightly into the rays of sunlight from the east window.

Joe hauled open the big bottom drawer of the desk, and glanced for reassurance at the splintered wood around the lock. The tin box he kept for the petty cash was there in the drawer where it had always been, its lid dented and scratched and open —and the box empty. Joe stood up and went over to the broken window to pick up the knife that lay there, shoved in near the wall as if somebody had dropped it and kicked it backward with his foot. It was in two pieces now, the elaborate carved handle separate from the well-honed shining steel of the blade. It had been snapped off about an inch from the hilt.

Joe picked the two pieces carefully out of the mess of shattered glass, went over and put them down on the golden-oak top of the desk. The steel winked brightly in the light and went dead again. For a moment Joe just stood there looking down at the knife. He was still looking at it—and smiling—when he reached out and hauled the telephone toward him.

"Give me Bob Haines," he said brusquely.

There was a moment's silence while he waited, wondering if Bob would be in his shop this early in the morning. Then the receiver at the other end clicked and somebody said:

"Hello?"

"Bob?"

"Ayeh."

"Well, listen, Bob, this is Joe Pettigrew. Just thought you ought to know someone broke into the office down here last night and cleaned out my petty cash. Musta been nearly fifty dollars."

"Oh, hell!" Bob said. "I spose—"

"Yeah," Joe said. "Seems I can furnish you with the proof you was complainin about the lack of."

"Well—" Bob hesitated. "Well, I'll be down and look it over."

Joe hung up and went out, not bothering to close the door. He went down to the head of the wharf and stared off at the sardine boat at her mooring. She sure was a pretty thing. Be nice to start out in one of those babies and keep right on going. Joe felt very much at peace with the world now, relaxed and interested in what was going to happen.

It hadn't taken Bob long to get started, he thought, hearing the first wheezing cough of Bob's old car. He turned to watch the big Reo grind in second down the steep hill.

Joe hesitated only a second when he saw that Bob had Hersh Baker with him.

"Well, Joe," Bob drawled the words out, trying to belie the concerned wrinkle between his kindly eyes. "What's all this about?"

"I'll show you." Joe led the way toward the office, Bob and Hersh trailing him. He and Hersh had looked at each other and nodded briefly, no other greeting. Joe pointed out the broken window. "See for yourself," he said.

Bob and Hersh went over and stood looking at the window and in through it at the broken glass on the floor.

"Where's the evidence?" Hersh said curiously. "Looks to me as if anyone coulda done it—or maybe they's fingerprints all over that glass and Joe's checked on em already."

He was looking obliquely at Joe when he spoke, but the words were apparently directed at Bob.

"I don't see much proof of anything, Joe," Bob said.

"Come inside." Joe jerked his head and preceded them through the door. The smashed desk drawer was open now and the tin box was in evidence. But Hersh's eyes found the broken knife on the top of the desk, and Joe, watching him, saw his face go blank and hard with recognition.

Bob reached out gingerly with one finger and turned the pieces over, almost as if he disliked touching them.

"Ever see that knife before, Hersh?" Joe asked.

"Good many times," Hersh nodded.

"Look!" Joe went over to the window. "You can see where he jimmied at the lock, trying to get it open. Probly broke the knife then and give up and just busted the window."

"Ayeh," Bob looked over Joe's shoulder at the marks on the window sill. "Looks as if that's what happened."

[249]

"Where'd you find the knife, Joe?" Hersh asked suddenly, his voice hard in the still room.

"Why, right there on the floor under the window," Joe pointed.

"Why, Hersh?" Bob said.

"Well," Hersh smiled tightly, "if I was doin anythin like this, I'd be mighty dam careful about what I left behind me. Only a dam fool'd leave anythin like that you could just look at an say who it belonged to. And Bub Dolliver ain't a dam fool whatever else he may be."

"Way it looks to me," Joe said quickly, "he was inside gettin the money an maybe he left the knife on the window sill so's he could get it on his way out. Then probly he heard some noise up at the spotter's shack or somethin that scared him off. He mighta kicked the knife off the sill an not taken the time to find it again, gettin scared off like that."

Bob nodded his head slowly and with emphasis. His face had stopped looking worried now and looked only mad.

"He's right, Hersh, it coulda happened like that."

"Yeah, it could of all right, but did it? You guys want to stop an think what you're doin. I wouldn't call that evidence; damned if I would. Anyone coulda put that knife there anytime. You can't prove nothin that way."

"Well, I dunno," Bob said. "I guess I'm comin to see it the way most folks do. We warn't havin this trouble before Bub come back. I admit I wanted to see him have a square chance if he'd straightened out, but I guess he's just plain bad all the way through."

"Look," Hersh began, "whatta you goin to do about it?"

"It's up to Joe, what he wants done."

"Well," Joe said slowly, "I dunno's I want to arrest him jest for fifty dollars. Seein how he had such a good record in the Marines." Joe glanced sideways at Hersh's face. "Maybe we could get up that committee I was tellin about an run him out of town. But I sure want to be in on it."

"Well, that's mighty big of you, Joe. Ain't many people wouldn't be frothin at the mouth to see him in jail because of somethin a lot less than this. Fifty dollars is still a lot of money."

"I know," Joe nodded thoughtfully, looking at the floor. "I

know all that, but I've had time to think it over an I ain't as mad as I was. Maybe he needs it worse than me. Maybe they was some reason. Anyways, I'm not goin to do anythin about it legally."

"All right," Bob said. "It's your money. I certainly can't do nothin if you don't want to. I'll talk it over with the fellers an they'll decide who's to tell him we had enough of him around here. Looks like you an Steve an Peterson ought to get a crack at him. We certainly don't want his kind around any longer, now we got proof."

"It's certainly dam white of you, Joe," Hersh said slowly, "to be so big about it. It's mighty white." His blue eyes, looking pale, were sardonically on Joe's face. "You must be coinin money here to let fifty dollars go like that."

"It ain't that," Joe said modestly, ignoring the sarcasm. "It's just I begun to like Bub an I don't want to make things any harder than they have to be. Now I know what he's been through an—well, maybe this is somethin he can't help. They get used to killin people an probly anythin like this just don't mean anythin to them."

"What's this about Bub?" Lou asked from the open door. The three men swung around to face her. She was standing there watching them, her face a cross between a frown and a look of worried curiosity.

"Well, see for yourself." Bob swung his hand at the desk, indicating the damage. "He made another break last night. This time we got him. He left his knife behind."

"Oh," Lou said, she was looking at Hersh now, "he did, did he? You believe that, Hersh?"

"Nope."

"Good god," Joe said loudly, "whatta you have to have for proof? Here it is right in front of your face an eyes, an you're too dam stubborn to see it."

"It ain't that," Hersh said. "I'm too smart. I don't believe he done it, but I can't prove he didn't."

"Then you better keep your big mouth out of it and let them handle it that can," Joe said sharply.

"I'm afraid he's right, Hersh," Bob said. "They's proof all

[251]

right, an if you can't do nothin about it, you better let it alone."

"I jest answered what Lou asked me," Hersh said. "I warn't talkin to you, Joe, nor to you neither, Bob. I was talkin to Lou."

"Bub will be glad to know he's got one friend in this blasted town," Lou said. She left the office abruptly before any of them could speak. Joe glanced once at Hersh and went after her. He caught her at the foot of the hill and brought her to a stop with his hand on her arm.

"Where you goin, Lou? You're goin to tell Bub, ain't you?"

"Why shouldn't I? If he's being accused of anything, who's got a better right to know about it than he has?"

"Howcome you're so interested all of a sudden in what happens to him?" Joe's eyes narrowed, watching her face, but her expression didn't change.

"I don't think much of seeing everyone jump on the under dog," she said coldly.

"Now, look, Lou, I know you been seein quite a lot of Bub since he got back—" Joe ignored the danger signal of her slightly narrowed eyes—"I ain't mentioned it to you much or how I feel about it, because I was hopin you'd get to see for yourself what he's like. But it seems like you can't."

"And what is he like?" Lou asked, her voice level and clear.

"Why, I should think you'd know after this. You know as well as I do the things that's been goin on here at the Harbor since Bub come back. I can't tell you nothin about that. Look, Lou, he ain't never been any good. Why can't you be sensible?"

"You laid for Bub that night and beat him up, didn't you?" Lou said.

"He had a chance to fight," Joe looked away. "He could've taken care of himself. He had a fair chance."

"Yes, I told him that once," Lou said thoughtfully. "I said the exact same words to him. But I guess I was wrong."

"Lou," Joe started pleading, "we were gettin along fine before he come back. Forget about him, why don't you? Everyone thinks you're crazy havin anythin to do with him. Why, look what his pa was like, and his old lady. Oh god, Lou, I—"

"I'm not interested in his family, Joe, I'm interested in him," Lou said stiffly.

"Lou, if you go to see him now, I'm warnin you, you and me's through."

"We never had anything to be through with, did we?" She pulled her arm out of his grasp and went on up the road to the shore path. Joe stood watching her go.

BUB had been in the store since early that morning. He heard the quick light steps down the wharf, and because they sounded unfamiliar at that time of day he was watching the door when she came in. For a moment, half-blinded by the gloom after the direct sunlight, Lou stood hesitating in the open doorway.

"Lou," Bub said, "What—"

She saw him then and came over to face him.

"Something's happened."

"Well, what?" he grinned slightly because he couldn't help himself, her face looked so puckered.

"There's—somebody broke into the factory office last night and stole fifty dollars Joe had in the desk there."

"Another one, huh?" That was bad, but he still couldn't see why she looked so bothered.

"Whoever it was had your knife, Bub. They broke it and left it there under the window."

"Oh." Bub's thin face grew wary. "Who knows about it yet?"

"Joe had Bob Haines down there when I got to work. Hersh was with him."

"Hersh," Bub said slowly. "Does he think I did it?"

Lou shook her head. Now that she'd got it out, she couldn't say anything else. Bub sighed deeply, she could see his ribs rise with the sigh under his heavy shirt.

"Oh, hell!" he said shortly. "That's goin to be bad."

"Bub," she began harshly, "you've got an alibi and you're going to use it."

"Talkin like a wife already, by judast, an you ain't got me roped and tied yet. I'm glad to find out what you're really like.

[253]

I bet you'll be awful bossy." He tried to make his smile look unconcerned.

One look at her face was enough to tell him he wasn't going to be able to handle it that way.

"No," he shook his head, "you know darned well I won't, Lou. An there's no use talkin about it. That was just goin to be between me and your pa. I ain't goin to use it like this."

She grabbed his shoulder fiercely and Bub winced under the clutch of her fingers.

"Bub, you listen to me. Don't you realize they can put you in jail? They can do anything they want to now. This is just what they've been waiting for, and you'll be a bigger fool than I thought if you don't tell them where you were last night."

"It ain't no use tryin to make me mad, Lou. I won't do it, and don't go worryin about jail. We'll find a way out."

"There isn't any way. It's fixed so there won't be any possible way unless you do tell. If you don't," she said, emphasis equal on each word, "I will. After all, we're goin to be married, aren't we? What does it matter what people think's the reason?"

"It matters one hell of a lot," Bub said. "I ain't goin to let you go through anythin like the talk there'd be, Lou. You tell an I'll say you're lyin, and then what'll people think? You don't realize what it'd be like. If you *do* marry me, it'll be bad enough, but if people think you *had* to—well—"

"What do you mean, if I *do* marry you?" she repeated the words with his emphasis. "Now look, Bub, don't go getting ideas like that in your head. If you think for one minute, I'm not going to—"

"My lord," Bub said, "you've certainly give me a good forecast of what I'm gettin into. I didn't know you were so managin, Lou."

"Please, please," she said. She was just standing there looking at him now, her hands clenched into fists at her side, her eyes bright with the effort of making him do what she thought he should.

"I've been in tougher spots than this," Bub made his voice calm, as calm as he could keep it knowing what was cooking for him, "an I handled them all right or I wouldn't be here to get

[254]

into this one. Now you stop worryin. You'll get me all right—you won't be able to get rid of me now."

"I hope not."

"Well, you won't. I'll see to that. It'll just mean maybe we better not talk to your father 'till this business gets cleared up."

"Darn you, Bub," she said shakily, "you're as stubborn as an old mule. All I hope is that you don't talk to my father through bars. He wouldn't like that."

"I wouldn't neither," Bub said. "Now you go on back to work, Lou, and stop worryin. For pete sake, it ain't the end of the world. It'll come out all right. Besides, we got back last night at midnight—that wouldn't prove anything one way or the other. The factory might have been broke into any time between night and mornin. So that's no alibi. But it'll be all right, Lou."

He stooped and kissed her lightly, but it wasn't the kiss she wanted. His lips were as impersonal as a stranger's. She stared up at him for a moment, turned, and went blindly to the door.

"I hope it will," she said over her shoulder. "I hope you know what you're talking about, Bub."

Bub wasn't half so confident as he'd tried to make her think he was. But he wasn't going to have her scared until there was something more to be scared about. This thing had been planted on him and he could see that in the eyes of the people he was obviously the guilty one. He stood trying to think when he'd seen the knife last and who could have got hold of it. He hadn't lost it, he was pretty sure, and he'd had it Friday afternoon here at the wharf.

He'd gone home that night—and then what? He couldn't remember. He'd been so excited about what he was going to do that week-end that he couldn't remember a pesky thing.

By the Lord Harry, he thought, it'll be mighty funny if this gets me. After all the things I've done an got away with, if this gets me an I didn't have a thing to do with it! He could feel his mouth curl into a humorless smile. Funny in a funny way, he thought.

Now who got that knife and how did he do it? He might have suspected Joe himself—Joe couldn't be arrested for taking his own money. He'd have suspected Joe in a minute if Joe hadn't come down to the shack and apologized about everything Friday night.

"Friday night!" Bub shouted suddenly. "Why, that thus an so —if he did—I'll—"

"Bub," Kelsey's foghorn voice said from the door, and Bub jumped. "What time d'you bring the truck back last night?"

"About twelve," Bub said.

"Hmm," Kelsey's mumbling roar filled the room. "Too darn bad it warn't this mornin sometime."

"News travels fast, don't it?"

"Just seen Bob Haines up to the post office. He figured I oughta know, seein's you work for me."

"Ayeh."

"If I was you I'd leave town mighty sudden," Kelsey said.

"That would be as good as sayin I done it."

"I know it, but nobody's goin to believe you if you say you didn't. Why, they even found your knife. Joe picked it up right under the window."

"I know that. I lost it Friday."

"Well," Kelsey shouted, "don't you remember where you seen it last?"

"That's the devil of it. I had it when I went home that night." I did, too, he thought, and the only person who had a chance at it was Joe, and how am I going to prove that?

"They'll be comin to jail you surer'n shootin." Kelsey's little bright eyes looked worried.

Bub shrugged.

"I got an idea they ain't goin to mention jail. I got more than an idea Joe ain't goin to want to see me in jail."

"I'll place a little bet on that," Kelsey said. "Joe Pettigrew ain't the boy to see fifty bucks of his walkin off on someone else's legs."

"That's right, he ain't. But you wait an see."

"I'll do that," Kelsey howled. "Now get to work an do what you can before they get the state cops down here to pick you up. By the holy hammers of Babylon, I'm goin to get my money's worth out of you."

When Lou went home to lunch at noon she was as tired as if she'd put in a hard day's work, when as a matter of fact she hadn't done anything all morning but sit there in the office and wonder what was going to happen. Joe had sent around one of the men with some lights of glass for the window, and the broken panes had been cleared away. Once or twice she'd seen Joe at a distance, but she hadn't spoken to him since early morning.

Bob Haines had come back down to the factory at eleven, and he and Joe had disappeared out toward the head of the wharf. They were gone half an hour, and when Lou left for lunch Bob came back down the wharf and offered her a ride uptown.

Neither of them had said much on the way up. Lou was too busy wondering what he and Joe had been talking about, and Bob himself was too concerned to want to talk to anyone. He let her out in front of her door and drove away. Curtis was sitting on the porch, well wrapped up, waiting for her.

When he saw Lou get out of the car, he began groping under his chair for his crutches, without looking down. He kept his eyes on her face.

"Hi, Dad!" She came up the steps and stood waiting while he hoisted himself out of his chair. She never offered to help him, and he was grateful for that. There were too many people always trying to help him, as if he couldn't get around by himself at all.

He looked down momentarily, his eyes defeated and puzzled. Having just one foot was an awful handicap, and he was going to be glad when he got the other one fitted. This waiting around was enough to drive a man crazy.

"Warn't that Bob Haines?" he asked Lou suddenly.

She nodded.

"He say anythin new?"

"You mean you've heard about the factory?" She glanced at him and saw that he had heard and was, in a way, glad it had happened.

"It's all over town!" Curtis swung the door open. "Guess people'll see now that I was right all along about that good-for-nothin kid."

"Guess they will," Lou said.

She stood watching her father's back, wondering what he'd say

[257]

if she were to tell him now where Bub had been last night and with whom. She actually opened her mouth to say the first words and then shut it again sharply.

"Hunh?" Curtis hesitated and glanced around at her. "You say somethin, Lou?"

"No, Pa. Come on, let's go eat."

Lyford was already at the table, eating busily, his eyes on his plate. He looked a little pale and rather subdued. He glanced up at his father and his sister, but looked down again without speaking.

"Where's the other one?" Curtis said.

Edna turned around from the stove, her face red and crumpled from the heat of it.

"She ain't home from school yet."

"Howcome you're not in school today?" Lou asked. Lyford looked up again, but his eyes slid past hers.

"Aw, I was tired," he said with his mouth full. "I didn't feel like goin."

"You oughta make him go, Edna." Curtis sounded petulant.

"He's too big for me to handle now," she said helplessly. "You won't say nothin to him. I can't do it alone."

They sat down at the table hurriedly. Lou took one look at her plate and knew that she wasn't going to be able to swallow a mouthful, even if she did have the energy to chew it, and she wasn 't sure of that. She pushed her chair back immediately and got up.

"I'm not hungry, Ma," she said hastily and left the room. Edna sat listening to her steps going up the stairs to her bedroom. The door closed above their heads and there was silence.

"What's wrong with her?" Curtis looked anxiously at Edna, who refused to meet his glance.

"I dunno. She's lookin sort of tired. Maybe them girls stayed up till all hours Saturday night."

"Crazy kids," Curtis said. "They ll find out sometime they got to get a good eight hours sleep every night."

Lyford looked up sharply, his eyes surprisingly like his father's, only clearer and expectant now, watching his mother's face. When she didn't say anything, he went on eating. His plate was empty when he pushed it away and got up to leave the table.

"Excuse yourself," Edna murmured, not having to think about saying it after years of using it automatically to one child or another.

"Excuse me, please," Lyford mumbled.

"That's more like it," Curtis said. "You kids have to have manners; honest, sometimes I think you shoulda been born in a pig sty."

"Well, I said it, didn't I?" Lyford snapped.

"Lyford! That's no way to talk to your father." Edna sounded shocked, and it made her voice louder than she'd intended.

"Well, I *did* say it."

He went out quickly, leaving the kitchen before they could think of anything else to hold him up. His mother stared after him for a moment in despairing silence and then looked at Curtis's face. It was red and congested with impotent anger, but he was looking down at his plate so he wouldn't have to meet her eyes.

Lyford went up the stairs on tiptoe, softly, so they wouldn't hear him from the kitchen. He stopped outside Lou's door and stood listening, but he couldn't hear a thing. Finally he lifted his hand and rapped lightly. He couldn't tell whether the muffled reply was "come in" or "go away"; but he shoved the door open a crack and peered in.

Lou was sitting on the foot of her bed staring out the window. She turned her head slightly, saw him, and her face changed from wariness to surprise.

"What d'you want?" The tone wasn't as short as the words sounded.

"I just wanted to ask you somethin, Lou." Hesitantly he went in and closed the door after him. "You know the dented cans that Joe keeps in that bin down to the factry?" he began.

Lou nodded, her heavy brows knit in puzzlement.

"Well, what would he do if he found out someone was takin them?"

"Nothing much," Lou said. "The men always take a couple of cans when they leave. That's what they're for. Joe can't sell them."

"I was wonderin,'' Lyford said slowly. He thought he'd better stick to that story and not tell her that he'd taken good cans. He crossed to the bed and put his hand awkwardly on the footboard and stood there, scraping his foot back and forth on the braided rug.

"Why?'' Lou's mouth quirked into a weak smile. "You haven't been helping yourself to them, have you?''

Lyford nodded.

"Well, I guess he won't put you in jail,'' Lou said. "Joe's got bigger things on his mind right now.''

"Who d'you like best, Joe or Bub?''

"What do you know about that? What're you trying to say, anyhow?''

"Well, I seen you with Bub, once or twice, around—you know—''

"I like Bub,'' Lou said miserably, not bothering to hide it.

"I figured you did,'' Lyford nodded wisely. "Well, I was down to the factry last night. A bunch of us kids thought we'd get some of them sardines an have a feed off'n them.''

Suddenly interested, Lou stiffened, staring at him. Lyford's eyes were perfectly clear and his thin, brown face was expressionless.

"What're you trying to say?'' she leaned forward.

"Well,'' Lyford gulped, "I don't see why Joe'd break a window in his own office, do you?''

"Lyford!''

"I see him do it.'' Lyford spilled it out now that he'd started. "He didn't know they was anyone around. I saw him break the window, then he went back up the hill.''

"How—how do you know it was Joe?'' Lou was tense now. Suddenly hope had come back and she was beginning to understand a good many things.

"He—he had a flashlight an I got a good look at him when he turned around.''

"Are you sure?'' Lou had him by the shoulders now and was shaking him, but she didn't seem to realize she was doing it.

Lyford nodded and Lou let go of him so suddenly that he staggered away from her. An instant later she was past him and

[260]

out of the room. He heard her feet on the stairs and the slam of the front door. He went to the window and saw her going down the road. She was walking fast, and he could tell how mad she was from the set of her shoulders under the dark cloth of her suit coat.

Lyford grinned. He went over to the door and then hesitated, glancing back at the bureau. Softly he went over and lifted the hand mirror. There was seventy-five cents there, in nickels, dimes, and one quarter. Lyford picked up the quarter and slipped it into his watch pocket.

"It ought to be worth that to her," he said, softly.

WHEN LOU found Joe, he was sitting at her desk as if he'd been waiting for her. She stood in the office door looking at him until he looked up and nodded.

"You look pleased," she said evenly.

"I am. Got somethin to do tomorrow. Maybe when I get it done, you'll come to your senses."

"What are you going to do?" Lou said each word so clearly that they sounded like stones falling into cold water.

"They's a bunch of us goin to see Bub Dolliver."

"Are you?"

Joe nodded.

"And I'm sure goin to enjoy tellin that bastard to get out of town. Sorry to use a word like that, Lou, but that's what he is. There's no two ways about it."

"Aren't you going to have him arrested?" she asked icily.

"Well, I got to thinkin about where he's been the last couple years an I guessed I wouldn't have him arrested. The fifty dollars —well, he can keep that. Just so long's he gets outa here an stops playin around with my girl."

"I take it you mean me," Lou said. "Joe, I *never* gave you any right to feel like that about me."

"Lou," he got up and came over to her, "be reasonable. I've

asked you to marry me more'n once, an all you've said is maybe. Now I'm askin you again. We could have a good time, Lou. I could give you a lot."

He took her arms lightly and bent over as if to kiss her. Lou doubled her fists, set them just above Joe's belt buckle, and pushed hard. Taken off balance, he staggered backward, away from her, saving himself from falling only by a wild clutch at the desk.

"What's the big idea?" Suddenly angry, he stood glaring at her. "You ought to know better than that. You used to be glad enough to have me kiss you. I never meant what I said this mornin about us bein through—I was just mad."

"I'm not glad to have you kiss me now, Joe," she said. "I don't want to have anything to do with as big a thief and liar as you are."

His eyes narrowed slightly and he didn't start to talk immediately. He waited a minute before he said carefully:

"What does that mean?"

"I mean you're goin to tell your citizen's committee or whatever it is that Bub didn't have anything to do with this robbery. You're goin to tell them who did, though."

"Well," Joe said stiffly, "who did, if he didn't?"

"You didn't know there was anyone around when you broke that window, did you, Joe?"

"There wasn't anyone—" instantly he saw his mistake. For a minute the look on his face frightened her. Then he said hastily, "What the devil are you talkin about?"

"You seem to know, Joe." Hersh's calm voice from the open door spun Joe around as if somebody had put a hand on his shoulder and caught him off balance.

"What the hell are you doin here?"

"Why," Hersh began softly, coming into the office, "I come down to have another look at the place, an maybe talk with you, Joe, but I see Lou beat me to it. Why don't we keep on from here?"

"Somebody saw him," Lou blurted, suddenly glad that she wasn't alone with Joe any more. "He did it himself, Hersh. He fixed it so it would look as if Bub did it. He robbed his own

[262]

office." She began to laugh, tautly and without amusement, but Hersh's steady voice stopped her.

"Who was it seen him?"

"Why, there were some kids down here after the dented tins of sardines last night. They saw Joe break the window. He did it. They saw him from the cartoning room window."

"Who's gonna take the word of a bunch of thievin kids against mine?" Joe said loudly.

"I am for one," Hersh said. He stepped to the window and glanced out. "You can get a real good view of this window from that shed, Joe. I'll be pleased to see you meet the rest of your dam committee, Joe. I'll be interested in seein what you say to them. An it ain't goin to be enough jest to say it warn't Bub. You're goin to tell them jest what happened."

"I am like hell," Joe said. "Who's goin to make me?"

"I hate to act like this in front of a lady," Hersh said softly, "but I guess she'll make allowances, seein you ain't much of a gentleman, Joe." He reached out and one of his big hands closed around Joe's wrist. Lou, watching, saw the veins in the back of Joe's hand stand out suddenly. Hersh brought up his other hand, open, and hit Joe apparently without force. But there was a sound like the light crack of a pistol, and the side of Joe's face flamed suddenly red.

"You—" Joe started, his voice high with rage and fear. He swung wildly at Hersh, but Hersh jerked his wrist easily and Joe spun away from him.

"I'll muss that nice, clean face, Joe. An your committee won't be able to recognize you."

Joe was silent.

"Go outside a minute, Lou," Hersh said, and Lou, only too willing not to witness what was coming, turned toward the door.

"No," Joe said suddenly, "I'll—it's—I'll tell them. No!"

"Joe!"

The one word hung in the air over Joe's head. There was nothing exceptional about the tone or the voice, but it stiffened Joe as if somebody had pushed a ramrod down his back under his shirt. He was standing on the wharf, hands in his pockets,

[263]

staring out at the big boat, but he wasn't seeing her. He was just standing there wondering how the devil he could get himself out of this mess without making more of a fool of himself than he already had. Somehow he hadn't been expecting the thing that he knew was going to happen as soon as the quiet voice behind him said:

"Joe!"

Joe felt the little hairs on the back of his neck prickle. He didn't turn around.

"What d'you want?" he said.

"I just come to get my knife you borrowed off me Friday night."

"Now wait, Bub—" Joe started talking before he turned, and he was in full spate when he faced Bub. Bub was standing there watching him evenly, but something in his eyes stopped Joe cold. He had a chance to think "My god, his eyes look yellow!" before Bub spoke.

"Wait for what?" he said. "I ain't touched you yet."

Bub's thin figure had a coiled, ominous look about it, and the yellow stare of his eyes chilled Joe's breathing.

"I can explain—"

"I don't know's I want to hear any explainin, Joe. Look what it got me, listenin to you Friday."

"Look, Bub, I—well, she was my girl, see? You come along an it made me so darned mad when she'd pass me up for you. I honestly figured you warn't much good. You didn't use to be—" Suddenly conscious that he wasn't helping his own case much, Joe stopped again.

"You had the nerve to come down there an shake my hand," Bub said. "You shook hands with me before you stole it. You musta had it all planned out how you was goin to fix me so's I wouldn't stand a chance."

"I wasn't goin to let them arrest you," Joe said weakly. "I just wanted to git you out of town. I wasn't gonna let them put you in jail."

"That's mighty white of you," Bub said. While Joe had been talking, Bub's face had got tighter and tighter, until the white lines in his forehead disappeared.

[264]

"I didn't know you'd got hurt. I never knew nothin about that when I tackled you that time. You don't hold that against me, do you?"

"You're darn tootin, I hold it against you. But that don't matter half as much as you comin down there an shakin my hand an havin it in mind all along to make out I was the one doin them robberies. That makes me mad. I never got real mad at you the night we fought. I figgered it was over Lou, an you had as much right as anyone. But, by the judast, this is different. I guess I wouldn't be so mad if you hadn't shook hands. Now I'm gonna teach you that ain't the way to do."

Bub took the first step, a half-shuffle forward with his right foot, hands open and tautly at his sides. Out of pure horror and desperation, Joe lunged. Even at that, his first swing took Bub high on the cheekbone under the eye Joe had blacked before. Bub staggered, hands waving wildly. Instead of following up his advantage, Joe started looking around for something better than fists. He was mad now and in a mood to tear Bub apart. He made a jump for the lumber pile and grabbed the short length of two-by-four that topped it.

Bub crouched, watching him, and what he'd been hoping for happened. When Joe's hands closed on the end of the club, something exploded redly behind Bub's eyes and he was raging. He went at Joe, not waiting to get up, going in crouched over; and in the impetus of his straightening up, his head took Joe in the stomach. The most satisfying sounds Bub had ever heard were the queer, horrified grunt of Joe's breath going out and the thud of the two-by-four when it hit the planking. Once the advantage had returned to him, Bub didn't plan on letting it go. He knew he had him now.

Joe was scared. When he let the club go, courage ran out of him like water. He put his arms up, but there wasn't any resilience in them. It seemed to him as if Bub had him surrounded and he didn't know where the ripping fists were going to come from next.

He could feel himself beginning to let go, and still the fists kept coming. His head felt like a melon full of light and pain, and so big he couldn't move it out of the way. The salty taste in his mouth was the taste of his own blood and it made him sick. He could hear himself retching under the hammer of blows. He couldn't see anything, all he could do was stand there and feel and wonder why he couldn't fall.

With a mighty effort, Joe gathered himself and let go a wild haymaker, hoping it would connect with something solid. It didn't, and the impetus carried him a step or two forward and turned him half around. He started to run, hearing a whimpering sound without knowing that he made it himself. But he couldn't get away from the thing that was pounding at him. There was no place left for him to run to—everywhere he turned, it was there before him. He felt the arm tighten around his throat and the fist pound at his face, but there wasn't any pain now. His knees went out from under him easily and he went down, not feeling himself hit the planks. Even then the pummeling fists didn't stop until the blackness came down over him and he couldn't even sense them any more.

"Here, boy! Here, boy!" a voice said soothingly, and the hand on his shoulder brought Bub up out of his blind rage, swinging like a man coming up out of water for the second time.

"Hey, don't take a swing at me," Hersh said, "an it looks to me like you'd took enough at Joe. You wanta kill him?"

"Gu-god, I'm glad you come, Hersh. I'd likely have done for him." Bub was sobbing for breath. He got up and stood looking down at Joe's quivering body, and his face twisted with disgust. He looked at his own spread hands and rubbed them hastily together as if they felt dirty.

"Lou—" Hersh said—"she told me where you was. She said you made her stay uptown. I can see why." He glanced at Joe and back at Bub. "Boy, you certainly got a beautiful eye there. People'll begin to think you wear it that way permanent. Come on, help me douse him."

Bub walked over and leaned, shaking, against the shingles of the office, and watched while Hersh hauled a bucketful of water up and threw it at Joe. Joe shivered and tried to roll over. He was starting to retch again, and the sound was like cloth tearing.

"Be better if you'd sit up," Hersh said. He leaned over to touch Joe's arm. "Sit up, Joe."

Joe pushed himself up slowly. He looked dazedly at Bub and the stiffness went out of his elbows. He lay down again, his breathing almost loud enough to be a moan, and he covered his face with one arm.

"Keep him away from me," he said.

"I ain't goin to do nothin more to you." Bub walked over and stood looking down on Joe. His gaze, though one-sided, was as impersonal as if he were examining some curious insect. Thoughtfully, he touched Joe's side with the toe of his shoe, then flipped Joe's protecting arm away from his face.

"Tomorrow you're goin uptown an tell Bob Haines the whole story, see?"

Joe shivered and made a shaking motion with his head, but it meant yes.

"I'm the one's walkin away this time, Joe."

Bub's knees felt limber, felt as if they were bending under him, but he walked away carefully, keeping them stiff, so stiff it made him swagger a little.

THAT NIGHT was cool and pleasant and June felt good. He swung himself up on the stone wall by the library and sat there swinging his heels against the masonry. He felt light all over, as if he didn't weigh anything. It was through now. There would be no more of those expeditions with Mack. And Bub would be out of the way and June could forget the whole business. But when he saw Mack come up around the corner and stand for a second looking up and down the road, June made an involuntary motion as though he wanted to get down and hide behind the wall. Then he changed his mind. What the heck, he thought. It's all over.

Mack came up past the movie house, angled across the road, and slouched carelessly against the wall beside June, who conquered an impulse to move his leg where Mack's sweater brushed against it.

[267]

"Had a little excitement down to the factory last night," Mack said.

"Yeah. That was a smart trick, Mack, leavin that knife like that so's they'd find it an be sure it was Bub."

"Don't tell *me* it was smart. I never left it there."

June started.

"You mean it warn't you done it at all?"

"Shutup, for pete sake," Mack said. "No, it warn't me."

"Well, then, who the hell was it?"

"How should I know?" Mack shrugged. "For all I know it really was Bub."

"I was pretty sure it was you," June said, softly.

"Why, June," Mack looked mock reproachful, "you know I wouldn't do anythin like that without your help. That's why I'm goin to need you tonight."

June squealed like a stuck pig.

"You heard me," Mack said.

"You crazy, you dam fool?" June felt as though he was shouting, but his voice came out in a whisper. His lips were too dry to form the words clearly. "For godsake, Mack, you'll get us both jailed."

"No, I ain't crazy. I'm smart, that's all. An if you can stop shakin long enough to listen, I'll tell you how smart I am. Now, look. They's just one more place I wanta get a crack at an tonight's the time to get it. See? They won't be lookin for nothin to happen tonight because it's too soon after the factory an they'll think he won't dare. After that, I'm leavin town. Since the hotel closed there ain't been nothin doin here, anyways. Now, this garage of your old man's down by the wharf, they's some new tires in there an I'm gonna have them. An you're goin to help, and that's all there is to it."

"I won't," June babbled. He was white with fear and almost incoherent. "I ain't gonna have nothin more to do with you. You'll have us both up on the Hill. God, I couldn't break into my own father's place! I'm through."

"No, you ain't," Mack said judiciously. "I'll be by that big old birch down by the garage at twelve. An you'll be there too."

"Mack—"

"I'll see you, June," Mack said over his shoulder.

At twelve o'clock June was lying on his bed, stiffly, his muscles twitching and his arms flat at his sides. He had decided not to go. He wasn't quite sure what Mack would do about it, but whatever it was, it couldn't be worse than this sitting around wondering when they were going to find out, wondering what his old man would do when he knew about it.

At twelve-thirty June went slowly down the road toward the wharves and saw the dim white shape of the big birch glowing faintly in the darkness. His hands were stuffed into the pockets of his jacket and he was shivering. His mouth was dry and he had to keep swallowing nothing because his stomach did a flip-flop at each step. The harbor was a still, flat stretch of black, and there was no light or sound across it. It was like a place where the world dropped off into nothing at all. He couldn't see much, but he could see enough to know that Mack wasn't beside the tree. There was no sign of him. For a moment June stood in undecided relief, thinking maybe Mack had changed his mind and wasn't coming.

"I counted on you bein a little late," Mack said behind him. "I figured just about right, didn't I?"

June whirled, and felt his feet take him, at no bidding, back up the road at a stumbling run. Mack caught him easily and jerked him around with a rough hand on his shoulder. He slumped forward and Mack hauled him up impatiently.

"Honest to god," he growled, "I don't know how I get mixed up with such awful fools. An you're a coward on top of that."

He waited a minute, then jerked at June's sleeve.

"Come on if you think you can manage to walk across the road."

Still in a daze of fear, June fastened his eyes on the blur of Mack's light sweater and followed its vagueness back up the road and across it into the wide field that let out on the water across the narrow neck of land connecting Old Point with the larger mass of land that backed it. His teeth started to chatter and he couldn't stop them, his whole head was shaking as if he had palsy. They were nearly halfway across the neck before Mack turned and started in a wide curve back to the road again. His judgment was accurate, and they came out through the little fringe of alders directly behind the dark windows of the garage. June leaned against the galvanized iron, feeling its roughness under his hands. He heard faintly, as if his head were inside a sack, the muffled crack and tinkle of breaking glass, and it was a familiar sound now.

"Come on, you sap," Mack whispered fiercely, and June crawled weakly in through the window. The row of windows was directly above the long bench that ran the width of the garage. June jumped off it, trying to land lightly and without sound, but feeling his legs give like macaroni under him.

"Go on down front," Mack said. "Take a look out an see if anythin's stirrin."

June went gladly. Halfway down the short length of the small garage he shied like a skittish colt at the big white blur of a sheeted car in storage. He reached the wide sliding doors in front and looked out, straining to see out the high windows. There was nothing moving up or down the road, as far as he could make out.

"Okay," he said, keeping his voice low, but knowing it would carry to Mack.

Mack stood beside the bench thinking. The tires were kept in the small storeroom off the back. He'd seen them there the other afternoon. He was trying to decide whether to tackle them first or to go up front where June was and take a look through the office. There might be a good deal to interest him up there. He stuck a cigaret in his mouth and lit a match to take his bearings. He lit the cigaret, too, noted the truck slightly to his left, and tossed the match away, over his shoulder.

Kelsey couldn't sleep for thinking about Bub and wondering what they were going to do to him. He wasn't so sure himself, now that Bub's knife had turned up where it had, that Bub wasn't the guilty one. It certainly looked that way, and the idea that he might have made a mistake in judgment like that grizzled him.

[270]

He was dozing off when he heard a door close somewhere downstairs and it took him a minute to wake up enough to realize what he'd heard. When he did, he sat up in bed with a grunt, and was perfectly still, listening for some further sound. There was nothing but silence now. Kelsey heaved himself out of bed and crossed to the window. His room was on the road side of the house and he looked out just in time to see and recognize June's back vanishing down the road into blackness.

Now what's that pesky kid up to, he thought, still half-asleep. Behind him, his wife tossed and said:

"Kelsey, what you doin up? For heaven's sake, come on to bed."

"I can't sleep," Kelsey said. No need to tell her what he was watching. "I'm goin down to the wharf to look around. You hear me?"

"I can't help but," she said pettishly. "You're foolish, though, traipsin around down there this time of night. Catch your death."

Kelsey climbed heavily into his clothes, and when he went out of the room, she was asleep again. He kept thinking, What's that kid up to? And he thought it steadily, trying not to think the other thing that he held just out of range of his fretting mind.

He opened his garage door, being unconsciously careful to make as little noise as possible because the quiet of the night pressed in around him like something tangible and not to be broken. The heavy engine answered to his foot with a muffled roar of power. He wasn't a good driver, but he got a lot of pleasure from handling motors. He backed out of the garage and turned, hearing with a click of annoyance, the gears whine under his clumsy hand. The half mile from the house to the shore was nearly all down hill, and once he'd given the truck headway, she'd coast the rest. He thrust the gear shift into neutral and sat back, his foot lightly on the brake. His lights were dimmed already, but when he neared the last curve before the wharves, something made him reach out and flick them off altogether. The truck was going slowly now, on the last lap, and she had a slight upgrade to make before the long narrow hill down to the wharf.

Going silently through the darkness like that, guided only by the faint lighter mark that was the road shoulder, Kelsey felt as if he had turned into an enlarged pair of ears and eyes. The rest of him didn't seem to be there at all.

As he neared the big birch that marked the turn, Kelsey glanced off to the left and saw a sharp spurt of light that seemed to come from the window of the garage, almost as if somebody had lighted a match. Reflection, he thought; then, but there ain't nothin it could be a reflection of.

He swerved the truck hastily to the road shoulder, jumped out, and ran for the garage door. It never occurred to him that it might be dangerous for him. He was too mad. He didn't stop to think that the heavy thud of his boots on the tarred road might warn whoever it was, waiting there, that he was coming. He was only afraid that it would be June.

It took him only a second to get from the truck to the garage. He passed the gas tanks, and just as he reached out to put his hand on the big rolling doors, the whole building seemed to shake itself before his eyes. Then it made a noise like a deep muffled cough, and every crack and window seemed to leap out at him. The brightness faded and came back again. The force of the explosion had jarred the doors apart, and as he stood there, too astounded to move, staring into the growing wall of flame that filled the back of the garage, something tall and dark against the light, something with a ring of fire around its legs, came screaming out of the open door and went past him on the run.

Kelsey came suddenly to life. He reached out and grabbed the running figure, throwing it with the force of his shoulders, and went methodically to work with gravel and his bare hands to put out the flames, paying no attention to the high hysterical whinnying sound the boy kept making.

He flipped the slight figure over and sat back on his heels staring down numbly at the face, clear in the light of the flames. The sound Kelsey made was hardly more intelligible than the high screaming June kept up. It was an animal sound of fear and utter horror. June sat up suddenly and the first intelligent word he said made Kelsey scramble to his feet.

[272]

"Mack's in there," June said, pointing to the blazing cave of fire.

Kelsey started for the open door again at a dead run, but this time he couldn't get within feet of it. The heat drove him staggering back again, his arms over his face. The building was a small one, and already the whole inside of it was ablaze. The flames were starting out through the door now and licking hungrily but without satisfaction up the rounded iron facade. The big doors were wooden, though, and they offered sustenance.

Shaking, Kelsey went back to stand looking down at his son. June's face was beyond the place where it looked familiar. He had stopped whimpering, but he was just sitting now, staring into the garage. His lips were drawn back tightly, and his teeth and eyes gleamed unpleasantly, the eyes showing a lot of white. His face looked twisted to one side, and Kelsey thought he didn't seem to recognize the fact that it was his father who stood looking down on him.

For once in his life Kelsey was speechless. There was nothing for him to say. The dull ache somewhere in his chest would have kept him silent anyhow. He lifted June bodily to his feet and half-walked, half-dragged him back to the truck. Then he started the big engine and hauled down the hill to the wharf. The nearest telephone was in the storeroom, and he supposed he'd better call the fire truck.

He unlocked the door and found his way to the phone, feeling as if he were trying to walk under water. His arms and legs had the heavy weightlessness of a dream. He had put his hand on the crank to ring the operator when he heard the fire siren start, loud through the still night; it rose brazenly until there wasn't any possible further note for it to hit, and then subsided. Kelsey put the phone down and stood listening to the wavering screech; there was no point in letting anyone know he'd been there when the fire started. There'd be time enough for that when he thought what to do. He went out, locking the door behind him. Up on the hill the flames were higher now, they were bright enough to show him June's white face peering out the truck window.

"You stay here," Kelsey went over to him, "an don't show your-

[273]

self. The fire truck'll be here soon. I got to go up and see if there's anythin I can do."

"He's probly dead," June said. "He couldn't get out of that." He started to laugh, an even sound that gave Kelsey a chill along his spine. Kelsey left the truck standing there and walked quickly up the hill, wanting to put space between him and June, not wanting to see the kid until he got back to where he'd know who it was who'd hauled him down to the wharf.

Going up the hill, Kelsey knew that he wasn't going to tell anyone how he'd found June. He couldn't do it. It was asking too much of any man to make him tell his own son was no good. It was his private fight and nobody could help him out with it. In the first few minutes he'd tried to make himself think that June had been there by chance, the way he himself had. But there was June's face to prove him wrong.

People had already begun to gather before the garage, and as Kelsey topped the hill, the firetruck drew up by the hydrant and the men started laying their hose. The pumping engine burst into a deep, throbbing roar. Kelsey stumbled over to the truck and stood watching the water turn to steam against the white heat of the corrugated iron walls of the building. It was a furnace now, but the flames were already dying down.

Bob Haines turned away from the truck to speak to him as he came up, but whatever he had been going to say lost itself in amazement at the sight of Kelsey's face.

"God, Kelsey," he said, "you look sick."

"I am," Kelsey said, his voice not his own because it was flat with weariness and the rising sickness in his throat. "I see it happen. I—I couldn't sleep, sort of uneasy, what with everythin that's happened. An with Bub still on the loose. Thought I'd come down an take a look around.". He stumbled on, getting his story out, and it came just as if he could really think about what he was saying.

"I see someone fooling around in there, so I snuck up on the window. I was tryin to see in when whoever it was lit the match. And then the whole garage just sort of exploded."

"Match?" Bob's eyes narrowed.

"Ayeh," Kelsey's breath came out in a whoosh of sound. "I

dunno who it was, Bob. But your burglar's in there, whoever he is."

"Oh, my god!" Bob said, his face going slightly green in the ruddy light. "Kelsey, there ain't anyone in that mess, is they?"

"I'm afraid so. I see him an I started for him, but I couldn't even git to the door." He turned his hands over, showing the blackened palms. "I couldn't get anywheres near him."

"Well," Bob said, "we'll know for sure when we find out who's missin."

"You—you think it was Bub?" Kelsey tried his best to sound curious—knowing who it was who had been trapped in the furious blaze.

"Who else?" Bob said. "That business down to the factry was pretty straight. Looks to me as if he got wind of what we was goin to do an decided he'd have one more try an then clear out tonight."

"I—I liked that kid," Kelsey tried to make it sound good. "I guess I never really b'lieved it till Joe found his knife today."

"Well," Bob shrugged and made a sick face, "he certainly got more'n what was comin to him if he's inside there."

By three o'clock the flames were out and the interior of the garage was nothing but a soaked mess of black ashes, with the bodies of the truck and the plows rising like skeletons, and a few reluctant curls of smoke still coming from them. But the iron shell was still too hot to let anyone safely inside.

Bob had spread the word that somebody had been caught inside by the fire, and the men didn't feel like going home until they knew who it was. It didn't seem right to go off and leave him, whoever he was; the poor devil certainly got more than his just deserts, they figured. So they waited around, looking a little like scarecrows in the pale beginning of daylight. The few women who had cowered around the outskirts of the gang of men had gone home; but the men waited on, unshaven, red-eyed, their faces black from smoke, dressed in whatever had been nearest at hand when the fire whistle blew.

By full daylight the place had cooled off enough to let the men in, and they went poking through the mess until somebody said, "Oh, good Christ!" Then they waited for the doctor, because none of them could bear to touch the thing they'd found. They didn't know who it was, they'd each taken a hasty look, but there was nothing left to tell who it might have been.

They were still waiting when Bub came down the road to work. He'd slept right through the commotion that had wakened the town—exhaustion from the fight had done that. He hadn't yet seen the garage. He had a black eye, he knew, where Joe's first punch had landed, and it was swelling more by the minute. He knew he wasn't a pretty sight, but he couldn't see how that accounted for the bunch of amazed men who surrounded him the moment he came in sight.

"Hey!" he said, not knowing what to say in the face of their astounded silence. Then he saw the blackened ruin of the garage. "Hey!" he said again. "Looks like you had a little fun here!"

"Judast priest, boy!" Bob Haines was the first to get his breath back. He waddled over and took Bub's arm as if he couldn't believe he held living flesh and blood. "Where was you last night?"

"Home, in bed," Bub said shortly. "You surprised?"

"I sure am."

"Well, that's where I was. Did you think I'd turned firebug, too? What's this all about, anyhow?" He shook off Bob's hand and stepped back to face them.

"We—I guess we got our burglar in there," Bob nodded toward the garage.

Bub glanced at the garage and looked away quickly.

"If he's in that, he's done for."

"We been sittin here waitin for the doc to come an see if we can't find out who it was. They ain't none of us can touch him."

"I see," Bub said. "You thought it was me. Well, this black eye don't make me a ghost."

"Howcome you didn't hear all the racket last night? Every man in town turned up sooner or later, an a lot of the women."

"I sleep sound," Bub said. "I never heard a thing."

They had been so sure they knew who it was, they had been so certain that what was lying there in the ashes was all that was left of Bub Dolliver that they acted a little stunned, seeing him now. Stunned, but friendlier than they had ever been before. When the doctor's big sedan pulled up alongside the smoking ruins, they circled around it like a flock of gulls around a dragger, all talking at once.

"My lord!" Doc Simmons climbed slowly out of the car and stood looking at them. "You certainly are a pretty-lookin bunch. If I didn't know the lot of you, I'd be scared to get out alone."

He looked casually at the ruins of the garage and turned to Bob.

"What goes on?"

"You mean to say you slept through it, too? We been havin one hell of a time down here. Started about one. Kelsey come along an see it start. He says the whole place sort of exploded."

Judast, Bub thought, remembering the gasoline.

"Yeah?" The doctor turned back to the car for his black bag, and the big cat lying neatly on the back of the front seat arched itself lazily and got out of the way. "I been havin twins—Ida Baker. Thought I'd got her all settled in with the first one an I'm blessed if she didn't go have another. I was too busy to hear anythin.

"You look all in one piece, though. Whatta you want to go draggin me out at this time in the mornin for? Someone cut his finger?"

Bob Haines shook his head, starting to turn green again.

"No, we just caught the robber, is all."

"Yeah?" Simmon's eyebrow barely flickered when he glanced over at Bub. "He looks all right to me—except for that eye."

"Twarn't him," Bob said. "The guy we want is in there, what's left of him."

This time the surprise was evident.

"You mean he ain't been doing it at all?" And then the full significance of Bob's words hit him and he started for the gutted building. "There can't be much left of anyone was in there," he said. His face was big and smooth, completely impassive, as he picked his way in through the door. Bob followed him, a couple of paces behind, wondering how he did it. Bob's own stomach was going over and over inside him like an excited butter churn.

[277]

"It's over there by that truck," Bob said hoarsely, and he couldn't have added another word if he'd been paid for it. He couldn't even say "he" instead of "it," because there was nothing there now but a thing you had to call "it."

He stood back watching the doctor go down on one knee, carelessly, not looking where the knee of his gray pants settled into the slush of soot and water. Behind them the men had surrounded the big front door and were peering in, trying to see what was goin on. They weren't talking, and they didn't offer to come inside the building.

Bob turned his head away so he wouldn't have to see what the doctor was doing. He heard the big man straighten up with a sigh, and side by side they went back out to the door, not saying anything, picking their way across the cluttered cement floor.

Simmons had something in his hand and he was polishing it with his large white handkerchief. Bob didn't look to see what it was, he couldn't look at those hands for a moment, knowing what they'd been doing just before. Simmons wiped his hands carefully on the handkerchief, balled it up and tossed it onto a pile of debris. Bob looked at it a minute, thinking, That's a perfectly good handkerchief.

"Well—" The doctor held up his hand with the thing he'd been polishing dangling from one finger. "This's all we got to go on right now. It's not much. One of them identification bracelets, but they ain't no name on it, just a Social Security number. Anyone ever see it before?"

Nobody said anything, watching the blackened metal tag swing idly. Then they all shuffled and turned to stare when Bub shouldered his way through the gang.

"I seen one like it," he said. He reached over and took the bracelet from the doctor's hand and stood turning it over and over in his fingers. It seemed to Bob Haines that Bub's good eye sank visibly deeper under his straight brow. "I seen this one before."

"Well, spose you tell us whose it is, then?" The doctor's voice sounded weary and brusque at the same time.

"I—it's my brother's. I remember seein it the first night I come

[278]

home an thinkin it was funny a kid that old wearin a bracelet, so I looked at it an it had this number on it. I—guess that's Mack all right."

"I'll be damned!" Bob said. "I wonder I didn't think of that before."

"No reason why you should of, was they," Bub managed a grimace, "with that knife an everythin?"

"Hey," Bob looked startled, "how about that?"

"There was a little mistake," Bub said. "You ask Joe. He wants to tell you about the mistake he made."

Bob's eyes looked blank, but that was deceiving; they always looked blank when he was thinking, and it seemed to Bub he could almost see the way Bob's mind kept turning over that piece of information.

"Joe, hah?" Bob said thoughtfully. "Well, I got to see about that. Seems to me that young Joe rode for a fall."

"He's had it already," Bub nodded his head. "Lit solid, too."

"Well," Bob said. "Well, I guess I better go take a look around your brother's place—just to make sure, you know. He was livin down to the hotel, warn't he? You want to come?"

Bub shook his head and turned away, looking down at the tarnished bracelet with its scrolled figures. It seemed funny to think that was all there was left of his only brother and he felt like this about it. There was no sorrow in him that Mack was dead, only a sort of vague pity that he had died the way he had, and a deep sense of relief because now the trouble was over. There was nothing standing in his way any longer. He knew that. It was evident in the casual accepting way the men watched him. Their eyes were different—calmer and not suspicious; just a little sorry because his brother had died. He spotted Kelsey and made his way through the crowd toward the big round dome of Kelsey's bald head. Kelsey had taken off his cap and he stood wiping his face with a large blue bandanna he'd taken from his hip pocket.

"I guess I better be gettin down to the wharf, Kelsey," Bub said. "It's near eight o'clock."

"No," Kelsey shouted, and spun on him wildly. Bub felt his

[279]

nerves tighten and let go with a startled snap. "Wait a minute," Kelsey regained his composure, "you take the day off, see. You've had quite a lot to put up with the last day or so. You just take it off today, Bub."

The last thing Kelsey wanted at the moment was for somebody else to go down to the wharf and find June there, particularly somebody who would put two and two together and get four as easily as Bub would.

"Why, I don't know's I better do that, had I?"

Kelsey's canniness got the better of him and he amended his first offer.

"Well, you take the mornin, anyhow. Come down around noon, maybe."

"Okay," Bub agreed hastily, in case Kelsey changed his mind again. He *did* want to see Lou as soon as he possibly could to tell her about what had happened. This would change everything, and he wanted her to know.

He was a little ashamed of himself because he felt as if somebody had suddenly given him something that made him weigh twenty pounds lighter. In spite of the stiffness in his muscles, he walked as if there were a spring in each knee. Poor old Mack, he thought, if only I'd thought of him before I mighta been able to stop him. But Bub knew it wouldn't have made any difference —there was nothing he could have said to Mack to change him.

He went up the walk to Curtis's front door and pounded on it loudly. Edna let him in. She couldn't say a word, she just let him in speechlessly.

Curtis had come to the kitchen door and he and Bub stood looking at each other along the length of the hall. Bub saw Curtis taking in every detail of his scarred face and his blackened hands and clothing.

"I—" Curtis began, but Bub stopped him there.

"You might's well not say it," he said. "I've come to get Lou. You've got to put up with me, Curtis, so you might's well make up your mind to it now. You see this?" he held the tag up on his finger. "Well, this is my proof that I warn't doin the robberies. You can ask Bob Haines. Now, where's Lou?"

He heard her coming down the stairs, he could tell her steps anywhere now, he thought. He turned to the living-room door and was standing there when Lou reached the landing.

"Darling," she said. "Oh, look at your face!"

Edna pulled Curtis back into the kitchen as Bub went in and closed the living-room door behind him.